THE HAUNTING OF ABRAM MANSION

ALEXANDRIA CLARKE

✿ Created with Vellum

ou'll be late to your own funeral. That was the heartily original greeting people usually recited to me upon my tardy entrance to any event, rather than a friendly hello or a kiss on the cheek. After twenty-eight years of being late to literally everything, I'd have thought people would start expecting me to show up a good half hour after everyone else. Instead, that damned societal expectations fairy kept batting everyone on the nose, and the repetitive comments about my perpetually delayed arrivals continued on. Though I had to admit, if I was going to pick one event out of my entire life to actually show up on time to, it should have been the meeting to finalize my divorce.

It wasn't my fault. I set my alarm for a good two hours before I was supposed to leave the house, and I only hit the snooze button six times. On the last snooze smash, I accidentally dismissed the alarm instead and slept for another forty-five minutes. Then the coffeemaker decided to pitch a hissy fit, spitting hot water everywhere but into the carafe, and I had to give it an attitude adjustment, which ended with the shattered glass pieces of the carafe scattered across the floor of our small kitchen. I learned my lesson not to mess with cantankerous kitchen appliances when time was already running short, but not soon enough. To keep me on my toes, my boots ran off as well, and it took me another ten minutes to unearth an alternate pair of shoes.

One of the worst parts about living in the small town you grew up in after the age of eighteen was that everyone—and I mean everyone—knew who you were as well as your entire personal history since the day you were born. It made getting around a nightmare because every person you passed in the streets wanted to ask you about your day. The blustery wind helped me out a little—I could pull my vivid purple scarf up over my nose and the hood of my jacket down over my eyes without looking like a serial killer—but there were one or two people who recognized the exposed bridges of my cheeks and stopped me to say hi.

"Peyton!" someone called with coffee-fueled positivity.

I almost didn't turn around, but in this town, if you snubbed someone, you'd forever be remembered as rude. "Annie! Hi, it's so good to see you."

Annie Phillips—a round-faced, pink-cheeked high school teacher that I'd known since we were toddlers because our mothers were best friends until a high-stakes cupcake incident in fourth-grade homeroom estranged them—engulfed me in a hug. The fake fur collar of her pink plaid puffy jacket went straight up my nose, and I tried not to sneeze into her ginger ringlets.

"How have you been?" Annie asked. Her grip around my shoulders had the same power and sensation as wearing a straightjacket. "I haven't seen you in so long. What have you been up to?"

I ripped myself out of Annie's grasp and scratched my nose.

The tickle of fake fur lingered. "Oh, you know. This and that. I would love to catch up, but I'm actually late—"

She swatted my shoulder. "Peyton Fletcher: always late. Didn't you win that superlative in high school? You haven't changed a bit."

My laugh came out with a poorly concealed nip of impatience. "Wasn't your superlative most likely to stay in high school forever? Isn't it wild how accurate those things turn out to be?"

"Wild!" Annie waved her arms like she was riding the tamest rollercoaster known to man. "Where are you heading?"

"The courthouse."

Annie sobered, stepping closer to me and linking her arm through mine, then asked in a hushed voice, "It's true then? The rumors?"

I didn't enable her weird secret-keeping cone of silence and asked, "What rumors?" at full volume.

"That you and Ben are over," Annie said. She burst into tears. "It's terrible! The two of you make me believe in true love. You're such a perfect couple, and you've been together for so long! Why would you ever get divorced?"

"Well, Annie," I said, trying to keep my voice level as people began taking notice of Annie's waterworks. "People grow and change. Ben and I got married at eighteen, when neither of us knew what we wanted. Now, we're giving each other the opportunity to pursue the things we should have done ten years ago."

"You mean like your photography?" Annie sniffled.

I searched my pockets and came up with a crumpled tissue. Whether it was clean or not was a mystery, but I handed it to Annie anyway. "Yes, my photography, but Ben has some things he wants to do as well."

She trumpets into the tissue. "Like what?"

"Like…" I racked my mind for anything that might placate Annie. "Scuba diving."

Annie scrunched her nose. "Scuba diving? Here?"

"Absolutely!" I clapped Annie on the back and guided her forward to get us both moving again. "Apparently, there are some really nice scuba diving places right off the coast. Who knew? Oh, look! Second street. School's thataway, isn't it?"

"It's Sunday."

"Education never sleeps," I assured her. The crosswalk at the intersection turned in my favor, so I took giant strides across the painted stripes on the road, putting as much distance between me and Annie as possible. "See you later, Annie! It was great running into you."

Once Annie had receded into the distance and I was safe on the opposite side of the intersection, I made a run for the courthouse at the top of the street. One quick, masochistic glimpse at my watch was enough to kick me into high gear, and by the time I plowed through the gilded front doors of the city building, sweat dripped down the line of my spine underneath my sweater. Inside, the historical radiators burned with the intensity of hellfire to combat the chilly wind creeping in. I shook my arms out of my winter coat as I pounded toward the front desk.

"Fletcher," I gasped into the face of the man in charge of directing soon-to-be-divorcees like myself to their court dates. "Big day. Getting divorced."

The man checked his computer. "Fletcher divorce. Second floor, Room 224 is reserved for you. You've got another ten minutes, ma'am."

I galloped up the stairs and raced through the corridor on the second floor, bumping into professionally-dressed women and men who weren't sweating puddles on the municipal carpet as I tried to find Room 224. I ran right past it then backtracked when I realized the numbers on the other room doors climbed too high.

"I'm here!" I announced, skidding into the room. "I made it."

Two blank faces stared back at me: Ben's, my almost ex-husband, and David's, our divorce mediator. Both of them were dressed for the occasion. David wore his usual sports jacket and slacks, while Ben dug through our closet for the one and only button-up shirt he owned. I heard him shuffling hangers around this morning before he left.

"You're late," David said. "We only have the room for another ten minutes."

"So I've been told." The last chair available was right next to the radiator. I dragged it to the opposite side of the room, intentionally placing myself on David's other side rather than next to Ben. "We can do this in ten minutes. No biggie."

As of late, I was all-too-familiar with Ben's disappointed face. Though I'd reached the end of my rope regarding our marriage, it was never my wish to hurt him, and his disappointed face packed all the wallop of sad puppy whimpers.

"I'm sorry," I whispered to him. Since David was sitting between us, the apology didn't sound quite as private and sincere as I hoped. "Why didn't you wake me up?"

"I tried," Ben said. "You smacked me with a pillow then rolled yourself up in a blanket burrito."

Ever since I'd asked Ben for a divorce, he'd been sleeping on the sofa bed in the living room. I'd offered to take the couch, but he insisted. Apparently, this was enough to qualify for our six months of separation before we were able to file for divorce. Everything was amicable. Neither one of us had cheated on or abused the other. We had simply grown apart.

"Sorry," I told Ben again. "It will get better, I promise."

Ben nodded, and David opened our file, filled with the agreements we'd worked out prior to our court date. Since Ben and I weren't at each other's throats over who would get what in the divorce, splitting up our belongings wasn't the nightmare it might have been in a worse scenario.

"Let's get down to business," David said, passing a summary of our divorce proceedings to each of us. "We've already sorted out most of the big stuff. The house will go to Benjamin, and the car will remain in Peyton's name. You'll be splitting your assets cleanly in half."

Ben turned his summary over so the details were hidden against the table instead of staring him in the face. "We got the gist, David. Can we just sign the papers?"

"Agreed," I said. "I'm ready to get this over with."

Ben frowned.

"Not our marriage," I added hastily. "Just the divorce, which I understand is almost the same thing, but you know what I mean."

"Not really," Ben said.

David jumped in, saving me from torturing Ben further. "I know the two of you intended on signing papers today, but something has come up. You have one more decision to make together."

Ben's eyebrows scrunched together the way they always did when he was confused or concentrating on something. No matter his mood, the expression usually made me laugh because the bridge of his round glasses morphed with his eyebrows and made it look like he had one long unibrow. Today, though, my giggles were trapped behind the wood panels of the stuffy courthouse room.

"You mean we can't sign the papers today?" Ben asked.

"I'm afraid not."

I clenched David's printout. "What's this last decision we have to make?"

David extracted a whole new file from his briefcase. "As it

turns out, the two of you have inherited a house from Peyton's grandfather."

"Grandpa Emilio isn't dead!"

"Your maternal grandfather," David clarified. "Andrew Anderson. He passed away some time ago. You didn't know?"

I thumbed through the file. "No. We don't talk to him. He left my mom when she was a kid. I've never even met him. Why the hell would he leave me a house?"

"Us," Ben reminded me. "He left us a house."

"Which makes even less sense." I closed the file and handed it back to David so he could return it to the suitcase. "It doesn't matter anyway. This is an easy fix. We'll do what we did with everything else. Sell the house and split the funds fifty-fifty. Right, Ben?"

"That's fine with me," Ben said.

"I'm afraid you can't do that." David took something out of the file that I skipped over: my grandfather's will. "You see, Andrew's will stipulates that the house cannot be sold until the two of you live there, together, for a minimum of six months."

"*What?*" I grabbed the will from David and look over it. Sure enough, one last sentence regarding the house sat on the white page like a tiny, grammatically-correct nail in the coffin of all my dreams. "So you're saying we can't get divorced unless we live at this" —I checked the paperwork again— "Abram Mansion place for six months first?"

"That is correct."

"This is ridiculous," I said, tossing the will across the table. "You can't force us to live together for another half a year. We've already done our six months of separation. There has to be some way to overturn this."

David collected the will, now a little crumpled from my rage grip, and filed it away again. "I checked, but nothing can be done. If you want to sell the house before you get divorced, you have to live there, legally, for six months beforehand. Change of address and everything."

"No way." I looked to Ben for help. "Ben, come on. Aren't you going to weigh in on this? It's insane, right?"

Ben shrugged and straightened his glasses. "I don't think it's that big of a deal. What's six more months?"

My jaw dropped. "Are you kidding me?"

"You said yourself you're not in a rush to 'get this over with,'" Ben continued, using air quotes around my damning words. "Six months will be over before you know it. Then we can finish this up and move on with our lives. Where is this place anyway?"

David jumped on board with Ben's cooperation since I wasn't giving him much to work with. He showed Ben the paperwork on the house while I craned my neck over David's shoulder to read a bunch of information I couldn't make sense of.

"The house is in Falconwood, Connecticut," David said. "It's about a five-hour drive from here."

"It's in a different *state?*"

Ben and David ignored me.

"The main problem is the house has been empty for about forty years," David continued. "I imagine it's not in the best shape. My suggestion is to get an inspector out there as soon as possible to make sure it's safe to live in. If it's not, there's a smaller cottage at the edge of the property. It was most likely meant for the caretakers of the house, but the two of you can hunker down there for a little bit while you get the house fixed up. The will says you *must* live in the actual mansion, but we can make an exception if the house isn't up to living standards."

"You can't make that exception now?" I asked David. "That sounds like a great loophole to me."

"Listen, Mrs. Fletcher," David said dryly. "I'm not a lawyer, though people keep telling me to become one if I stay in this line of business. If you want, I can put you in contact with an actual attorney, and you can fight with them over your grandfather's will."

"We said no lawyers," Ben reminded me.

"That was before my estranged grandpa dropped an entire mansion on us," I said. "It could be worth looking into."

Ben sighed and leaned back in his chair. "Fine. Do it your way. That's what always happens anyway."

David cleared his throat loudly, an obvious ploy to break up the tension in the air, but I duck around the mediator to get a better look at my husband's enigmatic expression.

"You really want to do this?" I asked him. "We're practically divorced, but you want to pack up and move to another state? Into a house that might be falling over?"

"What's the big deal?" Ben said, balancing on the back two legs of his chair because he knew I hated when he did that. "It's not like I'm selling the house here. I can have my mom check in on it while we're gone, and it'll be here for when our six months in Connecticut are up. We'll still have a place to come home to."

"I'm moving," I said. "I was going to make plans to get out of here and finally travel like I've always wanted to."

Ben's eyelids dipped, like he was going to roll his eyes but decided not to at the last second. "You've been talking about leaving for months, but you still haven't booked a plane ticket. This isn't going to put a wrench in any of your plans."

"Yeah, but—"

"If we don't suck it up and live at this place for a while, we have to hire a lawyer," Ben pointed out. "When you told me you wanted a divorce, we both agreed to make it as amicable and as inexpensive as possible. It was the one thing I thought I could count on. A lawyer is going to cost a boatload of cash, and now that we're splitting up our assets, I don't have that kind of money to blow."

"Splitting things evenly was your idea," I told him. "I offered to take less."

"And I promised to take care of you after your photography business failed," he shot back. "That hasn't changed because of this divorce. All I'm asking is for you to respect the agreement we made at the beginning of all this. No lawyers. No fighting."

The shot at my failed attempt at professional photography was the best ammo Ben had to fire at me. He knew it was a sore spot, and he also knew it was the only thing that might get me to agree to all of this. I was lucky he offered to split our assets in half when he was technically the only one paying the bills.

"Fine," I said. "Let's do it. Let's move to an entirely new town in a place we don't know because of some crazy stipulation in my crazy grandfather's will. That seems reasonable."

Ben didn't smile, but he did put all four of his chair legs flat on the floor again as David collected the paperwork and returned it to his briefcase. The mediator wiped his brow with his pocket handkerchief and tucked the moistened fabric away.

"That's settled then," he said. "Let me know when the two of you get to Falconwood. I'll need the date for my records. Now if you'll excuse me, our time is up in this room, and I've got another bickering couple to deal with."

Ben got up to hold the door for David then waited for me. A woman waiting in the hall butted in, looking Ben up and down.

"Thank you," she said. "Are you Mr. Brown?"

"No, he's not," I answered for him. "And we weren't finished with the room yet."

The woman stood her ground. "Oh, I'm sorry. We booked it for nine-thirty, and it's five minutes past. My mistake."

I matched her challenging stare. "Don't worry about it."

As Ben held the door for me, the woman glanced down at his wedding ring. "Hang in there," she whispered to him and winked.

Ben smiled. "Thank you."

With a huff, I headed for the stairs, possibly at a faster pace than how I arrived. Ben's footsteps followed me to the first floor and the main lobby of the courthouse.

"What was that all about?" he asked. "You were really rude to that woman. She's probably here to do something similar to what we're doing."

"She interrupted us," I said. "And if she's getting a divorce, she sure is bouncing back quickly. Did you see the way she looked at you?"

A gentleman through and through, Ben held the door for me to get outside as well. "Would it matter to you? You're the one who doesn't want to be married anymore."

"Ben, we've talked about this. Damn it!"

Freezing water gushed over the toes of my sneakers. I'd stepped right into a puddle of melted snow. My toes shriveled up instantly. Ben took my arm and helped me out of the pothole.

"Why aren't you wearing your boots?" he asked as I shook off my foot.

"I couldn't find them."

"They're in the coat closet."

"Why would they be in the coat closet?"

"Because that's where the boots go."

"You know I never put my boots in the coat closet," I told him. "I always leave them by the door."

"And then I always trip over them when I get home, so I put them in the coat closet," Ben replied. "We've had this discussion before."

"We've had all these discussions before. Ugh, great. I'm freezing now."

Ben zipped up his heavy workman's jacket. "You want a ride home? I'm parked right up the block."

"No."

"Peyton, come on. It's your car anyway."

Every time Ben said my name, it was like taking the DeLorean back to high school, when Ben and I first started dating. He had the warmest inflection I'd ever heard, and he always said my name with as much love as he could muster. When he was mad, he refused to say my name at all.

"Are you sure it's okay?" I asked him. "We're supposed to be separated."

He unraveled his scarf from around his neck and draped it across my shoulders to give me an extra layer of warmth. "We promised we'd stay friends, remember? Friends can give each other a ride home. Besides, we still live at the same address."

The longer I stood on the curb, the more likely it seemed my foot might solidify and fall off. "Okay. As long as you're good with it."

"I'm good with it." Ben nudged me with his shoulder. "I would've given you a ride this morning too, but *someone* tried to beat me up with a pillow."

"You know I'm violent before coffee."

"I sure do. Come on. Let's go tame the beast."

AT HOME, Ben made coffee for both of us because I liked his coffee better than mine, but after he handed me a steaming mug, he went into his office and shut the door. If I wanted a chance at discussing the Abram Mansion further, I'd have to fish one out later. Instead, I called my mother.

"Hello, darling," she cooed into the phone.

"It's not even ten in the morning," I said. "Are you already drunk?"

"No, why would you ever say such a thing?"

"Are you tipsy?"

"Much more likely," my mother replied. "But I'm having

brunch with the ladies, so in this case, my drinking is an example of totally acceptable social behavior rather than a cry for help from a functioning alcoholic. Besides, the restaurant was running a special on bottomless mimosas. Can I do something for you, my dear?"

I checked to make sure Ben was ensconced in his office before sneaking my coffee into the master bedroom. Ever since I spilled an entire mug across the white carpet a few years ago, Ben had banned coffee from our room. The stain was still there, like a giant reminder of how many times I'd disappointed my husband.

"Did you know Grandpa died?" I asked her as I settled onto the unmade bed.

"Emilio?" she gasped. "No!"

"Not Emilio," I said. "Andrew. Your father."

"Oh, yeah," Mom answered. "I got a notice a few years ago. Why?"

"He left me a house," I told her. "Actually, he left it to both me and Ben, and if we want to sell it, we have to live in it for six months first. Otherwise, we can't get divorced. Any ideas on that insanity?"

Mom slurped on her drink. "Hmm. No idea, kiddo."

"How did he even know about me and Ben? We never talked to him."

"Your wedding announcement in the papers, I guess," Mom said. "Maybe he thought he owed you something since he was never around before."

"Then why didn't he leave the house to you?"

"Because nothing could repair our relationship," she said. "He made that clear when he left my mother and never came back. Where's this house anyway?"

"Falconwood, Connecticut."

She groaned, and the ice cubes clinked in her glass like she'd drained the rest of her drink. "Of course it is. That's where he disappeared to on a supposed job assignment all those years ago."

I covered my feet with the blankets and rested my coffee mug on my stomach as I reclined on the pillows. "Do you know anything about this place? Have you ever heard of Abram Mansion?"

"Not a clue about the mansion," Mom said. "But Falconwood is supposed to be nice. Are you going to do it?"

"I don't think I have a choice," I told her. "Ben doesn't want to hire a lawyer."

"But he wants to live with you for another six months?"

"Why do you say that like it's such a bad thing?"

My mother sighed into the phone. "Because you broke his heart, honey. There's no other way to put it."

"Mom, we got married when we were eighteen. We were—"

"Too young," Mom finished for me. "Yes, I told you that on the day he proposed *and* the day you got married, but you didn't listen to me, did you?"

"I'm not in the mood to have an I-told-you-so battle."

On the other end of the line, a fresh stream of liquid rattles the ice in my mother's glass. "Honey, I get it. There's nothing wrong with realizing you made a mistake."

"I'm not saying our marriage was a mistake," I said. "I loved Ben. I still do in a lot of ways, but it's not enough. I have to get out of this town."

"Then do it," she challenged. "Go to Falconwood. Sure, Ben will be there too, but it'll help you dip your feet into a different area. Get to know some new people. Figure out what it might be like to live somewhere else, and when you get there, don't rely on Ben to take care of you."

"I am capable of caring for myself, thank you."

"I know that, but I'm not so sure that you do."

I hugged a pillow to my chest. "I'll think about it. Thanks for the talk. Enjoy your mimosas."

"I switched to bourbon."

"Bye, Mom."

I took a gulp of coffee. It seared off my taste buds and jolted me off the pillows. Coffee sloshed over the lip of the mug and tidal-waved across the expensive duvet cover that Ben bought me for my birthday last year.

"Great," I muttered.

I wiggled the duvet cover off the actual blanket, balled it up as tightly as possible, and snuck into the laundry room to wash it. As I crept past Ben's office, I heard him speaking softly on the phone and paused outside to listen.

"I know, Mom. *I know*," he was saying. "It's a crazy idea, but I think it might do us some good. Six months is a long time. Maybe I can prove to her that a divorce isn't the best way to handle things."

As he paused to let his mother reply, a lump rose in the back of my throat. No wonder Ben didn't want to fight David on the subject of the Abram Mansion. He thought it might be an opportunity to win me back.

"She's always wanted to go somewhere new," Ben went on. "Falconwood is somewhere new. If we stay there for a while, she might realize how good we have it here."

I withdrew from eavesdropping, unable to listen to Ben's hopeful tone any longer, and accidentally bumped into a nearby table, knocking over of Ben's old high school football trophies. The head of the tiny gold man popped off as the trophy hit the floor.

Ben emerged from the office and looked down at the broken trophy. "What happened here?"

"I guess I overdid it on the caffeine. I'm sorry."

Ben picked up the decapitated plastic head. "It's fine. I can glue it back on."

"Listen, Ben," I said. "About the Abram Mansion—"

Ben's office phone rang, and he held up a finger. "Hold that thought."

As Ben answered the phone, I attempted to balance the trophy man's head in place. A moment later, Ben stuck his head out of the office.

"Peyton, why is Annie Phillips asking me for scuba diving lessons?"

*a*ccording to the Internet, Falconwood was a tiny town in the foothills of the mountains with a population smaller than the crowd at a homecoming football game. From the few pictures I could find, it looked nice enough. It was surrounded by miles of natural forests, and the town itself had the cutest center square I'd ever seen. Though my first wish after divorcing Ben was to explore the biggest cities I could find, it was comforting to know that moving to Falconwood wouldn't be a huge change of pace. The hardest thing about moving from one small town to another was getting to know the locals.

A day after our meeting with David, Ben landed a big job with a high-paying client. He was a freelance technical writer who often worked from home, and though he had a steady income, opportunities as lucrative as this one were thin on the ground.

"Do you mind?" he asked me, covering the phone receiver with his hand so the client wouldn't hear our conversation. "The extra cash would help us both in the long run."

"Of course. Go ahead."

He accepted the position and got started right away, which left me to figure out how to get ready for our temporary move on my own. I unearthed our dusty luggage from where it was buried in the basement, wiped the insides with a damp cloth, and tossed a few dryer sheets in each pocket to get rid of the musty smell. The last time Ben and I went on vacation together was our honeymoon. Since then, I'd been begging Ben to take me anywhere in South America or Europe, but his answer was always the same; he couldn't take that much time off of work. When I offered to compromise with somewhere closer, like California, he shot me down too. His resistance to traveling was one of the reasons I knew we wouldn't work out in the long run.

The largest piece of luggage in my set was missing, so I returned to the basement to look for it. After sneezing years' worth of dust from my sinuses, I finally found the last suitcase hidden behind the massive toolbox Ben wanted for Christmas one year but never used once I'd bought it for him. When it became apparent that the toolbox would never become home to any screwdrivers or nail guns, I commandeered it for my own use. Back then, I took several rolls of photos every day, and the toolbox was the perfect place to store photography supplies and all of my prints. For nostalgia's sake, I opened the top drawer and rifled through the pictures.

Most of the pictures were prints I desperately wanted to be shown in galleries. After high school, I did an entire project on small-town life, photographing every inch of my hometown from Stan the Hot Dog Man to the rickety footbridge over the creek that was one good chomp away from succumbing to termite damage. But when I sent out the pictures to various galleries, no one wanted the story. They all told me the same thing. Photography wasn't about taking pictures of the things everyone already knew. It was about capturing raw emotion and making people feel something by looking at your photographs. My pictures weren't special enough. After that, I didn't pick up my camera for months.

Digging deeper into the toolbox, I found the collection of wedding and engagement pictures I did for my so-called photography business. If I had been more dedicated, the business might have grown to a decent size, but I found weddings so boring to photograph that I let the last few brides swindle me out of a fair price. They got their wedding photos for cheap, and I ran my business into the ground.

Beneath the wedding photos were the first ever pictures I took in high school with a DSLR that I'd borrowed from the yearbook department then accidentally stolen because I forgot to return it on the last day of school. In high school, everyone knew me as "the camera girl" because I was constantly shoving a lens in someone's face. It resulted in a thorough history of my high school years, though since I was taking the pictures, I wasn't in many of them. Ben, however, was the star of several of my photos. The first one I took of him was at tryouts for the football team. Ben, only a fourteen-year-old freshman at the time, was long and lanky, and he punted the ball with such strength and accuracy that the coach immediately put him on the varsity team. He was the star kicker for all four years of his high school career, and I photographed every second of it.

As I flipped through the pictures of Ben, nostalgia reared the ugly part of its personality and kicked me in the stomach. I had been infatuated with Ben since the day we met, and so had a hundred other girls in my grade. He was the cutest boy I'd ever seen. His curly golden hair was so long that it fell into his light-brown eyes, he had dimples on either side of his beautiful smile, and he had the tendency to wear hand-knitted sweaters that his mom made him no matter how much the other guys on the team made fun of him. Ben was always a class act like that. He didn't care that football inducted you into a club of popularity and renown. He had a few close friends on the team, but he mostly hung out with the yearbook staff. Lucky for me.

When I found mine and Ben's prom picture—he'd trimmed his hair and donned a perfect black tux for the occasion while I wore a backless red dress that my mother had deemed "too sexy for a high schooler"—I put all the photos away and closed the toolbox. It wouldn't do me any good to relive the better years of our lives. In a way, I missed the people we were in high school, but at the same time, we were the exact same couple as we were back then, and that was a huge part of the problem.

I packed Ben's things for him. I knew him well enough to pick out his favorite outfits, coats, and boots to bring with us. I included a few of his favorite books as well as a set of fresh notebooks. For all the technical writing Ben did at his computer, he matched with pages upon pages of handwritten poetry and prose, though he claimed he wasn't half as good at it as he was at his job. Once upon a time, he'd written love poems and left them around the house for me to find. Sometimes they were silly— roses are red, violets are blue kind of stuff—but other times, he wrote beautiful sweeping passages that, with a little refining, could have been published in a collection. No matter how many times I told that to Ben, he refused to look into it, insisting he needed a hobby that had nothing to do with making money.

When I finished loading the car late one night, I popped my head into Ben's office. He was finished with his work already, and he sat in the window with a notebook in his lap and a pen between his teeth. He wasn't writing though. He gazed outside instead, his eyes angled skyward to watch a fresh layer of snow float through the yellow light of the street lamps.

"Ben?"

He didn't look over. His noise-canceling studio headphones smashed his curls flat. When I tapped him on the shoulder, he jumped and nearly asphyxiated on his pen. He pulled his headphones off.

"You scared me," he said.

"Obviously," I replied. "I wanted to tell you that the car's all packed. Are you ready to leave tomorrow morning?"

"Already?"

"It's been three days since we met with David," I said. "I thought you'd want to check this place out as soon as possible. Isn't that what we agreed on?"

He set his headphones on the ledge of the window and fluffed up his curls. "Yeah, I just didn't realize you were so eager to get there."

"The sooner we start our six months, the sooner they'll be over." I took his pen and notepad from him and set them on the desk. "I packed your writing things. All you need is your laptop. Look around to make sure I haven't forgotten something you might need. We're going to be there for a while."

I turned to leave, but Ben slipped his fingers into my palm. "Peyton?"

Instinctively, I squeezed his soft, warm hand. "Yes?"

"It won't be so bad," he promised. "I'll stay out of your way. If you want, we can sleep in completely different sections of the house. The place is supposedly huge. You could have your own wing."

"Thank you," I said, letting go of his hand. "But that won't be necessary. It's not like I don't want to see you. I'm just—"

"Tired of being my wife?"

"No! Ben—"

As he shook his head, his curls bounced into his eyes, and he became unreadable once again. "I know already. You don't have to explain."

"But you don't understand—"

"I do," he insisted. "You have other interests, and I'm no longer one of them." He busied himself with his work things, packing his laptop into a padded backpack. "I want you to do everything you want to do. Hopefully, moving to Falconwood will be like a dry run for you. You'll see what it's like to live in a place where you don't know anyone."

"That doesn't have to be a bad thing."

"I didn't say it was."

I EXPECTED the five-hour drive to Falconwood to be some of the worst time I'd ever spent with Ben—we had so much to say to each other and no audacity to say it—but Ben was in a good mood. As our hometown vanished in the rearview mirror and we merged onto the long lines of the interstate, he casually chatted about his new job and the stray cat he'd befriended that lived behind his favorite sports pub. By the time we made our first pit stop, he still hadn't run out of conversation topics. Evidently, Watson the cat was a fat orange tabby who liked left-over cheese curds more than they liked him. Go figure.

As the hours wore on, we played the license plate game and a few rounds of I Spy before running out of things to spy because everything on the way to Falconwood looked exactly the same. An upward slope framed the road, at the top of which sat a line of naked, snow-covered trees. They looked down at us from their pedestal like the gods and goddesses of nature. Should any car dare to stray from the road, the trees were there to stop them.

"Hills like white elephants," Ben said when I casually asked if he thought trees were sentient. "That's what it reminds me of."

"What?"

"It's a short story by Hemingway," he replied, his eyes never leaving the road. "It's about an American guy and a foreign girl at a train station. The girl is pregnant, but the guy doesn't want her to have the baby. She says the hills look like white elephants. It's a metaphor."

"So the trees are white elephants?"

"No. They're every picture you ever took of me."

We fell silent after that, and it wasn't until I spotted the first green road sign with Falconwood printed on it that I spoke up again.

"Thirty miles," I said. "Almost there."

According to the map on Ben's phone, we have to drive through the little downtown area of Falconwood to reach Abram Mansion, which is located on the outskirts of town. As we exited at the proper ramp, the road tipped downward, putting us at the top of a shallow valley. Falconwood was nestled in the trough below. Craftily built so as to not disrupt nature's flow, the town was only visible if you looked at the spaces between the trees. As we drove closer, the twinkle of Christmas lights beckoned us toward the center of town, though the holiday season had ended at least a week ago.

"Wow," Ben said, gazing through the windshield as the town opened up in front of us. "This place is beautiful."

Like everywhere else, Falconwood had received a powdery layer of snow the night before. At home, it had already melted into gray slush, muddying the roads and making everything dreary and wet. Here, the snow retained its purity. The roads and sidewalks were cleared, but the drifts along the curbs went untouched, almost as if the locals purposely avoided them to ensure the dreamlike winter wonderland.

It was early afternoon, and Falconwood was popping with action. Post-Christmas sales lured deal-hungry mothers from their warm dens to buy discounted kitchen appliances for themselves and power tools to give to their husbands next year. The windows of the shops were outlined in frost and hand-painted with enticing messages like "Free hot chocolate with the purchase of any pastry!" and "Half-off Christmas decorations!" Children raced to and fro, shedding hats and mittens as they huffed hot breath across any glass surface they could find to draw faces in the condensation. Most of them were unsupervised. In a town as small as this one, where crime probably peaked at two percent, most parents were comfortable with letting their little ones go wherever their whimsical hearts desired.

In the center of the square, the town had erected a temporary ice skating rink. As we passed through the traffic circle around it, children and adults alike laced up rented skates and tiptoed onto the ice. Too soon, we passed the unimpeded joy of the skaters and crossed through the residential side of town. The neighborhood was just as picturesque as the rest of the town. The houses were quaint, snow-covered cottages, some still displaying Christmas trees or menorahs in the front windows. All of Falconwood was reluctant to let the holiday season go. As the houses thinned out, the trees thickened, and a hush fell over the car. We drove for a few miles longer, but there was no sign of civilization.

"Did we pass it?" I asked Ben, tapping his phone to check the map.

"Nope," he said. "It's up here."

He turned off the main road and onto an unpaved, one-way road that hadn't been cleared of snow. Thankfully, the all-terrain tires on our SUV were up to the job as Ben carefully navigated through the thick forest. At some points, the road disappeared amongst the surrounding natural elements, and Ben's phone lost our location. Thankfully, Ben's sense of direction kept us on the right track, and we trundled through the low branches into a huge clearing. I craned my neck for my first look at the house.

"You've got to be kidding me."

The Abram Mansion held none of the charm one expected out of its label, though it did deliver on size. It was enormous, branching off in different directions. From the front, I couldn't tell exactly how big it was since the bare gray branches of the trees and the low-floating clouds of fog obscured most of the mansion's construction. I could see, however, that the roof had caved in on the far left portion of the house due to forty years of snow and no maintenance. One of the chimneys was toppled over too. The entire mansion was made of white stones. Long ago, it might have shone brightly against its wintry gray backdrop, but the color had since faded, and the house sunk into the forested mountainside like it had given up on existing.

Ben parked in the circular driveway. A dilapidated double-sided staircase led up to the front door, the mansion itself elevated above ground level. Crumbling pillars held up a balcony on the second floor and a massive terrace attached to the right side of the house. Beneath the terrace was a room made of all glass windows, many of which had succumbed to the test of time. The garden inside had been taken over by invasive vines that roped their way up the columns and around the rest of the house. The mansion's many windows were boarded up or broken, the yard was thick with dead weeds, and every stone in the driveway was cracked. Everywhere I looked, the house was in a ridiculous state of ruin.

"It's big," Ben said once we stepped out of the car.

"That's all you've got to say?" I asked him. "Ben, we can't live here! This place is a total disaster area. Do you see that roof? One wrong step, and the whole thing comes down on us."

Ben tested the first step of the once-extravagant staircase. When it held, he started up to the house. "That's only one portion of the house. Places like these were built in segments. We can section the dangerous parts off and stay in one of the safe ones."

"If there are any safe ones."

"There's a reason it's still standing," Ben said as he reached the top of the steps and tipped his head back to take in the height of the mansion. "Craftsmanship back then was an art. They built things to last. I'm sure most of this place is fine."

As soon as I planted my boot, the stone beneath it cracked in two. I hopped off it and tripped up to the next step. "Not likely."

"Should we check inside?"

I frowned at the grand entrance. "I guess we have to."

The old key was cast out of iron, and when Ben slid it into the rusted lock, it grated horribly. The door popped open before Ben actually turned the key, welcoming us into the darkened foyer.

"We should probably get that fixed," Ben said.

"You think?"

With most of the windows boarded up, the entryway was shrouded in shadow. One timid beam of pale sunlight worked its way through to illuminate a single strip of dusty carpet. Ben flicked the nearest light switch, but none of the bronze sconces flickered on.

"No electricity?" I said. "We're going to freeze."

Ben turned on his phone light and shined it around the room. The entryway had a magnificently high ceiling, hand-painted with a variety of family crests. A mezzanine with a double staircase that mirrored the one outside looked over the massive hall. Beneath the open second floor was a seating area with high windows that presumably looked out into the court-yard. The furniture that hadn't yet been looted was covered with dusty white sheets, but for the most part, the interior was bare.

Something crunched under my foot, and I looked down to find a few pieces of pink confetti littered across the floor.

"Looks like they were party people," Ben said as he walked over to the enormous hearth at the head of the entryway. He yanked the boards from the mouth of the fireplace and peered up the chimney. "This looks okay. We could light a fire tonight."

"Be careful," I warned him.

But Ben thumped his head on the brickwork as he withdrew, and something skittered inside the chimney. Ben backed away slowly, rubbing his new bruise.

"What is it?" I whispered.

"I don't know," he said. "I didn't see anything."

A bat swooped out of the chimney and flew right between us, its wings brushing my face. I let out a yell, and the creature flinched in midair. With a spasmodic flutter, it found the open space beyond the front doors and lifted itself up and away from the house as my heartbeat settled back into its natural rhythm.

Ben started laughing. "You have ash on your face."

I swiped furiously at my cheek with the sleeve of my sweater. "Shut up. You would've screamed too if it attacked your face."

"It didn't attack you," Ben said, still chuckling. "It was probably scared. We shooed it out of its home."

"Good," I said. "He's being evicted. Is there anything else up there? Raccoons or possums who've decided to find a warm, cozy spot for the winter?"

Ben picked up one of the iron pokers near the hearth and rattled it around the bottom of the fireplace, but no other creatures decided to take their leave.

"It's not the last we'll see of the critters," Ben said. "The house is practically a part of the forest now. I bet there are a quite a few animals in here. Definitely rats."

The thought of tiny rodent feet crawling across my face

while I'm sleeping made me shudder. "Okay, that's it. There's no way I'm staying here."

Ben followed as I stomped out of the mansion, down the steps, and back to the car. I got into the driver's seat and rolled down the window.

"Give me the keys."

He handed them through the window. "Where are you going to go?"

"*We* are going to go find a nice bed and breakfast in the center of town," I said, starting the car and turning up the heat to warm my hands. "Get in. I'm not leaving you here."

I DROVE BACK to the center of town and parked near the first coffee shop I happened to see. It was a red brick corner building with a sign that read "Black Cat Café." Ben offered me his hand. If it were out of romance, I wouldn't have taken it, but the sidewalks were slick with ice, so I intertwined my fingers with his.

The coffee shop greeted us with a warm gust of heat. I stamped the snow off my boots on the rubber mat by the door before joining the line to the counter. As Ben peered up at the menu, I couldn't help but notice that every person in the coffee shop had turned to look at us.

"Uh, Ben?" I muttered, stretching up on my tippy toes to reach his ear. "Why is everyone staring at us?"

Oblivious as ever, Ben replied, "Are they?"

When we reached the counter, a teenage girl wearing a white apron with the minimalist outline of a cat on the front wrote the last person's order on a paper cup and asked, "Welcome to Black Cat Café. What can I get started for you?"

"One cappuccino," Ben ordered, digging into his pockets for spare bills. "And a regular black coffee. Right, Peyton?"

The teenager looked up from the register. "Whoa. Out-of-towners."

Ben offered her the money, but she was so enraptured by our presence that she didn't take it. "I take it you don't get a lot of visitors through Falconwood."

"Never," the girl replied. "What are you doing here?"

"This town sure is friendly," I muttered.

The teenager finally took our payment and tossed it into the cash register. "Sorry, I didn't mean to sound rude. You took me by surprise. I'm Hayden. And you are?"

Every patron in the coffee shop leaned in to listen to our reply.

"I'm Ben, and this is my wife, Peyton." He wasn't technically wrong, but it bothered me to let all these people think we weren't on the brink of a divorce. "We own the Abram Mansion a few miles away."

Maybe it was my imagination, but I could have sworn a mutter passed through the café in response to Ben's words. Hayden definitely wore a look of surprise.

"The Abram Mansion?" she said. "That place has been empty for years."

"We're moving in," Ben announced with a warm smile as Hayden gave him the receipt. "Hope to see you around, Hayden. My wife loves coffee, so we'll be in here a lot."

I mustered a smile, but it didn't have the same effect as Ben's. Hayden lifted her eyebrows at me.

"Your coffee will be out in a minute," she said.

Every table was occupied by a Falconwood local. Shopping bags cluttered the floor, making it difficult to navigate through the cramped café. Ben and I waited by the counter where the orders came out for pick-up. Each time I made eye contact with someone, they quickly looked away.

"This place is weird," I whispered.

"Can you relax?" Ben said. "You heard Hayden. They're not used to visitors. We do the exact same thing at home whenever someone new drops in. Small towns are all the same. Any news is big news."

"I don't want to stay here."

A father passing with his two children looked Ben up and down. Ben smiled and waved at the kids with his hand underneath his chin. The youngest child laughed and waved back in the same manner. The dad's expression thawed, and he grinned at Ben.

"You do remember what David said, right?" Ben said. "We have to live here, in the house, for six months. Legally."

"So we change our address to 101 Creepy Mansion Lane," I replied. "Then we find a nice house in the neighborhood down there to rent instead."

"That might work," Ben said. "But David said they'd send one of your grandfather's lawyers to check up on us from time to time."

"What? When did he say that?"

"He called me yesterday."

"And you didn't bother to tell me?"

"I didn't think it was that important." Ben collected our order from the baristas who dropped it off at the pick-up counter and scanned the crowded room. "No room in here. Want to sit outside?"

"It's freezing outside."

"They have warmers," Ben pointed out. "And the snow is so nice."

"I'm cold already."

Someone tapped on my shoulder. I turned to see an older woman wearing a hand-knitted sweater with a pattern of snowflakes across the front that reminded me of Ben's trademark winter wear. At first glance, the woman looked to be in her fifties. Her hands were muscled, and her legs appeared thick and strong beneath her snow pants. The lines around her eyes, however, gave away the amount of years she's actually been on this earth. If I had to guess, she was close to seventy.

"Hello," she said brightly, shaking my hand, then Ben's. "I'm Della Gordon. Would you like to sit down with me and my husband? We wrangled the best booth in the house, but it's far too big for just the two of us."

"Oh, that's all right," I said. "We'll find somewhere else. We don't want to inconvenience you."

"Nonsense!"

Della linked her arm through mine and pulled me along, leaving Ben no choice but to follow behind us. Della led us to a booth at the front of the café, right by the frost-covered window. From here, you could watch the ice-skaters glide around the temporary rink. A man nursed a steaming beverage in the booth already. Like Della, it was hard to tell exactly how old he was because he had aged so incredibly well.

"This is my husband, Basil," Della said.

"Oh, good. You convinced them." Basil grinned up at us. "I saw you two come in and knew you would be hard-pressed to find seats. Why don't you join us?"

"Thanks," Ben said as he slid into the empty side of the booth. "We appreciate it. We've been driving all day."

"I couldn't help but overhear you at the counter," Della said, sitting next to her husband. "Did you say you own the Abram Mansion now?"

Ben patted the empty seat beside his, a subtle gesture to get me to sit down. I almost excused myself. If all small towns were the same, then so were the locals. Everyone wanted to know your private business just so they had something to talk about to their friends later. But since we were going to be in Falconwood for half a year, I sucked it up and took my place beside Ben.

"We inherited it," I told Della and Basil. "We thought we'd stay in Falconwood for a little while, but it looks like that house is in no shape for anyone to live in."

Basil stirred a bit of raw sugar into his coffee then offered the container to me. "I can imagine. That place has been empty for a while now, hasn't it? I thought it had been abandoned."

Basil too wore a hand-knit sweater, though his was decorated with Christmas trees instead of snowflakes. Their outfits complemented each other in a way that spoke to their solidarity as a couple. Despite their introductions, neither one of them wore a wedding ring.

"Are you still going to stay?" Della asked.

"Yeah, we're in a bit of a pickle," Ben answered for both of us. "Not sure what we'll do about the house though."

"The Abram Mansion is a fortress," Basil said. "If you poke around a little, you'll find a few nooks and crannies that haven't been disturbed by the passage of time. It might feel more like winter camping than living in an actual house, but you should be able to get by."

Della chuckled at my wrinkled nose. "You don't look convinced. Did you have an alternate plan?"

"Check into the nearest bed and breakfast," I replied, getting a laugh out of both her and her husband.

"Falconwood's B and B is one of the coziest," Della said. "But I think you should give Abram Mansion a chance. It's about time that place got a little love and respect."

"Watch out for squatters though," Basil warned.

Alarmed, I asked, "Do you get a lot of that here?"

Della admonished Basil with a harmless tap to the back of his hand. "Not at all. Basil's a worrywart."

"That place is hidden in the woods," Basil protested. "You don't know who could be making their way through there. All

I'm saying is you might want to sweep the property before you settle down for the night."

"I'll make sure to do that," Ben promised.

"Get a dog," Basil said. "Dogs are great alarm systems."

Ben laughed as he brought his coffee cup up to his lips and accidentally dipped his nose into the cinnamon-dusted foam. "I'm more of a cat person, but I'll keep the suggestion in mind. I think we've got bigger issues than squatters anyway."

"Like what?" Della asked.

"No electricity," I replied dryly.

Della gasped and Basil groaned with sympathy.

"Or running water at the moment," Ben added.

My eyes widened. "There's no water?"

The table laughed again, this time at my panicked reaction. Della reached across the table to pat my hand as Basil recovered from his belly-shaking chuckle.

"I hope you two know how to dig an outhouse," he said.

Ben pulled me closer to his side. "We just have to make it through tonight. I can call the city tomorrow to get everything turned back on."

"Well, I admire you," Della said. "Taking care of a house that big is a huge challenge. I certainly wouldn't want to do it."

"Neither do I," I grumbled. "This was all his idea."

"You'll work it out," Basil assured me. He scribbled something on a napkin and slid it across the table. "Here's our home number. We know a couple of DIY construction guys that might be able to help you out, and Della's a wizard with interior design. Call us if you need anything."

I folded the napkin in half and slipped it into the inside pocket of my winter jacket. "Is everyone in Falconwood this friendly?"

"Pretty much," Della said. "We all like to help each other out.

It may seem invasive at first, but you'll get used to it after a while."

Basil poured the rest of his coffee into a to-go cup and scooted Della toward the edge of the booth. "We'd stay and chat, but we're hosting a forum tonight at the community center that we still have to get ready for."

"What's the forum about?" Ben asked.

"How to reduce your carbon footprint in a small town," Della replied as Basil helped her into her coat. "Are you two interested in coming?"

"Maybe," I said.

"For the record, the community center has both water *and* electricity," Basil added. "In case that has a role in your decision-making process."

WE SPENT the rest of the day shopping in town for things that might make tonight's stay at the Abram Mansion less terrible. Ben dragged me away from the Falconwood Bed and Breakfast and into a camping store instead, where we stocked up on battery-powered heaters, flashlights, insulated sleeping bags, two foldable cots, freeze-dried snacks, and a portable toilet that actually flushed. It was lucky Falconwood was surrounded by nature on all sides. Every employee in the store knew exactly the items we needed to survive the night.

Taking Basil's advice, Ben and I swept the mansion for any unwanted visitors. It took us a good hour to make our way through the main sections of the house, and we still didn't check every room. The mansion had at least a hundred doors, and when darkness fell, I was less inclined to discover the mystery behind each one. Though we didn't find any squatters, we did happen upon evidence that we weren't the first people to enter the house in forty years. Beer bottles and snack wrappers were scattered in one of the ballrooms, like the local teenagers held a party here once. In another hallway, we found a heap of dirty clothes and rags that formed a makeshift bed. A little farther on, we located the rest of the bat's family, hanging upside down from the exposed rafters. We also found the part of the mansion where the roof had caved in. From the looks of it, the room had been an office of some sort. Now, it was covered in debris and snow.

"I'm done exploring," I said, shivering as the moonlight streamed in from the hole in the roof. "Can we go back to the entryway now?"

We'd decided that the entryway was the best place to stay for our first night since it was well-protected by the rest of the house. I set up the cots as Ben lit a fire. He stacked fresh wood in the old fireplace and used old newspapers to get it going. In a few minutes, he had a perfectly contained blaze going.

"You made that look easy," I said, nodding at the fire.

"My dad used to take me camping." He rested the poker against the bricks and dusted off his hands. "You made the beds look homey."

I'd layered the sleeping bags and pillows on the cots to make it look like we were sleeping in actual beds tonight. "I put a few of those heating pads in there too," I told Ben. "To make sure it's not too cold when you get in."

"Good thinking."

I WENT to bed wearing two sweaters, thermal long underwear, and three pairs of wool socks, but the sleeping bag's insulated interior reflected my body heat and kept me warmer than I had expected it to. Ben fell asleep without issue, snoring lightly as the moon found its way through the boarded windows and cast eerie shadows. He could fall asleep on a building construction site with jackhammers and wrecking balls and still get a full eight hours. On the flip side, I was painfully aware of every little sound. The fire cracked and popped, burning down to mere embers. The wind howled outside, pushing the house around like a bully on a playground. The roof creaked with every little gust. Little feet skittered across the floorboards, and I squeezed my eyes shut to keep myself from identifying the creatures they belonged to.

But none of those sounds were quite as distracting as the whispers in the walls.

3

*W*hat was a restless, paranoid night for me was a perfectly uninterrupted eight hours of sleep for Ben. He woke up, rolled off his cot, and got the fire started again while I pretended that if I kept my face buried in the camping pillow for a few minutes longer, my dark circles might not match the intensity of a fat raccoon's. I burrowed deeper into my sleeping bag and covered my ears, sinking into the white noise of my own internal body mechanics. However, Ben had already entered productivity mode, and he was more than ready to start his day. With the shriek of nails being ripped from old wood, he wrenched a board off one of the windows near the front door. Sunlight fell across the foot of my sleeping bag, warming my toes but searing my eyelids. I poked my head out of the flannel fabric.

"Why?" I grumbled at Ben.

His golden hair was askew from sleeping on the same side all night long, his thick curls pushed skyward to sit atop his head like a nesting squirrel. He paid my grumpiness no mind, grunting as he worked to remove the second board.

"Why what?" he asked after he'd freed it.

"Why are you starting renovations at seven in the morning?"

He tossed the broken board on top of the first one in the corner of the room. "What renovations? I'm trying to get some light in here."

Oblivious as ever, Ben kept working. With one final yank, he freed the first window from its wooden prison. The light it brought into the entryway changed everything. Though the dust didn't magically disappear, the entryway looked cleaner with a bit of golden glow from the sunshine. Instead of unknown doom and gloom, I could see the beauty the house once bore. The textured wallpaper, intricate architecture, and what was left of the original owner's artwork were all from an earlier time. Though the designs had aged, there was no denying the amount of work a slew of people once put in to the Abram Mansion to enable its grandeur. Still, the expired elegance wasn't as invigorating as a cup of good coffee would be. I groaned and covered my head once again.

"Didn't sleep?" Ben asked as he moved on to the next window. "Was it too cold after the fire died out?"

"The temperature was fine," I said. "The voices were not."

"What voices?"

"You didn't hear them?"

More sunlight poured in. Ben tossed another board into the trash pile then planted his hands on his knees to take a breather. Manual labor wasn't the type of exercise Ben was used to. He was more of a calisthenics guy. Unlike all of his friends who trained their enormous biceps but never bothered to restrain their beer guts or squat deep enough to thicken their chicken legs, Ben didn't have a membership to the local gym back home. He tipped the coffee table on its side to do incline pushups, did pistol squats off the edge of a sturdy wooden box, and performed pull-ups on the archway that separated the kitchen from the living room. When he wanted to work in some cardio, he went swimming at the indoor pool. Earlier in our marriage, I would go with him and watch as his wiry body cut perfect laps from one end of the pool to the other. I usually brought my camera too, but I was too busy drooling to take many pictures.

A droplet of sweat glistened in the hollow of Ben's throat, balancing on his collarbone. As he swept his hair out of his face, the droplet ran down the middle of his chest and disappeared into his shirt.

"I was out like a light for the entire night," Ben said. "I didn't hear anything."

I shook my head, trying to remember what I was talking about. "I heard voices in the walls, like people were whispering to each other."

"Babe, there's no one in the walls. It was probably rats."

The mention of rodents cooled me off in less than the time it took for Ben to start sweating. I definitely couldn't go back to sleep now, not with Ben waging war against the house. As far as the whispering walls went, his explanation made more sense than my lack of one. As old as the mansion was, it was normal for things to occasionally go bump in the night.

"Ouch!" Ben huffed as he withdrew from another window board, this time unable to yank it off the wall. He studied his palm. "Got a splinter."

"Let me see."

He sat at the foot of my cot as I finally emerged from the sleeping bag. The chilly winter air took the opportunity to seep through the threads of my sweater and nestle next to my skin. Ben rested his hand in my lap. He'd downplayed the size of the "splinter." A sharp chunk of wood was embedded in the soft tissue of his palm. I checked the angle of entry before giving it a clean jerk to get it out of Ben's hand.

"*Ow!*" He pulled away, shaking his hand to redistribute the pain. "What did you do that for? Why didn't you warn me?"

"If I had warned you, you would've been a big baby about it, and it would've been harder to pull out." I carefully wrapped the splinter in one of the empty snack bags from last night. "This way, it doesn't bleed as much. How's it look? Do you need a bandage?"

"I think it's fine." He squeezed a tiny drop of blood from the wound and wiped it away. "Good as new. Thanks for doing that."

I swung my legs out of my sleeping bag, slipped my feet into my boots, and put on my puffy winter coat. "No problem, but I'm not playing nurse every time you get hurt because you're exercising your right to manhandle this house. If you're going to start ripping this place apart, you need gloves. Let's go into town."

Ben switched his flannel pajama pants for a pair of black, fleece-lined trousers. "Do you really want to go to town out of concern for my soft writer hands? Or are you jonesing for a cup of coffee."

"Coffee. Duh."

"I told you we should've bought the instant coffee last night."

"You know how I feel about instant coffee."

"That it tastes like dirty water." He pulled a crimson quarter-zip sweater over the top of his head and checked his reflection in the newly exposed window. With a few tweaks, he got his unruly curls to sit in perfect formation again. "I'm starving anyway. Are you ready?"

"Do I look ready?"

He checked me over. Puffy skin weighed heavily below my eyes. Cold, clammy sweat glued my inner thighs together. I wanted a hot shower and a real bed. A cup of coffee wasn't going to fix the issue, but it would at least postpone my breaking point.

"No," Ben said. "You certainly don't."

. . .

SINCE WE WERE ALREADY familiar with Black Cat Café, we went back for breakfast. This time, Hayden wasn't there to pester us with questions, but we drew just as much attention as the day before. As we stepped up to the counter, a petite man with no hair but a fabulous blond handlebar mustache waited to take our order. He wore a gray sweater with black stripes around the sleeves and a green scarf. The outfit combination along with his dark beady eyes made him look like a nosy pigeon.

"You must be Ben and Peyton," he cooed before bothering to welcome us in. "Everyone in town is talking about you. I'm so happy to meet you in person!"

"We're the talk of the town, huh?" I asked. "Super."

"You know how it is," the man said. "Falconwood is so tiny that whenever we get newbies, it's like having a celebrity in town. I'm Mason, by the way. I own the fine establishment you see before you." He beamed proudly, stretching his arms wide to showcase his assistant barista hard at work on the industrial espresso machine behind the counter as well as the many busy tables in the sit-down area of the café. "I heard you came in yesterday, but I had already left for the day. My husband caught that terrible virus going around, and he was dying for some chicken noodle soup."

"I hope he feels better," Ben said. "My wife turns into a tyrant when she's sick."

"Says the man who acts like he's dying of the plague every time he gets a cough," I shot back. "Don't listen to a thing he says, Mason."

Mason chuckled. "What can I get you today?"

After we ordered, Ben found a table in the middle of the shop and set paper napkins out for both of us. The café wasn't as busy as it was yesterday afternoon since everyone was at work and school. As I sat across from Ben, I stared absently through the window. The ice skating rink was empty except for a single woman practicing pirouettes.

"What is it?" Ben asked.

"What's what?"

"You went quiet," he said, handing me a packet of raw sugar for when my black coffee arrived. "That means something's wrong."

"I was just enjoying the sights."

"Peyton, just tell me."

I folded my napkin into a paper airplane and chucked it across the table. It nosedived into Ben's jacket. "You keep talking about us like we're still married."

"We *are* still married."

"You're giving people the wrong idea."

Ben leaned across the table, lowering his voice. "What am I supposed to say? 'Hi, this is my wife, but we're getting a divorce soon, and the only reason we're in this town is because of an obligation to sell the rotting mansion in the woods'?"

"That would be better than letting them think we're a happily married couple ready to settle down here," I whispered back.

"Would it?" he said. "We're not going to be here long enough for it to matter anyway, so who cares?"

"I care," I replied. "I don't want you to get confused."

He pulled away, like I was a bee that stung him on the nose. "Confused about what?"

"About us."

Ben scoffed and looked out the window. "Believe me, Peyton. I'm not confused."

"You called me babe this morning."

Mason arrived with our breakfast order, balancing two large plates on his forearm and carrying both coffees in the other hand. He set everything down with practiced perfection.

"French toast and freshly whipped cream for the lady, eggs and bacon for the gentleman, and coffee all around. Anything else I can get for you? Syrup for the French toast?"

"We're good," Ben answered. "Thanks, Mason."

"No problem. Holler if you need something."

After Mason walked away, I prodded the dry French toast with my fork. "Actually, Mason, I'd love some syrup. Thanks for asking."

"Why didn't you say anything?"

"You didn't give me a chance."

Ben went to the counter and waited patiently until Mason was finished with his next set of customers. Upon Ben's return, he tossed a few pre-packaged packets of maple syrup onto the table. One tumbled into my lap.

"Gee, thanks."

Ben unfolded the paper plane napkin and set it on his lap. "I was going to tell you something before you got all righteous."

"Boy, do I really want to hear about it."

"Fine then."

He dug into his breakfast and pretended I wasn't there. I drizzled syrup in an erratic zig-zag across the top of my French toast. Underneath Ben's layer of nonchalance, his bottom lip jutted out, and the line in the middle of his chin that only appeared when he was upset came out to play.

"Look, I'm sorry, okay?" I said, setting the packet on the table. The extra syrup leaked out, leaving a sticky brown mess next to my plate. "This is hard for me too."

"Doesn't seem like it," Ben muttered. "Ever since David told us about the house, you've been acting like it's a prison sentence."

"Because it was like getting to the end of a marathon and realizing they'd moved the finish line another twenty miles down the road," I told him. "I had plans, Ben—"

"What plans?" he asked. "You've been talking about all these things you're going to do after we're divorced like it's my fault you never got to do them before. I didn't stop you from traveling, Peyton. *You* were the one who never made plans."

"I couldn't leave," I argued. "What would everyone at home have said? What about the rumors that would've flown if I ditched my husband to pursue my career?"

I'd never seen anyone wipe their mouth so furiously as Ben did. He set the napkin and his fork on the table with contained rage, but the impact still rattled our coffee mugs.

"What do you think you're doing now?" he hissed across the table. "Back then, we were partners. We supported each other's decisions. When I said I wanted to go to the nearest university so I could stay close to my mom, you agreed. When you wanted to start up your photography business, I agreed. If you had told me you wanted to go to Argentina to photograph some rare species of monkey, I would have let you go and waited for you to come home. That's what husbands and wives do, Peyton." He took a sip of coffee in an attempt to do something that looked normal and calm. "Then, I wouldn't have seen it as ditching your husband to pursue your career. *Now*, that's exactly what you're doing."

My frazzled emotions, heightened by my lack of sleep, boiled hotter in the pit of my stomach than the coffee in Mason's espresso machine. I pushed my plate into Ben's, the clang of clashing porcelain echoing through the café, and left without another word.

We kept arguing about the same crap. Ben was content to stay in the same place we had both grown up in, work the same old job, and do the same things we did every single day until we both died. Meanwhile, I was suffocating. The world waited for me to explore it—all I needed was a one-way plane ticket—but Ben was wrong about my lack of initiative. All these years, I'd stayed home for him. I'd said yes to everything he wanted, with the single exception of starting a family. Long ago, I promised we could have a baby when I turned thirty, but as time passed, I couldn't envision myself being pregnant with Ben's child. If there was a surefire way to permanently tie myself to home, it was by having a kid.

Before I turned the corner, I paused to take one more look at Ben through the window of the café. His head was bowed toward the table, his hands tucked behind his neck. Our breakfasts were equally untouched. When the bell rang over the door as someone else entered, the coffee in Ben's cup rippled. He shoved the mug as far from himself as possible. It clinked against my own abandoned cup, and the lip of his mug kissed mine.

I walked off. Though the sky was clear of clouds and there was no more snow on its way for now, the crisp air stung my nose and dried out my lips. I stopped in at the corner store, bought a travel-sized Aquaphor, and smeared a heavy coat across the lower half of my face. With better skin protection, taking a walk through Falconwood's main street to clear my head wasn't quite so unbearable.

From what I could tell, not one of the shops in the town square was owned by a corporation or larger business. Every boutique, market, and bakery was managed by one of the local families. There was one bank and one pharmacy, and all three levels of education—elementary, middle, and high—were combined into one school building. The people were just as friendly and inviting as their shop windows. I passed stranger after stranger on the sidewalks, but every single one of them acted like we were acquainted in some way. They nodded or smiled or waved as we crossed paths. As someone who avoided as much human contact as possible in my hometown, returning the polite gestures was somewhat out of character for me, but the simplicity of settling into an easy smile caused my mood to tick upward. After a few blocks, I actually enjoyed exchanging pleasantries with the locals.

Hoping to avoid Ben wherever he might have gone after he left the café, I skipped the hardware store. I took a look in the furniture shop next door, where I spoke to the owner about a modular bed frame that could be assembled without any tools. The news had spread all over town about mine and Ben's arrival, so when I bought a full-sized bed instead of a king-sized, the seller gave me a long, scrutinizing look. Thankfully, he didn't bother to push the subject.

After visiting a few other stores, a tiny shop window caught my eye. It was a small photography shop, squished between the barber and the pharmacy. If it weren't for the display of antique lenses in the window, I never would have noticed it. When I went inside, a little bell over the door jingled to announce my entrance. As the owner glanced up, a raindrop of annoyance dropped onto my face and curled my lip upward. Couldn't anyone in this town leave me alone for five seconds? But the shop owner waved and went back to whatever he was doing, leaving me to peruse in peace and a little bit of guilt.

The photography shop had a little bit of everything, from used cameras dating years back to brand-new DSLRs. My own camera was a bit old. I'd bought it when digital cameras were just beginning to become more common than film, so it didn't have all the bells and whistles of the newer models. For years, I had shopped around for a new one, but when it came time to cough up the cash, I always reneged. I hadn't taken one picture since my business failed, and there was no point in calling myself a photographer anymore. Still, the familiarity of the shop cooled my head and calmed my pulse, which had been racing with anxiety ever since I left Ben at Black Cat. I wandered around, eventually making my way to the back of the store, where the shop owner tinkered with an old film camera. He was an older man, maybe Basil's age, who wore pince-nez glasses and a garish orange knit hat to keep his head warm.

"Need anything?" he asked without bothering to look up.

"Not at the moment. Just looking."

"Enjoy your gander."

As I inspected an old Leica lens, the bell over the door chimed and in walked Della Gordon. She didn't notice me as she beelined for the back of the shop. The shop owner set down his camera and beamed at her.

"Miss Della," he said. They kissed each other's cheeks over the counter. "Are you here to pick up your photos?"

"And to bring you these, Chester." Della set a picnic basket on the counter and folded back the gingham to show Chester the dozen freshly-baked muffins inside. The sweet scent of chocolate wafted across the store. "For putting a rush job on the pictures."

"Oh, you know I don't mind," Chester said as he ogled the muffins. "It's not like I have much to do here anyway. You two are the first visitors I've had all day, but I'll never say no to your muffins, Della."

"Us two?" Della looked over her shoulder. I waved when she spotted me, and a huge smile crossed her face. "Peyton! Would you like a muffin?"

"Like Chester here, I'll never say no to a muffin."

Della beckoned me over and offered me the basket. "They're vegan and gluten free. Basil and I like to eat as healthily as possible."

"It shows," I said, choosing a blueberry muffin out of the mixed bag. "You're both so fit. It's incredible. I hope I'm still in shape when—"

"When you're old?" Della chuckled as my cheeks turned pink.

The phone in the back room rang, and Chester excused himself from the muffin party to answer it. Della offered me a cloth napkin from her bag so I wouldn't get crumbs all over the floor of the shop.

"I admire you," I said. "You seem to like your life. A lot of people don't, you know?"

"Are you including yourself amongst those people?" Della closed the muffin basket and set it aside. "I'm sensing a little restlessness within you."

A blueberry stuck to the roof of my mouth, and I performed a series of tongue acrobatics to free my voice from its sticky prison. "It's a long story."

"I've got time."

"It all started when I was fourteen," I began in a poor imitation of a movie voice over.

Della laughed and rolled her eyes. "I suppose that is a long story. We'll have to get coffee sometime to talk about it. Just us girls."

While the thought of getting to know any other of Falconwood locals made me cringe, Della's offer took some of the weight off my shoulders. It might be nice to get to know someone who wasn't already familiar with the intimate details of my life.

"I'd like that."

"You'll have to tell me all about the Abram Mansion too," she said. "That place has been empty for so long. I hope you don't mind, but I've snuck out there to photograph it a few times."

I waved a hand to dismiss her apology. "That's totally fine. I probably would've done the same thing."

"It's such an interesting house. Beautiful too, even in decay."

"What else do you know about it?" I asked. "It's kind of a mystery why my grandfather left it to me. I don't know much about the property. Who were the Abrams anyway?"

Della leaned against the counter and picked up the camera Chester had been tinkering with. As she examined it, she said, "I don't know the whole story. Basil and I moved here about ten years ago, and the drama had long since subsided by then. From what I understand, a young family once lived there: Percy Abram, his wife Penelope, and their daughter Alyssa. They were picture-perfect from the outside. Percy hosted all kinds of parties at the mansion, and the whole town would show up."

"Then something tragic happened," I guessed.

Della nodded solemnly. "Percy and his wife grew apart, and soon the whole town knew Penelope had had an affair. She left Percy for the other man, and she took Alyssa with her. Percy was in such distress—"

She trailed off, her focus slipping to the camera between her deft fingers. I nudged her shoulder.

"What happened to Percy?"

"He died," she answered. "He couldn't take the grief of losing his wife to another man."

I let out a low whistle. "That's rough."

"The town was in bits," Della went on, now using one of Chester's miniature screwdrivers to maneuver a piece of the camera into a different place. "Everyone adored the Abrams. I imagine it was a bit of a shock to see their family fall apart."

A tiny screw fell out of the camera, and I caught it in my palm before it rolled off the counter. "What about afterward? My grandfather Andrew Anderson came to own the mansion. Do you know anything about him?"

She took the screw from me with a thankful tip of her chin. "I've heard the name a few times over the years, but just in passing. I'm afraid I'm not as familiar with him."

My phone chimed, and I checked the messages to find a text from Ben: *Back at the house. See you whenever.* I sighed heavily.

"Everything all right?" Della asked.

"Ben's gone home," I said. "Which means I don't have a ride."

"I'll drop you off," she offered. When I grimaced, she added,

"It doesn't have to be right now. We can go for a stroll if you like. I'll give you a quick rundown on the town."

"I'd like that."

By the time Della and I got back to the Abram Mansion, dusk had fallen. She'd helped me pick out a few things to make the place a little more homey—duvets, bath towels, and the like—but I didn't have any intention of taking them out of the bags until we cleaned up the house. I thanked Della for the ride and sent her on her way with the excuse that the house was too dirty to invite her inside. She took a raincheck and headed out. The interaction was so simple and uncomplicated for a small town. At home, anyone else would have pushed the issue.

A big white construction truck was parked next to mine and Ben's SUV, and to my surprise, there was a light on inside the entryway. When I went in, Ben was deep in concentration with a broad-shouldered man wearing fleece-lined buffalo plaid and heavy brown boots.

"Just keep an eye on it," the buffalo man was saying. "In a place this big, you're bound to get some leaks after forty years. I'll be back tomorrow with my crew, and we'll get things up and running in no time."

Ben shook the man's beefy hand. "Thanks, Jim. I appreciate you coming out on such short notice."

"It's no problem at all," Jim replied. "I love jobs like this. We don't see too much work in Falconwood. My boys and I usually travel elsewhere to keep busy, so this is the best commute I've had in years."

I cleared my throat. Jim and Ben turned to face me.

"This must be the wife." Jim beamed at me. With his rosy, plump cheeks and full brown beard, he looked like a younger version of Santa Claus. He shook my hand with both of his, which were surprisingly soft for a contractor. "Ben told me all about you. I can imagine you're not too happy living here for the moment, but we'll get everything nice and tight for you as quickly as possible. I've already got the power and the water back on for you, ma'am, so it won't be as rough as last night for ya."

For such a large man, Jim came off as a giant teddy bear. Evidently, all of Falconwood locals possessed genuine small-town charm. I let Jim keep my hand for a moment longer.

"Thank you," I said. "It's a pleasure to meet you."

"Pleasure's all mine." He extracted an earflap hat from his back pocket that matched the pattern of his coat and pulled it on over his tufty brown hair. "I should get going. My wife's waiting for me at home. I'll see the two of you bright and early tomorrow morning?"

"You got it," said Ben.

Jim saw himself out. The rumble of his engine faded as he drove into the woods. Ben didn't say a word to me, organizing a pile of tools and hardware Jim had presumably brought with him. The entryway looked both better and worse with the chandelier shedding actual light overhead. On one hand, the golden light warmed the room and gave it a cozier vibe than the chilling darkness of last night. On the other hand, it illuminated every flaw in the entryway. Each rip in the wallpaper, crack in the molding, and dent in the floorboards took center stage.

"You didn't tell me you were meeting with Jim today," I said to Ben.

"Meant it to be a surprise," he huffed, keeping his back toward me as he continued working. "Got the water running in the kitchen and the bathroom next to it."

"Where's the kitchen?"

"Downstairs. Electricity's only working in this section of the house, but I did clear out a room on this floor for you if you wanted to get some privacy tonight," Ben said. "I moved your cot in there already."

"Where are you sleeping?"

"Here," he replied. "I only had time to clean the one room."

"Thanks for doing that."

"Mm-hmm. I had Jim hook up the fridge and the stove too. If we get the kitchen cleaned up, you can start using it tomorrow."

Guilt crawled like a parasite into my brain. While Ben had been busting his butt to make the Abram Mansion livable, I'd been shopping with Della and making absolutely no use of myself. The shopping bags weighed like concrete in my hands, especially when Ben caught sight of them but didn't say anything.

"Which room?" I asked.

"First door on the left down the hall," Ben said. "Looks like it used to be a drawing room."

He didn't show me to it, a sign that things had definitely changed between us, and it wasn't my imagination. When we first looked into buying our house back home, Ben had swept me into his arms, lifted me over the threshold, and carried me into the bedroom. All of that whimsical playfulness was missing now.

Ben had cleansed the drawing room of every speck of dust and grime. Other than some general wear and tear, it was in pretty decent shape. Blank canvases were stacked in the corner, and an easel stood by the window. The window looked out on the snowy courtyard that Ben and I had yet to explore. The mansion was built in a large square with the courtyard in the center. Overgrown topiaries bordered a veiled pathway. Dead vines snaked around a huge trellis. In the center of everything, an empty pool lay cracked from disuse. In the moonlight, the courtyard was a magical land of mystery and snow. Years ago, it was probably a lovely place to spend hot summer days.

I set my new duvet and pillows on top of the sleeping bag already on my cot. Ben had done his best to arrange the room to my liking. He put the cot by the window, right next to the hot radiator. He'd also placed one of the side tables nearby and added a small lamp. He'd even folded my clothes and put them away in a large storage cabinet that he'd also purged of dirt.

"Got everything you need?" Ben's voice floated from the doorway.

"I think so," I said. "Where are my toiletries?"

"Already in the bathroom. Night."

He returned to the entryway and turned off the chandelier so the light spilling into the hallway extinguished itself. I coaxed the small lamp next to my bed on to combat the shadowy darkness, changed into pajamas, and went downstairs to brush my teeth. The lower levels were quite chilly, so I hurried back to my room as quickly as possible. Ben was already asleep in his own cot by the fire, his back rising and falling with the rhythm of his breath. A little pang hit my heart like a mallet on a steel drum. Though we'd been sleeping apart at home for a while now, it felt different in the big mansion. I almost missed him.

I snuggled up under my new duvet and stared up at the sky through the window. Since the mansion was practically in the middle of nowhere, there wasn't much light pollution, and the stars were more visible than anywhere else I'd seen. I traced constellations with an imaginary paintbrush until I dozed off.

THE WHISPERS CAME BACK in the middle of the night, and there was no mistaking it for rats or mice scurrying through the walls. Children's voices sang muddled songs in my head, pulling me out of sleep. In the hallway, a pair of footsteps scurried past my room. A high voice giggled.

"Ben?" I called.

No one answered. I put my slippers on, crept to the door, and peeked into the hallway. All was quiet and still until something rattled a few rooms away. As I snuck out, Ben was fast asleep in the entryway. I left him that way, sure he would call me paranoid if I woke him up for a few lousy noises, but I took a poker from beside the fireplace and followed the muted lullabies down the stairs.

At the entrance to the kitchen, I paused with my back to the wall. The singing and giggles had faded. Nothing moved or breathed. I was sure my head was playing tricks on me.

"It's nothing, Peyton," I muttered to myself. "Get yourself together."

I squared my shoulders, stepped into the kitchen, and screamed.

A little boy stood by the stove, gripping a butcher's knife in his small hand.

4

I swung the fire poker up out of pure instinct, but fear and shock sprang up in the boy's eyes in the form of copious tears. He dropped the knife and stepped backward, right into a pile of debris that Ben had swept up earlier. He tipped his head back and howled before sitting on the floor to cradle his bare foot in his lap. Blood dripped from the arch of his foot. I tossed the fire poker aside and went to the boy. He balked at first, but I stroked his thin blond hair, and he calmed down. He looked to be about five or six years old.

"Hey, kiddo," I said softly. "My name's Peyton. What's yours?"

"S-Sammy," he replied, choking back tears.

"Hi, Sammy. Can I have a look at your foot?"

Reluctantly, he extended his leg so his foot rested in my lap. A rusty nail was embedded deep in the skin. I hid a grimace. This kid definitely needed a tetanus shot.

"Hold on a second," I said, gently placing his foot on the floor. I wet a paper towel underneath the cold water from the faucet then sat with the boy again. "This might hurt a little bit, but you have to be brave, okay?"

Sammy sniffled and nodded.

"Ready? Three, two—"

Before I got to one, I tugged the nail out of Sammy's foot. Unlike Ben, who made a fuss over a splinter, Sammy flinched once before opening his eyes to get a look at the bloody nail. I pressed the wet paper towel against the bottom of his foot to stop the bleeding.

"Can I keep it?" Sammy asked, reaching for the nail.

"I'm afraid not, buddy." I tossed the nail into the nearby garbage pail. "It's dangerous. What are you doing in here—?"

Footsteps thundered down the stairs, and Ben entered the kitchen. "What the hell is going on in here?" he asked. "I heard screaming."

"And you *just* made it down here?" I asked as Sammy cowered behind me.

"I had to put my shoes on," Ben said. "Why is there a kid in here?"

"That's what I was trying to figure out before you thundered in here like an angry bear," I told him. To Sammy, I said, "That's just Ben. You don't have to be afraid of him. Ben, this is Sammy."

Ben took in Sammy's tearstained face and bloody foot. When he spoke again, it was with a more delicate tone. "Hi, Sammy. It's nice to meet you. Are you okay?"

Sammy nodded, his chin wobbling.

"He stepped on a nail," I said. "But he's going to be fine."

Ben knelt to get on our level, his instincts on dealing with children finally kicking in. "Sammy, how did you get in here?"

"The dog door." Sammy sniffled and wiped his nose on his sleeve. "That's how I always come in."

"You've been here before?" I asked.

"My friend lives here, but my Mama doesn't let me come play with her."

Ben wore the same confused expression I imagined I had on my face. "No one else lives here, buddy," he said. "Peyton and I just got here yesterday. The house has been empty for years."

Sammy shook his head with so much intensity that I was afraid it might spin right off. "No, that's not true. My friend lives here."

"What's your friend's name?" I asked him.

He pressed his lips together and looked away, tapping his fingers rapidly against the tile floor as if trying to expel some of the energy he was storing from concealing too many details.

"Never mind." I checked the state of Sammy's foot. Beneath the paper towel, his skin was all torn up from the nail, and it hadn't stopped bleeding yet. "Your mom doesn't know you're here, does she?"

"No, she's sleeping."

"Where does she live?"

"In town," Sammy says.

"You walked all the way here?" Ben asked, astonished. "Barefoot in the snow?"

"No, I took my shoes off before I came in," Sammy said. "She doesn't like it when you wear shoes in the house."

"Who doesn't—you know what? Never mind." I looked outside the kitchen door and found Sammy's boots dusted with a layer of snow. "Here they are." I helped Sammy wiggle his good foot into the first boot but hesitated at the second. "Wait here for a second, Sammy."

I left Sammy with Ben then returned to the kitchen a minute later with a pair of fluffy wool socks from Ben's duffel bag. With Sammy's permission, I wrapped his foot with a layer of clean paper towels, pulled the sock over top, then put his boot on.

"I think we're going to take you to the emergency clinic, Sammy," I told him as I helped him to my feet. "That way, we can get you fixed up and call your mom to let her know where you are."

Sammy pulled his tiny hand out of mine. "It's okay. I can walk home by myself."

"I don't think that's a good idea, buddy," Ben said.

"I've done it before." Sammy got down on all fours and crawled toward the doggy door. He was halfway out before we realized what he was doing.

"I don't think so, kiddo." Ben gently wiggled Sammy free of the doggy door and picked him up so he couldn't try again. "We'll take the front door."

"I'll get in trouble if Mama finds out I left," Sammy said as the three of us made our way to the entryway. "She worries too much."

I put on my boots and coat over my pajamas. Then Ben handed Sammy to me so he could do the same. For his age, Sammy was quite small and light, like he was made out of bird bones. As we stepped outside, his bright green eyes reflected the stars up above. I buckled him into the backseat of the SUV and sat next to him to make him feel more comfortable, and Ben drove us all into town.

The emergency clinic was the closest thing Falconwood had to a hospital. When we carried Sammy inside, the night receptionist gave him a lollipop to distract him while a pediatric nursing student dressed his foot with antiseptic gel and real bandages instead of paper towels. While Sammy was being taken care of, the receptionist phoned the police for us.

"An officer will be here shortly," she said. "Are you two going to wait?"

"No, I think we're going to head out if your staff has everything under control," Ben answered for the both of us. "It's late."

Upon hearing Ben's reply, Sammy's bottom lip quivered. A single tear hovered on his bottom eyelash, waiting to drop. "You're going to leave me here alone?"

I ruffled Sammy's hair while the nurse finished wrapping his foot with bright green gauze. "You won't be alone, bud. The nurse is going to stay with you until the police come, and then they're going to call your mom."

At the word "police," Sammy released the dam of his tears, and they poured down his cheeks. "I don't like the police," he said. "I want my mom."

"They'll find her," Ben insisted. "And the police aren't going to hurt you. They're here to help you."

"But I don't like them," Sammy blubbered, curling his knees into his chest and sobbing into his dinosaur-printed pajama pants. "P-please don't l-leave me."

"Okay, we won't," I said, squeezing Sammy's big toe to distract him from his emotions. "We'll say with you until your mom gets here. Is that okay?"

Sammy peeked at me from the shelter of his knees. "You p-promise?"

"I promise."

Behind me, Ben let out an annoyed huff. "Can I talk to you, Peyton? In private?"

"I'll be right back," I assured Sammy before following Ben down the hallway and into the waiting room. "What's your problem?"

He paced from the snack machine to the drink machine and back again. "My problem? My problem is that it's three in the morning, I'm tired, and a little kid broke into our house and got hurt. You do realized his mom might show up and decide to sue us, right? We could be liable here."

"That's what you're worried about?" I asked. "Ben, it's just a bandage and a tetanus shot. The kid's not dying."

"You know how parents are," Ben said. "They're vicious when it comes to their kids, and I'm not waiting here all night for his mom to show up. I mean, what kind of mother doesn't realize her son has snuck out of the house and walked over a mile in the snow?"

"Probably the kind that doesn't have any help," I answered. "In which case, she might be comforted to know that someone bothered to wait with Sammy until she showed up."

Ben stuck a dollar in the vending machine and pounded the key option. A bag of chocolate chip cookies fell into the drop zone. "You can stay," Ben said, reaching in for the bag. "But I'm not sticking around. If I don't get any sleep tonight, I'll be too tired to help Jim out tomorrow."

He stalked off with the bag of cookies before I could answer, forcing me to tail after him like a desperate stray puppy. "Are you serious? You're going to go home and leave me here alone?"

"Do you want to get this house in shape or not?" Ben asked. "Because the way I see it, we can either live in a dump for six months or actually do some work so the house is worth something when we're ready to sell it."

I would've bombarded him with more questions, but we arrived back in Sammy's room, where the nurse had just finished administering his tetanus shot. Ben forced a smile and tossed the bag of cookies to Sammy.

"Those are for you, kiddo," he said. "Figured you deserved a treat after being such a trooper all night long."

Sammy tore open the cookies and shoved one into his mouth. "Thanks, Ben," he said, spitting crumbs everywhere. "Is my mom here yet?"

"Not yet," I answered.

The receptionist popped her head into the room. "Mr. and Mrs. Fletcher? The police are here to speak with you."

Sammy paused with the next cookie halfway to his mouth, his eyes trained on Ben's back as he left without saying goodbye. I patted Sammy's knee.

"Don't worry," I said. "I'll be right back."

In the reception area, Ben was already shaking hands with a blonde police officer whose ponytail reached halfway down her back. She was nearly as tall as Ben with high cheekbones and shiny hazel eyes. Beneath her tight uniform pants, her thighs were thick enough to crush a watermelon between them.

"You must be Peyton," she said as I approached. She shook my hand too, nearly breaking it off in the process. "I'm Officer Spaughton, or Hillary if you're feeling a bit less formal. I was just telling your husband that this isn't the first time we've found Sammy Baker somewhere he wasn't supposed to be."

"Does he run away a lot?" I asked.

"All the time," Hillary replied. "I've personally picked him up twice in the last few months. It's a pretty regular occurrence."

"Where's his mom?" Ben asked, not bothering to hide his judgment. "Why does he keep running away from her? Shouldn't you guys be investigating that?"

Hillary bristled at his accusatory phrasing. "Sammy's mom is one of the best people in town, but she raises Sammy on her own and when you have a kid that likes to sneak out, it can be difficult to keep track of him. Anything else you'd like to ask me?"

Ben shut up, recognizing his mistake. I smirked. It wasn't often that he didn't have a comeback. The Amazon officer had scared him silent, and I respected her all the more for it.

"He doesn't want to stay alone with you," I told Hillary, then hastily added, "No offense."

Hillary softened her strong, broad shoulders and shrugged. "None taken. Sammy loves his mom more than anyone else, but he hates to disappoint her. He knows if the police pick him up, she's going to be notified he snuck out again. Who knows how many times he's made it out of the house and back in again without her noticing? You can take off. You've done your civic duty. I can handle it from here."

"I promised Sammy I'd stay with him until his mom got here," I told her. "But Ben was on his way out."

Ben stuttered as I pushed him toward the door. "Yeah, I've got some stuff to handle tomorrow. I would stay, but you know —" His eyes lingered a moment too long on the fine lines of Hillary's jaw. "Stuff to do."

"Sure," she said. "You should get on that."

"I'll see you around, Officer," he babbled. "I mean, Hillary."

Heat rose in my face to match Ben's as the reason for his blush became obvious. I shoved him outside. He struggled to put his coat back on, all the while glancing through the glass door for another look at Hillary. I snapped my fingers in front of his glazed eyes.

"Hello?" I said. "Can you wait to start checking out other women until after we're divorced? I know it was my idea and everything, but you're still wearing your damn wedding ring."

Ben blinked furiously as if to clear floaters from his eyes. "I wasn't checking her out."

"Then why are you blushing?"

"It's cold out."

"Whatever," I said, taking the car keys out of his pocket and putting them in his hand. "I know I don't have a right to be mad. Do whatever you want with Officer Hot."

"Peyton, relax," he said. "I'm not going to cheat on you."

"It's not cheating if we're separated," I reminded him. "We agreed, remember?"

"You agreed," Ben replied. "We've been married for ten years. I'm not ready to date someone new." He planted a kiss on my cheek. "I'll see you at home."

He hopped into the SUV and drove up the road, carving muddy tire tracks through the continually falling snow. For the second time today, I'd have to find an alternate ride home.

Inside, Sammy and Officer Spaughton—Hillary—were in the middle of a staring contest. The prize, from the looks of it, was the last cookie in the snack bag from the vending machine. Hillary leaned over Sammy and widened her eyes. Just as Sammy's eyelids looked ready to crack, Hillary made a big show of blinking.

"Gah!" She rubbed her eyes with a furious spasm. "Darn it, Sammy! You're too good at this game."

Sammy giggled gleefully and popped the last cookie into his mouth, chewing it with vehement victory. "I always win, Officer Spaughton."

"You're right," Hillary said. "I don't know why I even try."

Someone knocked into my shoulder in a rush to get into the treatment room, and a wave of silky brown hair flicked across my face like a whip.

"Sammy!"

The owner of the hair, a woman a few years younger than me with a heart-shaped face and wind-whipped cheeks, went straight to the little boy. She wasn't wearing a coat or a hat. Snow had settled on her hair and shoulders, but she was unconcerned with her own comfort.

"What happened?" she gasped, holding up his foot to examine it. "Did you get hurt?"

"He stepped on a nail," Hillary said. "But he's all fixed up now."

"*Where* did you step on a nail?"

"At my house," I offered. Ben's warning about parents wanting to sue at the drop of a hat circled through my mind, but I pushed it away. "I live at the Abram Mansion. There's a lot of debris around right now. Sammy got in through the doggy door."

"Sam." The woman took the little boy's face between her hands. "How many times have I told you not to sneak out at night? It's too dangerous for you to be out on your own. Look what happened to you. And you could have frozen to death!"

Sammy's lips were squished between his mother's palms, but he squeaked, "I'm fine, Mama. I just wanted to see my friend."

The woman threaded Sammy's arms through the bright red coat she had brought for him. "I've told you a million times. No one lives at that house. You have to stop going there."

"But Mama—"

"No." She zipped his coat up to his chin with a sense of firm finality. "I don't want to hear any excuses. You have to start listening to me, Sammy, or you're going to end up getting hurt." She pulled him into a tight hug, and his little arms encircled her neck. "Do you know what would happen to me if I were to lose you, little dude?"

"You would be really sad?"

"That's right," she said, nodding. "I would be really, really sad." She helped Sammy jump off the examination table and put up his hood. "Go wait in the hallway with Officer Spaughton. I want to talk to this nice lady for a minute."

Sammy took Hillary's hand, and she led him out of the room. Sammy's mother turned to face me since the first time she entered. I braced myself, ready for the onslaught, but instead of confronting me about the safety issues inside the mansion, the woman let out a quick, contained sob.

"Hey, it's okay." I offered her a tissue from the box on the exam counter. "Everything's fine. Sammy wasn't hurt too badly. They said his foot would heal up in a few days. He didn't even need stitches."

The woman blew her nose and wiped her eyes. "I know. I'm overreacting. It's just—Sammy and I have been through a lot. He keeps getting out of the house no matter what I do. I'm so sorry he turned up at your place. You said he came in through the doggy door?"

"Yeah, we found him in the kitchen," I said. I almost mentioned that Sammy had been holding a butcher's knife when I'd first seen him, but I didn't want to give the stressed-out mother any more nightmares. "I'm Peyton, by the way. Peyton Fletcher. We just moved here two days ago."

"Theo Baker. I'd shake your hand, but—" She brandished the snotty tissues. I pushed the waste basket toward her so she could deposit them. "I didn't know someone moved into the Abram place."

"Really?" I asked. "Because apparently everyone else does."

"That's the thing with small towns, isn't it?" she said, trying to smile. "Everyone knows everyone else's business."

"I'm pretty used to it. Our hometown isn't much bigger than Falconwood."

"It was different for me at first," Theo said. "I moved from Hoboken when I got pregnant with Sammy. I needed the support of a community like this. It's amazing. It's like I have three thousand babysitters at my disposal. Wherever Sammy goes, someone's watching over him. Anyway—" She spotted a bottle of hand sanitizer by the sink, pressed the pump, and rubbed it into her hands. Then she finally shook mine. "It was nice to meet you, Peyton. I should get Sammy back home and into bed."

"Yeah, I should call a cab," I said, taking out my phone.

"You don't have a car?"

"My husband drove us here," I answered. "But he went back home to get some sleep."

Theo wrinkled her nose. "I'll give you a ride."

"No, really. You have to take care of Sammy—"

She turned me around and marched me out of the exam room where Sammy was waiting with Hillary. They were playing another game. Sammy's hands rested on top of Hillary's palms. Every time she tried to lightly slap his hands, he pulled away with a ferocious giggle.

"Sammy," Theo called. "Say goodbye and thank you to Officer Spaughton. We're going home."

"Thanks, Officer Spaughton." Sammy saluted the officer then did a quick about-face. "See ya soon."

"I sure hope not," Theo muttered. To the cop, she added, "Thanks again, Hillary. I appreciate your help."

"Don't mention it, Theo. See you next time. Nice meeting you, Peyton. Do you need a ride back home?"

Though Officer Hillary Spaughton seemed perfectly nice, I couldn't stop thinking about the way Ben's brain devolved when he saw her.

"No, thank you," I said. "Theo's going to drive me."

Hillary walked us out and waited in the front seat of her cop cruiser until Theo had gotten Sammy buckled in. As Theo pulled out of the emergency clinic's parking lot, Hillary waved and turned in the opposite direction, back toward town.

"She seems friendly," I said.

"Hillary?" Theo flipped on the wipers to clear the windshield of snow. She drove a big green Jeep with giant textured wheels that made short work of the icy roads. "She's Sammy's favorite. She's actually babysat for him a few times."

"That's nice of her."

"If you ever need anything, someone in this town is guaranteed to help you out." Theo squinted ahead as the Falconwood lights faded behind us and the dark forest took over. "But first you have to help me out. Where am I going?"

"The turn is up there on the left, right after that big boulder," I said, pointing to the large, gray rock. "Can you see it?"

"Got it."

The Jeep trundled up the one-way road. Despite the bumpy journey, a light snore emanated from the backseat. Sammy was dead asleep, his head lolling on his shoulders. I reached back to roll up his hood and wedge it under his neck so he wouldn't be sore in the morning.

"Do you have kids?" Theo asked.

"No. It was never in the cards. Why?"

She nodded at Sammy in the rearview mirror. "You're good with him. He doesn't warm up to strangers easily."

"Well, I have to be honest," I said. "When I found him in the kitchen, he scared the living daylights out of me. I'm not used to being in such a big house. You hear things, you know?"

"I can't imagine," Theo said. "I'm so sorry."

"Don't be," I replied. "Everything turned out fine. I'm glad Sammy's okay."

The Jeep emerged from the trees and pulled into the front yard. Abram Mansion loomed above us like a huge gray castle. Ben had turned on the outside lights for me. The elaborate sconces cast a gloomy yellow light across the yard, like the snow was old and moldy.

"I've never seen this place before," Theo said, gazing up at the enormous house. "It's bigger than I thought it would be."

"You should see the inside." I opened my door just wide enough to let myself out, trying to keep the gusty wind from penetrating the Jeep's warm interior. "Thanks for the ride, Theo."

"Anytime," she replied. "And I still owe you one for getting Sammy to the clinic. Actually, I probably owe you another one for not freaking out when you found out he'd broken into your house."

I tightened my scarf around my neck. "It's not a big deal. Really."

"It is," she insisted. "At least let me take you out to lunch tomorrow while Sammy's in school. It'll give me the chance to thank you for real."

Since Ben was bound to be busy with his new job as well as Jim's construction crew, I didn't see any harm in going out for lunch with Theo.

"Sure," I said. "That sounds great. Take care."

"We will."

I waved goodbye as they pulled out of the yard. Then I made a run for the front door. The snow had picked up again, and the flakes were melting fast against my skin. The house was surprisingly toasty, since the radiators had been running all day now. As I kicked off my boots, I checked on Ben. Like Sammy, he was already fast asleep.

5

*W*ithout curtains, the sun came right through the window of the drawing room and laid across my face like a cold cat looking for a warm bed. Somehow, I'd wrapped myself so tightly in my new duvet that my arms and legs were bound to my sides. Though I appreciated the warmth, it took me a good few minutes to unravel myself. I put on my robe and slippers and went out into the entryway. Ben's bed was empty. He had folded up his sleeping bag and stored the cot against the wall, no doubt getting it out of the way of the construction crew. From the loud hammering above, I guessed Jim and his boys were already working on the leaky roof.

In the kitchen, Ben watched a pot of boiling water on the stove. He'd secured the dog door shut with duct tape. When I came in, I made sure to shuffle my feet against the floor so he knew I was there, but he didn't bother to turn around.

"Morning," I said, glancing over his shoulder at the simmering water. "What are you doing?"

"Making coffee," he grunted.

I picked up the little glass jar. "Instant?"

"We don't have a coffeemaker," he said. "So you're stuck with dirty water."

"Why didn't you go to Black Cat?"

"Because I have work to do, Peyton," he answered, barely masking his bad mood. "I can't drive into town every morning because you think instant coffee is beneath you."

I retreated from the stove. "I didn't say that. Why are you being like this?"

"Like what?"

"You've been in a funk since yesterday."

He opened the closest cabinet, where he'd stored two of our camping mugs. The kitchen, I realized, had been scrubbed clean. Ben must have gotten up early to wipe it down.

"Gee, Peyton," he said, now organizing the cabinets as if they were full of clutter and mess. "Why would I be in a bad mood after you left me in a café? After a little kid broke into our house so we were up all night taking care of him?"

"*We* weren't up all night," I reminded him. "You bailed."

"Because I can't do this anymore." He set the steel camping mug on the counter with more force than necessary. The mug bounced to the floor and twirled on its handle. "I tried to ignore it, but you keep acting like our relationship was always a mess. My only goal in our marriage was to make you as happy as possible. You can't blame me for not going after your dreams."

"Way to change the subject," I said. "You left me in town *twice* yesterday, Ben. I had to find two different people to drive me home."

"I've been thinking about what you said last night." He kept his back to me on the pretense of keeping an eye on the boiling water. "And I think you're right. I shouldn't feel guilty for looking at another woman. Not considering your past."

"What's that supposed to mean?"

He abandoned his water watch to confront me. "Do you

think I'm stupid? Do you think I don't know about the things you've done behind my back?"

My jaw unhinged and dropped to the floor. "I have no idea what you're talking about."

"Oh, yeah? How's Chrissy doing?"

"My old photography friend? I have no idea. Why?"

He scoffed. "You know why."

"I really don't."

"How'd you get home last night?" he challenged. "Did the cop give you a ride?"

"No, Theo did. Sammy's mom."

"So you found a new best friend," Ben spat like a venomous snake. "It figures."

The water in the pot boiled over, and the bubbly mess poured across the stove top. Ben's hand, planted on the counter, caught a bit of the splash. He yelped, flipped on the kitchen tap, and ran the burn under the cold water.

"Listen, Ben," I said, doing my best to keep my voice even. "I don't know why you woke up this morning and decided to get on my case. I know it's complicated between us right now, but you were the one who wanted to do this. We need to be able to get along because I can't fight with you for six months straight. If you—oh my God!"

Ben whirled around to see what I was staring at with such a horrified look on my face. "What? What is it? What did you see?"

"A face!" I pointed at the dirty window above the stove, set high in the wall to be right at ground level. "There was a face in the window, like a reflection." I checked behind me, but there was nothing lurking in the pantry. "I swear I saw it."

Ben wiped the window with the dish towel. "I don't see anything."

I pressed my palm to my chest, feeling my heart beat twice as fast. It had happened so quickly. For a brief moment, a small pale face had appeared in one of the square window frames. A second later, it was gone, almost as if it had never happened at all.

"Check outside," I said.

"Peyton, there's nothing there—"

"Check outside!"

With a heavy sigh, Ben unlatched the kitchen door and trudged up the stairs that led to the ground level. A minute later, he came back inside. "Like I said, nothing there. Peyton, watch out!"

As an ominous *rip!* echoed overhead, Ben tackled me. He wrapped his whole body around mine and dove into the hallway as a tremendous crash rocked the kitchen. We cowered on the floor, Ben using his own back to shield me as debris rained from the ceiling. He didn't move until everything was quiet. As the dust settled in the kitchen, it became clear what had happened. The light fixture—a miniature version of the chandelier in the entryway that was still rather large—had pulled free of the ceiling and fallen to the ground, taking the electrical work with it. Shattered glass was scattered around the kitchen and in the hallway.

As Ben got up, I planted my hand on the ground to help myself stand. A sharp pain kissed my palm. One of the glass shards had sliced through my skin. Blood dripped to the floor, but Ben didn't notice. He was too busy inspecting the fallen chandelier.

"Unbelievable," he muttered, picking his way through the mess. "Where the hell are we supposed to eat now? Jim said the work wouldn't disrupt anything inside. I'm going to go give his crew a piece of my mind."

Without another look back, Ben stomped outside, leaving me to deal with my bleeding hand all on my own. I stepped carefully across the kitchen to run the gash underneath the faucet. As the freezing water washed away the blood, I stared up at the window. A prickling feeling crawled up the back of my neck. Despite Ben's skepticism, I was sure I'd seen a face there, for however briefly it appeared.

Ben and I had brought a first aid kit with us, but when I opened the small plastic box, all I found were a few Band-Aids and a bottle of antibacterial spray. It wasn't enough to cover the two-inch slash on my palm. With my hand raised in the air to keep the blood flow at bay, I checked the nearest bathroom, the one Ben and I had set up for us yesterday. It was small and compact, without a shower or tub. My guess was this bathroom had been set up for the servants that once used to run the house, separated from the main rooms so guests of the Abrams family never saw the underpaid workers who served meals and changed sheets. I would have thought the servants' bathroom would be stocked with first aid supplies, but the cabinets were empty except for mine and Ben's toiletries. If there was anything here before, Ben had already thrown it in the trash.

Blood wept through the paper towels on my hand and ran down my wrist. I clenched my teeth, threw out the stained towels, and sacrificed one of our white bath washcloths to tie around the wound instead. I wrapped it as tightly as I could one-handed, hoping the pressure would help to stem the blood. Then I went in search of real first aid supplies.

I skipped the rest of the basement level, since all that was left down there was a maintenance room and a few storage closets full of moldy tablecloths and tarnished silverware. On the first floor, I swept all of the rooms branching off the entryway without luck. Where the corridors branched off to other areas of the mansion, I turned around. Ben and I hadn't explored the entire house yet, and I wasn't about to wander around those creepy halls by myself.

On the second floor, I finally found a huge, fully-stocked

bathroom connected to a guest bedroom. The cabinet beneath the sink housed a number of bandages, sterile pads, and antibacterial creams. Since they were expired by forty years, I skipped the creams, but the bandages and sterile pads were wrapped in individual packages. I unwound the towel from my hand. The bleeding had slowed, and I was able to see how deep the cut was for the first time. If I didn't want it to scar, the wound probably needed stitches, but I wasn't in the mood to go back to the emergency clinic. I used a few butterfly bandages to close the wound, then covered it with a sterile pad and wrapped my entire palm in gauze. The materials smelled a little weird from being around so long, but it was better to get the cut bandaged than let it drip all over the place.

Through the bathroom window, I caught sight of Ben and Jim in the front yard. Ben gesticulated wildly, mimicking the tackle he performed to get me out of the way of the falling chandelier. Jim listened to Ben's entire rant, and when Ben took a breath, Jim took the opportunity to place a steady hand on Ben's shoulder. Ben slumped, as if Jim's touch had an immediate soothing effect. Jim said something else, and the two of them went inside, presumably to check out the damage.

I didn't want to go back downstairs—I would only be in the way of Jim's work and Ben's annoyance—so I decided to keep going up. While the central part of the second floor opened up to the entryway with a huge mezzanine, the third and fourth floors were more private. If had to guess, the entire mansion had at least eighty rooms. It wasn't a house; it was a castle, one with an interior maze that begged to be traversed. The more I explored, the more obvious it became that the Abram Mansion had been built long before Percy Abrams and his family lived there. I wondered what kind of history it held in its walls.

On the fourth floor, an elaborate handwoven tapestry stretched a good twenty feet across the wall between the entrances to other rooms. The tapestry was old and faded, but the depiction of the Abram Mansion was still visible. The colorful threads made the mansion and the area around it look like a magical land. It didn't include Falconwood, another clue that the enormous house was erected before the town appeared in the valley below. I ran my uninjured hand across the intricate pattern, appreciating the texture of the artwork, but in the middle of the tapestry, I found something hard underneath. It was a handle.

I lifted the bottom of the tapestry and heaved it upward. It was shockingly heavy, and when I ducked under it and let it drop to my other side, it shrouded me in darkness. Only pinpricks of sunlight made it through the textured cloth, but it was enough to illuminate the handle I'd felt. The handle belonged to another door, but neither object matched the style of the rest of the house. The door was made of reinforced steel, and the handle was the type that swung open from a barricade, almost as if the room behind it was crafted to keep something violent inside. But there was no lock, so I expelled the scary thought from my head.

I swung the handle over and pushed the door open. The steel grated against the frame and red rust fell from the creaky hinges. For a reason I couldn't explain, I braced myself as the door revealed what was behind it, but it was only a set of stone steps. I turned on my phone light and started up. The steps were unusually steep, and at the top, I was already out of breath. A light switch was connected to a long wire that disappeared into the darkness.

With a flip of the switch, a low-hanging bulb in the middle of the room popped on. It was an attic, filled wall-to-wall with junk. From a cursory look, the room contained everything from broken furniture to full-sized carousel horses. One thing immediately caught my eye. A vintage camera was perched atop a pile

75

of cardboard boxes in the corner of the room. If it was as old as it looked, it was worth quite a bit of cash. Not to mention, if the camera still worked, I might be able to take some pretty cool photos with it. That was, if I decided to take up photography again.

To get to the camera required some fancy footwork. The room was so stacked with crap that the floor was hardly visible. I shoved aside cardboard filing boxes, bins full of toys, and luggage sets that looked like they'd been around since the beginning of time before I finally reached the camera. Though it was covered in dust, the viewfinder winked at me as I picked it up. It was a Canon SLR from around the fifties. There was still a roll of film in it, so I lifted the camera to my eye and took a look around the room for something to shoot. In the far corner, a child's rocking horse stood alone, so I snapped a picture of it.

In the second it took for the shutter to close and open again, a figure appeared in the viewfinder, tucked behind a rusty file cabinet. I quickly lowered the camera, but nothing stood in the space behind the cabinet that looked the same shape as the figure. I lifted the camera again, thinking there might be something wrong with it, but when I clicked the button to take another picture, nothing happened. The roll of film had run out.

"Hey, Peyton?" Ben's voice echoed from the fourth floor. He hadn't discovered the hidden antic entrance behind the tapestry. "Peyton, are you up here?"

With the camera in hand, I jogged down the steps and ducked under the tapestry. Ben backed away as I emerged.

"Whoa," he said. "What are you doing up here?"

"Exploring the attic. I found a camera."

"I can see that. What happened to your hand?"

I held it up so he could see the full extent of the bandages. "The chandelier got me. You were too busy having a conniption fit to notice."

He didn't take the bait, but he did give me a look that conveyed every bit of impatience he was harboring at the moment. "You shouldn't be up here. We don't know if it's safe."

"Is that why you came to find me?"

"No, I came to apologize." He offered to take the camera then ushered me toward the steps to a safer level. "I know I've been in a funk since we got here. I guess everything just hit me at once. I'm losing you."

When we hit the third floor, I nuzzled the back of his jacket with my forehead. "You're not losing me. We can still be friends."

"I don't think it works that way, Peyton." He urged me forward again when I stopped to look at a stone bust of a large woman in the hallway of the third floor. "Anyway, I was wondering if I could make it up to you. Do you want to go to lunch today? No divorce talk though. That's a promise."

"I would, but I already made plans with Theo," I told him.

His brow furrowed together. "You're going to lunch with a woman you met for five minutes? You don't even know her."

We reached the second-floor mezzanine, and I paused at the railing to get a look at the entryway from a different perspective. From up here, the floor below looked tiny. I wondered what the foyer would look like with hundreds of people arriving through the front door for some extravagant party hosted by the Abrams.

"Believe it or not, you can get to know someone by going out to lunch with them," I quipped, nudging Ben's shoulder to make sure he knew it was a joke. "Besides, she offered to do it in return for taking care of Sammy. I didn't want to be rude."

"You could have said you were busy."

"But I'm not." I trailed my fingers along the intricately carved wooden banister as we descended to the main level. "I don't have work like you do, and if I stick around, I'll only be in Jim's way. I might as well get to know the town. That's part of the reason why we came here, right?"

A car horn honked outside, and Ben craned his neck to check outside. "Does she drive a dark green Jeep?"

"She sure does."

As Theo pulled out of the driveway, she checked Ben out in the rearview mirror. "He looks mad. Should we have rescheduled?"

"He's fine. That's just his face."

Theo chuckled, piloting the Jeep through the slippery, winding road with one hand, as if this wasn't her first time navigating tricky territory. "Somehow I doubt that."

"How's Sammy?" I said, eager to change the subject as we veered closer to mine and Ben's divorce. "Is his foot okay?"

"He's great," Theo answered. "He made me change his bandage twice this morning. He said he was afraid of the germs, but I think it's because he wanted me to use the Buzz Lightyear Band-Aids instead of the plain ones."

"Well, Buzz Lightyear means business."

Theo drove us to her favorite restaurant in town, a place called Fitz's Pub that looked out on the frozen river. Inside was dark and broody, but the atmosphere was quite light. The host seated us at a booth by the window, and Theo handed me a menu.

"Everything here is good except for the jambalaya," she said. "Actually, I've never had the jambalaya, but I have this weird feeling that the only reason restaurants ever put jambalaya on the menu is so they can get rid of all the old food they couldn't sell from the day before. You know what I mean?"

"I don't particularly care for jambalaya anyway," I said, perusing the menu. Fitz's Pub had a hearty selection of classic bar food like burgers and wings, but there were also some more interesting selections available. "What's bangers and mash?"

"Sausage and mashed potatoes," Theo answered. "It's from

Great Britain. Ireland does it too, I think. There's lasagna and sushi on the menu as well. Fitz has a bit of everything."

"Fitz is the owner?"

"And the chef," Theo replied. "He's been all over the world, and he couldn't decide which cuisine to serve at his restaurant."

"So he settled for all of them."

"Exactly," Theo said with a smile. "But he puts his own twist on every dish. Like I said, everything's good here."

The waiter arrived to take our drink orders. Theo didn't hesitate to ask for an Irish coffee, so neither did I. Since we were so hungry, we ordered our food too, both opting for a burger served with fried leeks and mushroom sauce.

"So," Theo said after she'd handed her menu off to the waiter. "Want to play twenty questions?"

"Twenty questions?"

"To get to know each other."

"That's a lot of information," I said. "How about five questions?"

Theo tipped her chin down. "On one condition. You have to answer every question I ask you with absolute honesty. Does that make you nervous?"

Her eyes drifted to my fingers, which tapped a sporadic rhythm on the table top. I hid my hands beneath the table.

"Nope," I said. "You go first."

"Easy. What brought you to Falconwood?"

"We inherited the Abram Mansion."

Theo's lips twisted in a wry smile. "That can't be the whole story. No one moves into a rotting mansion without doing some renovations first."

I twiddled the paper wrapper from the straw between my fingers, shredding it to pieces. "According to my grandfather's will, we can't sell the house until we've lived there for at least six months. We wanted to get it over with as soon as possible."

"What was the rush?"

"Is that your second question?"

"No, it's a follow up to the first. Think of it as question one-B."

Theo was insistent, but she wasn't invasive. Though I'd agreed to the game, I had a feeling she would give me a pass if she asked a question that was too hard for me to answer. Then again, she'd started with the hardest question.

"Ben and I are getting divorced," I said. "And the mansion is the last thing we have to deal with before we're able to sign the papers."

Theo's wince of sympathy was the best reaction to our divorce announcement I'd received. While everyone else challenged my decision, questioning why I would let go of such a great guy if there was nothing inherently wrong with the relationship, Theo accepted our separation as fact right off the bat.

"That's tough," she said. "And kind of mean. You couldn't find a way around it?"

"Ben didn't want to bother with getting lawyers involved," I told her. "Since I was the one who sprang this on him, I figured I should go along with his decision."

One of Theo's perfectly angled eyebrows arched toward the ceiling. Her eyes were the same mossy green as Sammy's, though he didn't take after her in many other respects. While Sammy was the blondest of blonds, Theo had dark brown hair. Their noses came to the same cute point at the end, but the similarities ended there.

"Do you disagree?" I asked her.

"Kind of," she answered. "You served him divorce papers for a reason. That's not an easy decision to come to. Sounds like he's using the Abram Mansion as a way to keep you around."

"I know he is."

The server returned with our Irish coffees. I leaned over my mug and let the steam rise to warm my cold nose. The bold scents of dark roast and Irish cream tickled my nostrils. When I finally took a sip, it burned in all the good ways.

"My turn to ask a question?" I said.

"Shoot."

"Is Sam's dad still in the picture?"

Theo sucked on her teeth and nodded like I'd caught her with a difficult question as much as she'd caught me. "No, he's not. As soon as I found out I was pregnant, I moved away from him. Let's just say he wasn't the type of man you'd want around a child."

"How old is Sammy? Five?"

"He's six," Theo said, watching my reaction. "I can see you doing the math in your head. Yes, I had him when I was eighteen. It was a complicated time in my life, and I wasn't taking care of myself like I should have. Getting pregnant with Sammy was eye-opening. If it weren't for him, I don't know what might have happened to me."

"So there's more to the story?"

"There is," Theo confirmed. "But I'd rather not talk about it."

"I guess we all have things we don't want to talk about."

AFTER LUNCH, we left Fitz's Pub so Theo could show me her and Sammy's favorite areas of Falconwood. We shopped along the major avenue, walked to the frozen river, and visited the dog park. Apparently, Sammy was dying to have a puppy, but Theo was afraid she wouldn't have the time to take care of one. As a compromise, she took Sammy to the dog park once a week to fulfill his doggy desires. I learned more about Theo and Sammy as the day wore on. Theo worked as a part-time receptionist for Falconwood Dentistry. Currently, she was taking online courses to get her business degree. The part-time job afforded her enough money to scrape by and let her bow in and out as needed to accommodate Sammy's schedule.

"It's the best I could ask for right now," she told me as we strolled toward the school to pick Sammy up. "I don't want Sammy to be stuck in daycare all the time. I like to keep an eye on him."

"Otherwise, he finds trouble?"

"You guessed it. Hi, buddy!"

Sammy came tearing out of the school with his Power Rangers backpack bouncing around his shoulders. He ran up to Theo, wrapped his arms around her waist, and buried his face in her sweater. Theo stroked his fair hair.

"Everything okay, Sam?"

"I love you," he sighed into his mother's sweater.

"I love you too, little dude."

Sammy unearthed himself and grinned up at me. "Hi, Peyton! Look at my foot!" He lifted his boot in the air. Beneath the rubber, I couldn't see a hint of his bandages.

"Wow, I like your boots."

He stomped in the slush. "It looks cooler when I'm barefoot. Hey, can we go to your house? I want to say hi to my friend."

Theo squatted to zip up Sammy's coat and put his mittens on. "We talked about this, remember? Peyton and Ben are the only two people who live at that house. Your imaginary friend needs to move out."

"She's not imaginary," Sammy protested. "She lives there."

"How about this?" I said. "Why don't you come over so I can show you around? You can look for your friend, and if she's not there, you have to promise not to sneak out in the middle of the night again."

"Deal!" Sammy said with a tiny triumphant fist pump. "Let's go!"

. . .

JIM and his construction crew were still hard at work when Theo, Sammy, and I pulled into the front yard. About ten guys stood on the roof, hammering and power-stapling away like they all needed a good therapy session. As soon as we got out of the car and went up the steps, Ben—wearing a bright yellow hard hat— jogged out to meet us.

"Whoa, whoa, whoa," he said, spreading his arms as if to gather us all and prevent us from passing. "What are you doing here?"

"I invited them," I said. "I'm going to show them around the house. Sammy wants the grand tour. Isn't that right, Sammy?"

Sammy, quiet in Ben's presence, gave the smallest of nods.

"You can't do that," Ben said. "It's too dangerous. We've got guys on the roof, and we don't know if the rest of the house is structurally sound. I'm sorry, but I can't let you in."

"Ben, this is my house too," I reminded him. "You can't tell me not to have visitors."

"It's fine," Theo said, stepping in to defuse the situation. "We can come back another time when you're more settled."

"But what about my friend?" Sammy whispered, loudly enough for everyone to hear.

"Dude, no one else lives here," Ben told him. "Maybe you can stop by in a few months when things aren't so hectic."

"What does hectic mean?" Sammy asked.

Theo took Sammy's hand and gave me a one-armed hug while Ben peered on with a suspicious expression. "Thanks for having lunch with me, Peyton. We should do it again sometime."

"Definitely," I said. To Sammy, I added, "I promise you can come back to visit later, okay?"

"Okay!"

"I've gotta get back to work," Ben announced. "Be careful driving out of here. I don't want you to get a nail in your tire."

"The Jeep eats nails for breakfast," Theo replied coolly. "See you around, Ben."

As Ben walked off, Sammy pointed to the very top of the mansion, jumping up and down with glee. "There she is! There she is!"

I shielded my face from the sun and squinted up, following the line of Sammy's finger to one of the attic windows.

"Hi!" Sammy called, his arm waving wildly.

But there was no one standing in the window.

6

---

*A*s the days wore on, I settled into my new Falconwood routine. Every morning, I asked Ben if he wanted to come to Black Cat Café with me. Mostly, he claimed he had too much work to do to go to breakfast, but on the rare occasion, he set aside his laptop and joined me in town. If I didn't have Ben with me, I spent the entire morning at the café, researching online photography courses that weren't outlandishly expensive. The way Theo multitasked—juggling work, school, and Sammy at the same time—inspired me to jump back into learning, especially since I didn't have anything else going on. After researching programs, I'd meet Theo for her lunch break from the dentist's office. After a few meals at Fitz's Pub, we grew tired of burgers and fried leeks so Theo invited me over to her place instead. She and Sammy lived in a modest one-bedroom apartment above the town bakery. At any given time, the entire place smelled like chocolate chip cookies. We would make lunch and chat until it was time for Theo to go back to work. She always insisted I could stay in the apartment to continue my educational research, but I didn't want to impose.

To kill time and get in some exercise, I made a habit of taking an afternoon stroll around Falconwood. Just beyond the perimeter of the town was a fairly flat hiking trail a few miles long. I did however many laps it took to clear my mind before returning to civilization. Sometimes, I'd see another hiker on the trail, but I smiled politely and pointed at my headphones whenever any of them tried to strike up a conversation. I wasn't too committed to getting to know any of the locals other than Theo.

Once, Theo was running late to pick Sammy up from school. She called me in a complete panic, and she never actually got around to asking me to pick up Sammy for her. I offered before she could, and I met Sammy on the sidewalk outside the elementary school. I took him for an afternoon snack at Black Cat, where he enjoyed pretending his hot chocolate was a cappuccino "like what grown-ups drink."

When Mason, the café owner, stopped by to check on us, he said to me, "Theo must really trust you. She never lets anyone babysit Sammy without a background check first."

I laughed off the comment, but Mason shot me a meaningful look before he refilled Sammy's plate of cheese crackers. It didn't seem momentous for me to watch Sammy, but this town knew more about the Bakers than I did. I was just happy to have a friend in Theo, and by extension, in Sammy. He made me laugh more than I had in years, and he challenged me with weird questions only children thought to ask. In one conversation alone, he questioned what dreams were made of, where thoughts come from, and why lobsters don't have eyebrows. After I failed to answer, we made a game of searching for the solution on the Internet, and it became our new favorite routine whenever we spent time together.

"Where did the moon get its name?" Sammy asked one time as he colored at the kitchen table while Theo and I made dinner.

"I don't know, little dude," Theo said.

"Ask Siri," I told him, offering him my phone.

He wiggled off his stool to fetch the phone. "Hey, Siri!" he shouted. "Where did the moon get its name?"

"*Okay. I found this one on the web for 'where did the moon get its name.'*"

Sammy squinted at the results before turning the screen back to me. "I don't know what this means."

I clicked on the first link and translated the information to something Sammy might understand. "The word moon comes from different words in Old English, Dutch, and German that mean 'month.'"

"Oh, because the moon goes around Earth once a month!"

"Exactly," I said, grinning.

Theo leaned against the counter, sipping a glass of red wine as she waited for her homemade spaghetti sauce to reduce. "Is this what you guys do when I'm not around?"

"Yes," Sammy answered. "Peyton's so cool, and Siri knows everything."

"Scary thought," I muttered to Theo.

Sammy clung to my arm. "Can you come over for dinner every night? Mama, can Peyton come over for dinner every night?"

"Slow down, buddy." I picked Sammy up, turned him upside down, and shook him. His raucous giggles were so loud, the neighbors could probably hear. "If I'm going to come to dinner more often, you're going to have to cough up whatever loose change you have in your pockets."

"I'm broke!" Sammy insisted.

Theo roared with laughter as a single penny, a broken crayon, and a miniature dinosaur figurine fell out of Sammy's pockets. I set him down and pretended to collect my earnings.

"You're a Lego short," I told him. "And I don't do discounts."

He ran off without a word and returned with a plastic

building block. "It's not a Lego because Mom says they're too expensive, but she also says they're the same thing!"

I inspected the building block with one eye closed. "I suppose it's acceptable."

At the end of the night, I returned all of Sammy's things to him, told him not to default on his loan, and put my coat on to leave. As I walked to my car, Theo ran down the stairs after me.

"Peyton, wait up!" She caught me by the sleeve and lifted my hand to place my phone in it. "I don't think you want Sammy to keep that all day. You'd never get it back."

"Ah! Thank you."

"No, thank you." Theo's eyes glistened under the street lamps. She hadn't yet released my sleeve, holding on to my arm with gentle insistence. "Sammy hasn't snuck out of the house since you started hanging out with us. You have no idea how much that means to me."

"I'm sure it's a coincidence."

"It's not," she said. "He's so happy and tired by the time he goes to bed that he sleeps through the entire night now. That's never happened before. Never. He's always been the lightest of sleepers."

When I hugged Theo, she rested her head on my shoulder and squeezed back. "I'm glad to help," I told her. "Sammy's a great kid, and you're an amazing mother. You both deserve the world."

"Thank you," Theo sniffled. "So do you. I'm sorry Ben never realized that."

ONE MORNING during my usual breakfast at Black Cat, Della Gordon showed up with a heavy black case. She dragged her cumbersome baggage through the line, ordered a coffee and a croissant, then scanned the busy café for a place to offload. I waved from my two-top in the middle of the room. When she spotted me, I beckoned her over.

"Good morning, beautiful," Della said. "Is your lovely husband here today?"

"Nope. That seat's all yours."

"Are you sure, darling?"

"Of course." I pulled the spare chair out and helped Della put down all of the things she was holding. "You and Basil were nice enough to share your table with us on our first day in town. I'm returning the favor. What's in the case?"

"Camera equipment," she answered. "I have loads of it. Been collecting since I was twelve, but Basil thinks I'm a hoarder."

"Are you selling it?"

She stared wistfully at the case. "That was the plan, but I'm not so sure I can part with it. Chester would die to have some of the things in that case."

"The photography store guy?"

"Yes," Della sighed. "I love him so, and he's the only one I trust to make sure my things end up in capable hands, but it's just so hard, you know?"

"I totally get it," I said, stirring another packet of raw sugar into my mug. The coffee was stronger this morning than I was used to. "I haven't taken a picture in years, so Ben suggested I sell my DSLR. I put it up on eBay, but when someone bid on it, I had a legitimate panic attack."

Della chuckled. "Forgive my laughter. Were you an avid photographer? I meant to ask you the other day at Chester's, but we were distracted by the muffins."

"I used to be," I told her. "I started on the yearbook staff in high school, and I loved it. It was the only thing I was good at, and I wanted to do it professionally, but—"

"But finding professional photography gigs is about as difficult as locating the Holy Grail?" Della nodded in sympathy. "I've been there. It's a struggle for sure, but if you love it enough, you'll go after it with every fiber of your being." Mason brought Della her order. She buttered half of her croissant before offering the plate to me. "Want the rest? I can't eat the whole thing."

I'd been at Black Cat for so long that my breakfast had already digested, so I happily accepted the other half of the croissant. "Any advice for someone who wants to get back into photography?"

"Be persistent," Della offered. "Take hundreds of photos. Bring your camera everywhere with you. Shoot every day. You can't call yourself a photographer if you're not out there taking pictures."

"There's not much in Falconwood to photograph."

Della's expression mimicked that of a schoolteacher scolding a poorly behaved student. "Bite your tongue! First of all, a true artist can find beauty in anything. Second, Falconwood has some of the most amazing wildlife in the area. Get out on the trails and photograph some nature."

As if to emphasize Della's point, a beautiful swallow swooped past the window. She beamed at it like she was Cinderella.

"Is that what you used to do?" I asked Della.

Between her and her husband's somewhat wild appearances, I figured they were "of the earth" kind of people. They hosted their yoga class three nights a week, and though I had yet to attend a session, I'd overheard the yogis in town talking about how lovely and talented Basil and Della were. Through word of mouth, I'd learned the older couple lived on an acre of land, but instead of building a huge house, they lived in a sleek silver Airstream. Apparently, they'd driven all over the United States in it, found Falconwood to be their favorite, and bought a plot of land to park on. In the summer, they grew herbs on their property, made fresh juice from organic sources, and even raised chickens. In the winter, they weaved reusable bags out of recycled plastic. Every Sunday, they had their own stand at the Farmer's Market to sell their wares. I loved how simple and happy they were. Della found joy in educating the town about reducing waste while Basil, though quieter and more reserved than his wife, could always be seen reading a book from the library.

"Yes, I made it my mission to photograph some of the most secluded animals in the world," Della said. "With the exception of anything under the sea. That was never my forte. Every day was an adventure. I trekked to places you wouldn't believe, and I've received my fair share of scars to get the shot I wanted. See this?" She pulled down the collar of her sweater, revealing three jagged marks. "I got too close to a clouded leopard, but I also got the shot."

I grimaced at the thought of a leopard's claws buried in my neck. "Do you think it was worth it? All the traveling you did? All the times you could have gotten hurt?"

"Honey," Della said, letting her collar cover the scars again as she leaned across the table and patted my hand. "If you love something, you don't let it go because you might get hurt. You push through. What kind of photography did you want to do?"

"I did weddings for a while," I told her, "but I wanted to be a journalist."

"What would you have liked to report?"

"I never thought about it." I absentmindedly stirred my coffee, increasing the speed of my spoon until the whirlpool separated enough to see the bottom of the cup in the center. "It was a fantasy I had in high school."

Della relaxed in her chair and crossed one leg over the other. "When we're young, adults tend to dismiss our fantasies and dreams as unimportant, but if you work hard, you can turn dreams into reachable goals. Sounds like you never had anyone to push you to do the thing you really wanted to do."

"My mom encouraged me," I said. "But I got married so young."

"True love wasn't worth it?"

"True love made me compromise on a lot of things I didn't want to compromise on."

Della reached over the table to still my hand as the whirlpool of coffee in my cup threatened to spill over the edge. "It's not too late, honey. You're still so young. Get out there. Go see the world. Become a photojournalist. People waste so much energy wishing for things because they think they've run out of time to go after them."

A FEW WEEKS PASSED, and Ben continued his rigorous supervision of the renovation process. Jim's crew of guys worked exceptionally fast. In no time, the entryway, kitchen, and a few of the first-floor rooms had been gutted and rebuilt. They kept it simple for time's sake, but the updates made the house a hundred times cozier than before. In a day, the drawing room was transformed into a magnificent bedroom. The furniture store delivered my mattress and bed frame, and I spent that day turning my new room into the perfect place to spend some downtime. Ben seemed to be everywhere, constantly asking Jim for another favor or a new work order. He carried his laptop with him wherever he went, and I often spotted him wearing his hard hat as he worked on his technical writing job in the middle of whatever project Jim was engineering that day.

"I'm paying him double," Ben said when I asked him how Jim and his crew were so motivated to get the work done this quickly. "I wanted to expedite the process."

For the first time in several days, I'd convinced Ben to sit down and have dinner with me. Now that the kitchen was in better shape, I could actually get back to cooking. In an effort to bridge the gap growing between us, I'd offered to make Ben roasted chicken with lemon and rosemary. It was one of his favorite meals, and when I threw a loaf of garlic bread into the deal, he couldn't resist.

"It smells good," he said, glancing into the oven for a look at the whole golden-brown chicken. "We haven't done this in a while."

"I got some wine too." I took the bottle of white from the fridge to show him the label. "Who knew Falconwood had its own winery?"

"Apparently, you did," Ben said. "Did Theo take you there?"

"We went yesterday."

"Hmm."

I'd learned quickly not to bring up Theo's name or what we did together unless Ben specifically asked. For whatever reason, he was oddly jealous of her, and though he couldn't tell me what to do with my spare time upfront, I read his disapproval in every aspect of his body language. What his problem with Theo was, I had no idea. If I had to guess, he was unhappy that his plan to use the Abram Mansion to reunite us wasn't going to spec.

"It's a Sauvignon Blanc," I said hurriedly, trying to get off the subject of Theo. "Your favorite, right?"

"It just goes well with chicken." He checked the meat again. "Is this burning?"

I hurried to the oven and looked inside. The skin of the chicken was crispy and brown on top. One tiny spot had blackened. I resisted the urge to roll my eyes.

"It's fine," I told Ben.

"As long as it's not too dry."

He set the table with two of the new plates I'd bought in town a few days ago. Since we'd settled in, I figured we should be eating off of something other than camp ware. The plates were hand-painted by one of the locals and decorated with delicate purple flowers. I loved them, but something told me Ben wasn't sold. It didn't matter anyway, since I intended on keeping them after the divorce.

"How's Sammy?" Ben asked as he laid out the silverware. For all of his indifference toward Theo, he loved hearing about her six-year-old son. "Did his spelling test go okay?"

"He misspelled Virginia."

"How'd he spell it?"

"Vagina."

Ben, halfway through the process of opening the wine, snorted. The wine bottle knocked against the counter. "Well, you gotta give the kid credit for trying."

"He was upset," I said. "Then he got in trouble for trying to call his imaginary friend on the phone behind the teacher's desk. Theo's a little frazzled this week."

I checked the temperature of the chicken and took it out of the oven as Ben poured two glasses of wine and set them on the table. With a new knife, he carved the chicken, whistling as the blade cut through the meat with stunning precision. He served me first, making my entire plate before sitting down himself. He even lit a candle in the middle of the table like we were at a fancy restaurant.

"Cheers," he said, lifting his wine glass. "To finally getting a night together."

I tapped my glass against his and took a sip. The wine coated my tongue, but somehow it didn't taste as good as it did yesterday when I was at lunch with Theo.

"What do you think of Sammy's imaginary friend anyway?" I asked Ben. "It's normal for kids to pretend about that kind of thing, right?"

He inhaled a quarter of his chicken in one bite. "I had an

imaginary friend when I was his age. My mom let it play out. She set a place for him at the dinner table and everything. Eventually, I grew out of it."

"Sammy insists that his friend lives here," I said, cutting up my food into smaller pieces. The roasted carrots were too mushy, but the potatoes were too hard. "Every time Theo drops me off at home, he asks to come inside so he can say hi."

"We're talking about the same kid who walked several miles in the snow and broke into our house through the doggy door," Ben reminded me. "Sammy's weird. All kids are weird. One time, my niece yelled at me because I wasn't using magic markers to write at work."

"I can't help but wonder if it's not all in Sammy's head." I mashed the potatoes with the back of the fork, added a pat of butter, and kept mixing. "Ever since we got here, I've felt like this house has weird vibes. Remember when I told you I heard voices in the walls?"

"Yes, and I told you it was probably rats."

"There are other things too," I insisted. "The face I saw in the window that day the chandelier fell. Later, I took a picture in the attic, and I could have sworn someone else was in the room with me."

"Peyton, I've told you before, and I'll tell you again." Ben sighed, setting his fork on his plate to make sure I know I have his full attention. "This house is old. The pipes rattle and the floors creak. That's all there is to it."

"What about Sammy's friend?"

"He's a kid," Ben said as he went back to his chicken. "Let his imagination wander. Just don't let his imagination get into your head."

SINCE THE RENOVATIONS, Ben had been staying in the bedroom

across from mine. It was a comfort to have him right on the opposite side of the hall rather than all the way out in the foyer. We moved our toiletry kits to the larger bathroom on the same floor, abandoning the servants' bathroom downstairs. The new bathroom sported an enormous, claw-footed tub. Ben thought it was cumbersome to take baths instead of showers every night, but I loved it.

Late that night, after Ben had already gone to sleep, I got out of bed and ran a bath. Something had been keeping me awake, gnawing at the back of my brain, but I couldn't figure out what it was. Lying in bed only fed the restless thoughts. I filled the tub with warm water, added a bath bomb Sammy had picked out from the soap store in town, and slipped into the water. The bath bomb fizzled like a can of Coke underneath the surface, turning the water a shimmering blue hue. It smelled like lavender and eucalyptus. As I inhaled the soothing scents, my mind finally quieted. The candlelight flickered as I lowered my head beneath the surface of the water.

There was something calming about being underwater. It distorted the entire world. When I was a kid at camp, I'd hold myself under the lake and stare up at the sun, watching the pattern of the water warp the sky. It muted everything too, from the sounds around you to the thoughts in your head. I stayed under for as long as possible before coming up to take a breath.

When I surfaced, it was like turning up the volume on the TV. Everything seemed a hundred times louder. Water dripped from the faucet. The radiator hummed. The last pebble of the bath bomb fizzled out. And a voice echoed overhead.

I held perfectly still, straining to listen to the voice over the rippling water. It seemed to be coming from the floor above me. Across the hall, Ben snored loudly, so it definitely wasn't him upstairs. The voice sounded like it belonged to a woman anyway.

Water sloshed over the edge of the tub and poured off my legs as I stepped out. I shook off the excess, wrapped myself in my robe, and put on my slippers. I followed the muted voice down the corridor and into the entryway, where the aggravated tone became clearer. Up the stairs, I crossed the mezzanine, relying on my ear to locate whoever had taken up residence in our house without permission. At the end of the second-floor corridor, Ben had placed a strip of caution tape to block off the parts of the house we hadn't explored yet, but the voice radiated from somewhere beyond it. I stepped over the yellow barricade.

The east wing of the house was dark and drab. It had not yet been touched by Jim's crew and likely never would be. It would take months to redo the mansion entirely, and our stay here had an expiration date. This wing played host to more bedrooms and bathrooms. The long hallways and multiple doors made it look more like an ancient hotel than a house. The voice carried from somewhere down the hall. My heart thudded in my rib cage as I crept toward it.

It was definitely a woman, and she was upset. I recognized her bitter intonation as the same one I used with Ben when he was acting particularly righteous. I reached the last door at the end of the hall. A flickering light emanated from the crack at the floor, and the shadows of a pair of feet walked to and fro. I held my breath and listened.

"I can't take it anymore," the woman hissed from the room. "We're leaving, and you won't be able to stop us." There was a few moments of silence, as if the woman were listening to someone respond. Then: "Don't you threaten me. I've had enough."

My heart hammered against my chest. Who the hell had broken into our house to have such a heated argument with thin air? I hovered on the threshold, trying to decide what to do. The safest solution was to call the cops or at least get Ben as backup, but something kept me rooted to this corner of the expensive, hundred-year-old rug.

"Don't come near me!" the woman shouted. When she spoke again, it was in a whisper, as if raising her voice had been unintentional. "I'll shoot you. I swear I'll shoot you."

I swallowed hard. Did this woman have a gun?

"Stay back," she whispered, and her footsteps shuffled farther away from the door to the hallway. "I'm warning you."

The one-sided argument kept me so captivated that when a small, cold hand slipped its fingers into my palm as if seeking comfort, my first instinct was to squeeze it tightly. When the contact registered a moment later, adrenaline exploded through my body, racing through my veins as I looked at my side and realized there was no child there.

7

*B*en went into the room with a baseball bat and a fresh can of mace, then emerged thirty seconds later sporting an expression that was half-puzzled, half-irritated.

"Is this some kind of joke?" he asked me, the baseball bat swinging at his side. "There's no one in there."

"You're kidding."

I pushed past him, into the magnificent master bedroom suite. The canopied bed was large enough to fit at least four people comfortably, and the linens were fit for royals. Gold curtains trimmed with sparkling tassels covered the windows, keeping every bit of light, including the moon's, outside. I checked in the adjoining bathroom as well as the walk-in closet, but there was no sign of intruders.

"I saw feet!" I fumed, looking under the bed for good measure. "I heard her voice. Ben, there was a woman in here. I swear."

"Are we done with this game yet?" Ben gave the bat an impatient twirl. "Because I don't know how many times I have to go over this with you. It's an—"

"Old house," I finished for him, mocking his deep voice. "I'm bound to hear things go bump in the night. Yeah, I know, but this was different. Someone was up here. What are you doing?"

He punched a number into his phone. "I'm calling the cops. If you're so sure someone broke in, we have to report it."

"So you believe me?"

He shushed me and said into the phone, "Hello, I'd like to report a potential break-in."

TWENTY MINUTES LATER, Officer Hillary Spaughton stood in the middle of our entryway, her perfect platinum hair spilling out of her Falconwood P.D. knit cap like the tail of a unicorn. She'd already done a lap around the house, once inside and once outside. Like Ben, she'd come up empty-handed, but that didn't stop her from taking thorough notes in her official police notepad.

"You said you heard a voice from the bathroom?" Hillary asked.

"Yeah," Ben answered for me. "She said it was a woman speaking."

"Why don't you let Peyton answer the questions, Ben."

Ben blushed as Hillary stepped around him to where I was sitting on the bottom step of the mezzanine staircase. She took off her coat and draped it over my knees as she sat beside me. Ben, unlike Hillary, hadn't noticed I was shivering.

"It sounded like two people arguing," I told her as she flipped to a fresh page in her notepad. "But I could only hear the woman. I followed the voice upstairs to that bedroom. I even saw feet beneath the door."

"Two pairs?"

"Just one."

"And what did the woman say again?"

"She kept saying she couldn't handle it anymore," I explained.

"She sounded like she was frustrated with the other person's behavior. She threatened to shoot."

Hillary's worry gathered between her eyebrows and sat in the lines of her face. "Did you hear anything else to indicate she actually had a gun? Loading a chamber or anything like that?"

"No, nothing like that."

"That's good," Hillary said. "She could've been bluffing."

"Are we forgetting something?" Ben interrupted. "I went into that room, and no one was in there. No ruffled blankets or rugs either. It was empty."

Hillary flipped her notebook shut with an air of irritation. "Well, they could have slipped out when Peyton went downstairs to get you."

"Don't you think we would have seen them?" Ben said.

"There are probably a hundred ways in and out of this place that you don't know about," Hillary replied. "If I were you, I'd stop doubting your wife and spend that energy on something more productive. For instance, why don't you consider installing a security system?"

She stood and offered me a hand to help pull me up from the low step. I returned her coat to her, and she slipped her arms through it.

"I'll stay out front until the sun comes up," she said. "The cop lights will scare any unwanted visitors away." She clapped Ben on the shoulder, which made him seem shorter than he actually was. "Get that security system up and running tomorrow, would ya?"

"Will do," Ben said. "Thanks for coming out."

"No problem. You two stay safe and have a good night."

I LAY awake in bed until the first hint of sunlight came through my window. Then I went into the entryway and waved goodbye as Hillary pulled out of the driveway. Jim's crew showed up an hour later to begin work on the terrace at the west side of the house, but Ben was still asleep. I told Jim to do whatever he needed to do, got dressed, and headed into town.

I skipped Black Cat, too antsy to sit still in the café. The caffeine definitely wasn't going to help calm my nerves. As I walked up the main street, I wasn't sure what I was doing or looking for. I'd been to all the shops and eaten at all the restaurants. I'd mingled with the locals here and there. Without my regular routine, all that was left was a jittery feeling in my bones and a weird lump that surfaced in the back of my throat every time I thought of that cold hand in mine. It really had felt like a small child had walked up beside me and grasped my hand. I replayed the moment over and over in my head, trying to think of something—anything—to attribute that feeling to. But an imaginary draft sweeping through the second-floor corridor didn't have the same effect against your skin as flesh and bone.

Without a conscious plan, I ended up at Chester's photography store. I went through a stack of old photographs he had on the counter, looking at the subjects but not entirely seeing them. When the bell over the door jingled, I didn't register that someone new had come into the shop until Della showed up at my side. I jumped, scattering Chester's pictures across the floor.

"Oh, goodness," Della said, stooping to help me collect the photographs. "I didn't mean to scare you. I thought you heard me come in."

"I'm a little out of it today." I did my best to stack Chester's pictures in a neat pile then placed them where I'd found them on the counter. "How are you, Della? It's been a few days since we last saw each other."

"I'm well," she said. "But I'm finally biting the bullet."

With her, she carried the black case full of her old photography materials. She stroked the case with loving sincerity.

"Basil put his foot down?" I guessed.

"We don't have room for it," Della said mournfully. "As much as I like simple living, you sometimes have to make sacrifices. The Airstream just doesn't have the storage space for things like this."

"Tell you what," I said, helping her lift the case onto the counter so she didn't have to hold it any longer. "If you don't want to sell to Chester just yet, why don't you leave your things at my house? Believe me, we have plenty of space."

Della's eyes sparkled with glee. "Are you sure? I don't want to inconvenience you or your husband."

"It's seriously no trouble at all," I told her. "Bring it by whenever you like."

Della surprised me with a quick hug. She smelled like the bath bomb I'd used last night: lavender and eucalyptus. Her earthy vibe was the best antidote to my nerves so far. Something about Della was inherently calming. It was almost as if I was meant to run into her today.

"You are so lovely," she said.

For some unearthly reason, I started crying. Maybe I was so physically exhausted and mentally worn out from last night's escapades that I couldn't hold it in anymore, but all of a sudden, I was sobbing in the middle of Chester's store. Della cradled my head against her shoulder and let me get it all out.

"Oh, honey," she said. "Is there anything I can do for you?"

I was so glad she hadn't asked me what was wrong. It was a question that became increasingly hard to answer. These days, everything felt wrong, and it was a matter of wading through all the wrongness to finally find something that felt right.

"Will you help me get back into photography?" I sniffled.

"Sure! Do you need a camera? I have loads."

"I found an old SLR at the house," I told her as I drew away. "I've been wanting to see what it's got left in it."

She cupped my cheek and wiped a tear from beneath my eye. "Let's go have a look then."

"Right now?"

"Desperate times. Chester!" she shouted.

Chester emerged from his developing room wearing bulbous glasses that magnified his eyes to twice their normal size. "Hey, Della. Finally giving in to me? I'm dying for a look at your collection."

"You know what's in my collection," she replied, smirking. "But I'm not selling today. In fact, I'm buying. Get me a few fresh rolls of film."

"You got it."

"Make sure it's enough for both me and Peyton," Della said, pulling me closer. "We're going to go out and shoot some of the local wildlife."

"You don't have to do that," I assured Della. "I can buy my own film."

"Nonsense," Della said. "You're doing me a huge favor by storing my things for me. The least I can do is buy you a few rolls of film."

Chester put a few boxes of film on the counter and rang Della up. She paid with the wallet stored on her phone. The background was a picture of her husband covered in dirt with a cheesy grin on his face and a handful of fresh herbs yanked straight from the ground.

"About that local wildlife," I said to Della. "I should probably mention I'm not much of an outdoorswoman. Ben was always the one who wanted to go camping and live off the land. He bought me a pair of hiking boots, but—"

"That's all you need," Della told me as she nodded her thanks to Chester. "I promise we won't get into any terrain that's too tough. As a matter of fact, there are a couple of great trails right by the Abram Mansion. Want to check it out since we have to go get your camera anyway?"

THERE WAS no persuading Della to take pictures around town. She had her heart dead set on climbing the hills behind the mansion. When we got back to the house, Della stared open-mouthed through the windshield. Jim's crew was busy hammering away at the terrace, but the construction work didn't impede the effect of the enormity of the house had on Della.

"It's been a while since I've gotten this close to it," Della said. "I used to come take pictures here."

I put the car in park. "Why did you stop?"

"Basil asked me to." She rolled her eyes, but it was accompanied by a wry smile. She wasn't annoyed by her husband's request. Rather, she found it endearing. "He had a good reason. I stepped through some rotted wood on the second floor of the west wing and almost tore my leg off. The place is a bit of a death trap."

"Don't I know it," I muttered, slamming the car door.

Della shielded her eyes and peered up at the house. "It's bigger than I remember. How are the renovations going?"

"Quick and dirty." I beckoned her to follow me inside, and we went up the stone steps in the front. "Ben wants to do as much as possible in the time that we're here."

She squinted at Jim's crew, hard at work on the terrace, before we went inside. "Must be putting a lot of money into this. Is that what you wanted?"

"It's Ben's money," I told her. "I'm unemployed. He can do whatever he wants with his earnings."

Della cast an admiring eye around the newly-renovated

foyer. "It's certainly paid off. This looks almost as good as new. You could start hosting parties here any day now."

I snorted. "I don't think we're ever going to live up to the Abrams' popularity. Ben's not the type of guy to host extravagant galas. Besides, we're only here temporarily."

Della continued to inspect the new work as she followed me to my bedroom. "Did you ever find any more information about your grandfather?"

"No, but to be honest, I haven't looked." I rooted around in my new dresser, pushing aside layers of winter clothes. I had buried the camera at the bottom of the drawer, wrapped in old T-shirts to keep it safe. "I've had a pretty good routine going here, and it sort of slipped my mind."

"Yes, I've seen you around with Theo and Sammy." Della gazed around my room with her hands behind her back, almost as a show of respect for my territory. "How are the Bakers doing these days? Is Sammy still giving his mother a heart attack every thirty seconds?"

"Actually, he's been pretty well-behaved lately," I said. "Theo keeps him on a short leash. I think that's why he used to run away, but since we've been spending time together, he's too busy playing to run away. Here you go."

I handed the camera to Della. She took it with extreme care, turning it over to inspect it with a religious-like reverence.

"It's in great shape," she said. "You found it in the attic?"

"Just sitting up there," I told her. "I guess it's been there since the fifties."

"There's a roll of film in here." With practiced ease, she wound the film back into the canister then flipped open the back of the camera to take it out. "A little dusty. Wanna put that somewhere safe? I bet there are some cool pictures on it."

After placing the used film back in the drawer, Della urged me to find my hiking boots. Reluctantly, I laced them up then found a warmer coat. If we were heading uphill, it was going to get cold pretty fast.

"Where's Ben today?" Della asked as we made our way back outside.

"He's around somewhere," I told her, looping the strap of my camera over my shoulder. Della had chosen to bring her favorite DSLR with her upon the promise that we could trade off with every other roll of film I used in the old Canon. "He usually splits his time between pretending he's a contractor to boss Jim around and actually doing his real job."

Della chuckled lightly. "Men like to feel as if they're in control. It's best to let them play on their own. Are you ready for this?"

I looked into the thick trees beyond the house. "Are you sure there's a trail back there?"

"Positive," she promised, starting toward the woods. "Don't worry. It's not as scary as it looks."

It took about half an hour for me to finally believe Della's promise. As the trees swallowed the sounds of construction at the mansion, a hush fell over the woods. The gray trees whispered to one another, swaying in the light breeze. The snow wasn't too thick on the ground in most places, so our boots and pants weren't immediately soaked through. The air was a little harsh on my nose, but Della lent me a tube of Aquaphor to fix that. After a few trips here and there, I started to get the hang of walking across the uneven terrain. Della took pictures at every turn, clicking so madly with her camera that I finally asked her what she was photographing.

"Have a look," she said, handing me her camera.

I browsed through the pictures she'd just taken, shocked to find some truly astonishing shots of things I never would have thought to photograph. She framed shot after shot of weirdly-angled branches, wispy leftover spider webs, emptied bird nests, and one orange leaf that had miraculously survived the frost.

"Wow, you're amazing at this," I said, returning her camera. "No wonder my business failed. I could never do something like this."

"Don't sell yourself short," Della said. "I've been doing this for almost fifty years, and you never wanted to focus on nature anyway. Besides, if your business was shooting weddings, I'm not surprised it didn't do well. Everyone hates weddings."

"They were *awful.*"

Della grinned, letting her camera hang loose around her neck as she placed mine in my hands. "Here, let me give you some pointers. Take a look through the viewfinder."

I lifted the camera to my eye and peered through.

"Don't think about it," Della said. "Just focus on something and take a picture. It doesn't have to be mind-blowing. It just has to look interesting to you."

I lifted the camera up, staring into the sky through the viewfinder. Beyond the trees, the sky was a smooth blanket of white clouds, as if someone had laid a cotton bedspread over top of the world. I snapped a picture right as a black bird flew into the center of frame.

"Not bad," Della said when I lowered the camera. "Why did you photograph the sky?"

"I love when it's like that," I told her. "All white. When I was a kid, I always knew it was about to snow because the sky looked like that. Snow days were my favorite."

"Every kid's favorite, I'd imagine."

"For me, it was different," I told her. "I struggled in school for a long time. I didn't like it. I begged my mom to homeschool me."

"I take it she didn't go for it."

I shook my head. "My mom's always been a bit of a loose

cannon. She raised me on her own. Actually, Theo reminds me a lot of my mother, except Theo doesn't carry around a flask."

Della stomped her boots to keep the blood moving in her feet. "Did school ever get better for you?"

"When I started taking pictures," I said. "And then I met Ben, and I couldn't wait to go to school."

"Ah, young love."

"Naive love," I corrected. "What happens when you grow out of people?"

"You move on," Della replied lightly. If she caught on to the nature of my question, she didn't pry. "Both Basil and I were divorced from previous partners when we met."

"Really?" I said. "That gives me hope."

"The world's a funny place." Della climbed up a steep ridge, surprising me with her agility. She offered me a hand to help me up. "Sometimes, you just need a change of perspective. Take a look."

The trees opened up to a flat rock face on the side of the hill. Beyond it, the mountain dropped off at a sharp angle. I inched forward, scared to go any closer, but Della marched right up to the edge of the small cliff. From here, we had an eagle's eye view of the mansion. It was miles below situated right on the frozen river. At this height, the house looked half as intimidating. One might even mistake it for a beautiful castle hidden in the magical forest of Falconwood.

"There's Jim," I said, pointing to one end of the huge terrace. We weren't so far away that we couldn't see the people down below. "Which means Ben can't be too far behind. Aha!" I pointed my camera at the house and clicked a quick picture of Ben where he stood on the opposite end of the terrace. "Told ya he was nearby."

"Good instinct," Della said. She took a seat on the rock face, dangling her feet over the edge. When she saw my worried look, she added, "Don't worry. There's another level right below us. If I fall, it's only about a ten-foot drop."

"Oh, sure. Ten feet."

Della patted the ground beside her. "Come on, live a little."

I sat down before I reached the edge, and Della gave me a little nod of approval. After gathering my courage, I let my boots hang next to hers.

"There ya go," she said, patting my thigh. "Don't you feel like a bird?"

Though it was a bit of a stretch, I did feel a bit freer than usual. The air up here was crisper, and there was something about being so far above the people at the house that soothed my soul.

"Do you think the Abrams ever came up here?"

"Yes, indeed," Della answered. "Percy was an avid hiker. These trails are actually named after him, but they were closed to the public for a while. Not many people come up here anymore."

"Why's that?"

Della pursed her lips. "Maybe some other time."

"Della, just tell me."

She threw a rock as far as she could. It soared through the air and disappeared into the trees below. "Do you remember what I told you about Percy? How he died?"

"You told me he died of grief," I said. "But you didn't tell me how."

"He killed himself," Della said. "He hiked up here and threw himself off the side of a cliff, into the rushing river below. If you ask the locals, they'll tell you it was an accident."

"But you don't think that?"

"The police found a suicide note from Percy in the house," Della said. "I think the town convinced themselves it was an accident to make it less painful. Everyone felt Percy's death."

I imagined falling from the rock face and bouncing all the way down to the river. Poor Percy Abrams must have been half out of his mind.

"How do you know so much about the Abrams?" I asked Della. "You said you didn't move to Falconwood until after they were already long gone."

Della tossed another rock. This one bounced off a tree with a hollow thunk. "Have you ever heard of micro-obsessions?"

"I don't think so."

"It's common for people with depression or OCD to develop intense interest in one thing," Della explained. "Introverts are particularly susceptible to it. When I find something I like, I don't casually investigate it. I immerse myself in it. It used to be quite a problem when I was younger. I'd get obsessed over a TV show or a book and never come out of my room. My mother thought I was a recluse."

"So the Abrams were a micro-obsession?"

"Of sorts." Della snapped a few pictures of the horizon and the house below. "Once I got older, I learned to channel my obsessions into more productive avenues. That's why I practice photography so often. When we first moved to Falconwood, I found the Abram Mansion by accident while hiking. As soon as I saw it, I had to know everything about it. I asked everyone in town, scoured old newspapers, and dug up the Abrams's public records. All of the information was right there for me to absorb."

Her eyes glazed over as she spoke, and I got the feeling that her interest in the Abrams Mansion was still alive and well. Taking a leaf out of her book, I tossed a rock over the edge, feeling weirdly powerful as I did it.

"Did the locals mind you digging up information about the Abrams?" I asked.

"Most of them were fine with it," she answered. "But it was

the first time I got too wrapped up in something for Basil to handle."

"Why? What happened?"

"I was never present with him," Della said. "I was too busy combing over every bit of information I could find on the Abrams. I spent hours locked in my study, reading and re-reading about Percy and his family. I researched the house too, but there was surprisingly little to find. Anyway, Basil worried about me. When he finally got through to me, I realized how much time I'd been spending alone, away from him. I decided to give my obsession with the Abram Mansion a break."

"This is the first time you've been back since?"

"It sure is."

I chugged quickly from the bottle we'd brought along with us, but the water was too cold to sip for long. "Feel free to explore the house again if you like. It's a bit safer now that we've started renovations."

She gazed absentmindedly into the distance. "I'm not so sure that's a good idea."

"Well, if you change your mind…"

We sat in silence for a few minutes, listening to the wind pick up as it whistled through the trees. The white sky was no longer still. Dark clouds roiled above us, no doubt waiting to dump a fresh load of snow on the town. If we didn't get back to the house soon, it would be a much colder hike home.

"We don't have much time," Della said, noticing the sky. She slipped the strap of her camera off of her neck and over mine. "Here. Snap a few digital ones. It's got an amazing zoom on it."

I traded her for the old Canon and happily lifted her fancy DSLR up to my eye level. While Della aimed at the surrounding trees, I zoomed in on the house and focused the lens. Nature was fun for practice, but when it came down to it, I loved photographing people more than plants and animals. I snapped picture after picture of the construction workers in various stages of work. With a few adjustments to the camera, I could make the house and its current occupants look like toys.

After I finished with Jim's crew, I turned the camera toward Ben, who was still inspecting the older part of the terrace. He peered upward, and I traced the line of his sight up to one of the attic windows that looked out on the terrace. My heart dropped.

A little girl stared out of the window, looking directly at Ben.

"Della?" I tapped her shoulder and handed her the camera. "Do you see someone in that left upper window, right above Ben?"

Della peered through the viewfinder and fiddled with the focus. "Nope. Nothing there. You worried one of the construction guys is trying to rip you off?"

I took the camera back and focused on the window again. The little girl had disappeared. I checked on Ben. He walked the perimeter of the terrace, pausing every now and then to scuff loose tiles with his foot. He reached the corner and braced himself against the railing to check something beneath him. The railing wobbled.

"No!" I cried.

As the rusty railing gave way, Ben fell two stories off the terrace and landed on the frozen river below. He didn't get up.

8

---

*T*he hike back to the house took an hour. It was the longest hour of my life, and no matter how many shortcuts Della knew to get us through the woods as quickly as possible, it didn't ease my mind. With no cell tower nearby, I couldn't call 911. When we finally arrived at the house, no one seemed concerned with Ben's fall. The landscape around the mansion was so overgrown that I couldn't tell where Ben had landed from the ground.

"Jim!" I called up to the roof, cupping my hands around my mouth so the contractor could hear me.

He peered over the edge of the terrace. "Everything okay down there?"

"No! Ben fell off the terrace!"

"What? Where is he?"

"That's what I need you for," I called up. "I can't see where he landed from down here, but I know he's on the river. Can you see from up there?"

Jim jogged to the other side of the terrace where Ben had been patrolling an hour ago. He jiggled the faulty railing before glancing down. "I see him! He's about twenty feet to your right. How long has he been down there?"

I raced through the dead trees and bushes, dialing 911. Della was close on my heels.

"911. What's your emergency?"

"My husband fell off the roof of our house," I said. "Ben!"

I handed the phone to Della when I caught sight of Ben. He was splayed across the frozen icy river, one of his arms bent at an odd angle. Blood stained the ice dark red. I almost ran to him, but Della held me back.

"Go slow," she said. "You don't want the ice to break."

It took all of my willpower to take her advice. All I wanted was to get to Ben as soon as possible. He'd already been unconscious for an hour. Gingerly, I tested the ice at the edge of the river, stomping my boot down to see if it would hold. When it held firm, I slid across like I was ice skating and knelt beside Ben.

"Is he awake?" Della asked, no doubt repeating the question from the 911 operator. "Is he breathing?"

"He's breathing," I confirmed. "Ben? Can you hear me?"

Ben groaned, but each time he attempted to open his eyes, they fluttered shut again. "Peyton?"

"He's awake!" I told Della. "Should I move him off the ice?"

Della repeated the question to the operator then replied, "They said to leave him be. If you move him, you could risk injuring him more. An ambulance is on its way."

Jim jogged up from behind, breathing hard. "I didn't know he was up on the terrace. I kept telling him to stay put. My guys haven't gotten around to that side yet. I'm so sorry."

"It's not your fault," I told him. "You didn't know."

"I should have been paying more attention." Jim shed his workman's jacket and handed it to me across the ice. "Here.

Drape that over him so he stays warm. It can't be good that he's on the ice like that."

After five excruciating minutes, the ambulance ambled up the one-way road that led to the mansion, sirens screaming. They drove right up to the river, flattening the grass and bushes in their way. A team of paramedics filed out. The first one, a woman who had the same perfect bone structure as Officer Spaughton, gestured for me to get off the ice.

"Careful," she said as the ice cracked beneath my boot. "We don't want to trigger a worst-case scenario."

As soon as I was clear of the ice, she traded places with me. The other paramedics were beefier men. If they took one step onto the river, the entire frozen surface might shatter. The Officer Spaughton lookalike weighed the least, so she took point on the rescue while the others readied a stretcher.

"When did he fall?" the paramedic asked.

"About an hour ago." I wrung my hands, wanting to do something but afraid to get in the way. "We would have called sooner, but we saw him fall from up in the hills. Our phones weren't working."

"What's his name?"

"Ben Fletcher."

The paramedic waved her hand in front of Ben's eyes. "Ben, can you hear me?"

Like before, Ben groaned and made an attempt to open his eyes. The paramedic held his shoulders still.

"Try not to move," she said. "My name is Kate. I'm a paramedic. You've been in an accident, but we're going to get you to the hospital, okay? I just need you to work with me and my team."

Kate and her team got to work. They slid the stretcher across the ice, and Kate worked her magic to get Ben on it without compromising his injuries. His right arm was definitely broken, and he had an ugly bruise on the side of his head where he had hit the ice. Kate stabilized his neck, made sure Ben was strapped in tight, then pushed the stretcher across the ice all on her own. Once they could reach it, the other paramedics took hold of the stretcher to lift Ben off the ground and into the ambulance.

"You're the wife, right?" Kate asked as she stepped gingerly off the ice. "Are you coming with us?"

"Yes," I said. "Della, could you—?"

"I'll hold down the fort," Della promised, taking my hiking backpack from my shoulders. "I'll lock up too. If you have time to update me later, give me a call."

"Thank you so much."

The paramedics helped me step up to the back of the ambulance, and I sat next to Kate as the driver fired up the rig. The paramedics checked Ben's vitals and hooked him up to fluids. His eyes kept shooting open then fluttering shut again, like he was trying his hardest to stay awake. On the stretcher, with his head framed by the foam support, Ben looked smaller. His fluffy curls were wet and flat, pasted to his forehead with melted ice and sweat. I'd seen Ben like this once before. Over ten years ago, during the final football game of the regular season, Ben was tackled after a kick. The other player concussed him and took out his knee, ruining Ben's chance to play college football. Somehow, I was seventeen again, watching my high school boyfriend get carted off to the hospital without knowing what was wrong.

"You can hold his hand," Kate said. "The non-broken one obviously."

Since she seemed to be waiting for me to do so, I took Ben's cold fingers in mine. He didn't squeeze me to let me know he was going to be okay or anything like that. His hand was limp and clammy.

When the ambulance jerked to a stop and the paramedics got

out, I didn't recognize our surroundings. We certainly weren't at the emergency clinic in Falconwood. We had arrived at a bay door on the side of a huge hospital, where the paramedics shunted me aside to get Ben out of the rig.

"Where are we?" I asked Kate, hurrying behind her as she helped roll Ben's stretcher through the bay doors. "This isn't Falconwood."

"This is Moorewood," Kate answered. "Next town over. The Falconwood clinic doesn't have the kind of resources the emergency team needs to help him. Out of the way!" People parted like the Red Sea as Kate and the other paramedics piloted the stretcher through the hallways of the hospital. At another set of double doors, Kate held me back with one hand. "You have to stay here. I'll have someone give you an update as soon as possible."

They wheeled Ben through the double doors, leaving me to sit in the waiting room with no company aside from my racing mind. I sat in a cold plastic chair farthest from the other mourning family members. My socks were wet from the hike and the collar of my coat was stained with cold sweat, but I was too numb to address either discomfort.

I took off my gloves and fished my phone out of my pocket. Now that we were closer to civilization, I had full bars. I dialed Ben's mother, whose number wasn't in my phone but I'd memorized nonetheless.

"Hello?" she answered.

"Mrs. Fletcher? It's me, Peyton."

"What's wrong?"

I grimaced. Of course she automatically thought something was wrong. I never called her unless Ben asked me to. Ever since high school, Mrs. Fletcher thought I wasn't good enough for Ben. When he injured his knee, she found a way to blame his ruined football chances on me.

"Ben's in the hospital," I said, plain and simply. "He was working on the terrace of our house and leaned against a part of the railing that wasn't stable, and he fell."

On the other end of the line, Mrs. Fletcher's breath hitched. "What's wrong with him? Did they say he was going to be okay? I want to speak to a doctor."

"We just arrived. They took him back already," I told her. "He definitely has a broken arm and probably a concussion. They said they would update me when they knew more. I'll call you when they do."

"Don't you dare hang up on me!" Mrs. Fletcher said. "I know the only reason you called me was out of obligation, but as Benjamin's mother, I deserve more in this situation. Do you understand me, Miss Baus?"

When she was particularly angry with me, Mrs. Fletcher reverted to calling me by my maiden name, as if I wasn't worthy of the Fletcher surname.

"I didn't mean to—"

"He wouldn't have gone to that house if it weren't for you," she barreled on. "It belonged to *your* grandfather, not his, which means it's *your* responsibility. I warned him not to go, especially with this divorce looming on the horizon, but he was determined to make you see sense. He thought—"

"He thought I wouldn't divorce him if we lived in the mansion together," I finished for her, my patience waning. "Yeah, I know. I heard him talking to you before we left."

"Then you also know he loves you more than life itself, God forbid," Mrs. Fletcher spat. "He's always done right by you, and if he doesn't make it out of that house alive at the end of six months, I will never stop haunting you. Is that clear, Miss Baus?"

"This wasn't my fault—"

She hung up on me, and I found myself talking to my phone's home screen instead. I stared at the picture of me and Ben, never having changed it despite our supposed separation. It was taken about a year ago, right before I'd decided to end things, at Ben's favorite hometown bar. Behind us, Ben's high school jersey hung on the wall, as if to remind me of all the things I'd apparently kept him from doing.

The hospital closed in on me. The cloying smell of disinfectant invaded my nose. Various noises—doctors and nurses shouting over one another, babies and children crying, the wheels of a stretcher squeaking across the tile floor— bombarded my ears. I felt dirty all of a sudden, like my skin was crawling with every germ that had ever passed through this waiting room. I had to get out of here.

I made a break for the main doors, moving as fast as I could without accidentally taking anyone out, and burst outside. The cold air hit me like a truck, but it was a blessed relief from the stifling heat indoors. I was so overwhelmed, I didn't notice Theo walking up until I ran right into her.

"Peyton!" She steadied me by the shoulders before pulling me into a hug. "I heard what happened to Ben. Is he okay? Are *you* okay?"

Theo's soothing lemongrass scent staved off the hospital's sterility. I breathed in and out, burying my nose in Theo's hair until I felt like a normal human being again. "I don't know. They haven't told me anything yet. How did you know?"

"I was worried when you didn't show up for lunch," Theo said. "So I drove up to your house. Della filled me in. I figured they wouldn't take Ben to the clinic in town, so I came straight here."

I squeezed her tighter, glad that she cared enough to show up. "You should go. You have to get back to work, and Sammy needs to be picked up in a couple of hours."

"Della's going to take care of Sammy," Theo said, linking her arm through mine. "I'm going to take care of you. Have you eaten?"

"Not since this morning."

"Hospital food sucks, but we can probably find something edible in the vending machines. A nice cup of coffee wouldn't be horrible either—"

She began leading me inside, but I pulled her back. "No, please. I don't want to go back in. Not yet. I just need a few minutes."

Theo produced a tissue from a magical hideaway in her jacket and wiped my running nose. "Whatever you need, Peyton."

THEO STAYED with me until the hospital staff had news on Ben. Since I couldn't muster the anticipation of the waiting room, we wandered around the hospital instead. We hit the vending machines on every floor, ultimately sneaking into the nurses' lounge because theirs had the best options. We visited the maternity ward to look at the newborns through the glass window. Theo gave each one a name and made up a story about the baby and its parents. Then we sat in the trauma waiting room for no other reason than to remind ourselves that things could be worse. I could only stand to watch for a few minutes, especially when a doctor came out to inform a family of their loss. Though Ben hadn't looked anywhere close to death, I had no idea what was going on inside his body, especially since he'd been on the ice for an hour before anyone attended to him. We finally returned to our own waiting room, where it was only another hour before a doctor came out and asked to speak to Ben Fletcher's family.

"That's me," I said, raising my hand. "I'm his wife. Peyton."

As the doctor came over, Theo held me around the waist for extra support. "Everything's going to be fine," she whispered.

The doctor had kind gray eyes and a warm smile, and I wondered if he'd practiced those expressions in med school. "I'm Doctor Metcalfe," he said. "I'm relieved to tell you that Ben made it through surgery just fine. He should make a full recovery."

"What's wrong with him?" I asked. "No one told me."

"His arm is broken in several places," Doctor Metcalfe explained. "He'll need months of physical therapy to get normal motor function back. He also has a few fractured ribs, a collapsed lung, and a concussion. We re-inflated the lung and performed CTs. Thankfully, his concussion was relatively minor. No hematomas or anything like that. All in all, he's a very lucky guy."

"Is he awake?" Theo asked as she rubbed circles into my back. "Can she go and see him?"

"He's not awake yet," the doctor said. "He's still groggy from the anesthesia, but you're welcome to visit his room. I'll have one of the nurses show you the way."

As the doctor called over a nurse, I turned to Theo. "Please come with me."

"Are you sure?" she asked. "It's kind of intimate, isn't it?"

"I don't want to do this alone."

"Okay then."

Ben had a room with a window to himself. He lay passed out in the middle of the bed, his arm wrapped from elbow to wrist in a thick cast. His chest and head were bandaged too. On the upside, some of the color had returned to his cheeks so he didn't look as pale and corpse-like as he had on the river. His golden curls had bounced back as well.

"Wow," Theo whispered. "He looks okay, considering the situation."

More out of instinct than anything else, I stroked Ben's curls away from his eyes. "Yeah, he does. It could have been much worse."

"Do you want me to go?" Theo said. "Now that the hard part's over?"

"Can you stay a while longer?" I asked her.

"Sure." She pulled the armchair up to the side of Ben's bed and patted the seat. "Sit down. I'll steal another chair from down the hall."

A few minutes later, she returned from the hallway hauling another chair that she had pilfered from the nurse's lounge. She handed me a fresh coffee and a paper plate with a piece of chocolate cake.

"It was one of the nurse's birthdays," she said with a shrug.

I ate the whole piece. The snacks from the vending machine hadn't done much for me in the long run, and I was dying for a real meal. As I licked icing from the spoon and watched Ben breathe, an image popped into my head: that of the little girl in the attic window.

"Theo, when did Sammy start talking about his imaginary friend?"

"About a year ago," Theo answered. "It was the first time he ever ran away. He ended up at your house actually. Ever since then, he's been obsessed with her. He told me she's been living there for years."

"Does he know her name?"

"He calls her Alyssa." Theo rolled her eyes. "But there's a little girl named Alyssa in his class at school too, so I figured he named his imaginary friend after her."

"Has he told you anything else about Alyssa?" I asked. "The imaginary friend, not the girl in his class."

"Not really," Theo said. "He's been less adamant about

visiting her since you and Ben moved into the mansion, but he still mentions her once in a while. He's drawn a bunch of pictures of her."

"He has?" I said. "Can I see them?"

"Sure," she replied. "Come by anytime. He'll be happy to show them to you."

Not long after our discussion, Della called Theo to let her know Sammy was waiting for her, leaving me alone with Ben for the rest of the evening. When I started dozing off, I gave up on the chair and wiggled in next to Ben, careful not to jostle his bandaged injuries. He smelled like sweat and sterile bandages, with only a faint hint of his favorite mint-scented shampoo. I honed in on that and fell asleep.

"Peyton?"

Ben's groggy voice woke me up, as did a languid poke to my shoulder. I opened my eyes to see Ben's brown ones staring back at me. He was awake, alert, and talking. The sun gleamed against the window pane. We'd slept through the entire night.

"Hey there, sleepyhead," he said. Then he put on the winning star kicker grin that made me fall in love with him all those years ago. "Long time, no see."

I have no idea what possessed me to kiss him, but as soon as it happened, I realized it was a mistake. From the second I pressed my lips against his, I wanted to pull away again, not because it wasn't a nice kiss—on the contrary, it was very nice— but because I didn't want to give Ben the wrong idea.

"Wow," he said. "I must be hopped up on a lot of painkillers, because I'm definitely imagining things right now."

"I'm sorry," I said. "I shouldn't have done that."

"No, it's okay." He pulled me in with his good arm, cradling me against his chest. He winced when I brushed against his fractured ribs but refused to let me go. "It felt right, didn't it? I missed you, Peyton."

As I listened to his heartbeat, a single tear fell off my nose and landed on his clinical gown.

9

To my surprise, Doctor Metcalfe cleared Ben to go home, giving me specific instructions on how to care for him for the next several weeks. Between his broken ribs, tender head, and injured lung, Ben had to go easy on his recovery. He was prescribed a slew of pain medication and given advice on when to seek a physical therapy clinic.

"You should get moving as soon as possible," Doctor Metcalfe advised. "But not too soon. Take it slow and don't overwork yourself. Your body is fragile right now, and I don't want to see you back in this hospital for anything other than a checkup."

Since we didn't have a ride back to Falconwood, I called Della to ask if she was able to come pick us up. Not only did she arrive in Moorewood in Basil's eco-friendly car to get us, she stuck around once we made it back to Abram Mansion. She helped me get Ben into bed, set up his room so whatever he might need was within reach of his good arm, and whipped up a batch of chicken noodle soup for the both of us. After Ben took his pain medication, he was out like a light. Right before he fell asleep, he took my face in his hands and brought me closer to kiss me again. I pulled away.

In the kitchen, Della made tea. When the kettle whistled, she poured the boiling water over the fresh tea mixture she'd made herself and set the cup under my nose as it steeped. "Take a whiff of that," she said. "It'll perk you right up."

I inhaled the soothing scents, detecting orange and black pepper. "Thanks, Della. You have no idea how much it means to me that you're here."

"I'm just glad Ben's going to be okay." Della poured her own cup of tea and joined me at the table. "Are you all right?"

"Everyone keeps asking me that, but I'm not the one who fell off a terrace."

"Yes, but emotional health is just as important as physical health," Della said. "If Basil fell off a roof, I'd be elated to know he was going to be fine. You seem a bit put out."

"Not because of that," I answered quickly. "I'm glad Ben's okay. I don't ever want to see him get hurt. I did something stupid though."

"Honey, we're human. We thrive on stupidity."

"I kissed him," I admitted, lowering my head to rest on the kitchen table. "Right after he woke up."

Della whistled. "Wow, kissing your husband. What a terrible thing to do."

"We're basically divorced," I reminded her. "And now he probably thinks we have a shot at getting back together." I banged my head on the table. "Stupid, stupid, stupid!"

Della slid her palm between my forehead and the wood. "If you don't stop, you're going to give yourself a concussion too."

I groaned and slumped over in my chair. Della pushed the mug of tea toward me.

"Listen to me," she said. "That kiss happened in an onrush of emotions. You were happy Ben made it through surgery alive. There's nothing wrong with that."

"But he thinks—"

"Let him be for now," Della said. "As long as he's taking those painkillers, he won't be any kind of lucid. After a few days, explain that the kiss didn't mean what he might have thought. Remind him you're still getting divorced."

"He'll be crushed. I need to talk to him—"

Della forced the cup of tea to my lips to shut me up. "What you need is to get out of this house and away from Ben. As long as you're staring at his pretty bandaged face, you're going to let him play whatever card he wants. Go into town. Check in with Theo. Whatever you do, I don't want to see you here before dinnertime."

"But—"

"Go!" Della confiscated the cup of tea and pushed me out of my chair. "I mean it. Go get ready and get out of here."

Della's insistence shoved me out of the kitchen. With her blessing, I walked right past Ben's room without checking on him. In my own room, I dug out the rolls of film I'd shot on the antique camera and put them in my coat pocket.

ONCE IN TOWN, I dropped the film rolls off at Chester's photography shop to be developed then went about my usual routine. But when I showed up at Black Cat Café for a late breakfast, I discovered that the news of Ben's injury had spread far and wide. As soon as I stepped inside, Mason darted out from behind the counter to envelop me in a crushing hug.

"Peyton, you dear thing," he cried. "I heard the news. How are you holding up? How's Ben? Can I do anything to help? We love fundraisers here at the Black Cat if you need help raising money for the medical bills. Shall I set one up?"

"Insurance covered most of the cost," I said, squirming out of his claustrophobic grasp. "It's going to be a long recovery for him, but the doctors said he'll be okay."

"I'm so glad to hear that," Mason said, beaming. "What can I get you today? The usual?"

"Yes, please. I'd like something other than hospital coffee to drink."

"Of course! Go sit down. Anywhere you like. If someone's already sitting there, I'll make them move. Just say the word!"

"That's okay, Mason," I told him. "You take care of your other customers."

I did my best to go about my usual business, taking up residence in one of the cozy armchairs in the warmest corner of the café to read a book Theo had lent me. Mason soon brought me my coffee, an egg and cheese croissant, and a free cookie because I apparently looked like I needed it. Every few pages in my book, someone else came up to me to ask about Ben. From the sound of it, Jim and his crew had told the entire town about Ben's fall. Rumors of his supposed injuries spread far and wide, but I set the record straight and asked each of the locals to respect our privacy. Though everyone was polite enough, the constant interruptions got old quickly. I escaped Black Cat and gave Theo a call.

"Peyton!" she answered. "How are you? How's Ben?"

"We're both fine," I told her. "Ben's home on bed rest. Della's watching him, but she forced me to go out. Are you at work?"

"No, I picked Sammy up from school early," she replied. "He pulled someone else's hair and got sent to the principal's office. I haven't gotten the whole story from him yet though."

"I thought his behavior was improving?"

She sighed through the phone. "So did I. Do you want to come over? I made a vat of macaroni and cheese, and we could use the company."

"On my way."

. . .

THEO'S APARTMENT felt more like home than the Abram Mansion ever did. As soon as I got there, the smell of fresh cinnamon buns from the bakery below taunted my senses. Theo answered the door wearing a purple flowery apron with ricotta cheese smeared across the front and brandishing a cheesy spatula. She tossed the apron off to give me a cheese-free hug.

"It's so good to see you," she said. "I'm glad Ben's home and doing okay. How are you holding up?"

"Good and not so good," I told her as she took my coat and beckoned me inside. I flopped down on her couch. "I kissed Ben."

"Uh-oh."

"Yeah, uh-oh." I groaned and covered my head with a throw pillow. "Della thinks I should wait until Ben isn't taking painkillers to tell him how I feel."

"How *do* you feel?" Theo stirred the mac and cheese on the stove absentmindedly, not noticing when some of the noodles fell out. "I mean, are you going to get back together with him?"

"No!" I rolled to my feet, tossed aside the pillow, and sat at the breakfast bar to talk to Theo instead. "It was a relief kiss. I was glad he wasn't dead, you know? My emotions reared their ugly heads and went all Medusa on me."

"At least you haven't turned to stone. Taste this." She raised the wooden spoon to my lips, and I ate the piece of macaroni off it. "What's it need? More cheese?"

I wrenched my tongue from where it was glued to the roof of my mouth. "God, no. Add some milk, woman."

She added a splash of milk to the pot and started stirring again. The macaroni slowly unstuck from the sides of the pan and started to look more like pasta than a solid block of cheese.

"Not your usual healthy meal," I commented. "Where's the side of sautéed spinach or roasted broccoli?"

"Mac and cheese is Sammy's favorite," said Theo. "I don't make it very often, but he had a hard day."

"So you're rewarding him for pulling someone's hair?"

She set down the spoon and leaned against the counter to push her hair away from her face. "I asked him about it. He said the other kids were making fun of him. According to him, he didn't touch anyone's hair. The kids ganged up on him and lied to the teacher together."

"They're six. Are they really that cunning?"

Theo put her hair up in a ponytail and washed her hands. "I don't know, but Sammy's never lied to me. If he does something wrong, he tells me and apologizes. I just don't understand why he's being bullied, and he won't tell me."

I looked around the empty living room. Sammy's off-brand building blocks were piled neatly in his play corner, but there were no signs of the actual kid. "Where is he anyway? Taking a nap?"

"Probably," Theo said. "He fell asleep in the car on the way home. Do you want to go wake him up for me? Let him know his lunch is ready."

Quietly, I snuck into the bedroom that Theo and Sammy shared. Sammy lay in his twin-sized race car bed, but he wasn't actually asleep. He played with two plush dogs, silently mouthing a conversation between them.

"Hey, Sammy," I said.

"Hi, Peyton!" He jumped off the bed, upending the dogs to give me a hug around the waist. "I missed you yesterday."

"I missed you too. Aren't you supposed to be taking a nap right now?"

"I couldn't sleep," Sammy said. "But I know Mama didn't want me to get in the way in the kitchen."

I ruffled his hair. "Speaking of your mom, she wanted me to

let you know that your lunch is ready. I hear mac and cheese is your favorite."

"Yeah! Are you staying for lunch?"

"Sure, if you don't mind."

"I don't mind." He took my hand and led me back into the main room. "Mama, Peyton's staying for lunch!"

Theo clapped her hands together and beamed as if she hadn't already invited me to share the massive amounts of mac and cheese. "Lovely! Let's get this show on the road."

Sammy put away two bowls of pasta before taking a breath. Neither Theo or I could stomach more than half a serving of the cheese-laden macaroni, so Theo took a pre-made salad out of the fridge to share with me instead. As Sammy ate, he talked about the good parts of his day at school, which included P.E., English class, and Art.

"Mrs. Sable says I should show my clay pot in the winter art fair," he boasted, puffing his chest out proudly. "She says it's one of the best pots in the class."

"That's excellent, Sammy," Theo said, kissing her son's cheek. "But I thought you were going to submit some of your drawings for the art fair."

"Mrs. Sable says I'm better at clay than drawing," Sammy replied, almost as if trying to convince himself it was true. "I don't think she's right. I really like drawing, and I think I'm really good at it. But I like clay too, so it's okay, I guess."

"Speaking of your drawings," I said, "I was wondering if you had any of your friend Alyssa."

Sammy's entire face lit up. I guessed not many people encouraged his friendship with the invisible Alyssa.

"I have a lot!" he exclaimed, bouncing up and down in his chair. "Do you want to see them?"

"Sure, if you don't mind showing me."

"I don't mind." He hopped off the chair, realized he had abandoned the remainder of his food, and looked over his shoulder at his mother. "Mom, it's really cheesy. Can I finish it later?"

Theo smiled at him. "Of course you can."

"Cool!" He jetted off into the bedroom, singing to the tune of I Love Rock and Roll. *"I love mac and cheese, so put another bowl in front of me."*

I grinned at Theo. "Glad to see you're giving him an excellent music education."

"What can I say?" Theo shrugged. "I went through a Joan Jett phase. Lots of eyeliner. Had the girl mullet and everything in high school."

"Oh, I would love to see pictures of that. Did you learn to play the electric guitar?"

"I was a drummer actually," she answered. "Pretty good at it too."

"You amaze me."

Sammy came running out of the bedroom with a stack of construction paper. He clambered up to his chair again and laid the pictures out in front of me, one at a time so he could narrate each of them.

"I drew this after the first time we met," he explained, pointing to what looked like the most fragile drawing. Though the paper was water-damaged and the ink of the colored marker had run, I could see the rough outline of a little girl in a doorway. "She told me she was really lonely and that she didn't have any friends. Her mom's really strict, so Alyssa isn't allowed to play outside."

Theo caught my eye over Sammy's head. Alyssa's mother had similar rules to Theo. Sammy wasn't allowed outside or at a friend's house without Theo's strict supervision. I didn't have a child, so I couldn't judge Theo for the way she raised Sammy, but I definitely understood how rigid she was with his freedom.

"I promised her I'd come back," Sammy said, frowning as he

flipped to the next page. "I haven't been able to visit lately. She's probably sad."

I cleared my throat and pointed at Sammy's next drawing. "What's happening in this one, Sammy?"

"We explored the basement together."

The drawing was a little clearer than the last one. Sammy had put a lot of effort into two of Alyssa's prominent features: her bright red hair and a pink polka dot scarf around her neck. He had also drawn the kitchen of the Abram Mansion before it had been renovated in exquisite detail, right down to the old chandelier and the small doggy door. Alyssa stood by the stove, her uneven fingers gripping something Sammy had struggled to draw.

"What's she holding?" I asked Sammy.

"I don't remember," he said quickly. He hid the kitchen drawing beneath the others. "Here's Alyssa in the attic. She likes to hide there."

My chest tightened as I examined the drawing. Once again, Sammy managed to capture a rather detailed image of the inside of the mansion, all of the junk in the attic drawn in boxy six-year-old scribbles. Behind a crudely-drawn file cabinet, Alyssa stands half-hidden with her face in shadow.

"Sammy, did you go all the way up to the attic?" I asked him. "It's dangerous up there."

Sammy hummed, rocking on his chair. "I draw things that Alyssa shows me."

"You didn't answer the question, Sam," Theo said. "Did you go up to the attic?"

"No."

Theo took a deep breath. From the look of her expression, she didn't know how often Sammy had visited the Abram Mansion. "Go put your drawings away, Sammy."

Sammy, sensing his mother's distress, stacked his pieces of

construction paper, retreated to the bedroom, and did not return. Theo rested her forehead in her hands.

"I had no idea," she murmured. "He has at least fifty drawings of that house. How many times has he walked up there alone?"

I rubbed Theo's shoulders. "Hey, at least you know now, right? Maybe you should install an alarm system so he can't leave without setting it off."

"Yeah. I guess."

I gathered my coat and wallet. "I should get going. Thanks for having me for lunch and letting Sammy show me his drawings. Don't go too hard on him."

She hugged me goodbye. "I won't. Get home safe. Tell Ben to get well soon."

"I'll pass it on. See you, Theo."

As I left, Theo tossed the pan of mac and cheese into the sink to soak. I made my way down the stairs to the bakery. My car was parked across the street, but as I stepped out on the curb, a small hand grabbed mine. It was Sammy, out of breath from running after me.

"Here," he said, shoving a piece of construction paper into my hand. It was folded into fourths. "That's Alyssa too, but don't open it until you get home. I don't want my mom to see."

WITH SAMMY'S drawing tucked into the pocket of my coat, I picked up my developed film rolls from Chester and headed home. Della's car was still parked out front. She'd stayed the entire day to make sure Ben was okay. When I walked inside, the mansion was oddly quiet. I checked on Ben first. He was sound asleep in bed, his broken arm propped up on a pillow. I went down to the kitchen.

"Della!" I called, taking off my gloves one finger at a time. I tossed the stack of photographs onto the kitchen table. "Della, I'm home. Oh—!"

Basil stepped out from behind the refrigerator door, holding a knife between his teeth and a tomato in each hand. When he saw me, he carefully spat the knife out. "Whoops. Didn't mean to scare you. Della's in the bathroom. She left me in charge of the bruschetta." He held up the tomatoes. "Fresh from our hydroponic garden. They have quite the bold taste. Are you interested?"

I placed a calming hand over my rushing heart. "Yeah, that sounds great. How did you get here, Basil?"

"I walked."

"All the way up that hill?"

"Are you insinuating that I'm too old to hike?" he asked with a soft grin. He added one more tomato to his grip and began to juggle them, then nodded at the photographs on the table. "I see my wife has suckered you into her hobby."

"Don't listen to him," Della said, shaking her hands dry as she joined us in the kitchen. "He's such a spoilsport about photography. Just because *you* don't like having your picture taken, my dear" —she snatched one of Basil's tomatoes out of the air— "doesn't mean everyone else has to suffer."

"Of course, my love," Basil said. "Shall we cook dinner and get out of the Fletchers' hair?"

"Oh, please," I said. "You two have done so much for us already. I can't ask you to make dinner again. Go home. We'll be fine. I promise."

Basil checked with his wife. "Do we listen to the fine lady or do we proceed as planned? I have truffle oil that shouldn't go to waste."

Della patted Basil's arm. "Leave the truffle oil. I'm sure Peyton is eager to get to bed after such a long day. Let's head out, dear."

I walked the older couple to the door. Basil helped Della into her coat then offered his arm to her so she wouldn't slip on the ice outside. I waved from the doorway as they got in their tiny car and drove away. As soon as the car disappeared into the trees, I let my shoulders slump.

Back in the kitchen, a chicken sandwich waited for me in the fridge, no doubt Della's doing to make sure I had something to eat when I got home. Since Theo's mac and cheese hadn't been the best, I grabbed the sandwich and sat at the table to eat. As the sun lowered itself on the horizon, throwing the basement kitchen into darkness, I examined the photographs I'd had developed at Chester's.

The ones I'd taken in the woods weren't bad, but you could tell which ones were Della's and which ones were mine. Mine were clumsy, and the subjects were unclear, though the one of the sky and the single bird had come out as I wanted it to. At the bottom of the stack were the photographs from the roll of film I'd found in the old camera. Curious, I flipped through them as well.

Each photo was a picture of a room in the Abram Mansion as they had been before we had done any renovations. However, instead of the decrepit house we had moved into, the pictures featured the mansion before it had fallen into ruin. The photos were meticulously taken, almost as if to preserve the integrity of the mansion. The very last picture in the stack was the one I had taken myself in the attic. I slid it out from underneath the others to have a look.

My heart stopped beating. In the picture, half-hidden behind the file cabinet, was the fuzzy yet unmistakable outline of a little girl with red hair and a pink polka-dotted scarf. My hands shook as I took Sammy's drawing from my pocket and unfolded it. The image upon it made my blood run cold.

Sammy had drawn Alyssa lying in a puddle of blood.

10

*H*eart racing, I dialed Theo's number. It went straight to voicemail, so I hung up and tried again. Once more, it didn't ring, and I got Theo's voicemail instead. I couldn't stop staring at the photo and Sammy's drawing. I remembered that day in the attic not too long ago, when I'd taken that picture and swore someone was standing in the corner of the room. Had Sammy been right all along? Was a little girl living in the mansion without us knowing? And if so, why had Sammy drawn her in a puddle of blood? Without Theo to talk to, I needed someone else to discuss it with. I went to Ben's room and clambered onto his bed with the photo and drawing in hand.

"Ben," I whispered, poking his chest. "Ben, wake up. I have to show you something."

He murmured something incoherent, tried to roll over, and failed when his bulky cast got in the way. I patted his cheek impatiently.

"Ben, remember when I said there was something in the house?" I hissed. "I think I was right. Sammy saw it too. There's a little girl—"

With his good hand, Ben pushed my face away from his. I almost smacked him for being so rude before realizing he was still dead asleep.

"Ben!" I shouted.

He woke with a start, struggling to open his eyes as if they were glued together. "Huh? Peyton? What're you doing in here?"

"Trying to tell you something," I said. "If you would only listen. There's a kid in the house—"

He groaned and rolled over, this time completing the action by moving to his good side. He covered his head with the pillow then winced when he accidentally put too much pressure on his tender injury.

"Why don't you believe me?" I demanded. "I've been trying to get through to you practically since we moved in here. You brush me off or ignore me. Then you wonder why our marriage is falling apart. Oh, and by the way, that kiss at the hospital meant nothing. I was relieved you weren't dead. That's it. I'm sorry if you thought I was falling madly in love with you again just because you fell off a roof that you weren't supposed to be standing on in the first place."

Ben was quiet for a moment. Then he let out a delicate snore. I slumped against the pillows. It was useless trying to talk to him. He was so hopped up on painkillers and antibiotics that he wasn't a functioning human being right now. I tried calling Theo again, but for the third time, it went straight to voicemail. Was she already sleeping?

Somehow, I fell asleep right there in Ben's bed, clutching the photo and Sammy's drawing to my chest. I had strange dreams of winding hallways and shadowy figures wearing pink polka dot scarves. When a chill crept over the bedroom, sinking into my limbs as if the heater had suddenly stopped working, I slowly woke. It was the middle of the night now. Ben slept soundly beside me, blissfully unaware of the chill. Goose bumps rose all over my skin, and the hair on the back of my neck prickled. Something was going on in the house. A child was crying.

I slipped out of bed and made sure the blanket covered all of Ben. He looked impossibly peaceful with his cherub curls splayed across the pillowcase. Half of his hair was trapped beneath the bandage, but it didn't take away from the angelic illusion. I wished I was still in love with him, but the Ben I loved wouldn't have ignored me for six weeks every time I told him something was wrong about the Abram Mansion. As time went by and we spent more and more of our lives apart from one another, it seemed to be the right thing to do. After we finished our sentence at the mansion, I was more determined than ever to be on my own.

But being on my own meant starting now, with the eerie cries floating into the corridor from somewhere above. Like the last time, it sounded like someone was in the house other than me and Ben. I followed the voice to the east wing on the second floor. The cries went on, growing louder as I snuck along. This time, I didn't go all the way to the master bedroom at the end of the corridor. The cries seemed to be coming from another room closer to the middle of the hallway. I pressed my ear to the door.

No mistake about it, a child wept on the other side. I knocked quietly. "Alyssa? Is that you?"

The cries went quiet.

"I'm not going to hurt you," I promised. "Sammy told me about you."

With a deep breath, I reached for the handle and pushed the door open.

The room was empty. There was no little red-haired girl or anything else that might imitate a child either. I had happened upon yet another anomaly in the Abram Mansion. Either that, or I was slowly going insane.

The room had once belonged to a young girl. Everything was

a shade of pink, from the wallpaper to the trim at the floor and ceiling. The four-poster twin bed supported a dusty pink canopy, a rosy duvet, and several stuffed animals ranging from teddy bears to unicorns. The closet door, which was already ajar, revealed a collection of pink outfits. Even the books on the shelves were pink, although on closer inspection, I saw that each one had been wrapped in a protective layer of pink paper. Everything was coated in dust. Clearly, the room hadn't been touched in a number of years. For good measure, I got on my hands and knees to look under the bed. My heart pounded as I lifted the bed skirt...

A rat scurried out from under the bed, its beady little eyes gleaming as it ran past me and out into the hallway. I hurriedly stood, lost my balance, and grabbed the closest piece of furniture to hold me upright. It was a dresser, the top of which was decorated with a few homemade art pieces. I leaned closer to a plaster imprint of two small hands. A name had been scrawled into the plaster with a paper clip or something else: Alyssa. I reached for the imprint, letting my fingers coast across the cool plaster.

An invisible force ripped the artwork from my hands and flung it across the room. The plaster shattered, and a huge chunk of it flew at my head. I shrieked and ducked, but the sharp edge of the broken piece still caught the outside of my hand, ripping a huge gash in the skin.

A scream that didn't belong to me echoed through the room, so loud and piercing that I slapped my hands over my ears. I ran for the door, but the nearby bookshelf tipped itself over, and I dove across the room to avoid being crushed by it. The hardbacks tumbled to the floor as the bookshelf landed with a mighty crash and the door to the room slammed itself shut. Porcelain unicorns lifted themselves from the windowsill and pelted themselves at me, as if someone were throwing them with all of their might. One hit my back at a horrible angle, right on a bone in my spine. I flattened myself out and scuttled under the bed, gasping and crying. The chaos continued. Glass shattered inches from my face. Books hammered at the four-poster bed in an attempt to bombard me. The bed itself rattled and shook like an earthquake, though its legs remained on the floor. I huddled in my safe spot—back throbbing, hand bleeding—and waited for the onslaught to end.

At long last, the door to the bedroom swung open, and a pair of small feet stood on the threshold. Everything that had declared war on me fell to the ground as suddenly as the objects had taken up arms. Books landed splayed on the dusty carpet. Stuffed animals lay slumped on their sides. Broken glass and porcelain littered the floor. The small feet at the door picked their way across the debris, stepping carefully to avoid anything too big. My heartbeat quickened as the small sneakers paused near me and a small hand lifted the bed skirt. It was Sammy.

"Hi Peyton," he said, cool and collected. "We should probably get out of here."

I wiggled out from underneath the bed. Glass crunched underfoot as Sammy took my hand and led me from the pink bedroom. He looked sadly around at the destroyed room before closing the door.

"She doesn't like it when you go into her room," he told me.

"Who?" I gasped. "Alyssa?"

He shook his head then noticed my hand. "You're bleeding."

"Forget about that," I said, kneeling so he and I were at the same eye level. "Sammy, what is going on in this house?"

He scuffed the toe of his sneaker against the carpet. "Did you look at my drawing?"

"Yes. Why would you draw your friend bleeding?"

Sammy placed his hands on my shoulder, squeezing as hard as he could, as if trying to emphasize how serious the information he was about to impart on me was. "Because that's what happened to her. Alyssa's dead, and she needs your help."

The bottom dropped out of my stomach as I stared at Sammy's trembling lips.

"Don't tell my mom," he whispered.

11

Don't tell my mom.

The voice whispered to me every night now. Sometimes, it was familiar, belonging to six-year-old Sammy Baker, who was alive and well. Other times, the voice belonged to a little girl whose name was the only thing I knew about her. Oh, I also knew that she was dead. Her voice—high-pitched, wavy, and distorted as if she had soap bubbles in her mouth— followed me through the corridors of my dreams, corridors that were remarkably reminiscent of the immense mansion I lived in at the present time.

The Abram Mansion seemed older than time itself, and I had recently discovered that it was home to more than me and my soon-to-be ex-husband. In Falconwood, the tiny town that lay below the woods beyond the mansion, the Abram family tragedy was all but forgotten. Only a few retold the tale of Percy Abram losing his sanity and committing suicide on the mountainside when his wife, Penelope, took their young daughter Alyssa to live with Penelope's lover. The events occurred over forty years ago, but the mansion was much older than the Abrams. This was evident in its Victorian architecture and—as our lovely contractor, Jim, would say—its "old bones." The house and its secrets lay abandoned since the tragedy, and though Jim and his construction crew were doing their best to restore it to its former grandeur, the mansion did not go easily. For one thing, it was so large that Jim had to section it out room by room. In the two months that we'd been here, the construction crew had only repaired the front wing of the house and half of the terrace that faced the mountain.

Two months. Our sentence was six. Had it been my choice, I would have ignored my grandfather's instructions about the Abram Mansion. It was all a bunch of legal mumbo jumbo anyway. His will stipulated that Ben and I had to live in the mansion for six months before we could sell it. It was the only loose end left to tie up before we could finalize our divorce. Though Ben saw our time at the mansion as an opportunity to mend our relationship and get back on track as a married couple, I wanted less and less to do with him. It wasn't that Ben had been a terrible husband or that either one of us had sinned against the other. Simply, I had outgrown Ben and our life together, but it was getting difficult to separate the reasons from our divorce from the strange feelings that emerged between us at the mansion.

A mere week ago, Ben had fallen off the slippery tiles of the terrace. With a shattered arm, broken ribs, a collapsed lung, and a minor concussion, it was a miracle he survived the fall. When I lay awake at night, staring at the patterns of moonlight on the ceiling, I wondered if Ben's fall was some sort of cosmic warning to me, like a wake-up call from the universe that forced me to question whether our divorce was the right decision or not. When he woke up from his surgery, I'd kissed him out of pure relief. Ever since then, he'd been in an oddly cheery mood, reverting back to the smiley, good-humored Ben that I fell in love with once upon a time. The only differences were that we weren't in high school anymore and Ben was mostly confined to his bed while he recovered.

My relationship with Ben, however, was one of the last things on my mind. Mostly, I obsessed over the Abram Mansion itself, trying to figure out the discrepancy between what I knew and what the residents of Falconwood knew to be true. As was the way of the world, asking someone was out of the question. Little Sammy Baker had sworn me to secrecy.

"Please don't tell my mom," he'd whispered. It was the night following Ben's accident, when the voice of a crying child had led me to Alyssa Abram's old room. I hadn't told anyone what I'd experienced there. Who would believe an invisible entity had attacked me—throwing books and toys and furniture around the room like a tornado— anyway? Sammy had been the one to rescue me. He'd taken his hand in mine and led me from the room with a revelation about Alyssa Abram that I wish I'd never heard.

"Alyssa's dead," he'd told me. "And she needs your help."

Blood dripped onto the carpet outside Alyssa's room. My hand had been injured in the onslaught. I wrapped my sleeve around it and took two things out of my pocket with my good hand. The first was a picture I'd taken in the attic of the mansion not too long ago. It featured a mess of storage and the fuzzy outline of a red-haired girl wearing a pink polka-dotted scarf. The second thing was a drawing that Sammy had given to me. In marker, he'd drawn the same red-haired girl lying in a puddle of blood.

"Is this her?" I'd asked Sammy, showing him the picture. "Is this Alyssa?"

His eyes flickered toward the blurry image. "Yes, that's her. She hides in the attic."

"Why does she hide there?"

"Because she's scared."

"Of what?"

Sammy squeezed his eyes shut, shaking his head as he rocked back and forth on the toes of his worn-out sneakers. He was covered in a thin layer of snowflakes, evidence that he'd walked to the mansion from his mother's apartment in town yet again without her permission. I brushed the snow from his shoulders and pressed the back of my hand to his cheek. Surprisingly, his skin was warm and soft, but I worried for his comfort even so.

"Come on," I said, pocketing the drawing and the picture to take Sammy's hand instead. "Let's get a snack in the kitchen. Maybe you can tell me more about Alyssa."

Minutes later, Sammy munched happily on crackers and apple slices, his appetite unaffected by the scary events that had just occurred upstairs. As he ate, I applied antibiotic serum to the cut on my hand and wrapped it in a thick bandage. Every time Sammy's teeth crunched through a new cracker, I almost reached for my phone. His mother, Theo Baker, was the closest thing I had to a best friend in Falconwood. If she woke to find Sammy missing, she would panic, and I didn't want to be the cause of alarm for my only friend. On the other hand, I wanted to know more about Alyssa Abram, and Sammy was the only person who could tell me.

"How do you know this is Alyssa?" I asked him, tapping on the blurry figure in the photograph. "It could be anybody."

"I told you before," Sammy said. "Alyssa and I are friends. I met her the first time I walked here."

"Why did you walk to the mansion in the first place?"

His little shoulders met his ears. "Something told me to."

I shuddered and decided to ignore the implications of Sammy's answer. He was no ordinary kid, and I hated to think what doctors or psychiatrists might do to him if they ever caught wind of his ghostly communications. "Sammy, I need you to be entirely truthful with me, okay? According to the rest of the town, Alyssa Abram isn't dead. She left Falconwood with her mother forty years ago."

Sammy shook his head, sending cracker crumbs flying. "That's what everybody thinks, but Alyssa never left the mansion. She's still here. She's still five years old. I'm not old enough to help her, and I didn't think anyone else would understand" —he lifted his eyes to mine— "but you get it, don't you, Peyton?"

A shiver radiated down my spine. I wasn't sure if I wanted to understand what Sammy was talking about, but at the same time, my curiosity waved a checkered flag. Ever since Ben and I arrived at the mansion, I'd sensed there was more to it than met the eye. On our first night, I'd sworn voices were whispering to me in the walls. Later, I heard a woman arguing with her husband behind a closed door, but when Ben checked the room with a baseball bat in hand, he found nothing but an abandoned master bedroom. I wondered if the stress of our impending divorce and the renovation of the mansion was making me hear things, but with Sammy's insistence that Alyssa was real, I started to think it wasn't just my imagination.

"Listen, Sammy." I sat next to him at the kitchen table and almost reached for his hands, but he was busy with his apples and crackers. I opted for pushing his hair away from his forehead instead. His bangs needed a trim, but Theo hadn't found the time to take him to the barber lately. "This thing with Alyssa scares me. Do you understand why?"

"Because you've never seen a ghost before?"

My heart dropped into my stomach. It was the first time either one of us said the word out loud. When it came out of Sammy's mouth, it felt like a confirmation of what might have remained imaginary if neither of us had ever mentioned it. "You think the girl in your pictures is Alyssa's ghost?"

"I know she is," Sammy replied matter-of-factly. As he

chewed on his last piece of apple, one of his front teeth wobbled, on the cusp of loosening enough to fall out. "You know it too, but you're scared. Your face is pale. It's okay. She won't hurt you. She's just sad."

"You have to understand that none of this makes sense," I implored. "People don't see dead people unless it's in the movies. There has to be an explanation for this, a reason all these things are happening. Maybe the mountainside affects the pressure around the mansion or something. Pressure systems can really mess with people's heads—"

Sammy quieted me by placing one damp palm flat on my forehead. His skin smelled like baby wipes and granny smith apples. "That's the problem with grown-ups," he said. "You always have to have a reason for something. Sometimes, things just happen. Maybe there's a reason, or maybe there isn't, but a lot of the times, the reason isn't for us to understand."

"How old are you again? Forty?"

"Six," he replied with confidence, removing his hand from my forehead to finish off the rest of his crackers. "I don't ever want to grow up."

I slumped in my chair. "Who does?"

"It's not because it's hard to be a grown-up," Sammy went on. "It's because a lot of grown-ups can't see what's right in front of them. I don't want to lose that. If I grow up, I might not be able to help Alyssa, but since you can see her too—"

"Wait a minute," I interrupted him. "I've never actually seen Alyssa. I've heard her—I think—but the only time I might have seen her was in the attic when I took that picture. Even then, I saw her through the camera, not in real life. I'm not sure our abilities are the same, Sammy, or if we have abilities at all."

"I've seen her." Sammy pushed his index finger into the direct center of his last cracker, forcing it to shatter into four pieces on the plate. "She appears to me all the time. I bet she's scared of you."

"Why would she be scared of me?"

"Because you're a grown-up living in her house," he replied. "You're knocking things down and ruining her room. She's getting lost in her own house."

"Are you talking about the renovations? How were we supposed to know there was a ghost in the mansion who would take offense to it?"

"I'm not blaming you," Sammy said, his tone indicating that maybe he did blame me a little. "But Alyssa doesn't get it. That's why she's scared of you. That's why she scares you too."

I pick up a piece of Sammy's cracker and drag the pointy edge of it across the table, watching the crumbs disintegrate one by one. Sammy hastily eats the other three pieces, as if he doesn't want me wasting the rest. "What do you want me to do, Sammy? You said I'm the only person who can help her."

"*I'm* helping her," he reminds me. "You're helping me."

"Deal. What are we supposed to be doing?"

Sammy dusted cracker crumbs from the front of his sweater. "She needs someone to know the truth, to find out what really happened to her. Otherwise, she's stuck here forever."

"Why don't you just ask her what happened?" I said, feeling like this was the rather obvious way to solve the mystery of Alyssa's ghost. "Can't she tell you how she died?"

"I tried that," Sammy said. "She likes me, but she won't tell me much about herself. Every time I ask her something, she chases me out of the house."

"What do you mean?"

"She throws things at me," he said. "Like she attacked you in her room a few minutes ago. That's how I know she's angry. I don't get it." He held up both his index fingers, using each one to indicate a separate part of the situation. It was a gesture I'd seen his mother use more than once. "On one hand, I know Alyssa wants me to figure out what happened to her so she doesn't have to be trapped here anymore. On the other hand, she gets mad when I ask her questions about it. It doesn't really make sense. That's where you come in."

"Oh, is it?"

"Yes." Sammy patted the collar of my pajama top. "You can do stuff I can't, like go to the library and stay in this house and figure out all the things that I can't because you're a grown-up. Alyssa needs you."

"What if I can't help Alyssa?"

Sammy donned a mournful expression. "I don't think you can leave Abram Mansion until you do."

"On that note, let's get you back home."

As I lifted Sammy from his chair and wrapped a blanket around his shoulders to account for his lack of a snow jacket, he grasped me by my shoulders. "Please don't tell my mom," he said again. "If she found out, she would never let me come back here. She would send me to doctors and think I was crazy—"

"Sammy, your secret is safe with me," I assured him. "After all, it's our secret now, isn't it? I can't tell anyone either."

It was my truest intention to honor my deal with Sammy. If I had a spare moment, I sat down in front of my laptop to search through whatever I could find on the Abram family history. There was a stunning lack of information on the Abrams, as if their family tree began with Percy and Penelope and ended with Alyssa. It was as if the Abrams had appeared out of thin air. Either that or someone had wiped the Internet of all traces of them. The other problem with my research was that I kept being interrupted.

"Peyton?"

Ben popped his head into my newly-renovated office. The front of his wheelchair ran into the trim around the door, chipping off some of the fresh paint. Though he hadn't lost the use of his legs, the doctor recommended he use the wheelchair to get around until his lung and ribs were fully healed. Watching him wheel himself around the house reminded me of the last time Ben had been this injured after a fateful football play in high school. Then and now, he popped the chair up and skillfully balanced on the two back wheels, but he'd never gotten the hang of rolling himself from room to room without running into something. These days, it resulted in more swear words that usual.

"Shit." Ben backed the chair up and tried again to angle himself into my office. "This thing's impossible to steer."

I closed my laptop so Ben couldn't see what I was researching. "What do you need?"

"A shower," he replied with an apologetic grimace. "I'm starting to feel kind of ripe."

Between his shattered hand and various other injuries, Ben had a hard time getting things done for himself, including unzipping his pants to go to the toilet. After the tenth time of doing it for him, I went into town and bought him seven pairs of stretchy sweatpants that he could pull up and down without help, one for each day of the week. It was only the beginning of finding alternate ways for him to take care of himself, and we'd been avoiding the bath issue ever since he got home from the hospital. He wiped the parts of himself that he could reach with a wet towel every night, but it only did so much. His curls were limp with the amount of grease that had accumulated in them, and a distinct odor lingered around his person. He was right. He needed a real bath.

"All right," I said, standing from my desk and gesturing for him to back up. "Wheelie it into the bathroom. Let's see if we can find an easy way to do this."

The first-floor bathroom had yet to be renovated, but since Ben couldn't make it down the steps to the redone toilet on the floor below, he had to make do with the mansion's original outdated decor and appliances. On the upside, the bathroom was huge, easily three times the size of the one in the house we left behind when we moved to the mansion. It hadn't been too difficult to clean up either. The previous residents had a cleaning staff to keep the place immaculate, so there was no soap residue or mold to deal with. I'd had Jim replace some of the older copper pipes before turning the water back on to this part of the house, just in case of faulty plumbing. The pipes were all exposed, leading right up to the claw-footed porcelain tub that reigned supreme in the middle of the room. It was big enough to fit two people, something Ben noticed right away.

"Want to join me?" he quipped, throwing in a saucy wink to make sure I knew it was a joke. He rolled the wheelchair up to the edge of the tub and performed his classic balancing act. "You know I make this chair look sexy."

"You stink," I reminded him, though I couldn't help the smile that lifted my cheeks. This is what I'd been struggling with ever since I asked Ben for the divorce. In essence, he remained the perfect man: handsome, funny, smart, and willing to be an active partner in our relationship rather than a passive one. I kept having to remind myself that no matter Ben's charm, our marriage had kept me from doing the one thing I was passionate about—photography—and my regret was eating away at our relationship.

Ben's shoulders drooped, though he tried not to let his disappointment show on his face. "Figured it wouldn't hurt to give it a shot. I do kind of need a hand though. Can you get this shirt off of me?"

He lifted his arms as high as he could without disturbing his broken ribs, wincing when his T-shirt accidentally got stuck around one of his elbows as I worked it off of him. Beneath the fabric, his usual tan had faded to an uneven pale color, and he sported red splotches around his collar and chest. I rested my hand over his heart, feeling it thump against my palm in overtime.

"I think you're running a fever," I told him, withdrawing before he could read anything else into my touch. "We'll have to keep an eye on that."

"Good thing they have me hopped up on antibiotics." He glanced down at his legs. "What about the bottom half? How do we make this not awkward?"

"Can you transfer to the edge of the tub?" I asked him, reaching over to turn the taps. Hot water gushed into the claw-footed bath, the steam rising to tickle my nose. "Once I get your pants off, you can swing your legs into the tub."

Between his broken arm and ribs, Ben couldn't do much to move himself. He tried rocking himself forward, but that made his ribs hurt, and he couldn't push himself up from the chair with only one hand. In the end, I lifted him to his feet and sat him on the edge of the bathtub myself. Red-faced, he wiggled his sweatpants and boxers from around his waist, and I pulled them off the rest of the way, doing my best to avert my eyes.

"Swing it around," I ordered. It was the first time one of us had been naked in front of the other since we decided on the divorce, save for a single night during which too much bourbon resulted in a quick mistake. I figured as long as I kept my manner and tone professional, we could make it through this without too much embarrassment.

Ben lifted his legs over the lip of the tub and rotated so that his back was toward me. Like before, I lifted him from his armpits, his back resting against my chest, and deposited him gently into the water. He hissed as the steam hit his skin.

"Too hot?" I said, turning the cold tap on. "How's that?"

"Getting better." He turned over a bottle of liquid soap near the running faucet. Bubbles quickly appeared, censoring his lower half from my sight. He kept his broken arm—the plaster cast running all the way from his shoulder to his elbow—perched on the edge of the tub. "Sorry you have to do this. I know it's not exactly ideal."

"Tip your head back." I filled a deep cup with warm water and poured it over Ben's curls, using my fingers to make sure all of his thick strands got soaked. He sighed and closed his eyes. "It's not ideal, but I don't mind doing it. We're still married for now."

He reached back to run the rough, warm palm of his good hand up and down my forearm. A lump rose in the back of my throat. Gently, I took his hand and placed it beneath the water again. He didn't say anything, but his shoulders tensed up. I shampooed and rinsed his hair in silence, but when I dunked a washcloth into the soapy water and began washing his back, he pulled away.

"I can do it," he said. "Give me a minute."

"No problem."

Outside the closed door of the bathroom, I leaned against the wall and listened for signs of trouble on the other side. If Ben slipped or hurt himself, I could be there in less than three seconds. I hoped his dignity was intact, though I suspected the silent exchange between us had embarrassed him. Ben was so used to getting what he wanted because his confidence had always been sky high, but things were beginning to change. In a way, I still loved Ben—enough to put myself in such an intimate situation as bathing him—but I was afraid of giving him the wrong idea. If his maneuver in the tub was any indication, he was still trying to win me over.

He called me back in after a few minutes. He'd already drained the water, rinsed himself off, and draped a towel over his bottom half. I helped him out of the tub and back into the wheelchair. In his bedroom, he managed to get his pants on by himself but needed my help with a shirt.

"This will get easier," I promised him as I threaded his bulky cast through the sleeve of a fresh T-shirt.

"What will?" he asked. "Bathing myself or being embarrassed in front of my own wife?"

"Both, hopefully," I said. The sun had sunk below the horizon, and Ben's room was beginning to darken. I longed to leave the house, to find dinner by myself at one of the local restaurants or meet up with Theo and Sammy at their apartment for a homecooked meal. It had been too long since I'd seen my friend or her son. Sammy was probably wondering whether or not I was holding up my end of our bargain. For the past week, my focus had been on Ben. Every day, I made sure he ate three meals and took his medicine at the right times. Sometimes, I felt like the concerned wife I ought to be. Other times, I felt like a babysitter who'd been stuck with a particularly whiny charge. Either way, I wanted out.

"Your doctor recommended a few physical therapy clinics to me over the phone," I told Ben. "He says you need to look into them as soon as your arm starts to heal. Otherwise, you might not get full range of motion back. One of the clinics is right here in Falconwood. Another one does at-home care, so you wouldn't have to drive. That's more expensive, but since your new job is paying you more, it could be a good option—"

"I'm not thinking about physical therapy yet," Ben said shortly. He yanked the shirt down to cover the rest of his torso then turned the wheelchair sharply away from me. "My arm hurts too much. I can't even move my fingers."

"That's kind of the point of physical therapy," I told him. "Did you ask your boss about injury leave? Or are you going to use a voice-to-text application to finish your job?"

Ben was a freelance technical writer. Right before we moved to Falconwood, he had landed a huge contract with a high-paying company. It was the only reason we could afford to push through with the Abram Mansion renovations.

"I haven't told him," Ben said, wheeling himself to a pile of clothes I'd run through the washer and dryer for him but never folded. He set half the load in his lap, wheeled to the dresser, and dumped the clothes into a random drawer. "I figured he didn't need to know."

"How did you figure that?" I asked, incredulous. "You haven't worked at all this week. What was your excuse?"

"I said we went on a marriage retreat." He averted his gaze from mine, supposedly focused on his laundry task. "He understood."

"Ben, you're going to have a hard time keeping up with your previous pace," I reminded him. "Why would you lie to your boss about that?"

He finished throwing the clothes into the drawer and proceeded to try and close it, but the overflowing pile inside prevented him from doing so. "If he figures out I'm injured, this job is toast. He'll hire someone else."

"And what happens when you don't meet your quota?" I challenged. "What are you going to tell him then?"

"Why do you care?" he shot back. "Why does it matter what I tell him? You like living in this big-ass house, Peyton? Do you like how quickly the renovations are happening? Because if I lose this job, all that goes away. Say bye-bye to Jim and his wonderful crew of construction workers who couldn't bother to fix the terrace railing before I freaking fell through it."

The bitterness in his voice struck me like he'd slapped me across the face. Ben hardly ever lost his temper, even in the bleakest of situations, but he'd finally reached his breaking point.

"Don't talk to me like that," I warned him. "I'm not your punching bag."

"Then get out of my room."

I stood my ground for a fraction of a second, wondering whether I should challenge him, but someone hammered on the front door with the volume and gusto of a determined high school drumline. With one last look at Ben, I swept from his room to answer the front door. On the other side, pounding away, was Theo. She threw herself into my arms.

"Peyton, I don't know what to do," she said, gasping for breath. "You'll never believe what happened."

My heart took off, and I feared it might burst through my chest and sweater. Had Sammy told his mother about our secret already? Theo was the best keeper of a cool head I knew. A panic like this didn't spring up out of nowhere.

"What's wrong?" I asked, dreading the answer. I led Theo inside so I could shut the door against the biting wind whistling through the trees. "Where's Sammy?"

"I left him at daycare." She didn't make it past the foyer before she started pacing, shedding layers of clothing with each pass. "I know what you're going to say. 'But you never leave him at daycare!' Why should I? You know how Sammy is, running away every chance he gets. But I wanted to talk to you without him here. I didn't want him to listen in."

My heart, which already felt like it was sitting in my stomach rather than my chest, threatened to drop lower and exit my body through an entirely different route. "Why? What's the matter? You're freaking me out, Theo."

"My landlord raised the rent on our apartment."

My heart sprang back to its proper place as my chest expanded with relief. "That's it?"

Theo clapped a hand to her forehead. "What do you mean, that's it? Peyton, she added an extra two hundred dollars every month. I can hardly afford to live above the bakery now."

I sat on the edge of the couch. Since my own panic was over, it was time to focus on Theo's. "Did you ask her why?"

"Rent goes up every year when you re-sign a lease," Theo said. "Rose usually cuts me some slack, but she said the building needs a new roof. If she doesn't get the money to replace it, it's going to fall in, and we won't have a place to live at all."

"There has to be some rule about this in your lease," I said. "Something that ensures she can't take advantage of you like that."

"That's the thing," Theo moaned. "I know she's not taking advantage of me. She's raising the rent to what I *should* be paying if she hadn't been giving me discounts all these years. I would be a total ass not to pay it."

"What about cutting corners?" I suggested. "You could eat at home more often or clip coupons. Some people do online surveys for money. You could try that?"

"I've tried that. It's bogus," she said. "What I need to do is work more hours at the office, but if I do that, I don't have anyone to pick Sammy up from school every day."

I scratched a dry spot on my scalp and grimaced at the dead skin that came away beneath my nail. "I know you hate the idea, but every school has an afterhours daycare program."

"Sammy hates school as it is," she replied. "I can't imagine telling him he has to stay there longer. Not to mention, I don't trust the teachers at that place. They're always punishing Sammy instead of his bullies. It's heinous. Ugh, what am I going to do?"

I rolled around the possibilities in my head. Theo was the queen of overprotective mothers. It was one of the reasons she didn't leave Sammy in daycare unless she absolutely had to. She also didn't have any family around to take care of Sammy in her absence. That left one option, an option that put everyone involved in an advantageous position.

"What if I watched Sammy after school?" I offered. "I could pick him up and take him around with me. Then I could drop him off whenever you get home. It wouldn't be any trouble for me."

Theo stopped short, her boots leaving a black skid mark on the new flooring. "You would do that for me?"

"Yeah, for you and Sammy."

"I can't ask you for that," she said. "You have Ben to take care of."

"You're not asking. I'm offering. Besides, Ben needs to learn how to take care of himself."

Theo chewed the tinted balm off of her bottom lip. "Are you sure? He can be a lot to handle, and I can't afford to pay you."

"You don't have to pay me," I said with a little laugh. "And I like Sammy. We get along. When do you need me to start?"

"Tomorrow would be great."

"Tomorrow it is."

12

*B*en woke at dawn when Jim and his construction crew arrived to continue working on the terrace. They were almost finished repairing the broken tiles and faulty railings, though I wasn't sure why they had chosen to renovate the terrace at this point anyway. I was more concerned with the interior of the house, but if I asked Ben about the renovation plans, all I got as a reply were a few vague grunts. I also asked Ben to tell Jim to come an hour later in the day, so I didn't wake up with the birds to the deafening buzz of saws and pounding of hammers, but it was to no avail. Each morning, like clockwork, Jim showed up with the sun. I admired and loathed his work ethic.

This morning, Ben hadn't called me to help him with whatever task he needed assistance with—like dressing himself—so I found him in the foyer, talking to Jim in the same shirt and pants I'd helped him into last night. His hair had dried funny, and his curls all stuck up at the back of his head. His eyes were pink and puffy, as if he hadn't gotten much sleep last night. All in all, Ben looked worse than he had all week despite the bath.

"I need it done quick," he was saying to Jim, whose bulky

form and enormous beard were not indicative of his teddy bear personality. "I'm talking like one day. Would you be able to do that?"

Jim chewed on his bottom lip. "It's a lot of work for one day. That's a big bathroom. I'd probably need a few extra guys to get it done, and we'd have to expedite the shipping for the products we need. I hate to say it, but it's gonna cost you."

"I don't care what it costs," Ben said. "I need a bathroom on this floor that's accessible for me. All I want to know is if you can get it done in a day."

"I'll draw up an estimate for you," Jim offered. "Once I figure out how much extra I gotta pay my guys for working overtime, I'll let you know how much it'll cost. You might change your mind when you see the total."

As I leaned against the wall of the hallway that led to the foyer, Ben's eyes flickered toward me. He saw me there, but he made no acknowledgement of my presence. "I need this done as soon as possible," he said. "I don't see any other options."

"We could install the assistance tools in the old bathroom," Jim said. "It would be a lot cheaper for you, and we could get it done in a few hours."

"I told you. I don't want to put new equipment in that old bathroom."

Jim caught sight of me, and we exchanged a quick eyebrow lift that said everything it needed to say about Ben's pushy behavior. "I'll let you talk it over with your wife," Jim said, tipping his hat as he ambled toward the exit, eager to return to his real work. "I don't know about you guys, but I'm not allowed to do anything before I run it past my wife first."

"We're almost divorced," Ben said. "I don't need her permission."

"This house is a joint task," I reminded him. My morning voice was hoarse and rough, making my reply sound more severe than intended. "If you want to change something, I have to agree. What are you trying to do to the bathroom anyway?"

"Good luck," Jim muttered as he walked past me and jogged out into the snow to rejoin the rest of his team.

"I'm going to make the first-floor bathroom handicap accessible," Ben said, sifting through a pile of hand-drawn blueprints on his lap. They were messy and flawed—not Jim's work. Ben flipped them over before I could look at them. "I need to be able to bathe myself."

"Ben, you're not handicapped." I crossed my arms. "The doctor said your arm was likely to be fully healed in six months. As long as you start the physical therapy when they tell you to—"

Ben groaned and rolled his chair across the foyer, toward the stairs that led to the kitchen. "Enough about physical therapy! You're like an annoying parrot. 'The doctor said this, the doctor said that.' The doctor also said I couldn't start physical therapy until three or four weeks of healing. Did you hear that part?"

"Yes, but he said you should start reaching out to the therapists you're interested in beforehand so they're not booked when you need them," I replied, hurrying after him as he increased his speed toward the stairs. "Are you going to catapult yourself into the kitchen?"

"If I have to," he said. "I need breakfast."

He ended up stopping short of the stairs, the front wheels of his chair hovering on the first step. He gripped the railing with his good hand, as if gathering the courage to propel himself out of the wheelchair and down to the kitchen. I tickled the back of his neck, where his curls were thickest. Immediately, his whole body relaxed. He let go of the railing and settled in the chair again. The neck thing was an old trick of mine. Whenever Ben was feeling particularly stressed, I would squeeze or tickle him there. Every time, without fail, it would lessen the weight on his shoulders.

"I'll toast you a bagel," I offered. "But you have to put the cream cheese on yourself. Go wait in the living room. You can eat off the coffee table."

With a sigh, Ben rolled himself away from the stairs without another word. I went into the kitchen, listening to Jim and his crew bang away outside. As I opened a drawer to find a butter knife, something rattled beneath it. I ducked low for a look at the underside, but nothing seemed out of place. I slid the drawer in then out again. The same annoying rattle sounded, but no matter what I did, I couldn't find the source of it. With a roll of my eyes, I slammed the drawer shut again.

"Where's yours?" Ben asked when I brought a single onion bagel to the coffee table in the foyer with a side of cream cheese and set it in front of him alongside a glass of orange juice. "Aren't you eating?"

"I'm going into town," I told him. "I think it's best if I get back to my routine."

Ben flattened the bagel beneath his cast to frost it with cream cheese. "So Black Cat Café for breakfast and wandering aimlessly around Falconwood until dinnertime?"

"Actually," I said, offering no help as he maimed the bagel, "Theo asked me to watch Sammy after school."

"Does she have to work longer today?"

"She has to work longer every day," I said. "Her landlord raised her rent, so I'm helping out with Sammy."

Ben halted his crushing bagel work to look up at me. "You agreed to take the kid every day? Are you his nanny now? Is she paying you?"

I gathered my coat from the hook at the front door in an attempt to indicate that this conversation was over. "I'm trying to help my friend out. That's all."

"So she's *not* paying you?"

"That would sort of defeat the purpose of this whole arrangement," I told him, getting worked up. "She needs more money, not for someone else to try sucking it out of her."

"Did you ever think that you might need a job?"

"On the contrary, my husband always assured me he would take care of me."

Ben had yet to take a bite out of his bagel, too busy with glaring at me instead. "In four more months, you won't have a husband to take care of you, per your request. You might want to start making better business decisions before giving away your services for free."

"My services?" I laughed as I put on my hat and kicked open the front door. "You know what, Ben? You're totally right. I should get a job, and I already know my true calling. I'm going to become a sex worker."

I slammed the door in his stunned face.

"I HAVE a lot of respect for sex workers."

The Black Cat Café bustled with its early morning customers. Bacon sizzled, pancakes flipped, and eggs scrambled behind the counter as the industrial-sized espresso maker churned out cup after cup of fresh coffee. I'd managed to snag my favorite table, the one in the front corner of the café that looked out onto Falconwood's main drag. Today was a gross day. The snow had been stomped into muddy ice, and the gray clouds overhead threatened cold rain. On the upside, Della Gordon—my other friend in town—was already here when I arrived. Della wasn't the person I always pictured of befriending. She was an older woman in her sixties who lived with her husband, Basil, in an airstream on the outskirts of town. They were the type of people who knew enough about nature and living off the land to survive the apocalypse should it ever happen. Della was hardy and strong for her age. Both she and Basil were avid hikers. It showed in their matching wiry muscles. Though I had yet to visit their home, I was curious to do so soon. They cultured their own kombucha, had a hydroponic greenhouse, and grew their own herbs. Their lifestyle was strange and enviable, and I admired the Gordons' peculiarities because of how different they were from me and Ben.

In addition to her hippie-ish lifestyle, Della also happened to be a professional nature photographer who had worked in the industry for a number of years. Her pictures had been featured in magazines I drooled over. I'd probably seen her work a few times and never realized it. As someone who'd always wanted to make photography my career as well as my passion, I raved over Della's success. She was retired now, but she sometimes sent pictures out for publication. Today, she'd asked to borrow my laptop so she could check her email—she and Basil weren't connected to the Internet—and when she opened her inbox, she had a staggering two thousand unopened messages to read. This, for whatever reason, did not concern her.

"They're very brave," she went on. After listening to me recounting my less-than-regal comeback to Ben, Della had replied with all the dignity I lacked. "If you think about it, they're putting a tremendous amount at risk, and they're only doing what they have to do. It's admirable."

"I wasn't trying to discount sex workers," I said, lowering my voice to avoid stares from the other café patrons. I groaned into my coffee, which had gone cold in the last few minutes. "I guess I wanted to say something that would shut him up for once."

"Trying to get along isn't going well, I assume?" Della squinted over the top of her reading glasses at the laptop screen and deleted a few more emails. "Did he say anything about the kiss?"

My stomach lurched at the mention of it. The kiss of relief I'd bestowed upon Ben when he'd woken from anesthesia after his accident was nothing more than that. Della wanted me to break it to Ben easy, but with all the feelings rumbling around in my stomach like acid, I wasn't prepared to address it.

"He didn't say anything," I told her. "But he tried to make a move on me last night when I was helping him bathe. It didn't go so well."

"I know it's difficult, but try to be gentle with him," Della advised. "He's lost everything he's ever worked for, including you and his independence. That must be putting a lot of stress on him."

"He didn't lose me," I said. "We could be friends if he wasn't so curmudgeonly. Half the time, he's trying to woo me, and the other half, he wants to bite my head off."

Della closed the laptop and pushed it across the table. "Forget it. I can't take any more of these spam emails."

"How far did you get?"

"Not very."

I opened the laptop to check Della's progress. "Della, you still have 1883 emails left to read! And it looks like this one is about a potential job."

"Pah!" She waved her hand as if she were wafting away an unpleasant smell. "This is why we don't bother with technology. Everyone always wants a piece of me."

"That's because they know you're a talented artist." I clicked on the next email and skimmed through it. "Are you sure you don't want to read this? It's from National Geographic."

"They're always begging me for more content," Della said. "I keep telling them to find fresh talent. There are so many young photographers like yourself out there, waiting for a chance to prove themselves, and big magazines won't bother to print them."

"Fine. I'm deleting it. How about this discount coupon for essential oils?"

"Delete it," Della said. "Goodness, go through them and delete them all."

I kept my index finger on the delete button as I combed through the rest of Della's email until I happened upon one that caught my eye. "This one is from Falconwood's historic preservation society, concerning your request about the Abram Mansion. They said it was declined."

Della leaned across the table for a better look. "How old is that? I emailed them months ago, before you and Ben moved in."

"It's from July. What were you asking about?"

"Oh, I thought about picking up my photography project at the mansion again quite a few times." Della flagged down a busboy and pointed to our empty coffee cups to ask for a refill. "But Basil insisted it wasn't safe for me to go traipsing around the property. I propositioned the preservation society to make the mansion a museum. At the time, I thought it was public property, but it turned out your grandfather owned it. I guess that's why they denied my request."

"I forgot you loved the mansion so much," I said. "What did you call it again? A mini obsession?"

"Micro-obsession," Della corrected. "Yes, it was my greatest love for a year or so."

I pushed the laptop aside and folded my hands on top of the table. "Didn't you also research the house as well as take pictures?"

"Yes, I dug up everything I could."

"Would you be willing to share that information with me?" I asked her. "I've been trying to get a better understanding of why my grandfather might have left the mansion to me and Ben, but I'm having a hard time unearthing anything useful. I would love to take a look at your research."

"And I would love to give it to you." Della bowed her head apologetically. "But I'm afraid I got rid of all my photos and information on the Abram Mansion."

Disappointed, I slumped down in the booth. "Why would you do that?"

"It was Basil's request," Della said, sighing wistfully. "After I injured myself exploring the mansion, he asked me to take a step back from it. It was terrible at first, giving up the thing I'd obsessed over for so long. Then after a while, I grew used to being away from it. I tossed everything I had on the mansion, knowing it was for the best."

"I'm not so sure," I said. "The mansion is a big part of Falconwood's history, and you gathered more information than most. Meanwhile, I can't find a lick of knowledge about the Abrams. If you'd written a book—"

"It was never my intention to compile my findings," Della said. "But I am sorry that the information is no longer available to you."

"Any chance you'd want to take up your old hobby again?" I asked. "Help me find out what I need to know about the Abrams and their house?"

Della swirled her fresh coffee around, her eyes glazing over as she watched the liquid threaten to splash over the edge of the cup. "I don't think that would be a good idea. I would hate to get sucked back in, and I know Basil would certainly disapprove."

Disappointed but not surprised, I placed my hand over Della's to stop her anxious cup twirling. "It's okay. I'll have another look at the library." I caught sight of the time on Della's watch. "It's already two o'clock? I have to pick Sammy up in half an hour. I can't believe we spent all morning and half of the afternoon chatting."

"You've been holed up in the house all week," Della reminded me as she poured my coffee into a to-go cup and handed me my coat. "We had a lot to catch up on."

"Thank you," I said, jamming my hat onto my head. "I missed you this week. We should go for another hike soon. I enjoyed practicing my photography with you."

"As did I," Della replied. "Although I hope our next session doesn't end in such tragedy."

"We'll keep Ben safe at home," I agreed.

"For the record, I think it's great what you're doing for Theo," she added. "Ben might disapprove, but you're doing a noble deed by helping out your friend. You're a good person, Peyton Fletcher."

I planted a kiss on the top of Della's head. "Thanks, Della. I'll see you later."

THANKFULLY, Sammy's elementary school was right up the road, so I actually arrived early to pick him up. Parents honked at each other in the car pickup line, only masking their angry faces when their child arrived at the side door of their minivan. A grand total of six school buses puffed exhaust into the freezing air, two for each level of education. Falconwood was a tiny town, and its graduating senior class totaled to about fifty-five. Since I wasn't Sammy's actual parent, I had to stop by the front office to drop off an official document, signed by Theo, that allowed me to take Sammy home.

"Hi," I said to the front desk lady, a girl in her early twenties with a pin on her sweater that read in a jaunty font: *Ask me about drugs!* "I'm here to pick up Sammy Baker. His mom said I had to drop this paper off to you."

I handed over the document, and the bespectacled girl squinted at Theo's messy signature under her desk light. "Yup, that's Theodora Baker's handwriting. I'd recognize her illegible scribble anywhere. You're good to go. Sammy usually waits underneath the overhang in the pickup loop."

"Thanks." I leaned over the desk and added in a whisper, "Where can I get some drugs?"

As I left the office, the woman smacked her palm across the pin and hurriedly removed it from her sweater. It appeared Falconwood Elementary School needed to update their D.A.R.E program. I found Sammy exactly where the receptionist said he would be. He was by himself near the pickup loop, sitting on his backpack as he watched a group of kids play in the grass nearby.

"Hey, kid. Want some candy?"

"Peyton!"

He sprang up from his seat on the ground and wrapped his arms around my legs to give me a hug. I ruffled his hair and zipped up his coat.

"Did your mom tell me you'd be hanging out with me after school for a little while?" I asked him, picking up his Power Rangers backpack and swinging it over my own shoulder. "I hope that's cool with you."

"Yeah, she told me she has to work." He took my hand and bounded down the sidewalk. "It's totally cool with me! I like you. You're fun."

"Glad to hear someone thinks so." As we passed the other kids, Sammy switched to my other side so he didn't have to walk so close to them. "Hey, Sammy. Why don't you ever play with the people in your grade?"

Sammy's step lost its bounce. "I don't like them. They make fun of me."

"What do they say to you?"

"They tell me my drawings are weird," Sammy replied sullenly. "And that Alyssa's not real."

I tightened my grasp on Sammy's hand. "Did you tell them about Alyssa?"

"Not everything. Not that she's dead."

Once we cleared the schoolyard and the irritable honking parents, I knelt in front of Sammy to pull his hood over his head and straighten his jacket. "You're a brave boy, Sammy. A lot of other kids wouldn't be friends with Alyssa or want to help her. Here's the thing, though. You know how you don't want me to tell your mom about Alyssa?"

"Yeah."

"It's for the same reason you shouldn't tell those other kids," I said. "The things you've seen at the Abram Mansion are scary for other people. They won't understand you if you try to tell them, and they definitely won't believe you. It's better to keep it a secret."

"I know, but they look at my drawings."

"Can you make me a deal?" I asked him. "If you stop drawing Alyssa at school—just at school, you can still draw her at home—then I'll buy you one sticker pack of your choice every day I pick you up."

Sammy's eyes lit up. "Any sticker pack? Even the holographic ones?"

"Even the holographic ones," I promised. I offered him my pinky finger. "Do we have an accord?"

He linked his finger with mine. "I don't know what that means, but yeah!"

"Awesome. Come on, let's get you hooked up."

AFTER GETTING Sammy a pack of holographic planet stickers, I took him to the park and tired him out on the swings. Though it was freezing outside, I feared Sammy spent too much time indoors, either obsessing over his drawings or under Theo's watchful eye. Every time he jumped off the swings, his spindly legs buckled beneath him. He definitely needed more exercise.

"We should do this more often!" he hollered as he ran past me, sprinted up the plastic slide, lost his balance, and careened all the way down into the muddy mulch with a gleeful laugh. "I love the park!"

"We can come every day if you want," I offered. "But I should have gotten you a snack first. You're probably starving."

"I had school pizza for lunch." He tried his luck on the slide again. "It tasted like feet."

As he slid down once again, I suppressed a laugh. "You should start making lunch for yourself at home. You know how to make a peanut butter and jelly sandwich, right?"

"I hate jelly!"

"Oh, really?" I challenged. "Have you tried *all* the jellies?"

"I don't like any of them because they look like blood." Sammy kept up his maniacal pace around the playground, completely unaware of how creepy his reply sounded. He climbed up to the monkey bars and swung from the first rung. "When are we going to go to your house?"

"The Abram Mansion?"

"Yeah." He kicked his feet to propel himself to the next rung. "That's why you agreed to pick me up after school, right? So we can help Alyssa?"

"I agreed because I wanted to help your mom out," I told him. It was the truth, but not all of it. I also wanted to keep a closer eye on Sammy. "I don't think it's a good idea for me to bring you to the house."

"Why not?"

"According to what you've told me about Alyssa, she might get upset if you start asking her questions again," I reminded him. "If Alyssa starts causing trouble like she did the other night, she might accidentally hurt someone."

"Like she hurt Ben?"

My stomach flipped over. "What are you talking about?"

"The railing on the terrace was fine," Sammy said, sounding more like a contractor than Jim ever had. "I think Alyssa made Ben fall."

A terrifying flashback of the day of Ben's injury crossed my mind. Della and I had been hiking through the mountains, looking down at the mansion with a pair of binoculars from the cliffside. Right before Ben fell over the railings, I'd spotted a spooky ghostly face in the attic window, one that Della claimed she couldn't see.

"Why would she have done that?" I asked Sammy.

He tried to shrug, but his grip on the monkey bars was slipping. "Like I said, she's scared of you guys. You're changing things. You have to ask her what's wrong, but I don't know if she'll talk to you. That's why you should take me to the mansion, so I can ask her."

"I can't risk anything happening to you or anyone else," I told him. "Do you know what else Alyssa can do?"

"She moves things with her mind," Sammy said, concentrating on making it to the next rung. He was only three bars in so far. "She makes scary sounds sometimes. But I think doing those things makes her tired."

He grunted as he jumped for the next bar, slipped, and landed stomach down in the mulch below. I raced to his side and rolled him over.

"Are you okay?"

"Don't tell her I said that," Sammy groaned, holding his stomach. "Don't tell her I told you she gets tired easily. She'll be mad at me. Also, I'm really glad you didn't get me a snack."

"Do you have to throw up?"

"Nope. Nothing in my tummy."

Relieved, I put Sammy on his feet again and took his hand. "Come on. Let's get going. Your mom's going to be home soon, and I'm sure she's eager to see you."

. . .

THEO WAS ALREADY HOME when we arrived at the apartment, and she was so happy to see Sammy that I didn't want to stick around and ruin their reunion. She threw her arms around his tiny body and hugged him so tightly that his head looked like it might pop clean off.

"Oh, my precious boy," she cooed. "I missed you all day! Did you have fun with Peyton? What did you guys talk about?"

Sammy looked up at me over Theo's shoulder. I placed a finger to my lips.

"Stickers," he said, showing Theo the one he'd adhered to the back of his hand. "Peyton got me all the planets. This one's Pluto. My teacher says Pluto isn't a planet anymore, but it was in the pack of stickers! That means it must be a planet, right?"

I gave Sammy a thumbs-up as Theo planted a kiss on Pluto. "It must be," she said. "But there is a lot of misinformation out there, so you have to make sure you fact check. Do you know what fact-checking is?"

"When you check facts."

"Yes, sir." Theo tapped Sammy's nose before she dumped her armload of plastic bags on the kitchen counter. The sharp scent of soy sauce and kung pao chicken tickled my nose. "I can't thank you enough, Peyton. I got enough Chinese food to feed a small army. The least I can do is treat you to dinner. Are you interested?"

"I should probably get back to Ben," I said, though it was the last thing I wanted to do.

"Stay!" Sammy commanded, yanking on my arm.

"The prince has spoken," Theo said. "Sounds like you have no choice."

"I'm the prince! I'm the prince!" Sammy chanted.

I rolled my eyes and plopped in one of the seats at the

kitchen counter. "Okay, okay! I'll stay for dinner and *one* fortune cookie, but then I have to go home."

Satisfied, Sammy climbed into the seat next to mine and handed me a box of rice. "Open this, peasant."

"Say please," Theo chided.

"Please, peasant."

WHEN I FINALLY ARRIVED HOME, the sun was well on its way to bed. Jim and his crew were long gone, but they had replaced the lights on the terrace before they'd left, illuminating their hard work for all to see. With brand new red tile flooring and a sturdy wrought-iron railing, the terrace had regained some of its former glory. I could see the next family who lived here holding evening parties up there in the springtime, as long as the resident ghost didn't push anyone else off.

There were no lights on inside the house. I hung my coat and hat on the rack in the foyer and squinted into the darkness. "Ben! Are you home?"

It was a bit of a stupid question. Ben wasn't exactly in the position to drive, and I'd taken our car into town anyway. Technically, Ben could have caught a ride with someone else, but he hadn't made many friends during our two months in Falconwood. Jim was probably the only person he conversed with on a regular basis other than myself.

"Hello?" I called, elongating the last vowel sound. I flipped on lights as I made my way through the house. If I had to admit it, I was nervous about potentially being left all alone in the Abram Mansion with only Alyssa for company. "Ben, if you're here, this isn't funny!" I turned on the light in the stairway that led to the kitchen. "Oh my God!"

Ben sat at the bottom of the stairs, his back to me. The chair was tipped on its side on the kitchen floor. I rushed down.

"What are you doing?" I asked. "Did you fall? Why didn't you answer when I called? Are you hurt? Ben!"

He stared glumly up at me. "I was hungry."

"So you tried to make it down the stairs yourself?" Fuming, I set his chair on all four wheels. "You could have asked Jim or one of the other guys to help you."

"My wife was supposed to be here to help me."

"So I guess you didn't see the two sandwiches I set upstairs for you," I countered. "I can't stay home all day, Ben. You have to figure out how to do things for yourself—did you pee yourself?"

"Couldn't make it to the bathroom."

I seized him under the armpits and hauled him into the bathroom down the hall. He went like a limp ragdoll, not bothering to help push himself along. The shower in this bathroom was level with the floor, so I put Ben fully clothed right above the drain and turned the faucet on. It sprayed right in his face, soaking his hair and clothes in seconds.

"What the hell, Peyton?" He coughed and spluttered, finally giving me an emotion other than pity. "Are you trying to drown me?"

"You are not paralyzed," I reminded him. "You've had an entire week to get over this self-pity crap, but I'm done with it now. Stop acting like you'll never walk again. There's nothing wrong with your legs. You could have gotten out of your chair and walked to the bathroom in plenty of time. If you do this again—I don't care what my grandfather's will says about this stupid house—I will leave you before our six months here is up, and you can hire a nurse's aide to carry your ass to the bathroom. Do you understand me?"

In the past year, ever since I'd asked Ben for a divorce, he'd never looked scared. His expressions had read all over the place, from sad to disappointed to angry, but I'd never seen him look at me with fear on his face. Now, as he stared up at me through the unyielding rain of the showerhead, all I saw was fear. Above everything else—the frustration of his recovery, rebuilding the mansion, our eventual separation—he was scared to lose me. And as much as I didn't want to admit it, I was scared to lose him too.

"Do you understand?" I asked him again, this time in a softer tone.

"Yes, Peyton. I understand."

13

———

hough the forecast hadn't predicted it, that night hit us with the loudest of thunderstorms. Wind tore through the trees, lightning struck inches from the mansion, thunder rattled the window panes, and hail pieces the size of golf balls rained across the courtyard. They ricocheted off our car parked out front, no doubt decorating the roof with a number of dents. I lay in bed, unable to sleep with all the racket, and stared through my window at the courtyard to watch the chaos unfold. A hailstone hit one of the marble statues covered in dead vines and exploded. As another bolt of lightning struck close enough to shake my bones, I had the strangest inkling that the storm had specifically targeted the Abram Mansion. It was fodder, of course. When I checked the weather pattern on my phone, it showed all of Falconwood and its surrounding areas under attack. There was nothing to do but wait it out.

Just as I was getting used to the cacophony and had allowed it to soothe me to sleep, the overhead light turned on, flooding the room with its yellow glow. I covered my eyes with the blankets, letting them gradually adjust before I peeked out again. Near the door, the actual light switch hadn't moved. It was placed in the down position, as if the light had come on of its own accord.

"Peyton?" Ben pounded on my door then let himself in without waiting for me to reply. He wore a fresh pair of pajamas, the silk set I'd bought for him a few years ago, rather than his usual sweatpants. For once, he didn't ram his wheelchair into the molding as he came in. He rubbed his eyes, his frustration clear in the redness around them. "Do you believe this crap? I've got half a mind to call Jim right now to make him fix it."

"What are you talking about?" I muttered, my voice rough with sleep. "Because my light came on? It's probably just a fluke."

"It's not just your light," Ben said. "It's *every* light. Every damn light in the house has turned on."

"That's impossible. Jim only wired the front wing for new electricity so far."

"Or so he told us," Ben said. "Look out your window."

I kicked off the blankets and rolled over to face the window again. This time, beyond the storm's havoc, I could see that the entire mansion was lit up. Since the building formed a square around the courtyard, the light poured into the inner area. The overgrown topiaries and marble statues cast menacing shadows across the garden. The swimming pool had collected dirty rain-water, hailstones, and dead leaves in the deep end. The muck swirled around like a whirlpool that led to the world beyond this one. I gazed across the three other wings of the mansion. We had yet to explore the west and south wings, but I had made an unfortunate habit of sneaking off to the east wing. It was where I heard the voices of the dead the most, as if the Abram family had made most use of that section of the house. I scanned the windows of the east wing, searching the golden glow in each for an explanation of the sudden illumination. Toward the end, about three-fourths of the way to the south wing, I found what I was looking for. A small figure peered out of the window. She was no more than a silhouette, but her chin was tipped skyward, as if she too monitored the severity of the storm. When another clap of thunder hit, the silhouette jumped and dove away from the window. For some reason, it made a small smile cross my face.

"Why are you grinning?" Ben said, craning his neck to see what I was looking at. "Do you know something I don't?"

"Like I said, it's probably a fluke." I swung my legs out of bed, crossed the room, and tried the light switch. No matter how many times I flicked it up and down, the overhead light shone brightly. "Looks like we can't do much about it but hope for it to resolve itself. We'll call Jim in the morning."

"In the morning?" Ben said. "It's two o'clock. How on earth are we supposed to sleep like this? You know I'm sensitive to light at night."

"I remember." I stepped into my slippers and pulled a warm robe over my pajamas. "I used to have to cover the clock on the DVD player. Are you still hungry?"

"What?"

"Last we spoke, you hadn't had dinner," I reminded him. "I figure if we can't sleep, we might as well make use of our time. Let's see if we can figure out some cheat codes around the house for you. Teamwork, right? I hear that's what marriage is all about."

Without allowing him to answer, I left the room. As I expected, he followed me out, the wheels of his chair squeaking against the new wood flooring. When I pulled open the front door and a blast of cold air and hailstones buffered the foyer, Ben shouted and covered his head.

"What are you doing?" he hollered over the noise of the storm. "It's freezing out there, and if one of the hailstones lands on your head, I'm going to have to break out the first aid kit."

Grunting, I hauled in a big box that had been sitting on the porch since I got home yesterday. As soon as it was clear of the entryway, I shoved the door shut again, pushing hard to fight against the wind. I turned to Ben and patted the soggy top of the cardboard box as if it were a stray dog we'd let into the house to avoid the terrible weather.

"I ordered this a few days ago." Using my legs, I shoved the heavy box across the foyer and placed it against the wall by the stairs to the kitchen. "It was delivered yesterday, but I forgot about it. It was my first day with Sammy, and I had a lot on my mind. Anyway, I thought it would help you out."

Ben curiously eyed the box. "What is it?"

"It's a mini fridge," I said. "Like the kind you put in a college dorm room. I figured if it's too difficult for you to go down to the kitchen, then I'll bring the kitchen to you."

"That was nice of you." Ben picked up a box cutter—we had yet to unpack all of our things—and sliced through each side of the cardboard. The box opened flat to reveal the mini fridge. Ben whistled. "Sheesh, this thing belongs in a five-star hotel."

"The guy at the store was running a special," I said, handing him the manual. "You know how people in Falconwood are. If you make them fresh biscuits, they'll give you twenty-five percent of anything."

"Did you make them fresh biscuits?"

"No, Della did," I said. "But I reaped the reward."

For the first time in a while, Ben cracked a smile. "I'm glad you have friends in town."

"They could be your friends too," I told him, "but you're always holed up in this house. I know this injury has brought you down. I didn't mean to be so direct last night—"

Ben held up his hand to stop me. "No. Don't apologize. I needed you to say those things to me. You were right. I've been acting like a baby for the past week. I shouldn't have expected you to wait on me hand and foot."

"Well, that was the idea for the mini fridge." I wormed the cardboard out from under the fridge, unwound the power cord, and plugged the unit in to the closest outlet. The fridge powered on, humming happily as it began its work. "I thought if we kept a few of your favorite food items on this floor, where you can easily access them, you don't always have to be waiting around for me or anyone else to help you eat. However, I do think you should try to walk more. I know your ribs hurt, but you don't want to start relying on that chair more than you have to."

"I get it," Ben said. "I don't want to overdo it either though."

"You'll know if you overdo it."

He squinted toward the chandelier overhead then flipped the switch that controlled it. The light flickered once but remained on. Ben tried the dimmer next. No luck. "So weird," he said. "Do you think the electrical company did something?"

"No idea."

In the time since Sammy's revelation, I'd unconsciously made the decision not to tell Ben about Alyssa Abram. My reasons were similar to the ones I'd given Sammy to keep the secret from his classmates. For one, I didn't want to scare Ben, and two, I didn't want Ben to think I'd taken a dive off the deep end and landed in a pool of crazy. I also had the strange feeling of wanting to keep Alyssa to myself. I wanted to win her over. I wanted her to trust me, and I felt like telling Ben about her would betray her trust. After all, she'd only revealed herself to me in small ways, but she had never shown herself to Ben once.

"I'll check the electrical box in the basement in a few minutes," I offered as I wheeled Ben to the top of the kitchen stairs. "Up you get. Until that fridge gets cold, we have to work down there."

Ben lifted himself from the chair, and I slipped under his good arm to help him down the stairs. This time around, he made a significant effort to bear his own weight. Though he winced each time his ribs moved the wrong way, he didn't complain. Once in the kitchen, he lowered himself to sit at the table all on his own, beaming proudly. I left his wheelchair where it was.

"Alrighty," I said, rifling around in the refrigerator. "What sounds good? We've got roast beef and cheese. You could make a sandwich for yourself. That would be easy. Or we have some leftover Bolognese sauce from a few days ago. No pasta though. You'd have to boil some."

"Challenge accepted," Ben said, saluting me. Still seated in the kitchen chair, he used the table and his own momentum to slide across the floor and reach the cabinet where we stored the pots and pans. He took out a deep pan then slid himself to the sink to fill it. He continued in this manner, working his way around the kitchen for the things he needed, until it came time to reach the pasta, which was on the very top shelf of the pantry.

"I'll get it," I offered.

"No, no," he said. "Let me do it."

With the handle of a broomstick, he knocked the box of pasta off the shelf and caught it in his lap. Grinning, he tossed aside the broom and went back to the boiling water to get started.

"Looks like you're all set," I said, patting him proudly on the back. "Do you think you can hold down the fort while I check the basement?"

"Yes, ma'am."

The entrance to the basement was at the end of the hall. A set of rickety wooden stairs led into the damp, concrete-lined dungeon below. Thankfully, Alyssa had relieved me of the struggle to find the light switch. For good measure, I flipped the switch upward, just in case she decided to end her trick while I was downstairs. With careful footwork, I made my way into the basement.

The basement of the Abram Mansion was home to many

things, including the ancient and massive hot water heater that worked for this wing of the house. I had asked Jim to replace it, since its age and rust made it a fire hazard, but Ben had prioritized other renovations ahead of the heater. It chugged along, huffing and puffing like an old man with a cigar. Beyond the heater, the basement was cluttered with old hardware and tools. A circular saw with a rusty blade sat atop an old workshop table. A cleanly cut two-by-four waited for someone to finish cutting it, but from the looks of it, whatever project the wood belonged to had been abandoned long ago. Along the wall was a shelf piled high with old board games. Some of them looked as though they'd been sitting there since before the Abrams moved in. I didn't recognize many of the dusty titles.

The fuse box was in the far corner of the basement. I waded through the mess, carefully avoiding sharp corners and wayward items. When I reached the fuse box, I flipped each one out of ceremony rather than expectation. Somehow, I knew this wasn't actually a fluke with the mansion's electricity.

"Alyssa?" I whispered. "Can you hear me?"

I didn't expect her to reply, at least not immediately. If Sammy was right, she didn't like me very much, but maybe I could win her over with reassurances about the storm.

"You don't like thunderstorms much, do you?" I murmured, hoping my voice wouldn't travel up the stairs to Ben's ears. "I never liked them either when I was a kid. I didn't like fireworks too. New Year's Eve and Fourth of July were always nightmares for me. Loud noises made me jumpy."

I kept my tone low and soothing. Something flickered in the corner of my vision, as if someone had come down the stairs, but when I looked, there was nothing there.

"Balloons, champagne bottles, firecrackers." I shuddered, exaggerating the movement to catch Alyssa's attention. "Count me out. Not for me."

Another glint of movement caught my eye by the hot water heater. Again, when I looked directly at it, there was nothing to be seen. A real shiver crept up my spine, but I tried not to show it, lest my anxiety scare Alyssa away from making contact with me.

"But you shouldn't let a little bit of thunder scare you," I told the ghostly presence that had crept into the basement to accompany me. "That's why you turned all the lights on, isn't it? Because of the thunderstorm?"

This time, a hazy figure appeared by the shelf of board games. It was about Sammy's height, and I thought I caught a glimpse of red hair. I pretended not to see her, keeping my gaze focused on the stairway instead. When she nodded—an acknowledgement of our conversation—the hairs on the back of my neck stood up. I was talking to a ghost.

"The good thing about thunderstorms is that they're one of those things you can talk yourself out of being afraid of," I told Alyssa. "Let's go through it together, okay? First of all, we're inside. The big strong walls of your house will protect you from the lightning, so the storm can't hurt you, right?"

Another nod. Another ripple of fear across my entire body.

"You can also tell how far away the storm is by the amount of seconds between the lightning strike and the next boom of thunder." Little by little, I shifted my head toward the board games, hoping not to scare her. "For every five seconds you count, the storm is one mile away. Do you want to try together?"

The small figure nodded again. My heartbeat quickened as her image began to solidify. I could see her pink polka-dotted scarf now, just as Sammy had described, but I wasn't sure if I wanted to see more. A flash of lightning illuminated the hallway above us.

"One Mississippi," I whispered. "Two Mississippi, three Mississippi, four Mississippi, five Mississippi, six Mississippi—"

The thunder rang out, and the figure cowered against the board games.

"It's all right," I assured her. "That was six seconds, so that means the storm is over a mile away. It was a lot closer when you first turned on the lights. Now it's getting farther away, which probably means it's going to be over in another hour or so."

The figure took a step toward me. I stumbled backward. My arm ran into something sharp behind me—an ice pick sticking off of a shelf. The point of it pricked the back side of my arm, drawing blood. Alyssa's figure backed away.

"It's okay," I said hurriedly. "I'm scared too. You're not alone."

I clapped my free hand to the back of my arm to stem the blood. Another shelf rattled of its own accord. An old first aid kit fell off of it and sprang open to reveal clean rolls of gauze and antibiotic cream. The figure pointed toward it.

"Thanks, but I think that stuff's kind of old by now," I said. "We have some newer things upstairs. Are you okay? Do you think you can turn the lights off? If you want, you can keep the one in your room on. It won't bother me."

The figure tilted her head to the side as if considering it. I was still too scared to look right at Alyssa, terrified by what I might see. After a moment, the lights in the basement flickered.

"There we go!" Ben's voice carried from the kitchen. "Hey, Peyton! The lights stopped acting insane!"

Alyssa had left the basement light on for me, but as soon as she'd heard Ben's voice, she'd disappeared. Clutching my arm, I closed the fuse box and headed upstairs.

"What happened to you?" Ben asked when he saw the blood dribbling from my sleeve. He'd finished making the pasta and set the table for two.

"It's a mess down there," I said, rinsing the puncture wound at the kitchen sink. "I ran into an old ice pick."

"Ooh, is your tetanus updated?"

"I think so."

"Well, thanks for going down there." He spooned sauce one-handed over two bowls of pasta and nodded at the seat next to his. "I made enough for two. Want some?"

"Sure."

Before joining Ben, I pressed a paper towel against the cut and glanced through the window into the courtyard. As promised, Alyssa had cut all the lights except for the ones Ben and I had turned on ourselves. However, one light in the east wing—in her bedroom—remained lit.

BEN WOKE up early and worked in his office for most of the next morning. When I stopped to listen outside his door, I could hear the steady, slow plink of his one-handed keyboard work. Happy he was getting back to his normal self, I almost walked off to get ready for my day. I had the usual planned: breakfast at the Black Cat Café, a walk around town, maybe some photography practice, and picking up Sammy from school. Then Ben's phone rang.

"Hey, boss," he said, picking the call up immediately. "I'm almost done with the material you asked for—yeah, we're back on track. Why?"

There was a pause as his boss replied. When Ben spoke again, there was a hard edge to his tone.

"I told you," he said. "We were out of town for marriage counseling. It was a week's retreat. I thought you were okay with it—what do you mean you didn't approve it? We had an understanding—no, but—I think we can still make this work."

My shoulders tensed. I could see where this was going.

"You hired someone else?" Ben said. "Why the hell would you

do that? I'm getting the work done! No, you stop shouting, jackass!"

I jumped as Ben's cell phone hit the opposite side of the office door and clattered to the floor. I went inside to find Ben with his forehead in his hands, his wheelchair about four feet from his desk as if he'd pushed himself away from his laptop in frustration. He glanced up at me when I came in.

"How much of that did you hear?"

"All of it."

"Can you hand me my phone?"

I picked it up from the floor and turned it over. The screen was cracked from top to bottom. "I don't think you'll be making any calls on this for a while."

Ben groaned. "Can I borrow yours?" When I handed it to him, he dialed a number from memory and put the phone up to his ear. "Hey, Jim? Yeah, it's Ben Fletcher. Listen, I'm sorry to do this to you on such short notice, but I'm going to have to suspend construction. No, it's not your fault. My job didn't work out, and I'm not going to be able to pay you guys until I find a new one. Thanks, man. You have a good day too."

Ben hung up, handed my phone back, and returned his head to his hands. I rubbed his shoulders.

"You'll find another job," I said.

"Not like that one," he replied. "And I haven't talked to my other contacts in two months. I don't have any leads."

"Can they really just fire you like that?" I asked him. "It doesn't seem fair."

"We had an agreement," Ben said, rubbing stress and sleep from his eyes. "An agreement that I breached when I didn't turn any work in for a solid week. God, I'm such an idiot. I should have just told him about my injury."

I pursed my lip, holding in the *I told you so* that kept threatening to fall out of my mouth. Saying it wouldn't be productive, and it definitely wouldn't help to keep the peace between me and Ben.

"Why don't you come into town with me?" I said. "You don't have to supervise Jim today, nor do you have to work. It's not good for you to be cooped up in the house all the time. We can have breakfast at the Black Cat. Bring your laptop. You can work on reaching out to your contacts. You're a good guy, Ben, and a hard worker. Someone will hire you."

"I only have one hand," he reminded me. "Who's going to hire a technical writer who can only work at half speed?"

"Someone with enough grace to understand what you've been through." I wheeled him out of the office and into his bedroom, then pulled open his dresser. "Get dressed. We're going."

We parked the SUV right outside the Black Cat, which meant all eyes were on us through the windows of the café as I unloaded Ben's wheelchair from the trunk and helped him transfer to it from the passenger seat of the car. As soon as Ben took control of it himself and we went inside, everyone turned back around to mind their own business. Mason—the flamboyant owner of Black Cat—beamed at us as we approached the counter, his handlebar mustache bristling.

"The Fletchers, together again!" he said. "I'm so glad to see you out and about, Ben. I hope you're taking good care of yourself."

"Doing my best," Ben replied in a gruff tone. "What have you got for a guy who just lost his job?"

"Bourbon," Mason answered. To my surprise, he didn't latch on to Ben's job loss and ask more about it. "It warms the body and the mind. I'll pour a shot of my best batch into your coffee. Sound good?"

"Your best batch?" Ben said. "You make your own bourbon?"

"I sure do, and I reserve it for my best customers." Mason turned red and lowered his voice. "Just don't tell the government. It's my own private stash. Unmonitored. I don't sell it. I just share it, but it's technically illegal."

"Your secret's safe with us," I assured Mason.

"And I love strong coffee," Ben added with a wink.

Mason blushed as he rang up Ben's "regular" coffee and my usual breakfast order. "Oh, Mr. Fletcher, I'm married, you flirt! Anything else I can get for you?"

"Biggest stack of pancakes you have on the menu," said Ben.

"Coming up, handsome."

I wheeled Ben to the end of the counter to pick up our coffees. Ben took one sip of his and let out a relieved sigh. "There's Della," I said. "Let's go sit with her."

He put on the brakes. "I'm not sure I can take the town gossip."

"She's not like that," I told him, forcing the handbrake up and wheeling him over to Della's table. "Besides, we have breakfast every day. She's expecting me."

Ben pasted a smile on his face, one that Della matched when she saw us. She got up from the booth to give Ben a gentle hug. At her small height, she hardly had to stoop to reach him.

"Benjamin!" she said. "It's great to see you. You look much better than the last time I saw you, I have to say."

"Thanks, I'm feeling better too," Ben said. The bruises on his face were not as dark as they had been a few days ago, though they were taking on the unattractive yellow tinge of healing. "Do you mind if we join you?"

"Not at all!"

I slid into the booth across from Della while Ben parked his wheelchair at the end of the table. Within minutes, Mason served us our hot, steaming breakfasts, and we dug in.

"What brings you into town, Ben?" Della asked as she cut her sausages into perfectly-proportioned bite-sized pieces. "I usually have to rely on *this one* for company." She jokingly nudged me under the table.

"It just so happens I have a lot more free time on my hands as of this morning," Ben said. "I lost my job."

"Oh, that's awful!"

"It's a challenge," I said, stepping in when I saw Ben's sullen expression. "But we'll get through it. Ben has some good connections."

"You know," Della mused. "Basil's always wanted to write a book on independent hydroponic horticulture. He says he has all the information but none of the skill to write it down. If you like, I can ask him if he'd be interested in hiring you to do it for him."

"That's okay," Ben replied hastily. "Horticulture isn't really my thing. I usually work on tech manuals and stuff like that."

"Yeah, but you could adapt," I encouraged him. "A local job might be a good change of pace, and I'm sure Basil would be willing to work with your injury."

"He absolutely would," Della assured us. "Basil's a bit spacey himself, so you'd probably have to keep him on track, but the two of you would make a good team!"

Ben shot me a look that Della wasn't supposed to see. He didn't want to do this. His interest in hydroponic greenhouses was pretty low. I kicked his leg under the table, gently, and gave him a subtle nod. No matter how badly he didn't want to work with Basil, it was an opportunity he couldn't look over.

"Just consider it," Della said, sensing the disagreement between us. "I'll mention it to Basil, and if you're interested, give him a call. Sound good?"

"Sounds great," said Ben.

. . .

DELLA DIDN'T STICK AROUND for long. She finished her breakfast and bid us goodbye, saying she had a local photography job that needed attention. Knowing Della and her keen sense of perception, she could tell Ben wasn't in the mood for casual chit chat. He worked on his laptop for a few hours, typing emails out as fast as he could with one hand. Every so often, he would let out a deep sigh. When Mason heard him do it, he brought Ben another loaded coffee. Ben drank it too fast, turned bright red, and closed his laptop.

"I just had a thought," he said. "You're not supposed to mix painkillers with alcohol, are you?"

I immediately began collecting my things. "Let's get you home."

After getting Ben into bed and making him drink a liter of water to rehydrate, I Googled his medications to make sure he wasn't in immediate danger. Thankfully, he hadn't had enough bourbon to do much damage, so I left him to catch up on his sleep and returned to town. Since I was short on time, I drove the SUV to Sammy's elementary school and joined the line of minivans in the pickup loop. The process was similar to that of picking someone up at the airport. If you saw your kid waiting for you, you had permission to pull over at the curb. If not, you had to keep moving. At the end of the loop, you had to make a U-turn and repeat the whole circle again until your kid showed up.

I drove around the loop at least five times, coming in close contact with the bumpers of other mothers. On my next go around, there were significantly less cars to contend with and most of the kids had already been picked up. The buses were gone too. I checked my watch. The last bell of the day had rung thirty minutes ago. Sammy should be waiting for me. I parked near the front office and went inside. The secretary, bless her heart, had replaced her pin with one that plainly said *Say no to drugs!* in big capital letters.

"Hi, I'm Peyton Fletcher," I told her. "I'm supposed to be picking up Sammy Baker today, but I haven't spotted him yet. Did he get held up in class or something?"

The secretary checked a list of names on the clipboard in front of her. "Sammy Baker... Nope! His mom picked him up today. She was one of the first ones in the loop this afternoon."

"Theo was here?"

"So says my paperwork."

BACK IN THE CAR, I checked my phone. It was on silent. Ben must have accidentally switched the Do Not Disturb function on when he'd borrowed it that morning. I had a text message from Theo that read, *Got out of work early, so don't worry about picking up Sammy. Come over when you can?*

Relieved, I buckled my seatbelt and drove to Theo's. I stopped at the bakery on the floor below to pick up coffee and pastries then headed upstairs. Sammy answered the door.

"Hi, Peyton," he said, unusually subdued. "Wanna come in?"

Theo fiddled with the coffee maker in the kitchen. Her shoulders were drawn up to her ears. She put the glass pot in place then pushed the start button. The coffee maker groaned and sputtered.

"Damn it!" Theo said, kicking the counter.

"Whoa," I said as Sammy raced off to the other room. "Go easy on it. Looks like an off-brand. How long have you had that thing anyway?"

"All I wanted was a cup of coffee—"

"Lucky for you, I stopped downstairs." I set the fresh coffees on her counter along with the pastries. "Got a cinnamon roll for you too. It's your favorite, right? You want to tell me what's going on?"

Theo planted her hands on the counter. She didn't touch the coffee or the cinnamon roll. Something was off. When I brought goodies, she was usually the first one to drain her cup.

"I don't need or want your charity, Peyton," she said. "I know we're good friends, and I appreciate what you're trying to do, but it's not right."

"Theo, it was three dollars and seventy-five cents," I replied, confused as to where this was coming from. "If you want to reimburse me, more power to you."

"I'm not talking about the coffee."

"Then what are you talking about?"

She went to her coat hanging by the door and fished around in the front pocket for a regular envelope that had been folded in half. She tossed it onto the counter. "This."

I drew two hundred dollars from the envelope. "Whoa! Where did this come from?"

"Don't play dumb," she said. "I know you left it for me to find."

"Theo, I swear I didn't," I said, putting the money away. "I don't have this kind of cash lying around, and Ben just lost his job."

Theo's brow furrowed. "It wasn't you."

"No, ma'am."

"Then who—?"

"Someone who cares about you?" I suggested.

"No." She shook the envelope as if trying to get a stray cat off her front lawn. "Money doesn't land in your lap like this. It always comes with a price. Trust me."

14

"Why would I take a job about horticulture?"

Ben ambled around the kitchen, making coffee with one hand. His wheelchair waited at the top of the steps. It was his first attempt at navigating without it, something I'd made him promise not to do unless I was present. He was doing well so far, but I could tell it how much effort he was putting into his coffee-making. He walked with one shoulder higher than the other to keep one of his injured ribs from bothering him, and he took a deep breath between every four words, as if he'd just come inside after running a marathon. Still, I was happy to see him on his feet.

"Think of the benefits," I told him, getting the coffee filters off the high shelf in the pantry so he wouldn't have to. "It's local, so you don't have to go too far—"

"I didn't have to go anywhere with my other jobs," Ben countered. "Working remotely, I could stay in bed."

"I'm not so sure that's the best thing for you right now," I said. "You need to be moving around. It will quicken your healing process. Besides, the Gordons have been so helpful to us in the last two months."

"Maybe Della has." He filled the coffee pot with water then hit the top of the faucet with his cast to turn the water off. "But I haven't seen Basil around. What does that guy do anyway?"

"I think he's a bit of a hermit," I admitted. "According to Della, he stays home to work most days. Kind of like you, if you think about it."

"Are you comparing me to the town's hippie grandpa?"

"No," I answered. "Because there's nothing hippie about you. I can't remember the last time you pulled out a bong."

"Basil has a bong?"

I rolled my eyes as Ben struggled to fit the coffee pot into the proper slot. When he finally got it in, he slumped against the counter and wiped his brow. I tossed four pieces of bread into the toaster and tore open a package of bacon. For once, I'd decided to forego my usual breakfast at the Black Cat to spend time with Ben. Without Jim and his crew hammering away, the house was strangely quiet. It closed in on me, pressing against my ears like a fluffy pillow. If I listened closely enough, I heard the ever-present whispers that traveled through the walls. Sometimes, I tried to figure out what they were saying, but glimpses of the one-sided conversations fed my nightmares.

"I have enough money in my savings to get us through the next couple of months," Ben proposed once he'd caught his breath. "I can afford to let myself have a few weeks of vacation."

"I don't want you to spend all of your savings," I said. "What about the renovations anyway? Without a steady income, we can't continue fixing up the house."

Ben clicked his tongue. "Is that such a bad thing? We've repaired most of the parts we use on a daily basis. Why should we keep going?"

"It was your idea," I reminded him. "We were going to fix the house up and sell it for more money at the end of the six months. Do you want to give up on that now?"

"I'm assuming you don't."

"Not really." As the bacon sizzled, grease jumped out of the hot pan and singed my forearm. I hissed and wiped it away with a wet dish towel. "I had plans for the money from the house sale."

"Mm."

I turned the heat on the bacon down and gingerly flipped each piece. They were seared nicely on the other side, with crusty blackened bits just the way I liked. Toast, on the other hand, was not quite as tasty burned, so when the toaster started smoking, I accidentally shoved Ben out of the way with a little too much gusto to reach it. He clutched his side and let out a short grunt.

"I'm sorry!" The bread was far beyond burnt, so I left it in the toaster to check on Ben. "I forgot for a second. Are you okay? Did I break it again?"

Ben tentatively rubbed his ribs. "It's okay. You didn't mean it."

Something else hid behind the look on his face, and it wasn't his frustration with my lack of tact. "What's bothering you?"

"The left side," he said, lifting his shirt to show me his bruised midsection. The worst of it had faded, but his skin was a canvas of pink, blue, and yellow. "These ones aren't feeling much better—"

"I meant what's bothering you in your head," I said. "I can tell something's wrong."

Though the coffee pot hadn't finished filling, Ben shuffled over to the cabinet with the mugs, drew two of our favorites out, and poured servings for the both of us. "No cream, just sugar, right?"

"You know how I take my coffee," I said. "Stop deflecting."

Ben stirred a teaspoon of raw sugar into my black coffee, clinking the spoon absentmindedly against the mug. "To be honest, I don't like talking about money with you. Before all of this divorce stuff started happening, I didn't care that you weren't working. All I wanted to do was take care of you because I knew we were in it together. Now, every time you mention money or refurbishing the house, it's like you only care because we're splitting everything after the divorce."

My jaw dropped open. "Ben, no. Is that how you really feel?"

He lifted his shoulders. By now, the sugar granules had surely dissolved in the coffee, but he kept stirring. "You said it a minute ago. You have plans for the sale of the house, but I'm the one paying for the renovations. If we were planning to stay together after this, would you care how much money we might make off this place?"

I chewed on my lip. Thinking back on it—on my intentions for the money we earned once we sold the mansion—Ben had a point. I was so accustomed to Ben's sharing, I'd never considered he might feel as though I was taking advantage of him. It wasn't fair to him. He was doing all the work, pulling in all the money for both of us, while I did whatever I wanted without contributing to anything at all.

"You're right," I said.

Ben, stunned, finally stopped stirring. "I am?"

"Of course." I gave him a quick hug and playfully tugged one of his curls. "I never meant to piggyback off of you all this time. I keep telling myself I'll get back into photography and make money that way, but I haven't been walking the walk."

"You should ask Della if she has any contacts," Ben suggested. "She's your friend, right? I'm sure she would be happy to help."

I set the table for two and turned the bacon out onto a plate lined with paper towels. Distracted by the conversation, I'd let it go too long. It was burnt beyond my liking now. I sighed and put new bread in the toaster. "I don't think Della takes many jobs anymore. I'm not sure if she's in touch with any of her contacts."

"It doesn't hurt to ask," Ben said as he set out utensils. A minute later, he rescued the bread at the perfect moment. The toast was golden brown and just crispy enough. He set out my favorite passionfruit jam, and we took our seats. "I'll tell you what. If you ask Della about a photography lead, I'll call Basil about his book."

"You will?"

"Don't sound so excited," he warned, layering a piece of toast with jam before setting it in front of me. "I didn't say I would take it. It just means I'll consider it."

I squeezed his hand. "That's good enough for me."

AFTER BREAKFAST WITH BEN, the house began to close in on me. I itched to get away from the wooded seclusion of the Abram Mansion. Ben's foray around the kitchen had left him exhausted, so he fell asleep in his room soon after we had finished eating. I cleaned up our dishes and threw away the bacon that was too burned for us to consider keeping for leftovers. All the while, a strange humming sound buzzed around my right ear, like a fly that took a particular liking to me. I hadn't noticed it at first, but there were moments it became more pronounced. When I reached for the rattling drawer to put away a chef's knife, the buzzing became downright irritating. I clapped my hand to my ear and shook my head. Tinnitus, if that's what it was, did not run in my family.

The town of Falconwood was covered in yet another fresh coating of snow. It came in waves. One day, the dead grass poked its ugly little stems up to fight for a look at the sun, and the next, it was once again smothered in a blanket of snow. The worst part was in between these steps in the process, when the snow was stomped into half-melted ice. It was cold and wet, and no matter how thick your socks, it seeped into your boots to make your toes shrivel up. As I cleared a path to the car and swept snow from the windshield, I felt a chill on the back of my neck that had nothing to do with the weather. Someone was watching me. I scanned the woods, almost expecting to see a pair of glowing eyes staring back at me from the darkness, but there was no one there. Then, I glanced upward, toward the attic of the house. Someone was standing in the window, looking down at me. I waved. The curtains fluttered, and the figure disappeared.

With a shiver, I got in the car and drove away. No matter how many times Alyssa made her presence known, I couldn't get used to it. Ben was completely oblivious to her. He never mentioned the whispers or the strange sense that someone else occupied the house other than us. Maybe Alyssa's appearance in the window was what made me drive to the Falconwood library. I'd been meaning to check their newspaper archives for news on the Abrams, but it always slipped by the wayside. Since I had a few hours before I had to pick up Sammy, I figured I might as well hold up my promise to him and look into Alyssa's death.

The Falconwood library was small, and it catered mostly to the town's younger demographic. A reading circle took up the majority of the main room. Children's books lined the shelves along the border. The books for adults were confined to the outer limits, lined up along the walls so you didn't have to disrupt the inner sanctum if you wanted to find fiction that did not pertain to Harry Potter. I cruised through the shelves, scanning the titles for anything that might give me a hint into the Abrams' lives, but I only came up with one book about the "historic" town of Falconwood. As I read the back cover, the librarian—a tall man with round glasses and a slight hump to his back—came by to return a few books to their places.

"Are you looking for something in particular?" he asked. "I'm a wealth of knowledge."

"Yes, actually," I said, tucking the Falconwood book beneath my arm. "I was wondering if you have anything regarding the Abram family or the mansion. Newspapers, maybe?"

"You must be Peyton," he said. "I'm Baylor. It's nice to finally meet the new owner of the Abram Mansion. I can understand why you're interested in it. The place has a pretty dark past."

"You know about it?"

"A little," Baylor replied. "I've been working in this library for over fifty years. I remember the day we lost Percy."

"It must have been hard on the town," I said. "I know how much he meant to all of you."

Baylor bowed his head. "It was quite the blow, not only to the people, but the businesses as well. Percy invested a lot of his money in Falconwood. It took us a while to get our feet under us again. The library suffered too. Percy was our best contributor."

"How did you get back on your feet?"

"Lots of fundraisers," Baylor said, stretching his long arm up to return a book on local plants to the top shelf. "Falconwood loves fundraisers. Anyway, I can show you what we have left of our newspaper archives, but it's not much. We hired someone to help us go paperless a few years ago, and the guy turned out to be a total idiot. He claimed he lost the majority of our information before he could digitize it."

I followed Baylor toward the back corner of the library. "Who was the guy?"

"Some out-of-towner," he replied, reshelving books as he went. He knew the library so well, he did not pause to make sure the books were in the correct places. "He was desperate for work, so we gave him a chance. Falconwood is big on giving people chances, even when it seems like they don't deserve them. Come on in."

He ushered me through a back door and into the library's belly, where there were shelves upon shelves of adult books waiting for their chance to be read. "Here's where we keep the good stuff," Baylor joked. "The kids' books are more popular. You know how it is. These days, everyone's got an e-reader. Here's what's left of the newspapers." He pointed to a small, sad pile of yellowing papers. "I think there are one or two articles about the Abrams that survived. Let me know if you need anything else. Just close the door on your way out."

"Sure thing."

Baylor left me to discover the back end of the library on my own. I sat on the floor and pulled the pile of newspapers toward me, flipping through the corners to check the date on each one. According to what I'd been told, Percy Abram killed himself roughly forty years ago. Only two newspapers had dates that fit appropriately, one from 1973 and one from 1978. I carefully extracted them from the pile. The crisp pages threatened to tear as I separated them. As I unfolded the one from 1978, I realized I'd hit the jackpot. The front page featured an enormous picture of Percy Abram, along with a detailed obituary and personal piece. Percy had been a handsome guy despite his thin face and pointed chin. I'd always expected him to wear three-piece suits and expensive watches, but the picture featured him in a wrinkled golf shirt and chinos. It must have been taken before his wife left him because he wore a wide smile with the slightest gap between his front teeth.

The article told the story Falconwood wanted to hear about Percy. It detailed Percy's charity work and highlighted some of the town events that had occurred at the Abram Mansion. The journalist who'd covered the story spoke mournfully of Percy's "hiking accident" that resulted in his death. Della once told me the police had found a suicide letter in the mansion, but the people of Falconwood chose to believe a less-intense version of the story. Oddly enough, the article didn't mention Penelope or Alyssa at all. It was as if Percy's wife and daughter had never existed. I wondered why the journalist had excluded those details. Was it out of respect to Percy, since many believed his wife had left him for another, taking their daughter with her? That was another aspect to the story that didn't add up. Where was Penelope? Had she found happiness with the other man in her life? If her daughter was truly the dead spirit wandering around the Abram Mansion, I doubted it.

The 1973 newspaper appeared bereft of information on the Abrams at first glance, but after scanning the pages, I found Alyssa's birth announcement in a tiny article. Alyssa Elizabeth Abram was born on December 19th, 1973. Had she made it out of the Abram Mansion alive, she would be almost forty-six today, over ten years older than me and Ben. It was hard to process that she had allegedly been trapped in the mansion as a five-year-old for so long, so hard to process that I was starting to question whether the spirit at Abram Mansion was Alyssa at all. But if it wasn't Alyssa, who else could it be?

"How's it going?" Baylor had returned with more books to organize. "Find anything good?"

"Nothing too useful," I said, stacking the newspapers again. "You're right. There's not much left back here."

"Sorry about that," he replied. "Wish I could be of more use. Listen, I heard you dabble in photography. Is that right?"

It was remarkable how much information could spread through the town, even to the ears of people I'd never met. "I do. Why?"

He handed me a flyer from the top of his book stack. "We're looking for someone to photograph the town for our new website. Falconwood is such a nice place to visit, but no one knows we're here."

I examined the flyer, which advertised the job. The pay wasn't much, and the town committee was looking for roughly two hundred photos around Falconwood. Nevertheless, it was an opportunity that hadn't been open to me before. "I'm surprised Della Gordon didn't already jump on this."

"We asked Della," Baylor said. "She said she didn't take photography jobs anymore. She was actually the one who recommended you."

"Really? She didn't mention it."

"Well, give it a thought," Baylor said, "and let me know if you might be interested."

"I am interested," I assured him, "but I have to check on a few things first. My husband's hurt, and I have a nanny gig that I have to keep up with. One that I'm a little late for."

"No problem." Baylor moved out of the way. "If you have any more questions about the Abrams, don't hesitate to ask. I might be able to answer a few."

"I'll keep that in mind."

On my way out of the library, I ran smack into Della in the parking lot. She carried a stack of books to be returned, but a little bump from me sent them sprawling into the fresh snow.

"Oh, my!"

"Sorry, Della!" I helped her collect the books before the snow could get them too wet and caught sight of one of the titles —*Coping with OCD and Depression: When to Get Help.* "Is everything okay?"

She snatched the book from my hand and flipped it over so the cover was no longer visible. "Yes, my dear." She spotted the photography flyer tucked in my pocket. "Oh, did Baylor tell you about the job? Are you going to take it?"

"I'm thinking about it," I said. "Thanks for recommending me. Should I give Baylor my portfolio? Not that I have a recent one."

"No, he trusts my tastes," Della replied. "And I trust your style. You should do it. It would be a good project for you to cut your teeth on. I'm happy I ran into you. Basil and I were wondering if you and Ben would like to come over for dinner tonight."

"At your place?"

"That's the plan," Della said. "The airstream is small, but we have room for guests. Basil could show Ben the greenhouse. It might spike Ben's interest in the project."

"That sounds great."

"Excellent! How's six o'clock?"

"Perfect."

I PICKED SAMMY UP, took him for an after-school snack at the Black Cat, then spent the rest of the afternoon with him at the apartment. I shared what little information I'd discovered about the Abrams from the library, but he wasn't interested in anything other than Alyssa's current state inside the house. He asked to visit her again, but I shot him down. I still didn't think it was a good idea for Sammy to be anywhere near the mansion. When Theo got home, I bid them goodbye and headed downstairs. As I pulled out of the parking lot, a black rundown sedan cut me off and careened down the road at top speed. For Falconwood, it was an unusually rude show of poor driving habits, but I put it from my mind. I only had an hour to get ready for dinner at Della and Basil's.

"At their place?" Ben asked when I told him about our spontaneous dinner plans. "Don't they live in a bus?"

"An airstream," I corrected him, unwinding my scarf. The wind was brutal today, and my cheeks were burned pink. "People are doing that a lot these days. It's cheaper and more sustainable. I think it'll be cool to check it out."

"If you say so." He took the flyer from my jean pocket and smoothed it out. "What's this?"

"A job I might take."

He rolled up the flyer and tapped me on the nose with it. "Good for you! I'm glad you're putting yourself out there."

"Any news from Basil?"

"To be honest, I slept the whole day," Ben said sheepishly, "but apparently, we're going there for dinner tonight, so he can tell me more then."

I eyed his messy hair and wrinkled pajamas. "We have to be there in an hour. Are you going to shower?"

"Why? Do I look like I need to shower?"

"Yes, actually."

Again, he batted me with the flyer. "If you insist. Is this a formal dinner party? What are you wearing?"

"I don't know. Something nice, I guess."

"Something nice it is."

Ben rolled off to the bathroom. I kicked off my boots and piled my coat near the door. I wanted a hot shower too, but the mansion was fickle about two faucets running at once. It would be better if I waited until Ben was finished, so I sat on the couch in the foyer and pulled the Falconwood website up on my laptop. It was a sad little site without much information and too many broken links. If Falconwood wanted to attract tourists, they would definitely need more than a few catchy photographs. A soft thump distracted me from my job research.

"Ben?" I called. "Everything all right?"

No answer. The water continued running, and Ben's voice hummed an enigmatic tune. Besides, the thump had come from above. I looked into the mezzanine and caught sight of a pink scarf disappearing from between the railing.

"Alyssa," I murmured.

I set the laptop aside and carefully climbed the stairs to the second floor. On the mezzanine, I could never resist imagining what parties at the mansion used to be like. I saw people slow dancing under the chandelier and sneaking off to one of the many rooms for a private moment. I saw Alyssa playing with the other children her age, perhaps happening upon one of the sneaking couples. Now, I saw a pattern of small scuffs on the dusty carpet, as if a pair of child-sized feet had just recently run through. They led me to the east wing of the house, where Alyssa's presence was most profound, and up two flights of stairs. They disappeared at the foot of the huge wall tapestry, behind which the entrance to the attic was hidden.

"I've been up there already," I told Alyssa, sure she was listening from somewhere. "Sammy told me that's where you like to hide. Is there something you'd like me to see?"

The tapestry fluttered, which seemed like a solid enough answer to me. I ducked under the heavy fabric, pushed through the attic door, and made my way upstairs. Like the last time I came up here, the air was cold and musty, and it smelled faintly of cedarwood. The attic was full of odds and ends, as though the Abrams had used the space for storage and forgotten about everything that was up here. I spotted a corner dedicated to Alyssa that included an old crib, a rusty tricycle, and several cardboard boxes full of her baby clothes. A wave of cold air brushed by my left elbow, but none of the windows were open.

"I'm here," I told Alyssa. "What did you want me to see?"

A booklet fell off a stack of cardboard boxes about halfway across the room, spilling photographs from it. I picked my way past a broken laundry basket, a stack of mismatched china plates, and a bunch of hiking equipment. I bent over to collect the photos from the floor and shuffled through them.

"These are all of your parents?" I asked. Each picture featured either Percy, Penelope, or both of them. In some, Percy looked significantly younger than in the photo I'd found in the newspaper. Apparently, he'd known Penelope for a long time. "What about them?"

Another inexplicable gust of wind knocked most of the

photos from my hand. I peered at the one on top of the stack that remained. In it, Percy held Penelope around the waist. It had been taken at the Falconwood swimming pool, and both of the Abrams wore bathing suits. I studied the photograph, looking for whatever it was that Alyssa wanted me to see.

"I don't get it," I told her at last. "What am I looking for?"

A lump rose in my throat as something invisible folded over half the picture as I held it in my hand. I steeled myself not to drop it and run screaming from the attic. When Alyssa was finished, only Penelope was visible. She had folded her father out of the picture. I studied Penelope from top to bottom. Like Alyssa, she had auburn hair and a delicate face. Though she smiled, the expression didn't reach her eyes, and the hand she had around Percy did not rest firmly against his waist. She set her body slightly away from his, and as I scanned down her bare arms and legs, I realized why.

"She's bruised," I muttered, tracing the injuries with the tip of my finger. "All over. A hiking injury?" But the pattern of bruises along Penelope's arm—four over, one under—spoke of a different injury, and I could make out another faded handprint on the front of her thigh. More disturbing still was the slight shadow along her left cheek, which looked as though she'd covered up another bruise with makeup. "Alyssa, did your dad hurt your mom?"

A marble chess piece flew through the air and landed on my temple, the sharp edge of the knight's blade drawing blood. Before I could react, a heavy pawn was catapulted in my direction. I dodged it with a shriek, tossed the photos to the floor, and ran for the stairs. All the while, the chess pieces pelted me. Each time one landed, I knew it would be a bruise. I slammed the attic door shut and ducked under the tapestry, panting and in pain. The feeling of Alyssa's presence was gone.

15

*D*ella and Basil lived on a plot of land at the edge of town, as hidden away from everything else as the mansion was. Were it not for the tire tracks in the snow, Ben and I would have never found our way there, even with Della's detailed instructions. As we passed through a thicket of trees and emerged in a small clearing, I gasped at the sight. The silver airstream glowed with soft, golden light. It rested between the edge of a small, frozen pond and Basil's hydroponic greenhouse, which he'd built himself. The Gordons had drawn a canopy from the airstream, underneath which sat a picnic table set for four. They had cleared away the snow around the table and laid out what looked like portable flooring. Two space heaters warmed the area, and a string of fairy lights made it easy to navigate. Della was already outside when we parked the car, cooking something on the grill.

"Hi!" Della said, closing the grill as we got out of the car. She waded through the snow to give each of us a hug. "You found the place okay?"

"Sure did," Ben said. "Thanks for the instructions."

"Of course." Della beamed and squeezed my arm. "I'm so glad

the two of you decided to join us. Basil is inside, cooking up a storm. Would you like the grand tour?"

"Absolutely," I said.

She spread her arms wide and gestured to the clearing. "This is it." She chuckled at her own joke before waving at us to follow her. "Come on. I'll show you around."

The inside of the airstream was surprisingly roomy. A queen-sized bed took up the back quadrant, next to a tiny bathroom that had a shower and a DIY composting toilet that Della was proud to point out. Every bit of space had a purpose. Counters and desks folded out from the walls or could be rearranged to make one larger dining table. Beneath every seat was more storage space. The airstream even featured an entire kitchen, where Basil manned the stove.

"Ah, our guests have arrived!" He wiped his hands on a dish towel then flung it over his shoulder. "Would either of you like a glass of wine?"

"I can't," Ben said. He'd decided to forego his wheelchair for the dinner party since he was getting stronger without it. "Doc said no alcohol until I'm finished with the pain meds."

"Ooh, that's right," Basil said, shaking Ben's good hand. "How's your recovery going?"

Ben's gaze flickered toward me. "I had a bit of a rocky start, but things are getting better now. It's my first venture out into the real world without the wheelchair."

"Sit down if you have to," Della urged. "Don't stand to be polite."

"I'm okay for now."

"So a water for Ben," Basil said. "What about you, Peyton? Can I interest you in a glass of red wine? Or maybe some home-made bourbon?"

"Does everyone in Falconwood make their own bourbon?" I asked. "Mason put some in Ben's coffee the other day."

Basil laughed. "Mason gets his supply from me, but he doesn't mouth off about it. He thinks he's protecting me by telling everyone he makes it."

"He's a good guy," Della said. "A complete sweetheart."

Ben peered over Basil's shoulder for a look into the simmering pots. "What are you making? Something on the grill?"

"Oh, shoot!" Della raced outside.

Basil grinned and stirred his concoction. "She has a bad habit of forgetting she's cooking. We're having vegetable soup, grilled portobellos, salad, and garlic bread. I have some cheese and fruit for appetizers, and I made a chocolate mousse for dessert. I hope you guys don't mind, but we don't eat a whole lot of meat in this household."

"It's no problem for me," I told him. "I tried getting Ben to go vegetarian a few years ago, but he's a stubborn one."

"I'm sorry," Ben said, "but I really like bacon."

"As did I." Basil deftly chopped fresh herbs and dropped them into the bubbling pot of soup. "But then I started getting older and feeling my bones more. When I cut meat out, I started to feel better. That was all the reason I needed. It's not for everyone though."

Della came back inside, carrying a plate of grilled mushroom caps. "I hope you don't mind if your food is slightly charred."

"I prefer it that way," I assured her.

"Yes, Peyton likes everything blackened," Ben added. "You should have seen the bacon she made this morning."

I playfully flicked Ben's ear. "That was not intentional."

"Well, we will do our best to burn things to your liking." Basil popped the cork on a bottle of red wine and swirled it around. "We don't have fancy things like decanters so we do things the old-fashioned way." After he was satisfied with the improvised aeration of the wine, he poured three glasses, one each for me,

Della, and himself. He presented Ben with a glass of water instead, then raised his up. "To good friends," he toasted.

"To excellent food," Della added. Then the older couple looked at us, as if expecting each of us to add on a toast of our own.

"Oh, uh, to new opportunities," I said hastily, blurting out the first thing that came to my mind.

Ben was smoother than me. He tapped his glass against Basil and Della's and said, "To our hosts. Thank you for what's sure to be a lovely evening."

AN HOUR LATER, the cheese and fruit plate had been demolished. We finished up our dinner on the little deck outside the airstream. With the wind chill, I'd expected it to be the coldest dinner I'd ever had in my life, but the space heaters warmed the area enough to make the breeze feel pleasant. By the time we were through with the soup, I was huddled close to Ben, laughing and smiling as Basil and Della told us hilarious stories from their time traveling across America in the airstream. Ben had his arm around me, but it felt platonic rather than romantic, as if we were finally settling into the promise that we would remain friends throughout and after the divorce.

"Anyway, that's how we learned the *right* way to empty sewage at a travel stop," Basil finished off with a hearty chuckle. "Gosh, I probably should have saved that story until after dinner. Sorry if I spoiled your appetites."

I patted my bloated stomach. "Not at all. No story could have stopped me from eating all this. It was delicious. You two really outdid yourselves."

"You're flattering us," Della said.

"I'm not!" I promised. "I wish I could cook like this."

"Della could teach you," Basil offered. "She taught me everything I know. If it weren't for her, I'd still be eating microwavable macaroni and cheese."

Della kissed the back of Basil's hand as she held it in her own. "Nonsense. You began growing food long before I came along. You would've figured out what to do with it eventually."

"Perhaps," Basil said, returning Della's affection by tickling her fingers. "But it was more fun to learn all of this with you by my side, darling. Now, Ben" —he leaned forward and stacked the plates between him and Ben away from his field of vision— "I've heard you might be interested in helping me with a passion project. What do you know about hydroponic greenhouses and growing things?"

"Honestly?" Ben said. "Nothing at all, but I have years of experience with interpreting information and laying it out in plain text. As long as you can give me all the details you know, I can put it on paper in a way people would want to read."

"That's what I like to hear." Basil unwound himself with his wife and offered Ben a hand to help him stand up. "What do you say we check out the subject? A little greenhouse tour, if you're up for it. We'll deal with the dishes later."

Ben suppressed a grunt as he grabbed Basil's arm and stood up. When he peeled himself away from me, the cold wind tickled the side of me he'd been warming. Basil clapped a hand over Ben's uninjured shoulder. Together, they headed off to the greenhouse.

"There they go," Della said. "Hopefully Ben comes back with his ears still attached. Basil can talk about that greenhouse for hours."

"That's good," I told her. "It means he has a lot of material."

"I'm glad Ben came around," Della said. Across the yard, Basil pointed out construction details of the greenhouse, taking Ben around its perimeter before going inside. "It'll be good for the both of them. Basil needs to get out of the airstream more often."

"I think Ben and Basil have more in common than either one of them has realized yet." I picked at my third piece of garlic bread. Though my stomach was full, I couldn't help but keep nibbling. "So I took a look at the Falconwood website. It could definitely use some help."

Della poured herself another glass of wine. "Yes, it certainly could. Does this mean you're thinking of accepting the job?"

"Ben pointed out I haven't contributed much to the expense of the renovations," I confided in her. "And this will help me practice my photography."

"Two birds."

"Can I call you if I need your advice?" I asked. "I'm not familiar with Falconwood like you are. I'm not sure where to start."

"Wait here." She went inside and returned with a pad of paper and a pencil. When she sat down again, she began scribbling a list. "Here are some of the sites you should hit first. Some of them are obvious, and some of them are little hidden gems that everyone forgets about. The snow might make it difficult to get good exterior pictures, but give it a go anyway."

"Thanks, Della. You've been the best of help." I finished the last piece of garlic bread. "You and Basil have both been too good to us."

"It's no trouble at all, honey."

While Ben and Basil toured the greenhouse, Della and I had dessert on our own. The chocolate mousse was to die for, and I spent every mouthful marveling over the life Basil and Della had built for themselves. Without all the stuff that people tend to accumulate over the years, they seemed freer than most, relying more on their healthy habits than their belongings to get by. If Ben and I had tried the airstream lifestyle, we wouldn't have made it. Ben was the biggest homebody, and we'd never set foot out of our hometown until Abram Mansion came along. If I'd forced Ben into a nomadic existence, we would have the opposite problem of today. He would be divorcing me instead of the other way around.

"You wouldn't believe the setup Basil has in that greenhouse," Ben gushed when he and Basil finally joined us again. "It's amazing. They're completely independent. If the apocalypse hits, I'm coming to stay here."

Basil wrapped a blanket around Della's shoulders as he sat down again. "You're more than welcome. Peyton, I hope you don't mind, but I'd like to start getting ideas together with Ben as early as tomorrow."

"That's fine with me," I said. "I'm probably going to head back to the library to get started on the photography job."

"You decided to take it?" Ben said. "That's great!"

"Yeah," I replied. "I guess we'll see."

WHEN I PICKED up Sammy from school the next day, I had my camera equipment with me in the car. Sammy hopped into the back seat and immediately started rooting through it.

"What's all this for?" he asked, pulling out an expensive lens.

"We're going to take some pictures of the town today," I told him. "Does that sound like something you might like to do?"

"Sure." Sammy popped the cap off the lens and inspected the inside. "Are we going to take pictures of the Abram Mansion too?"

I pulled out of the pickup loop and joined the rest of the cars on the road that had already escaped the chaos of the elementary school. "I think you know the answer to that already."

"I want to visit Alyssa." He put the cap back on with a delicate touch and returned the lens to its place in my bag. For a six-year-old, he was conscientious of the fragility of the camera equipment. "You said we were going to help her, but we haven't done anything so far."

"Sammy, I'm trying my best," I told him. "As a matter of fact, I spoke to Alyssa in the attic yesterday."

Sammy wriggled happily in his seat. "Really? What did she say?"

"Actually, she didn't say much of anything. I did most of the talking."

"And?"

I thought back to my brief foray to the top floor of the mansion, rifling through the old pictures of Percy and Penelope until Alyssa had shown me the one of the pool. The shadowy bruises all over Penelope's body had haunted me all night, and the whispers in the walls seemed more agitated than usual. I had a mark in my hairline from where the first chess piece had struck my temple, and the more I thought about it, the more confused I became. If Alyssa had wanted me to know about Percy's potential abuse of Penelope, why had she chased me from the attic once I found out?

"I don't think you're old enough to know what I figured out," I told Sammy. "But rest assured, I might be making progress on the mystery around Alyssa's death."

Sammy blew a frustrated sigh through his nose, crossed his arms, and gazed out the window. I'd disappointed him, but I wasn't about to tell him that his dead friend's mother might have been abused by her father. It was a subject that no kid should ever have to deal with, and if Alyssa knew what was going on between her parents, I felt all the more sorry for her. Furthermore, I questioned what this meant about Percy Abrams. According to everyone in Falconwood, he was a stand-up guy, but what kind of stand-up guy beats his wife?

"I know this is hard," I said, peeking at Sammy in my

rearview mirror. "Remember that you asked me to look into it for a reason. Alyssa needed a grown-up to help her."

Sammy relented and peeled his gaze from the passing trees. "I know you're doing your best. I just thought I could help her too."

"You are helping her," I said. "By telling me what you know about her. For now, though, we've got different business to attend to. Do me a favor? Reach into the side pocket of that camera bag and grab the little piece of paper in there." Sammy did as told and extracted the Post-It note that Della had written all the photography sites on. "What's the first thing on the list?"

"Brighton Park," Sammy read off. "Ooh, if we go to Brighton Park, can we get sausages at Stan's?"

"We sure can."

Sammy and I spent the rest of the afternoon scouting locations around Falconwood. In Brighton Park, I got a few decent shots of the kids' playground, the community clubhouse, and Stan's Sausage truck, where Sammy happily chowed down on a bratwurst that was easily twice the size of his foot. Thankfully, it was too cold for kids to make use of the playground, so the snow from yesterday was perfectly preserved on the bright yellow slides. The clubhouse was similarly coated in snow. I took idyllic shots of the outside before asking the manager for permission to shoot the inside. Sammy played ping pong against the wall in the recreation center while I snapped pictures of the community room, gym, and indoor pool. A few families made use of the amenities, so I asked them if they would be willing to have their pictures on the Falconwood website. They all eagerly agreed, so I took several photos featuring smiling kids and their picture-perfect parents.

After Brighton Park, we hit the library and the town square. The library was one of the first buildings to be constructed in Falconwood, back in the 1800s, which made it rather historic. It had a plaque on the front door to share the details of its construction. Sammy read it aloud in a hilarious imitation of "an important old man" as I took pictures of the library's historic front porch and swinging bench. In the town square, I made sure to highlight the storefronts as well as the small ice skating rink that was full of kids blowing off their after-school energy. Then I brought Sammy to the Black Cat Café to warm up with a hot chocolate and take a few extra photos of the inside. Mason heartily consented to being featured on the website and put so many marshmallows on top of Sammy's hot chocolate that the kid started bouncing off the walls. As Sammy flicked sugar packets across the café and blew paper balls out of straws, I beckoned Mason over.

"First of all," I said, gesturing to Sammy, "that's your fault. Second, do you know where this garden thing is? Della said I should photograph it for the website, but I've never heard of it."

Mason squinted at Della's neat cursive. "Oh, the Garden of Marble. It's one of Falconwood's well-kept secrets. A lot of the locals plan weddings and other parties there. It's a few miles north of here. Make a right on Dean Road, go down a bit, and take a left at the ivy-covered wall. There's no sign, so you'll have to keep an eye out."

"Thanks." I folded up the note and slipped it back into my pocket. "Come on, Sammy. Let's get this show on the road."

I DROVE past the entrance to the Garden of Marble twice before I finally saw the driveway. It was hidden behind the ivy Mason spoke of, and the mirrors of the car pulled the plants away from the red brick wall surrounding the property. It had been a while since anyone had been through here. Apparently winter weddings weren't all that popular in Falconwood. Once inside, a hedge at least ten feet tall separated the parking lot from the actual Garden of Marble, keeping it a complete mystery. I parked the car in the first spot and helped Sammy out.

"This place is creepy," Sammy said. The sugar crash was hitting him quickly. He wobbled toward an opening in the hedge, the only sign of an entrance to the garden.

"You think this is creepy, but the Abram Mansion isn't?"

"What are we doing here?"

"Taking pictures, like we did around town," I said, slinging my camera bag over my shoulder. "Do you think we're supposed to let someone know we're here before we go in?"

There was no booth at the entrance to the garden or any information on whether or not this was a ticketed experience. Sammy tiptoed to the gap in the hedges and peered inside.

"Whoa," he said. "Come check this out, Peyton!"

I joined him at the hedge, looked in, and let out a surprised gasp. The Garden of Marble stood up to its name. It was equal parts nature and stone. Statues of all shapes and sizes were placed in a meticulous pattern, each one decorated with beautifully tended vines and flowers. The low hedge maze offered visitors a footpath through the garden that took you past the best places to view each statue. The middle of the maze was kept open, like an aisle for a wedding. At the very end, a statue of Aphrodite waited under a vine-covered archway, the perfect place to take your vows.

Sammy pranced off, dragging his fingers lightly across the tops of the hedges as he went. I followed after him, worried he might cut himself on a hidden thorn. The flowers in bloom were perennial, meant to withstand the harsh winter weather, though I found the remnants of Easter lilies along our path to the first statue. From the looks of a few different dead flowers, the garden was designed to bloom no matter the season. Sammy stopped at the first statue and attempted to read the plaque below it.

"'Moon in Winter' is an abstract form by Samuel B. Kross—we have the same name!—commissioned in 1998 by the Falconwood Board of Art for the Winter Fair," Sammy said, doing his best with the big words. "What's a board of art?"

"It's a collection of people who decide what to put in a garden like this," I explained, "though I'm surprised a town as small as Falconwood ever had one."

"Falconwood used to be bigger." Sammy stroked his chin with his thumb and forefinger, examining the statue with a narrowed eye. "At least, it used to be more important."

"How do you know that?"

"Alyssa told me."

The sculpture—Moon in Winter—was crafted out of steel despite the garden's title. It featured a huge orb that appeared to be floating above the hedges, though if you looked from just the right angle, you could see the support piece that kept the moon aloft.

"They used to have parties here," Sammy went on. He reached up to touch the support beam, as if to make sure it was actually there. "I remember now. Alyssa told me her favorite statue was right in the middle."

"Which one? Aphrodite?"

He shook his head. "Not in the aisle. In the middle of the maze."

With Sammy in the lead, we worked our way around the Garden of Marble, pausing briefly at each statue to determine if it was the one Alyssa spoke about. We passed busts of Falconwood's famous historical figures, nude statues so intricate that I covered Sammy's eyes, and more abstract sculptures that needed hefty help from the imagination to make any sense. At last, we reached a statue that jogged Sammy's memory. It was simple and beautiful, featuring a full-figured woman holding a newborn infant in her arms. Though she looked down on the child with obvious love, the woman's stone expression also carried grief.

"Is this it?" I asked Sammy quietly, as if to refrain from disturbing the woman in her moment of pain.

"Yes," Sammy said. "It's sad, isn't it?"

The sculpture was titled "With You, Always," but unlike the other sculptures in the garden, the plaque did not tell us who created or commissioned the piece. As I studied the infant's closed eyelids and slack fingers, I realized Sammy had grasped the point of the sculpture before I had. The mother's grieving expression suddenly made sense: her son was stillborn.

"Yes, it's very sad," I replied. My voice cracked. Why was this Alyssa's favorite statue? Death was a concept not many children her age fully understood. Then again, Sammy had immediately understood the sculpture as soon as we walked up to it. Maybe kids had a better understanding of life and death than the rest of us did.

Sammy walked up to the statue and dusted the snow off the infant's head and the mother's shoulders. Then he planted one kiss on the mother's forehead and another on the baby's. When he climbed down, he took my hand in his.

"I don't think you should take pictures here," he said. "We should go now."

"Whatever you say, Sammy."

After dropping Sammy off at Theo's—with no mention of the Garden of Marble to his mother—I swung by Della and Basil's airstream to pick Ben up from his first day of work. Since Ben and Basil were working late in the greenhouse, Della invited me inside for a cup of tea, the leaves for which she'd grown and dried herself. As the kettle boiled on the stove, she sat down at the tiny table across from me, groaning as she massaged her knees.

"Everything okay?" I asked.

"It's this weather," she said. "The cold makes my joints ache, especially when it's too windy to go hiking. Movement keeps you healthy. Remember that as you get older. How'd your first day of photographing the town go?"

"Pretty well." I offered her my camera for her to take a look at the pictures. "Sammy and I hit a few of the places on your list. What do you think?"

She browsed through the pictures, nodding her approval. "You've got a good idea for this stuff, unless Sammy set up your shots for you."

"A few of them," I admitted. "We also went to the Garden of Marble, but Sammy didn't want me to take pictures there."

The kettle whistled, and Della returned my camera to steep the tea. "You were alone, weren't you? That place whispers if you're alone."

"It whispers?"

"You didn't hear it?" She placed a spoonful of tea in a hand-made strainer, then lowered the strainer into the pot. "Places like that garden talk to you. It's like everyone who's ever passed through there leaves a word or a phrase, like the statues collect voices to use for themselves."

I suppressed a shudder. "Have you seen the statue of the mother and her child?"

"With You, Always."

"I was wondering if you knew who made it or commissioned it," I said. "There was no information on the plaque, and it looked familiar to me."

She swirled the pot with a practiced gesture to coax the flavor from the tea leaves. "I suppose you might have come across its image at the mansion. That sculpture was anonymously donated to the garden, but people always assumed Percy Abram was the one who commissioned it."

"Why would he have commissioned a piece like that?" I asked as Della poured the tea. It filled the air with the warm scent cinnamon and cloves. When she set it in front of me, I let the steam wash over my pores. "I didn't know he was into art."

"It wasn't one of his main interests," Della said, sitting across from me again. "But that sculpture was installed in the garden shortly after rumors swirled that his wife Penelope had had a miscarriage. They were expecting a son. It was early on in the pregnancy, but both Percy and Penelope were devastated."

I swallowed my voice with a sip of tea. With the assumptions I'd made about Percy and Penelope's relationship, I couldn't help but wonder if it Penelope had lost the baby due to natural issues or if Percy was somehow at fault. Before I found the courage to ask Della, Ben and Basil returned from the greenhouse. Ben's pink cheeks were smudged with dirt, and he carried a legal pad covered with cramped notes. His harried expression didn't match Basil's look of elation.

"First day in the books!" Basil announced, patting Ben on the back. Ben stumbled and caught himself on the back of my chair. "I might have overworked him, Peyton. My apologies."

Ben took a sip of my tea and replied, "It's no problem, Basil. Really."

I could hear the exhaustion in his voice, so I gathered my camera and coat. "Thanks for everything. I'm going to get this one home."

"Wait a minute." Basil ambled off to the 'office,' a pull-down desk near the back of the airstream, and came back with an envelope. He handed it to Ben. "That's for your hard work."

"Already?" Ben asked. "Shouldn't we do this every two weeks or so?"

"Think of it as an advance," Basil replied. "A gesture of good faith. Today went well. I'm looking forward to working with you in the future."

I helped Ben into the car as Della and Basil waved from the airstream. Once we'd pulled away from their little plot of land, I asked Ben, "So how did it really go? Because you look like you just buried a body."

Ben leaned his forehead against the window and closed his eyes. "I don't know if this is going to work out, Peyton. Basil just talks and talks. I don't think he knows what he's saying half the time. The notes I took? I have no idea what they say. Every time I tried to ask a question, I got an answer that made me think of a hundred new questions. That guy is senile, I'm telling you."

We drove through the town square. It was twilight on a Friday night, and all of Falconwood's teenagers were out for a night on the town. They loitered up and down the sidewalks, nursing iced coffees despite the dip in temperature. As we cruised past them, I saw a gaggle of boys wearing Falconwood High letterman jackets. They tossed a football between them while a group of girls looked up and giggled.

"God, do you ever wish things were still that simple?" Ben asked, gazing at the high schoolers with a forlorn expression. "Growing up sucks. I peaked in high school."

"Don't say that," I told him. "If you say it, you'll start to believe it. How much did Basil give you anyway?"

As we cleared the town square and made our way into the dark woods that led to the mansion, Ben fished the envelope out of his pocket and took out a handful of bills. "Holy crap," he said. "There's a thousand dollars cash here."

I nearly slammed on the brakes and made a U-turn. *"What?"*

He spread the bills out for me to see, counting them again in my line of sight. "Eight hundred, nine hundred, one thousand."

"We can't take that," I said. "We have to give it back. Basil must have made a mistake."

"He said it was an advance," Ben countered.

Something kept me driving toward the mansion, even as my mouth fought against it. "Ben, this is practically charity. We can't let them give us that kind of money."

"Why not? I'm working for it." He carefully put the money back in the envelope and tucked it safely away. "If he keeps paying me like this, we can resume renovations a lot sooner than we thought. Wasn't that our goal to begin with?"

"Yeah, but—"

"Look, I'll ask Basil to clarify what my pay is," Ben said, patting my thigh. "I can have him put something in writing if you want, but if he insists on paying me like this, I'm not going to say no."

I turned into our hidden driveway, thinking over our options in my head. As the mansion cast its shadow over the car, I caught sight of a little face in the attic window. Something about that face—always hiding in fear—caught my heart in a cage and squeezed tight.

"Fine," I told Ben. "But this time around, I want a say in the renovations."

16

*I*t turned out Basil had purposely intended to pay Ben as much as he did that first time, and though I argued with Della that it was too much, the Gordons refused to give us any less. It wasn't until Basil made the point that Ben was making almost the same amount of money for his last writing job that I finally gave up. We needed the money anyway, and if Basil was satisfied with Ben's skills, there was no point in wasting any more of my breath. As a result, Jim and his crew returned to work on the renovations two weeks later, and they dove back in with a dedication I hadn't seen since Sammy attempted to eat a whole bag of candy in the ten minutes it took his mother to order pizza from the closest pie place.

"Falconwood's a bore, ma'am," Jim told me one morning, covered in dust as his crew excavated a portion of the mansion we'd yet to step foot in. "Not much work to do here. We've traveled a few miles to fix a roof and mend a bathroom, but it's nothing like the project you got here. This is my dream job."

"I'm glad you're back at it," I told him.

The only problem with the renovations resuming was that Jim preferred someone to be home at all times to supervise. Just in case something went wrong or he had a question about our wallpaper preference, he requested either me or Ben to be available during business hours. Ben and I had since worked out an arrangement. I took the morning shift at the mansion while Ben gathered information with Basil at the greenhouse. They both returned to the mansion in the afternoon, working in Ben's study to put together ideas for the book while I went to pick up Sammy from school. Often, Della tagged along with Ben and Basil. While I was gone, she played maid around the mansion, cleaning up and putting our things away, as if she owed us a debt instead of the other way around.

"It's no trouble," she insisted one night after I'd returned from dropping Sammy off at Theo's.

I was exhausted. We had spent the afternoon doing reshoots all over town, since the snow had melted enough to see the ground. Baylor, the man who recruited me for the job in the first place, was picky about how he wanted the photos for the website to look. Often, I left Sammy to explore the children's massive section of the library while Baylor and I went through my pictures one by one. It was meticulous work. Baylor examined each picture with his nose so close to the camera, he fogged up the display with his breath. He had also tasked me with re-imagining the website, and I regretted ever mentioning that I'd maintained my own website a few years ago when I was photographing weddings and other events. He looked over every detail and link, obsessed over color schemes, and asked if I knew any graphic designers who could give Falconwood a logo that tourists would recognize "like Disney World." Then, at the end of the day, he wrote me a check for twenty-one dollars.

"Really, you don't have to do that," I told Della as she scrubbed the kitchen counters. She'd already made dinner for everyone under the roof, including Jim and his crew. The lentil soup warmed my insides and made my eyelids droop. Della, however, cleaned with unadulterated vigor. Her hands shook as she rinsed the sponge under the tap. "Are you okay?"

"Oh, I'm perfectly fine," she replied, dropping the sponge in the sink for the second time. "Old age gets to you every once in a while."

This wasn't particularly true in Della's case. I'd never seen a woman her age so strong and stout. No, her shakiness was definitely the result of something other than her age. "It's the mansion, isn't it? You've been here a lot in the past couple of weeks."

"Please. This old house doesn't scare me."

"It doesn't scare me either," I said, though it was half a lie. Most days, I didn't fear the mansion or its ghostly inhabitant, but every time Alyssa threw a temper tantrum, I questioned whether or not it was safe for me and Ben to make it to the six-month mark. "But I hear whispers in the walls, like the ones you mentioned about the Garden of Marble."

Della's furious cleaning came to a halt, though she remained facing the sink. "You hear them too?"

"Since the first night we arrived here," I said. "I told Ben about them, but he never heard it. You're the only person I've met who seems to understand."

She resumed scrubbing, slowly and on the same spot over and over again. "Are you... like me?"

I had no idea what that was supposed to mean. Through general observation, I'd gathered that Della worked hard to maintain her mental health. At the very least, she treated herself for Obsessive-Compulsive Disorder and depression. If I had to guess, there was some anxiety mixed in there as well. She covered it well, hiding her symptoms behind oddities that could easily be explained away. *Was* I like her? Did I have some undiagnosed illness that allowed me to see and hear Alyssa? If that was the case, did it mean Sammy was likewise inflicted?

"I think we both know this house takes certain people in and spits others out," I told her. "If spending time here affects you in a negative fashion, don't be afraid to avoid our home. I won't be offended."

Della squeezed the extra water out of the sponge and set it on the edge of the spotless sink. "You're right. It does affect me to be here. Something about this house pulls me in, but I can't quite put my finger on what it is."

"You've made me aware of your connection to this house in the past," I reminded her. "I just want to make sure you're taking care of yourself."

"I am," she promised. "In fact, it's good for me to spend a little time here with others. Before you and Ben moved in, long ago, I explored everything on my own. I had no buffer between me and the house."

"As long as you're sure."

"I'm here for you, Ben, and Basil," Della promised. "Not to feed my interest in this house or the Abrams. To me, that makes all the difference."

DELLA BECAME a frequent fixture at the house, appearing with Ben and Basil every afternoon. I grew used to her presence and stopped fussing over her constant cleaning. It was a soothing task for her, and it left me with time to tend to Sammy and the Falconwood website. Each day as I left the house, I bid goodbye to Ben, Basil, and Della as if they were all family.

Falconwood had had a particularly warm couple of days, so when I picked up Sammy from school, many of the parents who usually drove had walked instead. The pickup loop was far less busy, and I cruised right up to the curb. Sammy was nowhere to be found until I saw a gaggle of kids behind the bushes in the middle of the courtyard. In the middle, I caught sight of

Sammy's panicked face. I put the car in park and got out, much to the chagrin of the parents in line behind me.

"Miss?" One of the teachers manning the pickup loop hurried after me as I slammed the door of my car and navigated the sea of waiting students to reach the courtyard. "Excuse me, miss? You're not allowed to leave your car in the pickup loop. The whole point—"

"That's my kid," I snarled.

In the courtyard, the circle of bigger kids pushed Sammy around. He couldn't find a way out, though he pleaded with them to let him go. I stepped over the low hedge and emerged right behind a chubby blond boy who had Sammy in hand. Sternly but safely, I pried him off of Sammy. Sammy escaped the circle and hid behind me. I knelt down, gripping the blond kid's jacket firmly with one hand to ensure I had the attention of the whole group.

"Listen here," I whispered, deadly quiet. "You may fool your teachers and parents into blaming these fights on Sammy, but I know the truth. If any one of you ever touches or talks to Sammy again, I will make sure your parents hear about it. Do you understand me?"

One by one, the kids nodded. The blond boy looked especially terrified. "You're that girl, aren't you?" he said, voice trembling. "The one who lives in the Abram Mansion?"

"What of it?"

"That place is haunted."

"It sure is," I promised. "And I'm friends with the ghost. You wouldn't want to find a ghost in your room at night, when you're safe in bed, would you?"

The blond boy furiously shook his head.

I released his jacket and patted the wrinkles out of it. "Then I suggest you keep your hands to yourself."

"Yes, ma'am."

I stood up and took Sammy by the hand. "I'll be keeping an eye on all of you. Don't forget that."

As soon as I swung Sammy over the hedge, the rest of the kids huddled together and started whispering. Surely, they were conspiring how best to tattle to their parents about my threat of sending the ghost of Abram Mansion to haunt them. I didn't care. If the other Falconwood parents ended up at my throat, I would remind them that their children were liars and bullies. At least the blame would come down on me instead of Theo. She had too much on her plate already. Ever since she'd started working more hours at the dentist's office, I'd only seen her when I dropped off Sammy. Once or twice, she had invited me to stay for dinner, but she was clearly exhausted after such long days. I made sure they had everything they needed, even running to the grocery store a few times for them, before I took my leave and headed back to the mansion.

Today, like most every other day, I treated Sammy to his promised pack of stickers and an afternoon snack at the Black Cat. He picked out some glittery dinosaurs and happily stuck them all up and down his forearm as he ate his ham and cheese sandwich in our regular booth. Like always, Mason made him a hot chocolate. We were here so often that I began asking Mason to use a natural sugar substitute in Sammy's drinks to make sure he wasn't getting too much for his age. Sammy never noticed the change in taste, and he munched happily on his side of celery and peanut butter. Since Theo was so busy, I never knew what kind of diet Sammy was getting throughout the day, but I figured I might as well feed him like I would feed my own kid.

"Sammy, have you ever met Della Gordon?" I asked him as he rearranged the stickers on his arm in a pattern he liked.

"Sure," he replied. "She babysat me a couple of times. She's weird, but I like her. Did you know you can go ice skating on her pond when it freezes?"

"I did know that." I'd seen Della's figure skates tucked away in a corner of the airstream. "Why do you think she's weird?"

"She's not like other grown-ups," Sammy informed me. "She doesn't talk to me like I'm a kid. You know how most grown-ups do? Their voices get all high-pitched, and they talk to me like I'm a baby."

"Do I do that?"

"No. That's why I like you." He moved a stegosaurus from the back of his hand to his tiny bicep. "Actually, you and Della and my mom are all a lot alike. I think so, at least."

I stirred my cappuccino. The foam was gone, but the cup was three-fourths full. After rescuing Sammy from the bullies in the schoolyard, I hadn't been in much of a mood to drink it. "I think Della might be like us. At least, I think she can hear Alyssa when she comes to visit the house."

"Oh!" Sammy's eyes lit up as he finally tore his gaze from the dinosaurs all over his skin. "*That's* who Alyssa talks about all the time!"

"Alyssa's talked about Della?"

"Yeah, she used to tell me about a woman who would come visit the mansion," Sammy said. "Alyssa really liked her because she wasn't as lonely. She tried to talk to Della, but Della didn't understand what was happening."

"She thought she was going crazy," I muttered, more to myself than to Sammy.

"I guess so," Sammy said. "Because she stopped coming. Alyssa was really sad about it."

"Well, Della's at the mansion almost every day now," I told him. "If Alyssa wanted to say hi, she could. I'm not so sure it's a good idea though."

"Because Della doesn't get it?"

"No, she thinks it's all in her head."

Sammy peeled all the stickers off, stacked them into a single sticky mess, and wrapped them in a napkin. I admired that about him. Once he was done with the stickers, he made no attempt to save them, and he had no problem throwing them away when I asked him to. If we all learned to ditch certain attachments once they were of no more use to us, we'd probably be better off.

"Are you going to tell her about Alyssa?" Sammy asked.

"I wasn't planning on it," I said. "I don't want to scare her."

"That's good," Sammy replied. "Don't scare her."

UPON RETURNING Sammy to his apartment, I noticed Theo's car was already in the parking lot. She was home early. A familiar beat-up sedan was parked next to Theo's car. I pulled in next to it and peeked into the windows. The front passenger seat was full of fast food wrappers, half-empty soda bottles, dirty napkins, and a few items of questionable nature including a small baggie full of white pills. I hurried Sammy away from the vehicle and up the steps to his apartment, only to push him behind me when angry voices emanated from the open door.

"Theo?" I stepped inside, keeping Sammy fully hidden.

Theo stood across from an unfamiliar man. I'd never seen him in town before, and from the looks of Theo's angered expression, he certainly was not meant to be in this apartment. The man was around my age. His hair was shaved close to his scalp. He had thin cheekbones and a biting grin that never seemed to go away. He wore a baggy gray sweatshirt and kept his hands in his pockets.

"Who's this?" the man said, his grin spreading as his eyes raked me from my head to my toes. "The babysitter? Damn, Theo. Nice job."

Theo rushed me out of the apartment and shut the door

behind her, closing the three of us off from the suspicious man. "Peyton, I need you to take Sammy to your house for a while."

"Why? Who is that guy?"

"Please," Theo begged, rubbing Sammy's shoulders as he hugged her around the knees. "I don't want Sammy around him. Please just get Sammy out of here. Once I get rid of him, I'll come pick Sammy up."

"I don't like the idea of leaving you alone with him," I whispered. "What if something happens?"

"This isn't the first time I've dealt with him." She glanced nervously behind her as something shattered in the apartment. "Please. I'm begging you."

"Okay," I said at last. "But if I don't hear from you in thirty minutes, I'm calling the police."

Theo kissed Sammy on the forehead and pushed him into the safety of my arms. "That's fair. I'll see you later."

With that, she vanished once more into the apartment. Through the narrow gap in the door, I caught sight of the man's enigmatic grin again. Whoever he was, I hated him already. "Come on, Sammy," I said, piloting him away from the apartment. "Looks like you finally get to hang out at the mansion for a little bit."

In the parking lot, I buckled Sammy in but couldn't bring myself to drive away, not while Theo was alone in her apartment with that man. I dialed a number on my phone.

"Hello?" A familiar voice answered.

"Officer Spaughton?" I asked. "It's Peyton Fletcher."

"Hi, Peyton. How many times have I asked you to call me Hillary?" Paperwork rustled on her end of the line, like she was finishing up some stuff at the police precinct before packing up for the day. "What's the matter? Did someone break into your house again?"

Hillary Spaughton was the one and only officer in Falconwood that I was personally acquainted with. Before I knew about Alyssa, I was convinced squatters were breaking into the mansion to spend the night there. Hillary came out more than once to search the place and ensure Ben and I were safe.

"No, everything at the house has been great," I told her. "I'm actually calling about Theo Baker. There's a guy at her apartment who seems potentially violent. Theo asked me to let her sort it out on her own—I've got Sammy—but I'm worried about her. Is there any way you could—?"

"I'll swing by," Hillary said before I'd finished my sentence. "I'm about to leave the office anyway."

"Thank you so much."

"Not a problem. The Bakers are good people."

After hanging up, I finally pulled out of the parking lot. Sammy was unusually quiet, and when I checked on him in the mirror, his face was a pale, gluey color. "You okay back there?"

He craned his neck to watch the apartment disappear in the back windshield. "That was my dad, wasn't it?"

It was my guess too. Theo had never said a word to me about Sammy's father, so I always assumed he was completely out of the picture. When I thought about the kind of guy Theo might be attracted to, the man in the apartment was not what I pictured.

"I don't know, buddy," I said truthfully.

"Do you think he's going to hurt her?"

Falconwood receded in the background as I drove into the woods. "I hope not."

BASIL AND DELLA'S environmentally-friendly car was still parked outside the mansion when we arrived, but the house was quiet as I took Sammy in. I walked him inside with both hands on his shoulders. When we stepped over the threshold, I half-expected

Alyssa to materialize right in front of us to greet her friend, but we were only met with the warmth of the dark foyer. Ben and Basil's voices traveled to our ears from Ben's study, but Della was nowhere to be found.

"Come on, Sammy," I said. "I'll get you something to eat downstairs."

Della wasn't in the kitchen either. I wondered if she was off cleaning some other area of the house. Uneasiness stole through me, though I tried to stave it off. My nervousness for Theo had followed me to the mansion and applied itself to the situation here. Della's unusual absence had me on edge.

"Della usually makes dinner," I told Sammy apologetically. For once, the kitchen smelled of nothing at all. None of Della's home-grown spices or herbs filled the air. "I can make you a peanut butter sandwich?"

Sammy stared at the new door that led to the back of the mansion, where the courtyard opened up to overgrown topiaries and a massive swimming pool that stood empty save for dead leaves. The old door had featured a doggy entrance. Not so long ago, Sammy repeatedly snuck into the house through the small gap in security.

"Sure," he said, distant.

As I gathered the ingredients from the pantry, my phone rang, displaying Officer Spaughton's number. "Hey, Hillary. Is everything okay?"

"Seems like it," Hillary replied to my great relief. "I went by the apartment and knocked on the door. The guy bolted as soon as he saw me. My guess is he's got a record if he's that uncomfortable around cops."

"Theo's okay though?"

"She's shaken up," said Hillary. "She wouldn't tell me who the guy was. She did, however, assume you'd called me to check in on her, so I'm sorry for ratting you out. She said to tell you she's on her way to pick up Sammy, and she'll be there shortly. I'm waiting outside in my car until she leaves, just to make sure this guy doesn't show up again. Anything else I can do for you?"

"Nope. Thanks again, Hillary. I appreciate it."

"I appreciate women who look out for their friends," she said. "Thanks for the call, Peyton. Don't hesitate to use my number in the future."

I hung up, frosted peanut butter across Sammy's sandwich, and placed it in front of him with a bag of cheddar crackers and a glass of apple juice. "Your mom's okay. She's on her way."

He gazed through the window of the back door, seemingly entranced by the empty courtyard. "Uh-huh."

"Yo, Sammy." I waved a hand in front of his face. "You zoning out on me?"

Out of nowhere, he burst into tears, bawling his eyes out when he'd been perfectly fine two seconds ago. I shoved his plate aside and took his hands in mine, searching for a physical reason for his freak-out. "Sammy. Hey! Buddy, what's wrong?"

He continued crying, sobbing and heaving for breath. His chest rose and fell in sporadic bursts, but he wouldn't tell me anything, no matter how much I pled with him. His sandwich sat uneaten. The white bread looked pathetic against the white plate, as colorless as Sammy's face had been in the car on the drive home.

"Sammy, please," I begged. "If you don't tell me what's wrong, I can't help—"

A shrill scream cut into our conversation. I nearly jumped out of my skin, and Sammy's sobs increased in volume. The scream went on for several seconds, paused, then resumed in a similar fashion. It was coming from outside, in the courtyard. I left Sammy crying at the table, unable to help him at the moment, and barreled through the back door. It was the first time I'd walked into the courtyard since we moved into the mansion. The garden was so overgrown that I hadn't dared to take it on. Night had fallen, and the misshapen topiaries cast eerie shadows across the tangles of branches, weeds, and vines.

"Hello?" I called, swatting branches out of my way as I followed the hoarse scream through the immense garden. "Hello! I'm here to help! Where are you?"

The screamer did not respond except to take a deep breath and resume the constant, earsplitting note. The volume grew as I followed the sound. At last, I broke through the dead branches of a thick hedge and found the empty swimming pool. In the deep end, where the dead leaves had gathered near the drain, stood Della—eyes wide and blank, chin tipped toward the moon, and her cheeks drawn in tight lines to accommodate her dropped, screaming mouth. She kept her arms by her sides, as if they were bound to her body with a length of rope, but her fingers were spread wide and long as if she was suffering from a constant electric shock.

I ran to the deep end and jumped into the pool. Della screamed all the while, blasting my ear drums as I took her by the shoulders and shook her. "Della! Wake up! Della, it's me. It's Peyton!"

But the older woman went on screaming, her eyes wide with terror. Tears brewed in the corners of my eyes. Like Sammy, I suddenly felt the need to sob uncontrollably. Without reason, I wrapped my arms around Della and squeezed her in a tight hug. All at once, the screaming stopped and Della's body fell from its rigidity. I caught her as she collapsed.

"Della?" I said, rocking her gently. "Are you okay?"

Basil burst through the hole in the hedge, and Ben limped in a few seconds later. When Basil saw Della in my arms, he jumped into the pool and ran to us. "My dear! Della, what's the matter?"

Della lifted her heavy eyelids to watch all three of us peering at her. "Wh—where am I?"

"You're at the Abram Mansion," I told her.

"Ben and Peyton's house," Basil clarified. "The Abrams don't live here anymore. Darling, what happened? Why were you screaming?"

I steadied Della as she got her feet back underneath her, though I didn't let go until she gave me a sturdy nod.

"I fell into the pool," Della said. "It was an accident. I couldn't get out. That's all."

"You were screaming for at least a minute," I told her, "and you looked like you weren't—I don't know—*here*."

Della patted my hands. "What a silly thing to say. I'm right here, aren't I?"

"You know what I meant."

"I'm not so sure I do." Della went to Basil and rested her head on his shoulder as he wrapped a comforting arm around her. "Are you ready to go home?"

"Yes, let's get you to bed," Basil said, guiding his wife into the shallow end and up the steps. He kept a steady hand on her at all times. "Will you tell me what happened?"

"I fell into the pool," she repeated with the exact same inflection. "It was an accident."

"All right, my dear."

I followed them up to the main level of the garden, letting the older couple get a head start as I hung back to wait for Ben.

"What the hell was that?" Ben whispered. "No way she just fell into the pool and started screaming like that. Why was she out here anyway?"

"I don't know," I whispered back. "You should have seen the way she was standing out here when I found her. It was like something had possessed her."

He hushed me as we all met back at the kitchen. As Basil

helped Della into her coat, Sammy munched on his peanut butter sandwich. Inexplicably, he was calm. The only evidence of his freak-out were the tear stains on his collar.

"We'll be right back, Sammy," I told him. "We're going to walk Basil and Della out."

Outside, I helped Basil get Della situated in the passenger seat of their small car. Ben dropped a USB device into the cupholder. "That's the work for today," he told Basil. "Look it over if you get a chance. I hope you feel better, Della."

Della waved weakly in thanks.

"Are you sure you're okay?" I asked Della in an undertone as Basil made his way around the car to the driver's seat. "Was it the house? Did you hear the voices?"

"I'd like to go home now," Della replied. She pulled her door shut, forcing me to move out of the way. "We'll see you tomorrow."

As they pulled out of the driveway, Theo's car rumbled in. Basil waved to her through the windshield as they passed each other, and Theo waved back. As Theo parked in the spot the Gordons had just vacated, Ben kissed my cheek.

"I'll leave you to it," he said. "Hey, Theo."

"Hey, Ben," she said, getting out of her car. "Sorry for the trouble. I didn't mean for Peyton to be babysitting all day."

"Eh, you can have her," Ben joked. "I'll be in my office."

As Ben went inside, Theo hugged me hello. "How is he?"

"He's eating a sandwich in the kitchen," I said. "How are you?"

"Iffy," she admitted as I led her inside. "Thanks for calling Officer Spaughton by the way. I'm not sure how long he would've stayed if you hadn't. Can we talk up here? I don't want Sammy to hear this."

I leaned against the back of the couch in the foyer and crossed my arms. "What is it you don't want him to hear?"

"That guy in my apartment?" she said. "That was Dylan Miller, and you've probably already guessed that he's Sammy's father."

"It crossed my mind," I told her, "but I can't see you with a guy like that."

Theo paced across the floor runner that led from the front door to the kitchen stairs. "Things were different back then. I was young and stupid. I came from a cookie-cutter lifestyle where my parents set everything up for me. When I met Dylan, he made me feel adventurous and daring. It wasn't long before I ended up spending all of my time with him, and it wasn't long after that he started mistreating me."

A lump grew in my throat. "I'm sorry, Theo."

"It's fine," she said, though it obviously wasn't. "When I got pregnant, I knew I one thing: I couldn't let Dylan near the kid. One night, when Dylan was high off his ass, I ran away. I did my research. I found a town that was so small and insignificant that you couldn't find it on a map unless you had a magnifying glass."

"Falconwood," I confirmed.

"I changed my name," Theo said. "I dropped off the map, and I raised Sammy by myself. I didn't think Dylan would ever find us."

"How did he?"

"I still don't know." She squeezed the bridge of her nose as if she were trying to keep tears from falling. "He wouldn't tell me. Remember when I found that two hundred dollars in my mailbox? It was from him."

"What? Why would he give you money?"

"He says he wants to make up for the past," Theo said. "He found out about Sammy, and he wants to be a part of his life now."

"You said no, right?"

"I said hell no." She stopped pacing to lean her head against my shoulder. "What am I going to do? I don't feel like Sammy's safe as long as he's around."

I rubbed her back, doing my best to comfort her. "Sammy will never be alone. He'll either be with you, with me, or at school with his teachers. Dylan can't get to him."

"But he knows where we live," Theo whispered against my sweater. "He knows I lied to him all those years ago."

"It's okay," I said, cradling her close. "Everything's going to be okay."

But as Theo cried quietly into my shoulder, I thought of Sammy's outburst in the kitchen and began to wonder if this was just the start to all of our problems.

17

*W*hen Basil returned to the mansion the next day to continue his work with Ben, it was without Della by his side. He sported dark circles under his eyes and his step lacked its usual bounce. When he arrived, he attempted to slip past me and into Ben's study, but I followed along behind him.

"How's Della?" I asked him. "She didn't want to come today?"

"She's fine," Basil reported, walking briskly through the corridors. He'd been to Ben's office so often now, it was as if he too lived here at the mansion. "I'm not sure what Della's told you about her mental health conditions—"

"She's implied a few things."

Basil stopped short and pivoted on his heel to face me. "This house makes her unwell. I told her that years ago when she first discovered it, and I reminded her of it again last time. It doesn't matter who owns the house or how many times it's renovated. You could tear it down and rebuild it, and still Della would be trapped in its thrall."

"It's just a house, Basil."

"Not to her." He resumed his swift pace. "If you care about my wife's health, I would encourage you not to invite her around here again. I mean no offense. You and Ben are still more than welcome to visit us at the airstream. In fact, neither of you have anything to do with this at all. It's simply the house."

He knocked on the door of the office, and Ben popped his head out. "Hey, Basil. I didn't hear you come in. Are you ready to work?"

"Ready as ever," Basil said, saluting Ben as he receded into the office. Basil added to me, "I do my best to take care of my wife, Peyton. She's been so well ever since she stopped coming to this place. Please make sure the process is not reversed."

"Of course," I stammered. "I want Della to be okay."

"Then we're on the same page." Basil tipped his head in acknowledgement. "If you'll excuse me, we have a lot of work to do. Della is resting at home, though she expressed interest in visiting the Black Cat later. If you happen to see her, kindly remind her to check in with me every once in a while. I tend to worry."

"Sure thing, Basil."

The office door closed in my face before the words had fully made it past my lips. I gazed at the wood grain, picking shapes out of the squiggly lines. Never once had I experienced this side of Basil. He was strict and cold, whereas before he had always given off a goofy vibe of comfort. Did he blame me for Della's breakdown yesterday? Technically, Della had returned to the mansion at my request, before Ben and Basil started working together. Perhaps Basil thought it was my fault that she was in decline.

DESPITE BASIL'S clear indication that I should leave Della alone, I went looking for her. I drove out to their plot of land and knocked on the door of the airstream first but received no answer.

"Della?" I called, rapping lightly on the window. "It's Peyton. Just wanted to drop by and make sure you were okay."

There were no signs that anyone was home. Against my better judgement, I cupped my hands to the window and peered inside the back of the airstream, where the bed was. It was neatly made with the blankets tucked over the pillows. Della was not resting, nor was she present in the airstream at all. Had she headed to the Black Cat already? Basil had made it sound like she needed the morning to recuperate. For good measure, I walked the perimeter of their land, checking the greenhouse and Della's herb garden—which she tended to even in winter—for signs of her. She was nowhere to be found. Finally, I left the Gordons' place and drove to the Black Cat.

"Hey, Mason," I said, peeling off my gloves as I approached the counter. Mason was busy constructing a cat and a koi pond out of steamed milk foam on the surface of two adjacent cappuccinos. "Have you see Della Gordon around? Did she happen to come through today?"

"Nope," Mason said, his brow furrowing as he shaped a tiny fish with professional hesitance. "She's usually in here every day around nine o'clock, but she didn't show. With anyone else, I'd worry, but Della does this on occasion."

"Does what?"

"Disappears." Mason shrugged and accidentally decapitated his koi fish. He set down the milk. "Damn. Anyway, you didn't know?"

I sat on one of the high stools at the counter as Mason gave up his foam art and automatically started working on my usual order. "That Della randomly vanishes? No, I didn't. What's that all about?"

"I only know rumors," he said. "As long as the Gordons have lived in Falconwood, Della goes missing for a few days each year. No one knows where she heads off to. Some say she camps out in the mountains because she misses being in the wilderness. Others are less kind."

"What do the others say?" I asked, leaning in.

Mason checked to make sure none of his other customers were listening before he replied. "A few think Della's been to rehab. A few more think she admits herself to a mental health facility to maintain her state of mind. Either way, everyone suspects their marriage isn't as keen as it seems."

"That's ridiculous," I told him. "Have you seen them together? They're the definition of peas in a pod. They take care of each other."

"I'm not saying *I* believe any of it." Mason clutched a hand to his heart. "Basil and Della are always so sweet when they come in here. But you have to admit it's strange… don't you think?"

"Maybe," I murmured, watching espresso dribble into a fresh cup. "Or maybe there's something we don't know about the Gordons."

Mason fired up the steamer again. "You said it, honey."

AFTER A QUICK MEETING at the library to tidy up some loose ends regarding the new Falconwood website, I headed to Sammy's elementary school thirty minutes before the teachers opened the pickup loop. Theo's debacle with Dylan yesterday had me on edge. I kept expecting to see his ugly sedan pull around the corner and tail my bumper. In any case, I wanted to make good on my promise to Theo that Sammy would never be alone, so I parked on the curb just outside the loop and waited for school to let out. Last night, after we had put Sammy to bed in one of the guest rooms, Theo and I sat up for hours to talk about the situation.

"I can't believe he found us," she had said. The glass of bourbon I'd given her was pressed to her forehead, and the ice-cold condensation dripped down her temple. "When I left him, I left *everything*. Do you know what this means?"

"That he's a stalker?" I answered sharply. "It's the only way he could have tracked you down."

"He wouldn't confirm it, but I'm guessing he asked my parents where I was." She groaned, set the glass down, and rolled over the back of the couch so her legs were sticking up in the air. "I am *so* stupid."

"Why would your parents have told him where you were?" I asked her, sitting like a normal person beside her. "Don't they know the situation?"

"No, actually," she said. "As you might have imagined, my parents weren't particularly fond of my rebellious stage. When I told them I was pregnant, they demanded I marry Dylan because" —she used air quotes— "'we weren't those kind of people.' They said it was my only option. Getting rid of it was a no-no, and having a baby out of wedlock was the biggest social faux pas where we lived." She put on a Southern Belle type of accent. "The gals at the country club will have a field day when they hear about this!"

"You didn't tell them what a loser Dylan was?"

"Love is a tricky thing, Peyton," said Theo sardonically. "As is pride. Between the two, I was paralyzed. Too 'in love' and too proud to admit to my parents that I'd been wrong. They never met Dylan, but they were determined to make me ride out the consequences for my actions, and I sure as hell wasn't doing that by marrying him."

"And you never considered the other way out?"

"I did," Theo said pensively. "But it wasn't for me. My parents raised me religiously, and though I eventually stopped going along with it, I still feel something that ties me—ties all of us—to a bigger picture. I had to keep Sammy. I wanted him, even if I didn't want Dylan, and it's worked out better than I could have ever imagined. I love the person I've grown into because of the challenges of raising Sammy on my own. If I hadn't done all of this, I don't think I would like myself much at all."

"You're pretty amazing," I agreed, "but what are you going to do about Dylan?"

"As soon as he showed up, I had half a mind to pack everything up, move out of Falconwood, and disappear again." She ran her fingers through her long hair, separating the intricate tangles. "Then I realized Falconwood is mine and Sammy's home. Dylan is the one who doesn't belong here, and hell if I'm going to let him chase me out of the one place I've felt most comfortable."

"So you're standing your ground?"

"Damn right I am." She clinked her bourbon against my glass of water. "But I need your help to do it. Dylan's not going to give up easily. If I don't have a team to support me—you, Ben, Hillary—"

"You can count on me," I had assured her. "I won't let anything happen to you or Sammy."

NEAR DAWN, Hillary had come by the mansion to make sure Theo and Sammy were all right. Theo and I had fallen asleep on the couch, and Sammy slept soundly through the night in the guest room. Hillary had valiantly escorted them home, then checked the block to make sure Dylan wasn't hanging around in his creepy car. It was only after Theo and Sammy left that I realized nothing spooky had happened that night, despite Sammy's presence in the house. In fact, Alyssa had been quiet the entire time Sammy was at the mansion, and the only blip in my radar was Sammy's weird outburst during Della's simultaneous freak-out. My head kept trying to connect the two occurrences, but there was no immediate path from Sammy's cry fest to Della's screaming fit. All I could do was let Officer Spaughton walk Sammy and Theo out to their car and promise to pick Sammy up later.

Now, as I waited in the elementary school's parking lot, it occurred to me that perhaps one of the safest things for Sammy and Theo would be for them to move into our house until Dylan left town. Were it not for the ghost child that haunted the east wing, I would have invited them right away, but considering Sammy's sixth sense, it didn't feel like the best idea. I hated being in such a position, where one choice could either help or hurt my friend and her son in a dramatic fashion. The last thing I needed was for Theo to catch on to what Sammy experienced at the mansion.

As the end of the school day grew closer, the usual swarm of parents' cars and minivans came around the corner. I quickly pulled into the pickup loop so I could be first to pick up Sammy, but when the bell rang and the kids poured out of the building, Sammy wasn't among that group. I was forced to pull out of the pickup loop, make the U-turn, and try again. With every additional pass, my heart hammered faster against my rib cage. This had happened once before when Theo picked Sammy up, but today was different. Theo and I had agreed last night that I would be the one to fetch Sammy today, and there were no texts on my phone to inform me of altered plans. I dialed Theo, but she didn't answer, so I dialed Hillary's number next. Before she answered, Sammy's little head finally popped up out of the crowd. With a surge of relief coursing through me, I hung up the phone and opened the door for him.

"Hey, kiddo," I said cheerfully, trying to disguise my receding panic. "Good to see you. How come you're always one of the last kids to get out of class?"

"Mrs. Delacruz lets me stay after to finish my drawings." Sammy climbed into his borrowed booster seat and strapped himself in. "She knows I don't like going into the courtyard with the other kids."

"Oh. That's nice of her."

"Mm-hmm. Do you think we can go to a different sticker store today?" he asked politely. "I got all of the ones I liked from the other one."

I turned on my blinker to move off the curb and back into the pickup lane. "Actually, Sammy, I'm on strict orders to take you straight home and keep you there. It'll be fun though. We can make a pillow fort."

"Is this because of my dad?"

"Your mom doesn't want you calling him that."

"But that's who he is." He withdrew a plastic dinosaur from his coat pocket and made whooshing noises as he set it against the background of the window. "He's kind of creepy for a dad. I thought dads were supposed to be nice."

"Not all dads," I muttered.

At Theo and Sammy's apartment, I made good on my promise to build a pillow fort. We pulled all the cushions off the sofa, rearranged them into pillars, then draped sheets across the top for a roof. Inside, I stacked blankets and throw pillows to keep Sammy comfortable then gave him Theo's laptop so he could watch some weird animated movie about trolls that all the other kids were supposedly talking about. While Sammy camped out in the fort, I made him an afternoon snack—a hard-boiled egg, peanut butter crackers, and green grapes because he didn't like the red ones—then took up a watchdog position at the window that looked over the street below. All afternoon, I scanned the parking lot for the bakery downstairs, watching customers come and go. Not once did I see Dylan's muddy sedan, but when Theo's keys rattled in the lock, I jumped to my feet.

"It's just me," Theo said wearily. Grocery bags and exhaustion weighed her shoulders down. "Any trouble today?"

I relieved her of her load and started putting the perishables away. "Nope. Got him home no problem. Any on your end?"

"No sign of Dylan." Theo dumped her purse on the ground and surveyed the pillow fort. "That looks intricate. Is my kid in there?"

Sammy burst out from the sheets, hugged Theo, then returned to the comfort of the fort. I gave Theo an apologetic grimace. "I'll help him put everything back before I go."

"It's fine." She kicked off her heels and sat at the kitchen counter. "Thanks for doing this, Peyton. I didn't want to drag you into my mess."

"I didn't do anything differently today that I haven't been doing for a couple of weeks," I reminded her. "I don't mind watching Sammy, and if anyone tried to hurt him, I would throw *down*." Hoping for a laugh, I mimicked a professional wrestler slamming someone into the ropes.

Theo rewarded me with a weak smile. "You're too good to us. I talked to Hillary again this afternoon. She said she hasn't seen Dylan around either."

"That's great."

"Do you want to stay for dinner? I grabbed an extra microwaveable meal just in case. It's not much, but if you want…"

She trailed off, too tired to complete her sentence. I grabbed my coat and gloves. "I'm going to head home," I said. "I promised

Ben I'd rescue him from Basil's crazy horticulture lingo by six. Are you going to be okay on your own?"

"Yeah, I have Hillary on speed dial just in case."

"Perfect." I kissed the top of Theo's head then called, "See you later, Sammy!"

"Bye, Peyton!" came the little voice from the pillow fort.

AT HOME, the lights were on in the foyer and Ben's office, casting a golden glow across the dead grass in the front yard. Compared to the darkness in the surrounding woods, the mansion's shine was a surprising source of comfort. Basil's car was still parked out front, which meant he wasn't quite finished talking Ben's ear off. From the little Ben could explain to me about Basil's greenhouse, their project was going well. Ben had started to research the subject in his free time, and Basil was satisfied with Ben's interpretation of the information. He paid Ben every week in the same manner—cash crammed in an envelope—and he encouraged us to cheat on our taxes without saying it in such plain terms.

As I steeled myself to save Ben was Basil's frantic work ethic, the mansion's front door opened. Ben and Basil appeared, both in good spirits.

"Everything okay?" I asked as we crossed paths in the yard. "You finished early."

"Thought I'd get home to my wife," Basil said. "You two have a good evening. Get some rest."

Then Basil was off, leaving Ben and I alone. Ben took my coat and hung it up with his good arm. Ever since he'd stopped using the wheelchair, he was getting better and better at performing simple daily tasks. He'd stopped wincing so much too, a sign that his ribs weren't feeling so sore anymore.

"Everything okay?" Ben asked as I watched Basil's car disappear into the woods. "You look spooked."

"I tried to check on Della, but she wasn't at the airstream," I told Ben. "She wasn't anywhere. I'm worried about her."

Ben guided me across the foyer and into the kitchen. "I'm sure she's fine. She probably needed some alone time. That was one hell of a night she had yesterday."

"What do *you* think happened?"

He shrugged as he pulled leftovers out of the fridge and began lining them up for the microwave. "I asked Basil about it, and he said it's not the first time Della's done something like this. I guess she has some mental health problems. It's her business, Peyton. Don't go poking around in it."

"You're right," I said. "It's none of my business."

It became my business later that night as I was sleeping soundly in my bedroom. Usually, my mind raced with so many thoughts that I needed the help of a sleep aid to actually find peace, but I was so mentally exhausted that I fell asleep as soon as my head hit the pillow. I fell into a deep trance, the type of sleep that normal people were accustomed to. For them, the nothingness of unconsciousness was a common occurrence. For me, it was a blissful break from the fitful naps that generally filled my nights, but it was soon interrupted by a familiar voice.

"Peyton."

I woke with a start to find someone looming over my bedside. Before I could scream, Della clapped her hand over my mouth. Her eyes were dull and vacant, as they had been when she was screaming in the pool. My heart pounded as she pressed her hand against my lips before I remembered I could breathe through my nose.

"Shh," Della said, beckoning me out of bed. "Come with me."

She drifted off into the hallway, her long white nightgown floating along behind her. My vision swam as I swung my feet out of bed and into my slippers. I hurried after Della, who had made her way toward the foyer at a surprisingly quick pace. When I tried to catch her by the shoulder, she shrugged me off.

"Della, what are you doing here?" I whispered as she led me up the steps to the mezzanine. We had yet to renovate anything above the first floor of the mansion, and it wasn't safe to be up here. "Does Basil know you're gone?"

"She's here somewhere," Della muttered, but I had a feeling she wasn't talking to me. She walked in an erratic pattern, looping around in certain spots on the second floor as if she were searching for cell phone reception in a shoddy service area. "Here... or here..."

I mirrored Della's progress through the second-floor corridor. I had no doubt in my mind that Della was indeed like me and Sammy. She could feel Alyssa's presence, even if she didn't understand what or who it was. "Who are you looking for, Della?"

She didn't reply, but continued working her way through the hallway. She paused at each bedroom or bathroom door then shuffled along to the next one. Suddenly, she threw out an arm, striking me in the chest to stop me from moving any further.

"Wait," she ordered.

Then she disappeared into the room closest to us. I stepped up to the closed door and held my breath to hear what was happening on the other side. Della muttered under her breath, holding a conversation with someone who didn't exist.

"Show her," Della insisted. "It's the only way. No! You can't keep bringing me here. I won't! I'm trying to help you—I'm trying!"

Without warning, Della emerged from the room. I hurriedly stepped back, and she stormed past me, this time with more direction and determination. For the hell of it, I stepped into the bedroom, knowing that no one was in there but needing to see it for myself. Sure enough, the bedroom was empty. I turned around and hastened after Della, practically running as she made her way back to the mezzanine, through the foyer, and down to the kitchen.

"Where is it?" she mumbled, opening each kitchen cabinet and drawing out the contents. She shook her fist in the air and demanded again, "Where is it?"

"Della, what are you looking for?" As she made her way through the kitchen, yanking utensils, pots, and other items from the cabinets, I put everything back as she finished with each section of her search. "If you tell me, I can help you find it."

"Gotta be here somewhere," Della said, furiously searching through the drawers now. "I've seen it in my dreams—haunting me—nothing makes sense—"

"Della, please tell me what's going on." I stepped in front of her, trying to distract her from her frantic hunt, but she shoved me aside with enough gusto to knock over a small horse. "Please, Della! Is it her? Were you talking to Alyssa?"

The name triggered something in Della's mind. Her hands paused over the handle to the next drawer. "Alyssa? Alyssa Abrams?"

"Yes. Were you talking to her?"

"Alyssa's dead."

"I know that," I said, "but how do *you* know that? You were the one who told me that Penelope and Alyssa moved away from Falconwood after Percy died."

"It's all *lies!*"

She resumed her search in earnest and finally reached the one drawer with the rattle that had been driving me nuts for weeks. Though Jim had renovated the kitchen, we'd kept the old hardware to save money. The cabinets and drawers were the same ones the Abrams had once used, simply with a new coat of paint.

"Aha!"

Della yanked the drawer fully out of place and turned it over to dump the contents on the counter. Then she ran her fingers around the edge, pushed into the corners, and popped the bottom out. Something clattered to the floor: a chef's knife. It was of professional grade, something you'd find it a five-star restaurant, not in someone's house. The blade was clean, silver, and shiny. The only hint that it was not new was the dust that had accumulated in the secret compartment the knife had been hidden in.

As soon as Della picked the knife up from the floor, adrenaline pushed through my veins. Quickly but cautiously, I took it from her grasp. For all the fervor of her search, she gave it up easily enough.

"You needed to find it," she told me, her eyes still glazed over. "She didn't want me to show you—scared—desperate—I'm so tired, Peyton. I think I'll go home now."

MY HEAD SNAPPED up from my pillow with all the whiplash of a car crash. Panting, I propped myself up. The bed was soaked in sweat, and the sheets were twisted around my legs and torso as if I had been thrashing around for hours. I struggled to detangle myself, listening to my pulse pound in my ears. Something caught my eye in the corner of the room. If my voice wasn't stuck in my throat, I would have screamed.

It was Alyssa. All of Alyssa. Not a glimpse of an outline from the corner of my eye. Not a feeling or a presence in the air. She stood in the darkest corner of the room, enshrouded in the shadow of the tall wardrobe beside her. Every nerve in my body stood at attention as she slowly raised a hand and untied the pink polka dot scarf from around her neck. As it fluttered to the floor, she stepped out of the shadows, and the moonlight bathed her in silver paint.

This time, I did scream. Alyssa's throat was slashed. Blood poured down her chest, staining her white nightgown crimson. She collapsed on the floor, and a bright white light took the whole room with her.

18

*B*en found me in the kitchen at dawn the next morning. As the sun cast pink rays of light across the countertops, I stood in the corner of the room with a cup of coffee I'd yet to touch. The kitchen was spotless. The cabinets and drawers were all in place, not left in disarray like I expected when I first walked in. The dishes and utensils were neatly stacked. The rattling drawer still rattled, but when I poked and prodded at the bottom as Della had done last night, no secret compartment revealed itself. The chef's knife was nowhere to be found. It was as if Della had never been here. That, combined with the horrible nightmare of Alyssa, made me feel more off-kilter than I ever had in my entire life. It wasn't until Ben lightly tapped my shoulder that I ripped my gaze from the rattling drawer.

"Peyton," he said. "You okay?"

I almost spilled everything I knew about the Abrams and the mansion on the spot. After last night, I wanted to tell Ben everything. I didn't want to be alone in this place anymore, especially not when a dead little girl made her way into my bedroom to show me how she was murdered. The problem was I didn't know whether last night had *actually* been a dream. It all felt so real, but there was no evidence to show Ben that I wasn't crazy, and I was starting to believe that maybe—like Della—I wasn't so sound of mind after all.

"Ben, do you like this house?" I asked him. My voice came out a lower register than usual, like I'd been sick for a while. "I mean, do you like living here?"

"It's too big for my taste." Ben poured himself a cup of coffee from the pot, took a sip, and set the cup down. "It's cold already. How long have you been up?"

"Seriously, Ben. The house?"

"I told you, it's too big," he said, dumping the cold coffee and putting on a new pot. "I miss our old house back home. This place is fine, but I don't understand how the Abrams did it. Why did three people need so much space?"

"But you don't feel uncomfortable here," I said, searching Ben's face for clues. "You don't hear or see things that seem...unusual?"

Ben set the pot down to give me his full attention. "Is this about the stuff you heard in the walls when we first got here? It's been a while since you mentioned it."

"I'm not talking about me," I said. "I want to know if *you* hear anything."

"I don't, Peyton," he replied. "I don't want to be that crappy guy who tells you you're being paranoid, but I do think this is one of those things where you're letting your anxiety get the best of you. Do you remember when we first moved into our other house after we got married? You told me someone had died in the living room."

"Because someone did," I insisted. "I know it—"

"How?" Ben asked. "The realtor is obligated to report things like that when they're selling the house to a new buyer. There was no record of anyone dying in that house."

"I just knew. I don't know how."

One-handed, he filled the new filter with fresh grounds and set it in the coffee maker. "You're intuitive, Peyton. It was one of the things I always liked about you. But just because you're intuitive doesn't mean someone's died at every place we've lived."

It was weird that he'd touched on the subject before I brought it up. Though I'd told Ben more than once about the whispers in the wall, I'd never mentioned the fact that people had died here. He landed on that matter all by himself.

"I'm supposed to meet with Basil in a half hour," Ben went on. "Jim and his crew will be here soon. Are you going to be okay until then? You seem a little off this morning."

If I was honest, I didn't want to be alone at the Abram Mansion ever again. The image of Alyssa coated in blood was burned into my vision. Every time I turned a corner, I expected to see her again. Ultimately, it was best if Ben didn't know these things.

"I'll be fine," I told him. "Sorry for freaking you out. I'm not trying to put extra stress on you."

He gave me a light hug. "I know that. Don't apologize. This house *does* have weird vibes. I think Della can account for that too. Just ignore it. We're here for three more months. After that, we can sell this crazy place and you'll be free to go wherever you want."

His intonation dropped at the end of his last sentence. It was the first time he'd said something to that effect out loud, actually acknowledging that—after all this was over—I wouldn't be returning to our little house in our hometown with him. His arm dropped from my shoulders as he cleared his throat and pretended to fuss with the finicky coffee pot. Once he got it going, he excused himself from the room to get dressed, leaving me alone with my haunting thoughts.

SHORTLY AFTER BEN left to meet Basil, Jim and his crew arrived. They brought noise and donuts with them, both of which I appreciated. The donuts were from the bakery beneath Theo's apartment, hot and homemade. The noise of the construction—all the banging and drilling and shouting—reminded me that I wasn't alone in the mansion. As long as Jim's crew joked and worked, I felt safe from the mansion's apparitions. For the first half of the morning, I took advantage of the warmer weather and sat out on the front porch to enjoy my coffee and donuts. The warm sun and the crisp breeze worked in tandem to keep me comfortable. I curled up in a big sweater and watched the birds flit through the trees. Did they know what lurked within the mansion? Could they sense it? I had never seen a bird land directly on the mansion. Maybe it was a sign. After all, people always said animals knew things about the universe that humans couldn't comprehend.

"Hey there, Peyton." Jim—cheery and gruff as always—emerged from the house with a heavy blanket from the foyer. "Couldn't help but notice your toes turning blue out here."

I thanked him as he draped the blanket across my legs. "How's the work looking, Jim? What kind of progress are you making?"

He lowered himself to the chair next to mine with a groan. "What specifics would you like to know? I figured Ben was keeping you updated."

"We initially agreed that he was going to be the head of this project," I told him. "But after a few months of living here, I'm more invested in the house. You're almost done with the front wing, correct?"

"With the bare basics," Jim reminded me. "We tore out whatever carpet we could find and put hardwood floor instead. Pulled out rotting drywall, sanded peeled paint, fixed the leaky pipes. It's not as much renovation as you might think, Peyton. I hate to disappoint you, but when you're on a deadline of six months and the place is this big—"

"Don't worry, Jim." I patted his enormous hand. "I didn't expect you to turn the Abram Mansion into Versailles. I'm just curious as to what you're thinking about tackling next."

"Well, I thought we'd do a general sweep to make sure everything is safe." He began to draw imaginary blueprints in the air as he explained his process. "We've got the front of this place all fixed up, but these other three wings need a lot of work. We're going to get our inspector out here to see what needs to be done, but if I had to guess, we'll have to get going on the east wing next. Lot of damage on that side of the house. Very unsafe. If something happens—an electrical fire or a burst pipe—it could ruin the entire house."

"Wait, the east wing?"

"Yup. It's a wreck."

I gestured to the right side of the house. "This part, right?"

"That would be the east. Yes, ma'am."

I remembered what Sammy had told me—that Alyssa was scared of me and Ben because we were changing her house around. If we started renovating the east wing before I figured out why Alyssa was haunting the mansion, it would be a recipe for disaster. That east wing was Alyssa's safe place, and I wasn't about to send a bunch of strange men into her space to tear apart her childhood bedroom.

"I would prefer if you started on the west wing," I said to Jim. "Every time I set foot near that part of the house, it feels like the ceiling is going to fall in."

Jim's mustache bristled with curiosity. "Where, exactly? I haven't noticed quite as much damage in the west wing."

I took a sip of cold coffee and feigned a coughing fit to buy myself time. Eyes streaming, I replied, "Just off the mezzanine. Uh, near the library."

"Huh." Jim settled his back against the chair, brows furrowed in thought. "The last time I checked, the library was in decent condition. I did see some water damage up on the fourth floor though."

"That's what I meant," I revised hurriedly. "West wing, fourth floor. That's my main concern. I'd like to leave the east wing for last if at all possible."

One of Jim's crew members—an older woman named Maureen whose biceps were bigger than Ben's—popped her head out of a window on the third floor and called down, "Jim, we need your opinion up here!"

Jim glanced up, shielding his eyes against the pale sun. "I'll be right up, Maureen."

"Can't wait," Maureen replied. "Hey, Peyton. Hanging in there?"

"Oh, I'm doing swell, Maureen."

"That's what I like to hear."

As Maureen withdrew, Jim cleared his throat and readied himself to stand up. The porch chair was a low bucket seat, and Jim was so large that he had to propel himself upward with an exaggerated push of his hands. "We'll talk about the east wing with Ben later," he said, pulling his workman's gloves back on again. "Just to make sure everyone's on the same page."

Though his tone was polite, I heard the implications behind it. Ben was the one who had spearheaded the construction so far, which meant Jim considered him the first point of contact. If Ben decided the east wing should be renovated first, that was what would happen.

"You should head inside too," Jim advised. "You're looking a little pale."

I hadn't realized how cold I was. A layer of clouds had appeared in the sky, veiling most of the sun's warmth. Shivering, I picked up the blanket wrapped around me, gathered my coffee cup, and reluctantly followed Jim inside. He gave me a polite nod as he headed up the steps to the mezzanine to meet Maureen on the third floor. Once he was gone, I stood in the foyer with the heavy blanket wrapped around me like a cape. I had to admit it to myself: I was afraid to go anywhere in the house. No matter how much I wanted to help Alyssa, I feared seeing her again. I much preferred dealing with her when she was too shy to stand in my direct eyeline.

Of course, the things I feared had a way of creeping up on me. Maybe Alyssa had felt it in the air as I'd re-entered the house. Maybe she'd sensed that I'd considered backing out of all this. The mystery around Alyssa's death felt unsolvable. There was no information to track, no leads to follow. I'd spent more of my time trying to convince Sammy that I was playing detective than actually doing any detective work. If I had to guess, Alyssa was even more perceptive than Sammy, because when she showed up on the mezzanine, where Jim had just passed through, she made sure to only show enough of herself to let me know she was there. She was a pair of eyes peering down into the foyer from behind one of the banisters, something I'd imagined she'd made a habit of when her parents held parties at the mansion that she wasn't invited to. My teeth clacked together as I felt her presence wash over me. I kept my eyes on the carpet.

"You scared me last night," I whispered, knowing she could hear my voice no matter what volume I used. "That was you, right? Not a nightmare."

"I didn't mean to show you like that."

Startled to hear an actual voice respond, I glanced up at the mezzanine. Alyssa kept herself out of sight, but she didn't back off. "Did you just... talk?"

As if the question was too stupid to merit a reply, she remained silent, peering at me from her lookout spot on the mezzanine. Tiny fingers wrapped around the railing. With a single one, she beckoned me toward her.

"You want to show me something?"

With Alyssa, I got more of an answer out of the feelings she gave me than her actual voice. I felt her nod more than I saw it, and though every part of me wanted to run away and forget about everything I'd seen in the mansion so far, I couldn't do it. Instead, I dropped the blanket on the couch and headed up the stairs. As soon as my feet reached the mezzanine, Alyssa vanished from behind the banister and reappeared up ahead. I caught sight of her pink scarf, tied firmly around her neck once again. Hopefully, she kept it there this time.

"Are you going to throw another tantrum?" I asked her, tiptoeing along the corridor as she led me into the east wing. "Because to be honest, I'm not quite over the chess piece debacle."

"That wasn't me," Alyssa's voice floated back to me.

"Sure. Who was it then?"

No reply. I rolled my eyes as we walked on. Alyssa kept up her sporadic transparency. Sometimes, I caught sight of her staring at me from behind a curtain, but she would vanish as soon as our eyes met. Whether she did this for my benefit or hers was beyond me. Eventually, we reached the door to a room I had not yet explored. Alyssa pushed it open but kept herself invisible, so it looked like it floated open on its own. I stepped inside.

Long ago, the room had been someone's recreational outlet. A craft desk stood in one corner, stacked high with scrapbook materials, blank photo album pages, and brightly-colored pipe cleaners. An old sewing machine sat on the windowsill. The bookshelf was stacked with romance novels, cookbooks, and do it yourself manuals, though one of the shelves was reserved for Alyssa's art projects.

"You have to be quiet," Alyssa whispered. She hadn't shown herself in the room, but the white linen curtains by the window flickered, and a floorboard nearby creaked as if someone had stepped on it.

"What am I doing in here?" I whispered back. I didn't dare touch anything. Every time I'd snooped around in the Abrams' old things, something random had attacked me of its own accord. All this time, I thought it was Alyssa's doing, but now I wasn't so sure.

The floorboard creaked again. This time, one end of it popped up. I cautiously crept toward it and used my heel to press down on the opposite end. The floorboard flipped up to reveal a hidden pocket beneath it. With a deep, steadying breath, I reached in and pulled out a red steel box.

"Am I supposed to look inside?" I asked Alyssa.

The curtains fluttered again as Alyssa retreated behind them and nodded. I pried open the rusty box. Inside, there was a stack of letters in different colored envelopes. The steel box had kept them clean and dry, and whoever had stored them here had been delicate with the pages. I carefully pulled the letter from the first envelope and read it aloud:

"My dearest Penelope," I whispered, tracing my fingers across the elegant handwriting, "I write to you in tears. I can no longer bear the thought of you in that cold, ghastly manor or in the presence of such a beast. Once more, I must implore you to make better choices for yourself and your daughter. Come to me—bring Alyssa with you—and I promise to care for you for all of my days. I care little about the judgements and opinions of other people. I have no shame in our relationship. On the contrary, I am proud of our love. Please have the courage to find your pride in it. Yours forever, Charles Rainer."

I looked up from the letter. One warm tear ran down my cheek. Alyssa had finally taken a corporeal form, though she did not step out from behind the curtain.

"Charles Rainer," I repeated, holding up the letter. "I heard your mom was in love with someone other than your dad. Is this him?"

Alyssa nodded. I put the first letter—the most recent one—back in the steel box and shuffled through the other ones. They were all from Charles, and from what I could tell, he declared his undying love for Penelope in every one of them. Though Charles never spoke of Percy directly, he mentioned him every so often, and never in a positive light. I took a picture of Charles' home address.

My alarm chimed on my phone. It was time to pick up Sammy from school. I wiped my eyes and put the letters back where I'd found them, making sure to place them gently in their home.

"I have to go," I whispered to Alyssa. "But thank you for showing me this."

Alyssa peeked out from behind the curtain. Her cheeks were pink and round as she gave me a small smile and waved good-bye. As I left the room, I realized my anxiety from this morning had faded.

SAMMY, once again, was nowhere to be seen in the first rush of kids fleeing the elementary school. This time, I waited him out in the parking lot instead of subjecting myself to the chaos of the pickup loop. Gradually, the schoolyard emptied itself out and the minivan moms went on their way. Still no Sammy. When the secretary left the office—lunch box and school bags in hand—I rolled down my window and called out to her.

"Excuse me, miss?" I said. "I'm here to pick up Sammy Baker. Did he stay late in his last class again?"

"The teachers are gone already," the secretary said. "Everyone's on their way home."

My pulse quickened. "That's impossible. Sammy hasn't come out yet."

"One second." She balanced her bags in one hand to look at the office's paperwork in the other. "It says here that Sammy was picked up by his father."

"His father?" I repeated, jaw dropping. "His father doesn't have custody over him! And he definitely doesn't have Theo's permission to pick him up."

"According to this, he does." She showed me the permission slip and pointed to Theo's name scribbled at the bottom.

"That's not Theo's handwriting," I growled. "He forged it."

The secretary examined the signature. "Oh. Oh! Oh my God, should we call the police?"

I swiped the falsified permission slip from her. "I'll handle it. Next time, try to do your job a little better."

Her bottom lip quivered as I rolled up the window and reached for my phone. It wasn't entirely her fault—Dylan had been crafty—but I didn't have time to console her. I dialed Hillary Spaughton's number and got her voicemail. I called the Falconwood police station next.

"Hello?" answered an unfamiliar voice.

"My friend's son has been kidnapped," I reported, feeling my chest tighten as I said it. "Sammy Baker. His father picked him up from school."

"If his father picked him up from school, then he hasn't been kidnapped, ma'am."

"No, you don't understand." I gritted my teeth. "His father

isn't in the picture anymore. He hasn't known Sammy since he was born. I'm supposed to be the one who picks him up from school, but he's missing—"

"Ma'am, if the child is with his father—"

"Are you listening to me?" I shouted into the phone. "Are you some kind of idiot whose ears don't work? Where is Hillary Spaughton? I need to talk to someone competent."

In a smaller voice, the man replied, "Officer Spaughton called in sick today. She's not coming in. Word is she has a massive case of food poisoning."

"Then you have one job today," I hissed. "Find Sammy Baker. You should already have a file on him. Call this number if you track him down."

I hung up. Despite my ferocity, I wasn't entirely sure the police would start looking for Sammy unless I came in and filed an actual report. Even then, the only officer I could count on was Hillary, and she was mysteriously ill. With a heavy heart, I called Theo next, dreading the moment she answered, but her phone went to voicemail too. I wasn't brave enough to leave a message. It was better to do this in person. I put the car in drive and almost backed out of the space before something shiny caught my eye on the sidewalk. I got out of the car to examine it. It was a glittery dinosaur sticker. Fifty feet down the sidewalk, heading toward the edge of town, was another sticker. Sammy had left me a trail of breadcrumbs.

I left the car at the school, grabbed my scarf, and set off down the sidewalk. The stickers were placed erratically, as if Sammy had only stuck one down when Dylan was distracted enough not to notice. A couple of times, I lost the trail, once at an intersection where I had to search all three pathways before finding the next sticker and again when the trail led me through a nature hike trail where the path was all dirt. Here, Sammy had dragged his heels instead of dropping stickers. Every so often, I found gouges in the path that were roughly the size of his tiny shoes. The farther I walked along the trail, the darker it became. The trees overhead were so thick that they blocked out what little of the sun could be seen. After an hour of searching, the trail went cold. No stickers, no footprints, and no other clues to let me know where Sammy might be. But the path only led one way.

I emerged from the hiking trail and into a small cemetery. It was unmarked and had no border, and I wouldn't have known it was a cemetery at all were it not for the short headstone that I almost tripped over. I had no idea where I was in relation to the rest of Falconwood, but I didn't care. A tiny figure was huddled next to a gravestone in the middle of the cemetery, wearing Sammy's trademark red sweater but no coat. Heart racing, I hurried over.

"Sammy?" My voice cracked as I knelt down. "Sammy, it's me. It's Peyton."

Sammy's lips trembled as his eyes fluttered open. "P—Peyton?"

"Hey, buddy. I've been looking for you." I took off my coat and wrapped it around Sammy instead. His skin was pale and freezing, and he barely had enough strength to hug me as I brought him closer to my body to warm him up. "Let's get you warmed up, huh?"

"He took me," Sammy whimpered, his nose pressed against my neck. "Dylan. I don't like him."

"I know, buddy, but you did such a good job of helping me to find you," I said. "Thanks for the stickers. Where's Dylan anyway?"

"I don't know," Sammy said. "I ran away from him near the road. He couldn't find me in the woods. That's why I came this way."

"You're such a smart boy."

He wiped his nose on his sleeve. "Alyssa's here too."

"What?"

Sammy pointed to the gravestone he'd been leaning against. I shuffled forward to get a look at the faded name carved into the rock: *Percy Abrams, Beloved Husband and Father, 1949-1979.*

19

"*I* can't believe this."

Theo paced back and forth in her tiny kitchen while I sat exhausted at the counter. After bringing Sammy to the clinic to make sure he hadn't crossed over into hypothermia, I'd returned him to his mother's apartment and filled Theo in on the drama from that afternoon. Needless to say, she was furious.

"I can't believe this!" she said again, slamming her fist on the countertop. "Dylan waltzed into that school like he owned the place? He forged my signature! That bastard! And the cops? They were absolutely useless. I swear, Hillary's the only officer with half a brain in Falconwood—"

"Theo, try to calm down," I said. "Everything turned out okay. Sammy's safe at home, and you can give the cops more information on Dylan tomorrow. They'll keep an eye out for him, though from what I got out of Sammy, it's doubtful he's going to try this again."

Theo paused her rampage through the kitchen. "What do you mean? What happened?"

"Sammy's a smart kid," I reminded her. "It's not like he *wanted* to go with Dylan. First, he tried making a scene at the school. He told the secretary that I was supposed to pick him up, but I guess Dylan outsmarted the poor girl. Dylan tried to carry him, but Sammy kept kicking at him. When Dylan let him walk, Sammy put stickers on the ground so I could find him."

Theo sat next to me and rested her forehead in her hands. "Then what?"

"Apparently, he tried to get Sammy into his car."

"Ugh, that car! It's probably full of drugs."

"Well, Sammy wasn't having it," I assured her. "He made himself throw up in the front seat before Dylan could even get the piece of crap started. Then he got out and ran off into the woods. Dylan doesn't know this area like Sammy does, so I guess he gave up when he couldn't find Sammy."

Theo's teeth ground together. "I hate him. I hate that man with every fiber of my being."

"Hey." I pulled her hands away from her face so I could look her in the eye. "I know you're angry and scared, but the important thing is that Sammy is safe. Tomorrow, we'll call Hillary again. She'll know what to do about Dylan. You can take out a restraining order."

"What did I do to deserve this?"

"Nothing," I answered fiercely. "You did nothing wrong. Do you hear me? Dylan's a jerk, and from the sound of it, he's also psychotic. This has nothing to do with you or the choices you've made. You're a great mom, Theo. Don't let some asshole make you forget that."

Theo gave a feeble laugh. "I didn't mean what did I do to deserve Dylan stalking me. I already know the answer to that question—I gave him access to my life. I meant what did I do to deserve a friend as good as you?"

"Oh." The question took me by surprise. I didn't feel like I'd gone above and beyond to be a good friend to Theo. I simply cared for her and Sammy. "I'm not sure what you mean. You and

Sammy are two of my favorite people. I would do anything to make sure the two of you stayed safe."

"I'm so grateful for you," Theo said. "Truly. I owe you so much."

"You don't owe me anything," I told her.

A frantic knock on the door interrupted our conversation. Theo nearly leapt out of her chair. "It better not be him," she hissed. "I might murder him on the spot."

"Check the peephole," I whispered.

Theo peered through the tiny window in the door. "What the hell? It's Della Gordon. She never comes over unless she's watching Sammy."

"Answer it."

Theo opened the door. Della stood on the doorstep, wringing her hands. Her hair—usually neatly tied away from her face—was frizzled and messy. Pink circles decorated the skin beneath her eyes. She looked as though she hadn't slept in three days.

"Is Peyton here?" she asked Theo. "She's not at home."

"I'm right here, Della," I said, getting up from the kitchen counter. "Is everything okay?"

Della peered around Theo. "I need to speak with you. Alone."

I gathered my coat, hat, and keys and hugged Theo on my way out. "I'll check in with you tomorrow, okay?" I told her. "If you need anything, let me know."

"Thanks, Peyton. You've been amazing."

"Tell Sammy I'll see him later."

"Will do."

I helped Della down the stairs. With every step, she wobbled as if her age had caught up to her in the amount of time since I'd seen her last. I kept my hand on her elbow as we made our way into the parking lot. She refused to say anything until we were safely within the confines of my car.

"Did you find it?" she asked, once I'd fired up the heat and her teeth had stopped chattering. "Did you see where it was hidden?"

"Della, I'm not sure I know what you're talking about," I said. "I had a rough day. Sammy went missing, and we're worried that Theo's ex-boyfriend might still be in town. Last night—"

"Last night!" Della grabbed my hand, squeezing hard enough to cut off the circulation to my fingers. She certainly hadn't lost the strength in her grip. "Last night, you saw it. I remember."

My memory circled back to last night's chain of horrible nightmares, so vivid that I hadn't been able to tell whether or not they were real. "Were you actually in my house last night? Did you wake me up?"

"Yes, yes, yes!" Della released my hand, and all of the blood rushed back to my fingers. "I knew it. I knew you were listening. Did you find it?"

Stumped, I replied, "Did I find what?"

"Think," Della pleaded. "What did I show you? Remember?"

Reluctantly, I dug through my fuzzy memories of last night. "Are you talking about the chef's knife? In the drawer that rattles?"

Della snapped her fingers, a weird gesture that I interpreted as triumph. "You know it's true, don't you? The other story."

I stared at Della's wild eyes and crazy hair. "Della, I have no idea what other story you're talking about. You have to give me longer sentences here."

She leaned across the center console and took the collar of my coat in both hands, yanking me forward until we were only inches apart. "You know what really happened to Alyssa Abram."

A familiar lump rose in my throat. It tasted like bile and backwash. No matter how many times I tried to swallow it, it remained stuck near my tonsils, threatening to explode at any second. "What do *you* know about Alyssa Abram?"

"She was murdered," Della whispered, her eyes growing wider with every word. "In her own home—that poor, sweet little girl—I can't go there anymore."

"You've seen Alyssa, haven't you?" I asked her. "At the mansion?"

Della violently shook her head.

"You can tell me." I unfurled Della's fingers from my coat collar and held her hands in mine. "I can see her too. I don't think you're crazy."

"Not Alyssa," Della said.

"Last night, you spoke to someone upstairs in the west wing," I reminded her. "I heard you talking to them. Alyssa talks to me too."

Della pulled her hands out of mine. "It wasn't Alyssa."

"Then who was it?"

"I can't tell you," Della said. "It's for your own good. Alyssa doesn't talk to me anymore. Not since I stopped visiting all those years ago. I think she's mad at me."

"She doesn't understand why you left her," I told Della. "She's young. She's still only five years old, no matter how long she's been trapped in that house. I'm sure if you apologized to her—"

"No, I can't go back to the mansion." Della trembled in her seat. I turned up the heat, but it didn't make a difference. Her shivers weren't weather-related. "I can hardly live in Falconwood anymore. I hear that voice everywhere I go. It's following me."

"What voice? Who's following you?"

Della's eyes focused again, and her frantic energy radiated throughout the car. "You have to find out the truth about Alyssa —what really happened to her. That's the only way all of this stops."

"All of what?"

"Everything," Della whispered. "The voice in my head will go away. Alyssa Abram will find peace. Sammy Baker won't run away from his mother anymore. All you have to do is figure out the truth."

I let out a long sigh that fogged up the driver's side window. Night had long since fallen, and I was ready for a good night's sleep. Then again, a good night's sleep was never guaranteed in the Abram Mansion. "Della, what do you think I've been trying to do? Ever since I realized Alyssa was trapped there, I've been trying to find out how she died, but there are no records of the Abrams that I can find. There are hardly any clues, and the ones that I have found don't make any sense. For instance, why did you show me the chef's knife last night and then hide it away again? I couldn't open that weird compartment in the drawer."

"Do you know why I showed you?"

I thought of Alyssa's neck without her scarf. "I have a guess."

"Someone else showed me the knife," Della said. "I had to show you. It's important."

"Well, without it in my actual hand, I don't have anything to go on," I told her. "If that knife is a murder weapon, the police need to see it."

"No!" Della hit the dashboard hard enough to rattle the plastic spoons I'd been hoarding in the glove compartment. "No police. They're incompetent. They'll make this harder."

"I don't know what to tell you then," I said. "I don't know what happened to Alyssa after Percy died. We all thought Penelope Abram took her along when she left Percy for Charles—"

Della snapped her fingers again. Another moment of triumph. "Charles! Charles Rainer."

"How do you know that name?"

"You have to find him," Della ordered. "He might know something. Go to him."

"The address I have for Charles Rainer is printed on a letter

278

from over forty years ago," I said. "Who knows if he even still lives there?"

Without warning, Della got out of the car. It had begun to rain, and within seconds, the moisture had flattened her crazy hair against her forehead. "Find Charles Rainer. Ask him what happened to Penelope Abram. Come to me when you know the truth."

"Penelope? What about—Della, wait!"

She slammed the door and walked off, her gray sweater blending in with the dark, foggy evening. The rain grew heavier, bouncing off my windshield with a vengeance. As I pulled out of the bakery's parking lot, I expected to find Della again, walking along the sidewalk, but it was as if she had dissolved into droplets and absorbed into the concrete, just as the rain did.

To MY RELIEF, Basil's car wasn't parked in front of the mansion. He'd already finished his work with Ben and left for the day. When I went inside, Ben was making dinner in the kitchen. I admired him as he stirred a pot of pasta sauce with his good hand. With the other, he squeezed a stress ball to strengthen his grip. He was making decent progress with his physical therapy, but he had a long way to go before he was back to his usual self. As I shook off my wet coat and sank into one of the chairs at the kitchen table, I wished things were as simple as they used to be. A simple house, a simple husband, and a simple life. Then again, I hadn't been happy with simple either.

"Do you think I'm making the right choice?" I asked Ben.

"About what?"

"About you and me."

His grip tensed around the wooden spoon. "I'm not sure why you would ask me that."

"Because you have a good head on your shoulders, and you know me better than anyone else."

Ben lifted the spoon from the sauce and tapped it against the pan. "Peyton, I'm not sure what good this conversation will do for either one of us."

"It's just a question."

He sighed and turned the burner down to low. "Are you making the right choice? I don't know. I guess it depends on who you're making that choice for. If you're making it for me, it's the wrong choice. I love you now as much as I loved you the day we got married, but that doesn't matter if you're making this choice for yourself. I know being married to me stopped you from doing a lot of the things you wanted to do. If I could go back in time and listen to what you wanted, I would have given you the freedom to travel and come back to me when you needed a safe place to land. I know that now, but it's too late."

I could tell from the slump of his posture that my question was hurting him more than it was helping me. I cleared my throat. "What are you making?"

"Arrabbiata," he answered, his tone lighter now that I'd changed the subject. "Do you want some? I didn't make it too spicy."

"Sure."

For the rest of the evening, we kept to pleasant topics, narrowly avoiding our impending divorce every time the conversation veered toward it. When we had finished eating, I helped Ben clear the dishes.

"I might have to go somewhere tomorrow," I informed him as I rinsed sauce from our bowls. "Out of town."

"Oh. For a photography job?"

"Not quite." At this point, I wasn't sure how much to tell Ben about the Abram Mansion, but it was getting to be too complicated not to tell him. "I'm trying to track someone down who might know more about the house."

"A friend of your grandfather's?" Ben asked. "That's pretty big. Are you sure you want to go alone? I can come with you."

"I'm not sure if they were friends," I said. "They might not know each other at all. This guy—Charles Rainer—knew Penelope."

"Penelope?"

"Penelope Abram," I replied. "You know, the wife of the mansion's last owner?"

"Oh, sure. Penelope." He spooned the leftover pasta into a plastic container. "I don't need to be worried about you, do I?"

"Why would you be?"

He set the pasta in the fridge before turning to examine me. "Between Della and Sammy, I'm starting to believe that this house does have an effect on some people. Just wondering if you're starting to feel those effects too."

"No. Are you?"

Ben shrugged. "I don't think so. This place seems normal to me. Big and creepy, sure, but nothing out of the ordinary."

"Good." I finished loading the dishwasher, wiped my hands, and kissed Ben on the cheek. "Let's keep it that way. In two and a half months, we can move out anyway."

"Counting down the days."

THAT NIGHT, as Ben's snores floated across the hallway and into my room, I sat by the window and let the moonlight from the courtyard wash over me. With my computer perched on my lap and the photo of Penelope's letter beside me, I searched the Internet for Charles Rainer. It was tedious work. Though I had Rainer's address, I quickly determined it was no longer current. It did, however, tell me a few things about Penelope and

Charles's relationship. He once used to live in the next town over from Falconwood, far enough to avoid controversy but close enough to attend the events held at the Abram Mansion, which explained how he met Penelope. In the letters, they spoke of a hiking trail near Charles's house. If I had to guess, their interest in hiking was a cover for what they were actually doing together. All Penelope had to do was tell Percy she was visiting her friend to traverse the wilderness together, and if she was talented enough to deceive him, Percy wouldn't have found out about the affair for years.

There were things that didn't add up. I had questions for days and no one to answer them. For hours, I scoured the web for Charles Rainer. There were so many men with the name that I had to fish out extra details: where they lived, what age they were, and whether or not they had ever resided at the address I had on record. Finally, at three o'clock in the morning, I found a golden nugget of information in an article about a new art exhibit that was installed in the Garden of Marble two years ago. The statue—a naked woman who sat with her back to the viewer that I remember shielding Sammy's eyes from—had been commissioned by one Charles Rainer of Hartford, Connecticut. It was too much of a coincidence not to be the same guy. I tried a new search, this time including Rainer's name, his location, and the title of the statue. I clicked on the first link that popped up—Rainer's profile on LinkedIn. He was a retired art dealer, and from the information on his profile, he still lived in Hartford. Getting his exact address wasn't too hard. All I had to do was sign up for a free trial for a "people-finding" website, type in Rainer's name and city, and press enter. Right away, his records popped up, including his current address. I typed it into my phone and checked my watch. Hartford was less than an hour away. If I left now, I'd show up at Rainer's house before dawn.

Something told me that if I did that, Rainer wouldn't even consider answering my questions.

I set my laptop aside, got under the covers, and propped my head up to look at the stars through the window. Behind me, a light chill told me that Alyssa had crept into my room.

"You can come closer," I whispered, closing my eyes.

The chill and strange displacement of air that happened when Alyssa was nearby neared the window. Then it climbed into bed with me. I felt a tiny hand rest against my arm. To my surprise, it was warm. I kept my eyes closed, just in case Alyssa had taken her scarf off again.

"I won't be home tomorrow," I told her. "I'm going to look for Charles Rainer. I promise I'll be back though. Is that okay?"

The tiny hand squeezed my arm. I felt Alyssa turn over and bury her cold nose into my back. Gently, I tried to place my hand over hers, but there was nothing to touch except for my own skin.

AFTER A FEW HOURS of restless sleep, I hugged Ben goodbye and started my drive to Hartford. It was a Saturday, so I didn't have to worry about being back in time to pick Sammy up from school. That in itself was a relief. After Sammy's near kidnapping yesterday, Theo needed some well-earned alone time with her son. After getting a coffee to go from the Black Cat, Theo rang my phone.

"You're leaving town?" she asked when I told her I was on my way to Hartford. "Why? When will you be back?"

"Later this afternoon," I replied. The quasi-lie I'd given Ben yesterday was the perfect cover to tell everyone else too. "I'm trying to find out more about my grandfather—why he would have left the Abram Mansion to us."

"Or why he ended up with the mansion in his care in the first place?"

"Exactly." That was another question that kept bothering me more and more often. My grandfather—Andrew Anderson—had to have known *something* about all of this before he died. After all, he somehow inherited the mansion from Percy Abram. Were the two of them acquainted? "Maybe this contact can help me shed some light on the situation."

"Why the sudden interest?" Theo asked. "I thought you were planning on selling the mansion right after the six-month mark."

"We are," I said, "but something's bugging me about this. My mom never had a relationship with my grandfather. If this is a way to find closure for all of it, I'm going to check it out."

"Good luck," Theo said. "Just so you know, Sammy and I would hate for you to move out of Falconwood after all this. You should consider staying. Maybe not in that house—"

"I'm not sure what I'm going to be doing," I told her. "But my main goal is not to get tied down. Who knows? Maybe I'll invest in an airstream like Della and Basil."

"As long as you drive it by our apartment every once in a while."

"Are you kidding?" I said. "I'll take you both on a road trip."

Once I'd reassured Theo that I had no plans to chuck her out of my life when our time at the Abram Mansion came to an end, I hung up and focused on the road. I practiced what I might say to Charles Rainer. I had a million questions to ask him, but they were all jumbled up in my head. I should have prepared for this better. I should have taken notes on what I already knew versus what I wanted to know. Nevertheless, when I pulled up to the address I had on file for Rainer, I was anxious to ring the doorbell.

Rainer lived in a fancy neighborhood, where all the houses were made of gray stone and about the size of one of the mansion's enormous wings. Rainer's house, on the other hand, was quite modest compared to the rest of the neighborhood. While the other properties boasted tennis courts and pool houses, Rainer's plot of land had not been filled in with so many extras. It was simply his house and his lawn, which was impeccably tended. As I approached his front door, my heart skipped several beats.

A woman answered. She was perhaps in her fifties, and she held a feather duster in one hand. "Yes? May I help you?"

"My name is Peyton Fletcher. I'm looking for Charles Rainer."

"I'm afraid Mr. Rainer isn't taking appointments today." The woman looked me up and down, taking in the handful of papers in my grasp. "In any case, Mr. Rainer is no longer looking to buy anything. How did you get this address?"

"Please, Miss—"

"Gupta."

"Miss Gupta," I said. "It's not about an art sale. I'm not a solicitor. I was wondering if I could talk to Mr. Rainer about Penelope Abram."

Miss Gupta's feather duster quivered. "How do you know that name?"

"I live in the Abram Mansion now," I answered. "My grandfather, Andrew Anderson, left it to us, and I was hoping—" The door opened further, and a man appeared behind Miss Gupta. I recognized his neatly trimmed goatee and impressive head of hair instantly. "Mr. Rainer? Hi, I'm—"

"I heard you the first time," he said. "Are you coming in or not?"

20

*C*harles Rainer was an odd man. First of all, for an art lover, his house did not contain many examples of great art. From what I'd ascertained during my Internet research, he specialized in sculpture, yet there were no sculptures on display or, I assumed, anywhere at all. In fact, Rainer's house was strangely bare. The walls were white or a greenish shade of gray. His furniture was clean and minimalistic. The white tile floors gleamed underfoot, reflecting my face back up at me when I looked down. The only decoration were plants. Every room featured at least three plants each: towering indoor palms, hanging spider plants that reached for the opposite corners of the room, and lucky bamboo that had been guided into beautiful twists and abstract shapes. As Rainer led me into a sitting room, he gently caressed the fronds of a tall palm tree on his way past it. I suddenly understood. The plants *were* Rainer's art.

"Can I offer you something to drink?" Miss Gupta said, abandoning her feather duster as she followed us into the house. "Water, tea, coffee?"

"I'm—" I began.

"I'll get it," Rainer interrupted. "Genevieve, what have I told you about serving me or my guests?"

Miss Gupta—Genevieve—gave Rainer a timid smile. "That it's not in my job description."

"Precisely." Rainer patted Genevieve's hand affectionately. "Please take a break. Have an early lunch. Something tells me you skipped breakfast this morning. Was William late to school again?"

Genevieve rolled her eyes. "You know my son. It takes him three hours to wake up and five minutes to get ready. Do all fifteen-year-olds sleep like the dead?"

"I wouldn't know," Rainer replied. "I made roast beef last night. If you warm it in the oven, it tastes almost as good as it does fresh. Help yourself." As Genevieve went to the kitchen, Rainer turned to me. "Make yourself comfortable. I'll be right back."

I took a seat on one of the white couches, found that I couldn't stay still, and wandered around the sitting room instead. A large glass door stretched across the back wall, yielding to an impeded view of the backyard. Here, Rainer's small garden waited to bloom. The only other thing on the property was a modest greenhouse. Rainer returned shortly, carrying two glasses of water. He set them down on the coffee table and gestured for me to sit across from him.

"My husband's a writer." I shuffled my papers and photos off to the side of the coffee table, not ready to show him what I had in hand quite yet. "He's working on a book about hydroponic greenhouses right now."

"Does your husband garden?"

"No, he just writes."

"Then I'm afraid he won't grasp the true joy of growing things in his book," Rainer said matter-of-factly."

"Well, it's not *his* book," I modified. "Our friend Basil is the one with the greenhouse. My husband's helping him—anyway, that's not the point."

"I heard the point when Genevieve opened the door," Rainer said. "I'll ask you the same question she asked you with a slightly different angle. How did you discover my connection to Penelope Abram? It's been years since I've heard a whisper of her name."

"I assume you also heard me tell Genevieve that I own the Abram Mansion now." I handed him a picture from my stash. "I discovered a few things hidden away in the house, including old photos of Penelope... and your letters to her."

His eyes whipped up to meet mine. "Letters?"

I pushed a folder toward him. "From what I can see, she kept every single one that you sent her. I think she was very much in love with you."

He opened the folder to find the forty-year-old letters. Earlier that morning, I'd rescued them from beneath the floorboards with Alyssa's help. Rainer's eyes glossed over.

"She kept them," he murmured.

"All of my questions stem from one," I told him. "Where is Penelope Abram?"

Rainer thumbed through the letters, even lifting one to his nose as if hoping to inhale whatever was left of Penelope's essence. "To be honest? I believe she's dead."

A cramp started in my chest, like someone had stuck a pencil into my lung. "What makes you think that?"

Rainer turned the letters so his handwriting faced me. "I assume you read through these? And if you live in Falconwood, the older members of the town would have filled you in on the Abrams' drama. Penelope Abram was the love of my life. She disappeared with her daughter shortly before Percy's death. People called me for years—her mother and father, friends, random acquaintances—demanding to know where she was. They all thought she had left Percy to be with me."

"Did she?"

"Admittedly, that was our original plan." He placed the letters face down on the coffee table. "We never wrote about it, lest Percy discover what we were up to, but Penelope and I agreed that she would leave him."

I showed him the picture of Penelope where she was covered in light bruises. "I found a few more like this, and from some of the things you wrote in your letters, I have to guess that Percy Abram wasn't the stand-up guy everyone in Falconwood thought he was."

Rainer swallowed hard before replying. "He was an upstanding gentleman to everyone but his wife and child. He beat them, carefully enough to hide the evidence from the community."

"Why didn't Penelope report him?"

"Who would have believed her?" Rainer asked. "Everyone though Percy was faultless. He had the police in his pocket. Besides, Penelope was terrified of Percy. She feared retribution if she sought justice for his abuse. She was afraid he would put Alyssa in danger."

"So no one else knew about Percy's abuse?"

"Not that I know of," Rainer answered. "When Percy died, it was lauded as a tragic accident. The community mourned him. They reserved no thought for Penelope and Alyssa or what might have happened to them."

"Because they all assumed Percy was the victim?"

"Indeed." Rainer stood, perhaps no longer able to discuss the topic without moving, and roved around the sitting room like an automatic vacuum cleaner. "I was the only one who knew something was off. Penelope and I had everything planned out. She told Percy she was taking Alyssa to visit her grandmother in

Hartford for a few weeks, a girls' trip, as it were. Really, she was to meet me at my previous address. From there, we had planned to flee. Penelope had always wanted to live in California. It was so far away from Falconwood that Percy wouldn't consider looking there. Once we arrived, Penelope planned on serving Percy divorce papers and a restraining order."

"Then what happened?"

Rainer stared through the glass doors and into his garden. "She never arrived. I did all I could to get in contact with her, but she did not answer her phone. I even drove to Falconwood, planning to confront Percy myself, but the mansion was empty. A week later, I heard the news that Percy committed suicide—that everyone believed Penelope and Alyssa were with me. I reported them missing, but the police refused to take the case seriously. Eventually, everyone but me forgot about them. They had little family, and Penelope's mother refused to speak to me. I hired a P.I. to find them, but years went by without any information. At last, I had to give up the search, as it was taking a toll on my mental health."

"You said you thought Penelope was dead," I reminded him. "Why?"

"Because it's the only explanation that makes sense," Rainer said. "I knew what Percy was: an abusive man who hid his insecurities behind an inscrutable mask. He was a monster, and I have no trouble believing that he killed his own wife and daughter before he committed suicide himself."

A rush of heat flooded my body. My palms and the soles of my feet were sweating. It was as if I'd needed Rainer to confirm a hunch that had been sitting in the back of my head all along: Percy's abuse had escalated, and he'd murdered both his wife and daughter in cold blood. It was the most logical conclusion, yet I'd avoided thinking about it because of how terrible it was.

"Why did you want to know all of this?" Rainer asked me as

he observed my shaking fists. "Surely you don't need this information to sell the mansion."

"No, it's for my own research," I said, my voice quivering. "I was curious. My grandfather—Andrew Anderson—did you know him? Percy left him the mansion after he died."

"Andrew Anderson was Percy Abram's best friend," Rainer answered. "He moved out of Falconwood after Percy killed himself. No one's heard from him since."

AFTER RAINER'S REVELATIONS, I couldn't find the strength to drive back to the mansion right away. I sat in a café in downtown Hartford with my head in my hands for so long that the barista came over to ask me if everything was all right. By the time I got back in the car, dusk had already fallen, and I had two missed phone calls on my cell: one each from Ben and Theo. I called Ben back first.

"Hey," he answered, warm but rushed. "I just wanted to tell you not to wait up for me when you get home. Basil and I are observing how the temperature in the greenhouse changes overnight, so we're going to camp out at the airstream. Where are you?"

"Hartford," I said. "I'm coming home soon. Make sure you eat something."

"I will," he promised. "There's leftover pasta in the fridge if you want it. Are you okay?"

"Hmm. Why?"

"You sound sad."

"I'm fine. See you tonight?"

"Tomorrow morning," he reminded me.

"Right. Love you—I mean—you know what I mean."

Ben cleared his throat. "Uh, love you too. Bye."

I took a minute to clear my mind before I dialed Theo. The

conversation with Rainer had completely destroyed me. I didn't know which way was up.

"Peyton!" Theo answered, automatically excited to hear from me. "Are you still out of town? Sammy's been begging me to see you all day. Please don't make me tell him no again."

It was the first thing to put a smile on my face all day. "You know what? I'll be home in an hour. Do you want to meet somewhere for dinner?"

"Is it terrible if we invite ourselves over to your place?" Theo asked. "Normally I'd say let's go out to eat, but I'm still crunched for cash."

I hesitated. Things at the mansion had always been kind of dicey for Sammy. I hadn't forgotten his random crying attack from a few days ago. Then again, with Alyssa under better control, maybe Sammy wouldn't have too much of a problem. I was too exhausted to hang out in town anyway. At the mansion, I could wear sweats and lie with Theo and Sammy on the couches in the foyer while we watched a movie on my laptop. It sounded like a great evening.

"No problem," I told her. "I'll pick up some pizza on my way home. If you get there before I do, just let yourself in. You know the code to the door."

WHEN I ARRIVED HOME, Theo's car was parked outside the mansion and the light in the foyer was on. My heart swelled with warmth as I zipped my coat, grabbed the pizza, and went up the porch steps. I left Penelope's photos and letters in the car, hoping I could leave my emotions about the issue with them.

"Hey, honey!" I called jokingly from the front door. "I'm home!"

No one answered. I set the pizza on the table by the door and hung my coat on the rack. The light on one of the side tables in the living room was on, and someone had started a cozy, crackling fire in the hearth even though we were well into March. Pillows and blankets were piled on the floor in front of the fireplace, along with a few of Sammy's books, but neither Sammy or Theo were to be seen.

"Hello?" I called, walking down the stairs. The kitchen was empty too. "Sammy? Theo? Is this some kind of a joke?"

No reply came. I went back upstairs and followed the corridor down to the end and back, checking each room for a sign of my guests.

"Guys, seriously," I said, my patience waning. "I had a long day, and I'm not in the mood to play hide and seek."

Still, no one emerged. I checked my phone, wondering if Theo and Sammy had stepped out for some reason. It didn't make sense. Theo's car was parked outside. Her keys and purse were next to the pizza on the table by the front door. Her coat was hung on the rack next to mine and Sammy's. They were definitely here somewhere. Had they gone to explore the rest of the mansion? My heart weighed heavy in my chest. If they went on a tour of the mansion without me, there was no knowing what Alyssa might do to them. I climbed the steps to the mezzanine, instinctively heading for the east wing—

An arm looped itself around my neck from behind as I passed a dark corner. The muscled bicep pressed against my throat, trapping my breath in my chest. I struggled in the darkness as an unfamiliar voice hissed in my ear:

"So you're Peyton, huh?" The voice was deep and raspy, like its owner was a fan of smoking hard substances. "I've been waiting to get you alone."

In the dark window of the second-floor corridor, I caught sight of a shaved head and tattooed neck. I wriggled my hand in between my throat and the arm holding me. It loosened just enough to allow me to speak. "You must be Dylan. I'd say it's a pleasure to meet you, but—ach!"

Dylan tightened his grasp again, forcing the air out of my throat. "Shut up, you stupid bitch. You're the reason Theo won't come back to me."

"Where is she?" I forced out, feeling the veins in my forehead bulging. "What did you do to her? Where's Sammy?"

"I was hoping you could tell me." Dylan dragged me across the hall to the windows that looked out on the front yard. "See, I followed my lovely girlfriend here. Watched her go inside and get all cozy. Looks like she's real familiar with your place, Peyton. How'd that happen? Does she play for the other team now? I always thought something was weird about her."

"We're friends, asshole," I gasped.

He shook me roughly, and I coughed all over the window. "I wouldn't disrespect the man with his arm around your throat. Just a friendly piece of advice."

"What the hell are you doing here?" My phone was in my back pocket. If I could keep Dylan talking long enough, maybe he wouldn't notice if I tried to call the cops. "Have you been stalking her all this time?"

"I'm not a stalker," Dylan said, his tone softening in a way that was more creepy than comforting. "All I want is my baby back."

He kept his arm flexed just enough to let me breathe and talk. I took a deep breath and said, "You might be Sammy's biological father, but you'll never be his dad."

"You think I was talking about the stupid kid?" Dylan whispered. "I don't need a kid in my life. I want Theo. That's it. *Did you just roll your eyes at me?*"

"Sammy and Theo are a package deal," I told him. "You won't get her without him too. Actually, you won't get either of them because you're a drug-addicted psychopath."

He whirled me around and slammed me against the wall. Even bracing myself, the impact took it out of me. As my head spun, Dylan pressed his forearm against his chest and leaned in until he was only inches away. From such a close distance, I could see parts of Sammy in Dylan's features, but the similarities ended there. Dylan was a scumbag, and Sammy was an angel.

"Are you playing with me?" Dylan demanded. "You better not be playing with me, because I've got a gun in my back pocket, and I intend to use it tonight."

I inched my phone out of my jeans. Dylan was too close to pay attention to anything other than my face. "My husband's on his way home. He'll find you."

"I can't wait to meet your husband," Dylan said, his eyes widening wildly. "I'm sure he's a lovely fellow. The two of you will look great dead—don't think about it!"

As soon as I'd unlocked my phone, it had made a sound to welcome me to the homepage. Dylan hammered his fist on my arm before I could dial 911. He hit the nerve in my arm, causing it to spasm. The phone jumped out of my hands and fell over the edge of the mezzanine. I heard it shatter on the first floor.

"I'm not playing your game, Peyton." Dylan's eyes were dilated, and his gaunt cheeks dripped with sweat. When he opened his mouth to speak, his breath wafted over me. The smell alone could have taken out an army. "You're playing mine. Where's Theo?"

He shook me again to emphasize the importance of his question. My eyes felt like they were going to pop out of my head. "I don't know!" I gasped. "My guess is she hid when she saw your dumb ass come through the door."

"Damn it!"

To my surprise, Dylan let me go, only to throw me to the floor. He paced across the short width of the hallway, rolling up his sleeve to scratch the track marks on his arm. If I had to guess, he was itching for a hit of whatever it was he couldn't get enough of. That worked both for and against me. On one hand, drug addicts were unpredictable. I didn't know what Dylan was capable of or if he really meant to kill me. On the other hand, drug addicts didn't make the fastest or best decisions under pressure. Sometimes, if you got lucky, their reaction times sucked.

I stayed on the floor, curled into a ball both to protect myself from a potential attack and to keep Dylan thinking that I wasn't able to move. Then, when his back was turned toward me on his next pass, I aimed a hard kick at the tendon behind his knee. His leg collapsed underneath him. Before he could recover, I sprang to my feet and slammed both hands against either side of his head. My palms hit his temples, and he went sprawling to the floor with a yell.

I ran. Right as I reached the entrance to the east wing, Dylan pulled a gun from his waistband and fired down the hallway. The bullet imbedded itself in the wallpaper, inches from my head. I chanced a backward glance. The idiot was still on the floor, cradling his head as he fired the gun blindly.

Breathing hard, I sprinted as fast as I could through the hallway. Dylan's grip on my neck and the subsequent wall slams had done some damage. It wasn't long before I had to slow down to let my body catch up, but I could hear Dylan's staggering footsteps following behind me. I didn't have much time. I needed a phone, but the landlines in the house didn't work, and my cell lay shattered on the foyer floor. My next best plan was to get out of the house and drive away, but where were Theo and Sammy? I couldn't leave without them.

"Peyton!" Dylan's garbled yell echoed through a nearby hallway, making me jump. He was closer than I thought. "Come out, come out, wherever you are!"

I picked up my pace again, reached the stairs that led to the third floor, and headed up, Hopefully, Dylan would keep moving through the second floor and into the north wing. If he went that way, I'd have enough time to make it back to the foyer before he realized I was gone. I screamed when a hand shot out from a random room on the third floor and yanked me inside. The hand covered my mouth, and Theo emerged from the gloomy darkness.

"Theo!" I gasped and threw my arms around her. "You're here! Dylan—he's downstairs. I think he's trying to kill you—us —I don't know. Where's Sammy?"

"I locked him in the attic."

"You *what?*"

Theo's eyes watered, but she held back her tears. "I saw Dylan through the foyer windows a split second before he got into the house. I'm an idiot. I should have locked the door. I did what I thought was best. I took Sammy and I ran. I took him all the way up to the fourth floor. He was the one who found the attic door hidden behind the tapestry. He wanted us both to hide—"

"Slow down," I said as Theo started hyperventilating. "Stay calm. Then what?"

"Sammy wanted us both to hide until Dylan left," Theo said, "but I couldn't let you walk in here without knowing what Dylan was up to. I was trying to warn you from the window when you parked the car, but you didn't see me."

"Where's your phone?" I demanded. "Why didn't you call the cops?"

"I stupidly left it in the living room," Theo answered, hiccupping. "Peyton, Dylan's the one who made Hillary sick. He saw her at the Black Cat and dumped a laxative in her coffee when she wasn't looking."

A thump echoed from the hallway. I shoved Theo into a closet, where a collection of dusty fur coats muffled our whispered conversation. "We have to get to your phone, Theo. This house is huge, and we can use it to our advantage. I'll lure Dylan away from the foyer so you can find your phone and call the police."

"I won't leave you alone with him—"

"He won't touch me," I told her. "I promise."

"What about Sammy?"

"He's safest in the attic," I said, hoping I was right. "He can stay there until we handle Dylan."

Theo wiped her streaming eyes on the sleeve of a coat. "I'm scared, Peyton. I'm really scared."

"Me too, but everything's going to be okay," I promised her, hugging her tightly. "We have to be brave. We have to do this. Are you ready?"

She squared her shoulders and nodded. Quietly, I opened the closet door and listened for Dylan. Everything was quiet, so I inched down and beckoned for Theo to follow me. We waited at the door to the room. A minute passed, then two. Then a voice called up the stairs.

"Oh, Theo!" Dylan sang, his vocal chords straining. "Peyton! Why don't you tell me where Sammy is, huh? I think we're going to be best friends."

Theo growled low in her throat. "I'm going to kill him."

"Stick to the plan," I whispered. "I'll go out first. He'll follow the sound of my footsteps. You go downstairs and get the phone."

She grabbed my arm as I reached for the doorknob. "Wait—"

We locked eyes. Her fear was right there, etched in the color of her pupils for anyone to see. I rested my hand against her cheek for a short moment. "Trust me, Theo. We're going to make it out of here."

Before she replied, I made a run for it, letting my feet fall heavily on the creaky wood floors. At once, Dylan's footsteps sped up, and his voice echoed through the corridor. "Oh, I love a good chase. There's no fun in an easy capture."

His words sent a shiver down my spine, but I kept running. He was stupid enough to lumber after me no matter where I set my path, so I led him down to the second floor and around the north wing at the back of the mansion. As I gasped for breath, I desperately hoped Theo had made her way back to the foyer. By now, she should have been able to reach her phone. If she hadn't, I was in trouble. I was running out of gas, and Dylan was closer than I wanted him to be. When my lungs were burning too much to keep going, I ducked into a supply closet and blocked the door with a broom handle. My heart hammered against my rib cage as Dylan's footsteps passed in the hallway just outside. I clapped a hand over my mouth to keep him from hearing my heavy breathing. He paused, and I watched the shadow of his feet wander back and forth through the crack between the floor and the door. After what felt like an hour, he continued in the same direction he'd been chasing me, and his footsteps faded out.

I waited another minute to make sure he wouldn't loop back then slipped out of the closet and ran in the opposite direction. When I reached the mezzanine, I saw Theo in the foyer down below. At the sound of my footsteps, she dropped to the floor and rolled under the couch. To my utter relief, she had her cell phone in hand. I jogged down the steps as quietly as possible and crouched beside the sofa.

"It's me!" I whispered when she let out a soft yelp. "Move over."

She shuffled to the left to give me room to join her under the couch. "Where did he go?"

"Into the west wing, but he'll make his way back around soon," I reported. "Did you call the cops?"

"They're on their way," she said. "They said they'd be here in less than five—"

She was interrupted when Dylan seized her by the ankle and dragged her out from under the couch. As he tried to control her, Theo screamed and thrashed like a demon escaped from hell. Dylan couldn't get a good grip on her, and when she nearly gouged his eyes out with her fingernails, he threw her across the room. She landed on the coffee table, which broke under her weight. I rolled out from under the couch and lunged at Dylan's legs. He fell backward and bashed his head against the wall behind him, but it wasn't enough to render him unconscious. For the second time, he pulled his gun from his belt, but he didn't aim it at me or Theo. Instead, he aimed it at the top of the stairs. When I looked up at the mezzanine, my heart stopped.

Sammy stood there, bracing himself on the railing as he measured the chaos in the foyer below.

"No," Theo gasped. "Sammy, what are you doing? I told you to stay hidden!"

"Alyssa let me out," Sammy said, staring blankly at the gun pointed right at his head. "She said you needed help."

"Sammy, go—"

"Shut up, Theo!" Dylan roared. Theo flinched as he caressed the trigger of the gun. "Let the boy speak. Go ahead, Sammy. What else did you want to say?"

Sammy's bottom lip trembled. "You're a bad man."

Dylan chuckled humorlessly. "I understand why you might see it like that, little man, but I'm just trying to take back what's mine. You're not a part of that deal. I'd say you'll understand when you're older, but" —he brandished the gun— "I guess we'll see how about that."

"Dylan," Theo gasped from across the room. "Put the gun down. He's just a kid. I'll go with you. I'll do whatever you want."

"Theo, no," I said.

"Shut up, Peyton," Theo ordered sharply.

"Yeah, Peyton, shut up," agreed Dylan. He had a glimmer in his eye now, like he knew he was about to get what he wanted. "Theo, come here."

Theo lifted herself up on trembling legs. Some of her hair hung loose from where Dylan had ripped it from her scalp. Blood ran down the side of her neck and face. Her ankle was already swollen from where it had banged against the leg of the coffee table, but she made her way across the foyer until she was within Dylan's reach. He grabbed her around the neck and pulled her close.

"Don't you miss this, baby?" he whispered in her ear, brushing her hair away from her neck so he could kiss her. His lips came away bloody. "When it was just the two of us?"

Theo caressed him, running her hands across his biceps and arms. She got closer and closer to the gun in his right hand. "Yes, Dylan. I missed you. Take me with you. Just leave Sammy."

Dylan leaned his head against Theo's skin, nuzzling in her neck. He didn't lower the gun. "You really want me to leave the kid?"

"Yes," Theo said. "You have me. You just said it yourself. It's better when it's just the two of us."

"Just to be sure: leave the kid?"

"Yes, baby."

Dylan grinned against Theo's neck, baring his teeth. "Nah, I don't think so."

He pulled the trigger.

Theo screamed.

The air turned cold.

Sammy collapsed.

And Dylan's head snapped back as, at the last second, something hit his elbow and forced the gun up under his chin. The bullet ripped through his face, and he fell out of Theo's grasp.

Dead on the floor, Dylan began to leak blood all over the new foyer carpet. Theo covered her mouth, sobbing into her hands. Together, we both turned our eyes to the mezzanine.

At the top of the stairs, a ghostly figure helped Sammy to his feet. It was a woman—tall and thin—wearing a silk nightgown that flowed all the way down to the floor. Once Sammy was standing upright again, she held tightly on to his hand and looked down at me. My heart stopped.

"Penelope?" I whispered. "Penelope Abram?"

*P*urgatory was a police department. More specifically, it was the Falconwood police department, where I'd been waiting all night while the cops checked out the crime scene in my house. I'd expected to be bombarded with questions the second I got here, and I mentally prepared myself to give the answers, but how do you explain that a ghost made your best friend's ex-boyfriend shoot himself after he threatened to kill his own son? Thankfully, the town of Falconwood was so small that there weren't enough officers to monitor the crime scene *and* babysit me at the department. That, at the moment, was for the best.

My husband—almost ex-husband—came crashing through the front entrance of the police department, slamming the door so hard that the wide window behind it shuddered. "Peyton!" he gasped, wrapping me up in his arms when he saw me. "What happened? I got your call in the middle of the night, but when I went to the mansion, there were a bunch of cops outside. They said you were here? What's going on?"

I rested my head against his chest, listening to the blood pumping through his heart. The plaster cast on his arm chafed against my shoulder as he hugged me, but I didn't care. I needed the contact, to be held by someone who loved me. I burst into tears, sobbing into Ben's sweater. They were tears that I'd been holding back all night without realizing it. Ben tightened his hug until all I heard was the steady, muffled beat of his heart. I let it lull me into a more peaceful state of mind, counting the beats until I could control myself. My breath hitched two or three times before it settled, and my pulse stopped bouncing erratically around in my neck. Ben held me until I calmed down, his chin resting on the top of my head. When I was ready, I pulled away and wiped my eyes on the back of my sleeve.

"Are you okay?" Ben stole a stack of tissues from behind an officer's desk and handed it to me. "That's the first thing I need to know. The police said you'd been beaten up—" His voice cracked and broke off, and he bowed his head to hide his look of pain. "God, Peyton, I should have been there, and I don't even know what happened."

I'd practically forgotten that I'd been manhandled just a few hours earlier, dragged around the mansion like a rag doll. From what I could see of my reflection in the window, I had bruises all around my neck and on the backs of my arms. My aggressor, however, had gotten what he deserved.

Ben's warm hands caressed either side of my face, turning me gently so that he could examine the damage. "Tell me you're okay. Do we need to go to the hospital?"

I took his hands in mine. "No, the medic at the house checked me out. It's all superficial. I don't have a concussion or anything like that. It's nowhere near as bad as when you fell off the roof."

Ben's own wounds were healing well. I'd spotted him trying to scratch underneath his cast with a pen, but the plaster reached all the way from his hand, past his elbow, and up to his shoulder.

After his fall, the bones is his arm were shattered, and he needed surgery to put it all back together again. He had a long way to go before he regained full mobility, but it was the last thing on his list to improve. The bruises around his face were gone completely now, and his broken ribs only bothered him every once in a while—if he turned the wrong way or moved too abruptly—during his daily routine. When he'd first returned home after his injury, he had been bound to a wheelchair and had a bad attitude. In just under two months, he'd come so far.

"Forget about me," Ben said. "It isn't a competition. I just want you to be okay. Will you please tell me what happened? I mean, can you? I won't make you talk about it if you don't want to, but I'm dying from the suspense, Peyton. Your voicemails didn't make much sense."

I couldn't remember what I'd rambled over the phone to Ben's message box. Everything that happened between leaving the mansion and arriving at the police station was a blur. "Theo and Sammy came over last night to keep me company while you were at Basil's, but when I got there, I couldn't find them. Then Dylan showed up—"

"Who's Dylan again?" Ben led me to a comfortable ergonomic chair behind one of the police officers' desk and sat me down. He kneeled in front of me, making sure to stay right in my line of vision, and kept his warm hands on my knees for comfort. "I'm a little behind on the story, baby."

"He's Theo's ex-boyfriend," I told him, going through tissues like nobody's business. "Sammy's father. She ran away from him when she figured out she was pregnant with Sammy. Anyway, he found her here in Falconwood a few weeks ago. She didn't keep me updated, but I guess he started harassing her. He tried kidnapping Sammy, but thankfully that kid's smarter than your average six-year-old boy."

"I remember." Ben patted my knee reassuringly. "It was only a few days ago."

"Oh, right." At this point, the four months we had already spent in Falconwood felt as though they had stretched into four years. I'd lost track of when things had happened. "Anyway, we thought Dylan had given up after Sammy gave him the slip that day, but I guess it only pissed him off more. My guess is he was stalking Theo, and he followed her to the mansion last night. He broke in, so when I got there, he attacked me—"

"Wait, where were Theo and Sammy?"

"They hid," I said. "I got away from Dylan and ran. When I found Theo, we split up. I distracted Dylan while she went to the foyer to get her phone. She called the cops, but Dylan found us before they got her. We attacked him, but he aimed—" I choked up as the moment flashed before my eyes. "He aimed a gun at Sammy."

Ben cupped his head in his hands, as if he couldn't bear to hear what happened next. "And then what?"

To tell him the truth would be to admit that I'd been lying to him for months. The truth was hard to believe, and it didn't make much sense to me either. The truth was that a ghost had turned Dylan's gun away from Sammy and onto himself. The truth was that the ghost had forced Dylan to pull the trigger when the muzzle of the gun was under his chin. Dylan had died in an instant, and the woman at the top of the stairs holding Sammy's hand vanished as quickly as she had appeared. It was easier to believe she hadn't been there at all.

"He shot himself instead," I answered. This was not a lie. It only omitted the portion of the true events that Ben wouldn't understand. "He turned the gun up and shot himself under the chin."

"In front of you?"

"In front of all of us," I said. "In front of Sammy."

"Oh my God." Ben crouched over me at an awkward angle to cradle me against his chest. "I'm so sorry, Peyton. I'm so sorry you had to see that. What can I do?"

"Can I put my feet in your lap?"

He rolled another office chair across from mine, sat down, and drew my legs into his lap. As he massaged my calves, he scanned me with a worried look. "So when did the police show up?"

"About two minutes after Dylan shot himself," I told him wearily. "He still had the gun in his hand. We tried to explain what happened, but Theo was in shock."

"What about Sammy?"

"He seemed fine."

Also true. As adults, we always expected children to react with more fear in situations like these. We forgot that a child's innocence protected them from mature emotions. Sammy didn't know how to react to watching someone shoot himself. It was Theo who had dissolved into a bag of emotions after Dylan's death. She was so frozen with fear that I went to Sammy first, pulling him into my arms at the top of the stairs to the mezzanine. In that moment, as Sammy buried his face in mine, I saw the ghostly woman vanish around the corner and into the next hallway.

"Where are Theo and Sammy now?" Ben asked, pulling my head out of the past few hours and back to the present in the police station.

"At the clinic," I said. "The medics wanted to make sure Sammy wasn't hurt, and Theo wasn't responding. They wouldn't let me go with them."

Ben's brow furrowed in frustration. "That's crap. You're Theo's best friend, and you're practically Sammy's other mom. Not to mention, you got injured as well. You should be at the clinic too. I swear, when those cops get back, I'm going to give them a piece of my mind—"

I tickled Ben's side with my foot. "Don't worry about it. I told you—the medics checked me out at the house. I think they wanted someone here at the police station to question once they were finished at the house."

"So let me get this straight," Ben said, untying my boots and pulling them off so he could rub my feet. "There's a dead guy in our house, bleeding all over the floor in the foyer?"

"Yes."

"That flooring is brand new."

A laugh barked its way out of my throat. "There's a dead guy in our house, bleeding all over the foyer, and all you can think of is the new flooring?"

"What?" Ben said innocently. "It was expensive! Can you imagine what Jim is going to say? He's going to have to do it all over again."

I had a feeling Ben was ramping up the importance of the renovations we'd been doing at the Abram Mansion to get my mind off of Dylan's suicide. At the very least, it was a solid attempt to cheer me up, and to my surprise, it was actually working.

"Are you kidding?" I sniffled. "Jim will be thrilled. He gets double the money for the same floor."

Ben's chuckle faded quickly, and he settled into a pensive expression. "Do you think it's worth it anymore? The renovations?"

"I'm starting to wonder why we tried to keep up with them in the first place," I admitted. "According to my grandfather's will, we only have to live in the mansion for another two months before we can sell it. We're never going to finish upgrading it by then. We should have stopped after our own living space was finished."

"It seemed like a good idea at the time," Ben said. "A little paint, and that place isn't nearly as depressing as it first seemed. Whoever owns it next should turn it into a museum or something. The construction is amazing, just... not for me."

"You miss home, don't you?"

Before our journey to the Abram Mansion, Ben and I had lived in our high school hometown, where we co-owned a small two-bedroom house. While I needed more, Ben was perfectly content to stay where we had always been. It was why we were on the verge of divorce.

"I do," Ben sighed. "I miss normalcy. Falconwood doesn't feel normal."

"Not at all," I muttered.

Car engines rumbled in the parking lot and headlights flashed through the window as the police returned to their small office. Within seconds, the police team that had been investigating the scene at the mansion swarmed inside, chatting rowdily about Dylan's death. When they spotted me and Ben in their chairs, they came down on us with a ton of questions.

"Where were you at ten-fifteen p.m.?"

"Did you know of the deceased's history of mental illness and drug abuse?"

"Was the child present at the time of the shooting?"

One cop—a leggy blonde who looked better in the Falconwood P.D. attire than any of her male counterparts—broke through the crowd. Officer Hillary Spaughton was the one and only cop I trusted in Falconwood. "Back it up, everyone," she said, and though she spoke at a regular volume, everyone heard her and listened. The cops—even the detective—bowed out of her way. Hillary looked paler than usual, but that was probably due to the fact that Dylan had dropped more than the advised dosage of laxatives in her coffee the day before.

"Let's go to the office," she said, beckoning me and Ben to

follow her. "We'll have more privacy there. You don't mind, Beckworth?"

Beckworth, Falconwood's lonesome detective and the only guy in the department with his own private office, shook his head. Hillary patted his shoulder in thanks—she was taller than him—and led us away from the horde. In the relative peace of the office, she sank into Beckworth's chair with a surprising amount of familiarity.

"Everyone knows I deserve Beckworth's job," she said in reply to my silent question. "But the chief decided to hire an out-of-towner, which was a mistake because I know this place better than the back of my own hand. Anyway, how are you two holding up? Anyone barf yet?"

"We just want to know what's going to happen next," Ben said. "Is Peyton in trouble? Do we need to get a lawyer?"

"Probably not." Hillary swigged a blue electrolyte drink from her water bottle and puffed out an exhausted breath. "I'm ninety-nine percent sure Dylan's death is going to be ruled a suicide. He still had the gun in his hand. No one else's prints were on it. It's impossible to read the evidence any other way. What you might consider instead of a lawyer is a therapist."

"No," I said right away. "I don't want to talk to some stranger about this. I don't need to."

"You say that now," Hillary replied, "but I can guarantee you're going to change your mind later. I've seen a lot of crap go down in my line of work, and I thought I could handle it all by myself at first. Trust me, it's better to talk to a professional."

"We'll consider it," Ben said, placing his hand over mine before I could argue any more. "What happens next?"

"We had the crime scene team clean up the area already," Hillary reported. "You can go home as soon as you're ready to do so."

"It's gone?" I clarified. "The body? The blood?"

"You can't even tell something happened there," she confirmed. "Listen, I know it might be hard to go back there right away, so I called the local inn just in case. They have a room available if you'd like to stay there instead. We'll cover the cost."

"Thanks," Ben said. "We'll consider it."

"What do *you* think about all of this?" I asked Hillary. "About Dylan shooting himself?"

Hillary gazed over the desk at me, folding her fingers together. "I think it was only a matter of time before Dylan ended up the way he did. He was a heavy drug user, and my guess is he was going through withdrawals when he came to find Theo at your house. We pulled his records" —she entered Beckworth's password on his computer and got access to his files— "and Dylan's been in out and out of prison for years. Theft, assault, possession. You name it. I don't know what the hell Theo was doing with this guy, but she was smart to get Sammy out of that situation. " She patted her stomach, burped, and took another sip of her drink. "I might be speaking out of turn, but I'm glad he's gone. Theo doesn't need a guy like Dylan harassing her, and I sure as hell don't need some idiot dumping laxatives in my coffee every morning. He was on my shit list as soon as I met him."

"Do you know if Theo and Sammy are okay?" I asked her. "I tried calling the clinic, but they wouldn't tell me anything because I'm not family."

"They're doing better," Hillary said. "I checked in on them before I went to the mansion. Theo's no longer in shock, but they're keeping her overnight just in case. Sammy is... well, he's Sammy. That kid bounces back from everything."

"When can I see them?"

"They'll be released tomorrow morning," she answered. "You can make plans with them then, but don't push it. They need their rest, and so do you two. Where did we land on the room at the inn?"

"We'll pass," I said.

"Are you sure?" Ben asked me in an undertone. "I know you don't always sleep well at the mansion. It wouldn't be a big deal to share a room at the inn for a couple nights."

"We made a promise to my grandfather to stay at the mansion for six months," I reminded him. "We have to go back at some point. Why put it off?"

"As long as you're certain," Ben said.

"I'm certain."

"That's that then," Hillary said, logging out of Beckworth's computer. She stood up to walk us out. "I'll keep you updated on the case, but I don't expect there to be any surprises. Now that Dylan's out of the picture, the two of you can rest easy."

DESPITE HILLARY'S attempt at comfort, there was to be no resting easy at the mansion that night. When Ben and I returned home, the foyer smelled strongly of disinfectant and the laminate wood flooring bore wet streaks from where the cleaners had mopped up Dylan's blood. The smell carried through the corridors and into my bedroom. It was so prevalent that I asked Dylan if I could stay in his room instead. Not only was his bedroom farther from the foyer and therefore less smelly, but I also didn't want to sleep alone that night. I didn't want to be alone at all.

There were times when Ben was perfect, and I asked myself why we were getting divorced at all. Tonight was one of those nights. He stood in the bathroom while I showered, kept me company in the kitchen as I refilled my water bottle, and even walked me back to the bathroom and kept watch outside the door when I had to pee again. When I couldn't fall asleep, he held me close. Though his plaster arm extended up at an odd angle over the pillowcase, he didn't move until I'd drifted off to the sound of his heartbeat. I woke up a few hours later as the sky was just beginning to lighten. Ben was passed out against the pillows, his good arm draped over my body. Carefully, I slid out from beneath his weight and tiptoed into the hallway.

In the foyer, I walked around the part of the floor where Dylan had died then flopped onto the couch. I gazed up the steps to the mezzanine. Just hours ago, Sammy had stood there with a gun pointed to his head. We could have lost him in a second. What kind of man aimed a gun at a child?

"The crazy kind," I muttered to myself.

The curtains fluttered, and a cold draft wafted across the room. A chill crept across my spine, a sure sign that I wasn't alone in the foyer.

"Alyssa?" I whispered. "Is that you?"

A small child emerged from behind the curtains. She was of the adorable variety, with chubby cheeks, auburn hair, and a pink scarf tied around her neck. She also happened to be dead. A hazy light outlined her figure. Until recently, Alyssa never appeared in my direct line of vision, nor did she often speak to me, but I had a feeling the rules were changing.

"That was your mother I saw last night, wasn't it?" I asked her, keeping my voice low. "She was the one who saved Sammy?"

Alyssa nodded before flitting to the other side of the room like a hummingbird. She hid in the alcove beneath the mezzanine, peering out at me with wide-eyed curiosity.

"Her friend—Charles—told me what he thought happened to you and your mother." It seemed so long ago that I had met with Charles Rainer to discuss what he knew about the Abram family. "Your father… did he hurt you?"

Alyssa nodded again.

"Is he the reason you're still here?" It was the easier way to ask what I really wanted to know. Did Percy Abrams kill his wife and daughter before he committed suicide?

Once more, Alyssa nodded. As soon as she did, a pain ricocheted through my heart as if someone had shot an arrow clean through me.

"I'm so sorry," I told her. "You shouldn't have had to go through that. Your mother didn't deserve it either. Has she been here all along with you?" Another nod. "I didn't know. I thought it was just you. I guess it makes sense though." The more I thought about it, the more obvious it became that Penelope had been in the house all along. She just hadn't shown herself to me like Alyssa did. "It was your mother who always chased me out, wasn't it? In the attic and your bedroom? Every time something was thrown at me, I thought it was you, but it was your mom."

"She doesn't like people in her house."

As always, when Alyssa did choose to speak to me, it startled me so much that my bones tried to jump out of my skin. Her voice was soft and warbly, like a songbird who was unsure of its tune. I tried to hide my discomfort from the little ghost.

"I'm trying to help her," I said.

"She doesn't think so," Alyssa whispered. "She says you bring bad things into the house."

"What bad things?"

"People."

"Alyssa, I wouldn't invite anyone to the mansion if I didn't think they were good people," I assured her. "What happened last night with Dylan was a fluke. We didn't bring him here."

"Not him."

"I don't know who you're talking about then." With Dylan on my mind, I had another question for the little ghost. "Alyssa...is Dylan going to come back like you did? Because he died here?"

As the light of dawn brushed the foyer with golden strokes,

Alyssa shook her head and came a little closer. "There are rules. He died by his own hand. We were wronged. That's what Mama says anyway."

"So you can't pass over because you were murdered?"

"I guess not."

"The man who killed you is also dead," I reminded her. "Isn't that enough retribution for you to move on?"

Perhaps it was different when the man who killed you was your own father because Alyssa shook her head again. "We remain here. We can't go. We need your help."

"I can't help you unless you tell me what you're looking for," I said. "You have to give me more to go on. Just tell me what I need to do."

"Alyssa!" The stern voice rang down the second-floor corridor from the east wing of the house, where the Abrams' main living accommodations had been. "Come here this instant!"

It was the unmistakable tone of a mother ready to scold her daughter. Alyssa turned bright pink, and the fuzzy outline around her grew blurrier. I knew she was about to vanish.

"Wait—!"

It was too late. Alyssa disappeared from the foyer and reappeared at the top of the stairs of the mezzanine. She put her finger to her lips before running off, the pitter patter of her little feet fading into nothing. Seconds later, Ben emerged from his room with a loud yawn.

"Oh, it's just you," he said, patting my shoulder affectionately from behind the couch.

"What's just me?"

He headed down the stairs into the kitchen. "I thought I heard voices."

"You did," I muttered under my breath.

. . .

315

ACCORDING TO THE POLICE, the best thing to do after a traumatic experience was to get back to your normal routine as soon as possible. On one hand, that seemed impossible. A man had killed himself right in front of me and I was supposed to have coffee like it had never happened? On the other hand, what else was I supposed to do but head into town like I did every other morning? The Black Cat Café was one of my main sources of comfort anyway, and as soon as Ben left for work, I didn't want to be alone at the mansion anymore. Of course, the events of last night had spread through the small town like wildfire, and the owner of the Black Cat was the first to ask me about it.

"Is it true?" Mason said as soon as I stepped up to the cash register. "Did you kill Theo's ex-boyfriend for trespassing at your house?"

I set my debit card on the counter with a quick snap. "Now Mason. If I had killed a man last night, do you think I would be standing in your café today? I need a double shot of espresso and the largest stack of French toast you've ever made. I'm talking record-breaking here, buddy. Can you do that?"

My quick tone told Mason not to mess with me, and the message must have spread through the rest of the café because no one else approached me as I carried my coffee to my regular table near the front windows. Not long after, Theo and Sammy came in. Mason caught my eye as they walked up to the counter, and I drew a finger across my throat. He caught my drift and took their order without mentioning the events of last night. Sammy spotted me in the corner booth and ran over.

"I'm glad you're okay," he said, climbing into my lap. "You're okay, right?"

"Yes." I smiled down at his cute, pink cheeks. "Forget about me. What about you?"

"I'm fine," he said. "Mom's scared though. I think she might have seen what really happened last night. She keeps trying to talk to me about it—"

I hushed Sammy as Theo made her way over to us from the counter, balancing her coffee, Sammy's juice, and a tiny jug of creamer. When she set everything down, the jug tipped over, sending creamer across the table.

"Damn!" She threw a pile of napkins over the spill before the liquid could reach mine and Sammy's side of the table. "Of course. Can't anything go right?"

I lifted Sammy over my lap so that I could slide out of the booth. Then I coaxed Theo to sit next to him. "Just relax, Theo. I'll take care of it."

I mopped up the rest of the creamer, tossed the soggy napkins, and got fresh creamer from Mason. As I set it on the table, Theo covered her hand with mine. "I truly don't know what I would do without you, Peyton. You've been a literal life-saver these days."

"How are you holding up?" I asked. "Did you spend the night at the hospital?"

"We did, though I didn't want to." Theo poured creamer into her coffee then took a long sip and sighed. "Apparently, I went into shock. I hardly remember what happened."

"Well, don't expect me to give you a refresher course," I said, half joking. "I don't think I'm ready to talk about it yet."

Theo shifted uncomfortably in her seat. "Actually, there is one thing I wanted to talk to you about. Hey, Sammy? Would you mind sitting at the counter for a while? Ask Mason to give you some crayons and a coloring menu."

Sammy, who was too smart not to know that he was being sent away, rolled his eyes and crawled past his mother to get out of the booth. Theo watched as he hopped onto one of the stools at the coffee counter and blew a straw wrapper at Mason to get his attention. Mason pretended to get mad, waggling his finger as Sammy laughed and laughed.

"He seems okay," I said to Theo, "considering last night's events."

"It's like he didn't see it happen," Theo replied, her eyes on her son. "I swear I'm more messed up than he is. Do you think I should take him to a therapist?"

"Hillary thinks we should all go."

"Yeah, but kids are different," Theo said. "I don't want to force him to talk about it if it's going to make it worse, you know?"

I watched Sammy turn on the milk steamer for Mason. "Maybe you should ask Sammy what he wants to do. He's advanced for his age, you know. He can make his own decisions."

"You're probably right." Theo fiddled with a sugar packet. "But what about that thing at the top of the stairs?"

A cold wave washed over me, as if someone had tipped an iced coffee into my lap. "What thing at the top of the stairs?"

"Come on, you had to have seen it." Theo checked to make sure no one was listening, then leaned in to whisper, "The *ghost.*"

If there was a way to play this well, I hadn't figured it out. I stared across the table at Theo for several long seconds, my face blank as my brain flashed through thousands of questions. Had Theo really seen Penelope with Sammy on the mezzanine? Did that mean everyone could see the ghosts in the Abram Mansion, or did they only appear to certain people when they wanted to? *Or* did Theo have the same weird ability that me and Sammy did —the stupid sixth sense or whatever you wanted to call it?

"I'm not crazy," Theo said, misreading my vacant expression. "I know what I saw. There was a woman holding Sammy's hand right after Dylan shot himself. She was all blurry, but I swear she was there. Didn't you see her? Tell me you saw her."

The last sentence sounded like a plea. Theo needed her assumption validated. Otherwise, she had to face the idea that maybe she *was* crazy… or hallucinating.

"Theo," I began gently, stretching my hand across the table to reach hers. "Last night was the worst thing you've witnessed in your life. It makes sense for you to have seen something you didn't understand. You said yourself that you were in shock."

She pulled her hand away from mine. "This happened *before* I started losing it. Peyton, someone was standing with Sammy, and I have this weird feeling that—you know what? Forget it. You're right. It's crazy."

"It's not crazy," I insisted. "Tell me."

Theo sighed and looked out the window to watch the unbothered citizens of Falconwood go about their regular lives. "I have this weird feeling that the woman—whoever she was— somehow stopped Dylan from shooting Sammy. You saw him, Peyton. You and I both know he intended to hit Sammy when he pulled that trigger." Her voice hitched, and she quickly glanced at the counter to make sure Sammy was still there. "Something changed at the last second. Something made Dylan shoot himself instead. He was too vain to commit suicide."

"Listen to me, Theo." This time, I took both her hands and held them over the table top until she looked at me with teary eyes. "You're looking for the reason behind a miracle, and your head is filling in the gaps for you. Do yourself a favor. Appreciate that Dylan is gone and that you still have Sammy, because what happened last night *was* a miracle. Focus on that."

She squeezed my fingers and allowed one tear to drop from her eyelashes before wiping them away with a fresh napkin. "You're right. Sammy matters most, and so do you, Peyton. You matter most too."

22

On the following Monday and Tuesday, Theo called the elementary school to inform them that Sammy was sick and unable to attend classes. Sammy was fine. He didn't have a hint of a sniffle, and when Theo told me she had also called out of work two days in a row, I realized what the real trouble was. On Wednesday morning, I showed up at their apartment over the local bakery to see what I could to do solve it.

Theo answered the door with a look of surprise. "What are you doing here? It's eight o'clock in the morning. Aren't you usually at the Black Cat by now?"

"I thought I'd swing by here instead and check on Sammy." I lifted the box of fresh breakfast sandwiches that I'd bought from downstairs as an offering, and as she accepted them, I took the opportunity to squeeze past her and into the apartment. "Oh, Sammy! Where you at, dude?"

"He's sleeping," Theo answered hurriedly, depositing the breakfast sandwiches on the kitchen counter. "I told you earlier. He's been sick for the past two days. He's only just started to feel better—"

Sammy burst from the bedroom that he and Theo shared and sailed into my arms. His cheeks were pink, his eyes were healthy and glowing, and there was no breathiness to his voice when he said to me, "Hi, Peyton! Guess what me and Mom are doing? Playing hooky!"

I swung Sammy up to my hip. He'd had a growth spurt in the last couple of weeks, so his feet knocked against my knees now. The lengthening of children always struck me as sad and exciting at the same time. Sammy was finally starting to look his age, but it came at the expense of losing his cute, compact figure.

"Playing hooky, huh?" I ticked Sammy around his neck, and he ducked his chin with a giggle to ward me off. "Do you know what that means?"

"Yeah, it means I don't have to school and Mama doesn't have to go to work. But" —he hushed me— "don't tell anyone because it's a secret."

I glanced over the top of Sammy's head to see Theo doing her best to hide her guilty expression. It wasn't working.

"Okay, fine!" She tossed her hands in the air. "We're playing hooky. Sammy's not sick. Are you happy now?"

I set Sammy on the ground and ruffled his hair. "Hey, buddy. Let me talk to your mom alone really quick?"

"Sure." He beckoned me toward him, and I leaned down to his level so he could whisper in my ear. "She hasn't gone to bed for three nights in a row. She sits by the window over there." Subtly, he jerked his head in the direction of the window that looked out onto the parking lot of the bakery. "I think she's scared."

"I'll talk to her about it," I whispered back. "Get out of here, squirt."

I patted his butt as he ran off. Once he was ensconced in the room and the sound of cartoons emanated from under the door, I straightened up to address Theo.

"What did he say to you?" she asked. Her posture—arms crossed, shoulders hiked up to her ears—was defensive. "Whatever it was—"

"He says you're scared," I reported. Hopefully, Sammy wasn't listening from the other room, lest he think I was betraying his trust by relaying his whispers to his mother. "That you haven't been sleeping at night. Is that true?"

Theo sank into the worn-out armchair she got off Craigslist for fifty bucks and leaned her head over the back of it to stretch her neck. "Can you blame me? First, Sammy almost gets kidnapped. Then his own father tries to kill him before shooting himself right in front of all of us. Before that, Sammy ran off at every chance he got. I feel like every time I let Sammy out of my sight, something terrible happens."

"Theo, you can't keep Sammy out of school just because you're scared of what *might* happen to him." I sat on the mismatched ottoman and playfully swatted her knees as if to admonish her for her actions. "The one good thing about what happened is that Dylan is no longer in the picture. Sammy isn't in danger, and he needs to go to school."

"He hates it anyway," Theo said. "The kids still bully him, God knows why, and the teachers won't do anything about it. I picked up his homework from the school and taught the lessons to him myself for the past few days. He does so much better when he's homeschooled."

"Maybe, but *you* can't homeschool him every day," I said. "You have a job, remember? One that you need to keep in order to afford this apartment. I'd invite you to stay at the mansion, but—"

"I couldn't ask that of you." She glanced through her fingers at me, and the hope on her face was obvious. She wanted me to insist on her and Sammy moving in with us. "It's too much to put on you."

"I would do it in a heartbeat," I assured her. This was true, but with all the ghostly action going on at the mansion, I wanted Theo and Sammy to be far away from it. Sammy was especially prone to witnessing the dead's jaunts. "But even with the renovations we've completed so far, a lot of the house just isn't safe. Sammy has the tendency to wander, and I would blame myself forever if he ended up getting hurt in our home."

Theo's shoulders buckled as she blew out a sigh. "Yeah, Sammy's pretty oblivious when it comes to judging the danger of a situation."

"Besides, going to school is good for him," I said. "It's unfair that he gets bullied, but he needs regular social interaction. If you keep him cooped up at the house—sure, he'll be Mama's little boy forever—but he's not going to learn how to cooperate with kids his own age. Homeschooled kids go on field trips and do all sorts of stuff to make sure they're learning social skills too. I love how much you love Sammy, but you can't be his best friend for the rest of his life. Believe me, once he hits puberty, you won't want to be."

That got a laugh out of her. She swung her legs into my lap. "You're right. I can't be afraid of letting Sammy out of my sight, but it's a hard habit to break. I feel like I've been looking over my shoulder for Dylan ever since I moved away from him. I've always been overprotective of Sammy."

"Well, now that Dylan's gone, maybe it's time to take a breath," I suggested. "The biggest danger to Sammy is gone, you know? You can relax. Let Sammy figure things out on his own."

"I want to," Theo said, threading her fingers through her long, shiny hair. "But he also just watched his own father die. I have no idea how to handle that. I still think it might be a good idea to get him to a therapist."

I pulled on her pinky toe until the joint popped. "Then take him to a therapist. There's no harm in trying it out. If Sammy feels uncomfortable, he'll let you know."

"I think I will," Theo said.

"And, uh, what about the whole ghost thing?"

She winced as I cracked the knuckle of her big toe. "I don't know. I keep thinking it's too crazy, you know? Like maybe my mind hallucinated the whole thing as a coping mechanism. God, maybe I should be the one to go to therapy."

"You should both go." I didn't know what the best thing for Theo was, but finding out that the Abram Mansion was haunted by its previously murdered occupants probably wasn't on the list of things that would make Theo feel better. "At least try it out. It couldn't hurt, right? You have nothing to lose." I checked my watch. "I better get going. I only meant to stop by for a couple of minutes."

Theo nudged my midsection with her foot. "Sorry, I didn't mean to keep you."

"I never mind seeing you two," I said, "but I've been trying to catch up with Della Gordon for a while now, and my best bet is to find her at the Black Cat for breakfast."

"How is Della?" Theo asked. "I heard around town that she had another episode."

"Is that common knowledge? Her, um, mental disorder?"

"Pretty much." Theo got up to inspect the breakfast sandwiches I'd brought for them. "No one talks about it specifically, out of respect for Della, but the whole town knows that she's had some trouble in the past."

I tugged on a loose thread of the armchair, trying to weave it back into place. "I'm worried about her. The last time I saw her, she seemed kind of... off."

The last few times I'd seen Della, she seemed straight up out of her mind. Like me and Sammy, Della also knew about the dead residents of the Abram Mansion, but the spirits affected her in ways that turned her personality upside down.

"She'll bounce back," Theo said. "I've known Della for as long as we've lived here. She's gone through a few rough spells before. Don't worry about it, but make sure you're available to her. Everyone loves the Gordons, but no one's very close to them. Actually, I think you and Ben are the only two people they've ever invited over to have dinner at the airstream. They're super private about their personal lives."

"Thanks for the tip," I said, putting my jacket back on. I stole a bite of Theo's breakfast sandwich. "Take Sammy to school and go to work. I'll be there to pick him up this afternoon like always. You don't have to worry."

"Thankfully, I never worry about Sammy when he's with you."

"Good to hear."

FOR THE PAST SEVERAL DAYS, Della Gordon had not shown up at the Black Cat Café for her usual breakfast and coffee. Nevertheless, I came each morning and sat for longer than I usually would have just in case Della decided to drop by. I finally got lucky. Just as I had resigned myself to another disappointment and was gathering my things to leave, the bell over the café door gave a cheery chime as Della walked in. She was positively glowing. The fading winter chill made her cheeks pink and bright, her eyes were clear, and her hair was kept away from her face with an intricate Dutch braid that made me jealous about my own lack of styling skills. She ordered from Mason, who beamed and patted her hand to welcome her back, then she turned around to search for a place to sit. I waved from my usual corner.

"Look at you," Della said once she'd made it over and hugged me tight. "Back to your usual schedule. Seems like things are finally looking up, am I right?"

"They definitely are." I looked Della over, taking in the new plumpness of her figure. There was something different about her, but I couldn't put my finger on it. "How are you doing? It's been a while since we've seen each other." What I really meant to ask Della, I couldn't say out loud. What had happened since she last left the mansion?

"I am fabulous." She swept her arms above her head, brought her hands together at her heart, and bowed to me, as if she was still in yoga teacher mode after a class she taught at the local community center. "I've never felt better actually. It's like I've been renewed. It's amazing what a little green juice and meditation can do, isn't it?"

"I'm glad to hear it." I gestured her toward my table. "Do you want to join me? I've got plenty of space."

She glanced over the rest of my breakfast and my empty coffee cup. "Looks like you're about ready to leave. I don't need to keep you."

"I can order another cup of coffee," I said, urging her into the booth. "It's worth catching up with you. Please?"

Della unzipped her denim jacket and draped it over the back of the booth before sliding in. "I suppose I need a place to sit anyway."

I waited until Mason brought my new coffee and Della's breakfast. Then I waited while Della dug into her veggie omelet. It was a relief to see her eat. The last few times I'd seen her, her face had become sallow. I much preferred this new version of Della.

"Not to dive right in, but are we going to talk about what happened?" I finally asked her in a low voice when I couldn't take the suspense anymore. "About what you told me regarding the Abrams?"

"I heard what happened." Della munched happily on her fries. "It's tragic that young man couldn't get his life together, but I suppose Theo and Sammy are much better off without him."

"I'm not talking about Dylan," I said. "You told me that I had to find out the truth about Alyssa Abram so she could find peace... so that the voice in your head would stop following you around."

"Shh!" Della's mask broke. Her fork clattered to her plate. "Don't say that out loud."

I lowered my voice. "You asked me to track down Charles Rainer. I did that. You also told me to find you when I knew the truth about Penelope Abram. I've been trying to do *that* for days, but you've been incommunicado. Are you with me or not? Because I don't think I can do this without someone by my side who understands what's happening."

Della gulped her water. "I—I want to help you, Peyton. I can tell you're making progress too."

"How?"

"Because she's been quiet lately."

"Who? The voice in your head?"

"Yes."

"It's Penelope Abram, isn't it?" I guessed. "She's the one who you've been talking to at the mansion. I can't imagine there are more than two ghosts running around the place. What has she told you? Why does she talk to you but not to me? I'm the one—"

Della slammed her empty water glass against the table top. "I can't speak for Penelope, but she's never trusted anyone who has set foot in the mansion since her death. She won't ask you for help."

"She doesn't hate Sammy," I said. "She saved him."

"Because Sammy is Alyssa's friend," Della said, "and Penelope refused to see another child die in that house. What did Charles tell you about the Abrams?"

327

"He confirmed a hunch of mine," I answered. "He thinks Percy killed Penelope and Alyssa. Is that true?"

Della suddenly became infatuated with her veggie omelet again, shoving away huge bites so her mouth was too full to talk.

"Why won't anyone tell me anything?" I hissed across the table. "I'm tired of having to piece everything together by myself when it seems like everyone else already has the information. I found out the truth, so now it's your turn to hold up your end of the bargain. What are *you* going to do to help Alyssa and Penelope pass over?"

"Pass over?"

"Do I look like a freaking ghost whisperer to you?"

Due to her frantic feasting, Della ran out of omelet to distract herself with. She patted her lips with a paper napkin. "What you need is the item of information that Penelope specifically asked me to keep from you. She doesn't trust you with it, but I do. I'll tell you, but you have to promise not to go to the police."

"Things would be so much easier if people didn't say that," I muttered.

"Promise?"

"Yeah, yeah. I promise."

Della beckoned me toward her, and I got out of my seat to lean across the table. She cupped her hands around her mouth and whispered, "Percy Abram is still alive. He faked his own death. That's why Penelope and Alyssa can't move on. He goes free for his crimes against them."

I lowered myself into the booth. "That can't be."

"Oh? And why not?"

"He wrote a suicide note," I reminded her. "He jumped from a cliff edge. The Falconwood police found his body in the river by the house."

"Not so," Della countered. "Yes, Percy left a suicide note and staged his death. Penelope thinks he actually climbed up that mountain and left his gear there to lead the police astray, but they never located his body, Peyton. Percy Abram is alive."

"Say I believe you," I said. "Say the information we have is actually true. What are we supposed to do about it?"

"We have to locate Percy Abram," Della answered, as if it was the most simple thing in the world.

I stirred my cold coffee with a straw. "Della, he's gone. Disappeared. That guy was rich enough to buy himself a new identity. How do you figure we're going to find him?"

"That's where you come in," she replied. "Your grandfather, Andrew Anderson. How much do you know about him?"

"Barely anything at all," I said. "We didn't speak to him. He left my grandmother for a job here in Falconwood and never came back, so he was basically shunned from the family. I never met him."

"He was also Percy Abram's best friend," Della said.

I stretched my legs underneath the booth. I'd been sitting here for far too long. "Charles Rainer mentioned something to that effect. Makes sense. Apparently, my grandfather wasn't much of a stand-up guy either."

"His personality matters not," Della said. "The information he might have on Percy does."

"One small problem with that," I said. "My grandfather is dead. That's why I ended up in this mess to begin with, remember?"

Della stacked her plates and put them on the edge of the table for a busser to collect. "I never said we needed him alive. All we need is what he knew about Percy."

"Andrew Anderson was a hermit," I said. "He disappeared and never spoke to us again."

"Sounds like it was the other way around," Della pointed out.

"You just said that your family shunned *him*. Maybe there was a misunderstanding."

"Yeah, well—"

"Your grandfather may be the key to this investigation," she interrupted. "All I'm asking you to do is look into his last-known whereabouts. Whether you knew him or not, the two of you are connected by blood. You inherited his property. That means you probably have legal access to his information. Use it." She stood up, tossing her crumpled napkin onto the stack of plates. "I'm ready to put the Abram Mansion to rest if you are, Peyton. All you have to do is step up."

Outside Sammy's elementary school, I enjoyed the crisp spring weather. As the end of April neared, the snow—which had been dumping buckets since we arrived here in January—was finally dying off. There were still traces of it around. Big mounds of it were piled on the sides of the road, but the warmth in the air was finally taking a stand. I turned my face into the cool breeze and let it cool the heat on the back of my neck. I was trying not to think of anything at all, a sort of mindful meditation exercise that wasn't going as well as I planned.

Della's sudden turnaround was nothing short of suspicious. In a few days, she had gone from crazy, stumbling, and unkempt to fully healthy and determined. I wondered if Della was always bouncing back and forth between her two states of mind and this was just the first time I'd witnessed it. My new quest—tracking down my grandfather's last whereabouts—wasn't something I wanted to think about, but I knew where I had to start: with my mother. We didn't have any other family. My grandmother—Andrew's wife—has already passed away when I was younger. I wasn't sure how much help my mother was going to be anyway; she was a functioning alcoholic who lived off of disability, and the only time she ever talked about my grandfather was when she wanted to hurl insults at his memory.

It seemed impossible that my family was connected to the mystery of the Abram Mansion. If everything had panned out in a less graphic way, I might have even known Penelope and Alyssa personally. After all, Alyssa's father and my grandfather were apparently close buddies. It was weird to think that if we'd all lived in the same area, Alyssa might have been my babysitter or older friend as we grew up. Now, she was trapped in the same five-year-old body for all of eternity unless I dug up whatever information was left about my weird, dead grandfather.

I was lost in thought until the school bell rang and momentarily freed me from the confines of my old mind. I knew better than to expect Sammy to come out to the front courtyard with the first rush of kids. He almost always stayed behind in his last class. He usually blamed it on having to finish up an art project, but I guessed that the true reason he stayed behind was to avoid the bullies outside. More than once, Sammy's potential tardiness had turned into a "boy who cried wolf" scenario, but there wasn't much I could do about it. Once the pickup loop cleared out, I spotted Sammy as he stuck his head out from a classroom door, peeked in either direction, and—sensing freedom—made a run for the parking lot. He ran straight into my arms and pressed his cold nose into my neck when I picked him up.

"Everything okay, buddy?" I asked, patting his messy hair. "How was school?"

He sniffled in my ear. "Everyone's saying mean things about Mama."

"What kind of things?"

"That she took me out of school because she's crazy."

I helped him into his booster seat and did up his belt buckle. "Sammy, we've been over this before. The kids at your school are mean. Don't listen to them. All that matters is you know the truth. Also, ice cream matters. What do you say?"

He perked up and wiped his eyes. "Mint chocolate chip?"

"Whatever flavor you want." I finished strapping him in and climbed into the driver's side. When I checked on Sammy in the rearview mirror, he grinned back at me. "We haven't talked about what happened at the mansion that night."

He pulled two dinosaur figurines from his backpack and made them fight each other. "Yeah, I know. But Mama's always around."

"And you don't want to scare her."

"Nope," he said. "I want to be brave."

"You're the bravest," I assured him. "Sammy, did you know that Alyssa's mom was also in the mansion?"

His dinosaurs went still. "Will you be mad if I say yes?"

"No, I won't be mad, but I would like to know why you didn't tell me."

He pursed his lips and wiggled them back and forth like a rabbit sniffing out its next carrot. "She scares me. She was the one who always chased me away from the mansion when I tried visiting Alyssa."

"She also saved your life," I reminded him.

"I know," Sammy said. "That's when I realized she's scared, too."

"What is she scared of?"

He tapped the noses of the dinosaurs together, like they were kissing. "She's afraid they're going to be stuck there forever."

My heart clenched. That was the thing about ghosts. Sometimes, you forgot that they used to be actual people. "Sammy, I'm going to do my best to make sure Penelope and Alyssa get to leave the Abram Mansion."

"I know you are."

At a red light, I twisted around in my seat to look at him.

"Listen, your mom might take you to a doctor to talk about all the stuff that's happened so far. If she does, it's probably best not to mention Alyssa or her mom. The doctor—"

"Won't believe me," Sammy finished. "It's okay. No one ever does."

23

*T*hat night, the first real rainstorm of the season hit Falconwood. It pounded against the windows and flooded the garden in the courtyard of the mansion and made a mess of the trees and plants outside. When Ben and I woke up the next morning, it was to a muddy front yard that had captured the wheels of our car with determination so fierce that we needed several scrap pieces of wood to bolster the car high enough to free it. After we were through, we were covered head to toe in mud. It was all over the plaster cast that covered Ben's arm from hand to shoulder.

"Oh man," I said, wiping fruitlessly at the mud that had saturated the plaster. "We're never going to get this clean."

"It's okay." Ben pushed the slick hood of his raincoat away from his face for the tenth time. I remembered telling him that coat was too big for him when he bought it, but he insisted on going a size up. He finally gave up and pushed the hood off entirely, and I watched as the rain loosened his golden brown curls. "I'm getting it off today anyway."

"You are?" I asked. I hadn't heard the news yet, but me and

Ben had been spending a lot of time apart lately. "Why didn't you tell me?"

He attempted to clap some of the mud off his hands, but only succeeded in rubbing it further into his skin. "I forgot, I guess. Besides, you've been busy with Sammy and Theo. I've had my job with Basil. We both had a lot on our minds."

"Well, what did the doctor say?" I asked. "Did you go for a checkup?"

"A couple weeks ago." Ben gestured me up the steps to the porch so we wouldn't keep standing in the mud and rain. "Once it comes off, I'll be doing a lot of physical therapy to get my grip strength and mobility back. Would you be able to help me with that stuff?"

"Of course."

"Great," he said, taking a seat on the swinging bench beneath the porch overhang to assess the situation of his drenched, muddy boots. "I'll need some motivation, and I know you're the best person—" Ben's phone buzzed, and he pulled it out of a dry pocket on the inside of his raincoat. "It's Basil. Hello?"

Though he wasn't on speakerphone, I could still hear Basil's aggravated tone babbling across the front porch. Ben held the phone away from his ear with a grimace.

"Basil, hold on," he said. "Slow down. What happened?" As Ben got up and paced back and forth on the porch, Basil yelled some more. Ben ran his fingers through his hair—something he did when he was stressed—spreading mud through his curls like crusty gel. "Okay, don't worry. I'm on my way. We'll figure something out. No! Don't do anything until I get there. I need to see how much damage has been done."

"What happened?" I asked when Ben hung up.

He stepped back into his drenched boots with a long sigh. "Basil says the storm flooded his entire garden *and* the greenhouse."

335

"Oh, no. That's terrible. Della's probably upset about losing her herbs."

"Della's upset? I'm upset!" He kicked a rock off the porch. "We've been studying that greenhouse for the past two months, Peyton. It's the basis of our entire book. If it's ruined, there's nowhere for us to go with the material."

The reason for Ben's anger sank in. Basil was our only source of income at the moment. If Ben was no longer able to write Basil's book for him, then we were back to square one for the second time since we moved into the Abram Mansion.

I grabbed Ben's arm before he could step off the porch and into the rain again. He looked startled when I pulled him for a hug, then he relaxed into my grip. "Everything's going to be okay," I told him. "We'll figure it out."

He lightly kissed the top of my head. "Thanks for your support. I'll keep you posted on the damage. Don't get into too much trouble today."

"Me? Never."

WITH BEN GONE, I spent the rest of the cold, dreary morning in the huge clawed bathtub in the first-floor bathroom. Of all the rooms we'd had remodeled, this bathroom was one of my favorites. When you shut the door, it felt as though you were underground in the catacombs of some historic castle. If I sang, my voice echoed off the tiled walls and came back to me in a chorus, as if there were ten more of me in the room. I stripped off my muddy clothes, filled the tub with hot water, and tossed in a bath bomb that Della had made herself. As it fizzed and dissolved, the calming scent of fresh lavender filled the air. I climbed in, hissing as the hot water came in contact with my cold skin, then settled my head against a pillow made out of a towel. Slowly, I drifted off.

Someone knocked on the bathroom door, jerking me out of my meditative sleep. My arms flew up to grip the side of the tub, sending a tidal wave of foamy water across the floor. The bath bomb had long since fizzled away and my fingers were wrinkled and pruny. I wasn't sure how long I'd been lying in the water. My heart pounded as I watched a shadow walk past the closed door of the bathroom.

"Ben?" I called, my voice shaking. "Is that you?"

Ben did not answer, and I didn't expect him to. I knew whoever was out there wasn't Ben, and though I liked to think I'd fostered a relatively positive relationship with the dead people who lived in Abram Mansion, it was times like these that made me question that fact. The shadow paused outside the door. My skin grew goosebumps as the handle began to turn itself.

"Alyssa?" I whispered.

Abruptly, the handle clicked back into its original place. I jumped as a folded piece of paper slid under the crack in the door and settled right out of my reach. The shadow lingered in the hallway, as if waiting for me to pick up the paper, but my fingers seemed affixed to the sides of the tub. Paralyzed with fear, I couldn't move or even feel my body until the shadow made its way down the hallway, its footsteps fading with it.

When I felt the nerves in my fingertips again, I slowly stood up. Lukewarm water cascaded off my body as I gingerly stepped out of the tub, dried my hands on the nearest towel, and stooped to pick up the folded piece of paper. With shaking hands, I opened it up.

Check the Yellow Pages.

The handwriting was scribbled and hasty, not how I expected Penelope Abram's handwriting to look. From her expensive education and even more expensive taste in husbands, I thought Penelope would have learned calligraphy early on in

337

her girlhood. Nevertheless, here was this note with a cramped, cryptic message that made no sense at all. What could I possibly find in the Yellow Pages?

I wrapped my robe around myself, stepped into my slippers, and stood by the door to listen. The hallway was silent, so I cautiously made my way out of the steamy bathroom and down to the kitchen, where my laptop rested on the table. I boiled water, added one of Della's homemade tea mixes to it to steep, then sat down with the curious note and my computer.

Phone books were such an outdated concept that it took me a minute to figure out how the information was organized online. Though Falconwood was such a tiny place, there were a surprising amount of businesses listed. I scrolled through them from A to Z over and over until my eyes felt like they were going to fall out of my head, but I couldn't find anything about Percy Abrams or his business.

A thump echoed overhead, like someone stomping their foot on the floor above. The noise felt like a shock to my brain, and that's when it hit me. I didn't need to be looking at the phone book for today's businesses. I needed a phone book from forty years ago, when Percy Abram was a huge part of the Falconwood business world. But how to find one? If there was one around the mansion, I needed help to get to it.

I made another cup of tea and set it at the place across from mine. As I added a ton of honey to it, I whispered, "Alyssa? This one's for you. I need some help, if you don't mind."

Nothing happened for a minute or so. Then I felt a cold spot behind me. I didn't turn around, instead letting Alyssa come into the kitchen on her own. A lump rose in my throat as the ghostly little girl toddled over to the table, climbed into the chair, and leaned her face over the cup of tea to inhale the soothing aromas. Her pink scarf dipped low—if it were made of real cloth, it would have dipped into her tea—and I caught a glimpse of the gashed skin below it. I averted my eyes. I did not want to think about how Alyssa died.

"I'm looking for a phone book," I told her. "It's for adults. It's a big, thick book like this" —I held my hands about four inches apart to indicate the width— "and the pages feel kinda funny, like you can tear them really easily. Did your mom or dad ever keep something like that?"

Alyssa stuck her tongue into the tea then sat back with a grouchy look on her face. She couldn't taste it. "Daddy's office, probably."

It always shocked me when Alyssa actually spoke. In the past several months, she'd uttered maybe a grand total of fifty words to me. We had only just started this part of our relationship— where I asked for help and she responded with real words.

"Where's his office?"

She waved a brisk hand over the top of the tea cup as she got off the chair. Though she couldn't touch the tea cup, she could move it with the force of her will. It knocked itself over and clattered to the floor. The mug cracked in half. Alyssa froze, like she hadn't meant to break something.

"Oops."

"It's okay," I told her. "I'll clean it up later."

She led me into the foyer and up the stairs to the mezzanine. This part of the house was familiar to me even though we had yet to start renovations up here. I'd spent a lot of time tracking Alyssa and Penelope through these hallways. The second floor east wing, which included Alyssa's bedroom, was where the Abrams spent most of their time, but Alyssa kept leading me upward. When we reached the third floor, she made her way to a door in the center of the corridor, then waited outside for me to open it.

Percy's office was a grand affair. It was one of the larger rooms in the house, spanning at least thirty feet across. The enormous window looked out onto the courtyard, but dusty curtains framed either side of it in case Percy needed a dark, cool place to think. An enormous desk took center stage, its dark wood hand carved into woodland creatures. The top of it was lined with green felt dotted with cigar ash. It was still stacked with paperwork and folders, which I assumed had to do with Percy's work.

"What did your father do for his job?" I murmured to Alyssa.

"Art," she said.

That was all she gave me. Perhaps that was all she knew about her father's career. I'd heard about Percy's interest in art—he'd apparently commissioned a statue in a nearby garden for Penelope—but I never suspected that it was his job. Then again, as I looked around the office, it made more sense. Priceless paintings were displayed on one wall of the office, as if it were a gallery. A strange-looking storage unit decorated the other wall. When I examined it closer, I saw that it featured a temperature and humidity gauge that had long stopped functioning. I pried open the door to find at least fifty paintings stacked on their own individual shelves.

"You'd think these would have been sold after Percy died," I murmured. "Then again, if your dad's still alive…"

Alyssa sniffled, and I realized she hadn't fully come into the room. She stood in the doorway, scuffing her toes against the old carpet.

"Are you coming in?" I asked her.

"Daddy didn't like me in his study," she said. "He said it was only for grown-ups."

"Let me guess," I said, observing the guilt in her eyes. "You snuck in here a few times to see what all the grown-ups were talking about."

"And to look at the garden," she insisted. "Daddy has the best view."

I wandered over to the huge window and looked down at the garden. It was overgrown, and at the present time, completely flooded from the storm last night. I imagined what it used to be like when the Abrams had gardeners to tend to it throughout the seasons and could understand why Alyssa liked it so much.

"He sure does," I said. "Where would the phone book be?"

She pointed to a row of low cabinets lined up beneath the window. I opened the one closest to me and found a pile of paperwork that had never been filed. The next cabinet was stacked full of old books that looked like priceless first editions. Finally, I located the phone book. The only problem was that there were about thirty of them.

"Are you kidding me?" I muttered to myself as I yanked out the ones piled on top. They looked like they were about to fall apart. "How am I supposed to look through all of these?" I realized I was half-asking Alyssa, but when I turned around, she had disappeared, leaving me on my own to figure out the phone book clue.

With a sigh, I settled into Percy's leather throne and pulled the first phone book into my lap. I did a cursory search of the businesses listed under the letter A but didn't find anything. The second phone book did not yield any clues, neither did the third or the fourth. As frustration built up in my chest like a volcano ready to erupt, I grabbed the fifth phone book with too much ferocity, lost my grip, and accidentally flung it halfway across the room. It landed face down, the spine split down the middle, on the musty carpet. I had half a mind to leave it there and storm out of the room until I saw a small piece of paper sticking out from under the yellow pages.

It was a business card for a company called Anderson & Associates. Other than the title of the company and a phone number, there was no information to indicate what kind of work the company did. However, it did have my grandfather's last name on it, so I pocketed the card anyway and hoped it was what I was supposed to find in the phone book. I put everything back where I found it, lest Penelope resented me snooping in her killer husband's office.

IT WAS STILL RAINING and dreary by the time I had to pick up Sammy from school, so I stopped by Theo's apartment and got a spare outfit for him just in case. It came in handy: when Sammy emerged from his classroom, his entire front was splattered with mud. As I helped him into the car, the dirt fell off in chunks.

"What happened, buddy?" I asked him. "Did you slip and fall at recess?"

"No." Sammy crossed his arms and hung his head. There were no dinosaur figurines to play with today. "Bradley pushed me over."

I froze with the key halfway to the ignition. "You were bullied again?"

"Yeah." He rested his forehead against the window. "I'm tired."

"This is ridiculous." I got out of the car and opened Sammy's door. "Come on. We're going to the front office."

He stared up at me. "Why?"

"Because clearly no one's doing anything about this situation," I said. "Your mom isn't here to say anything, so I have to do it."

I reached to undo Sammy's buckle, but he took my hand to stop me. "No! If the other kids know I ratted them out, they'll never leave me alone."

His little cheeks puffed out. He was serious.

"You really don't want me to go in there?" I asked him.

He thought about it for a second before he nodded.

"Fine," I said. "But if it happens again, you have my permission to stand up for yourself. You have to defend yourself, buddy. If they're not getting caught, you won't either."

It wasn't the best lesson to teach a first grader, but I wasn't sure what else to say to Sammy. He was such a timid kid, which was probably why the other kids kept using him as their punching bag. Maybe it was best if Theo *did* take Sammy to therapy. It was always the quiet ones that ended up shooting their classmates when they couldn't take it anymore, and I didn't want Sammy to be the next national news story. The thought made me cringe.

As always, we ended up at the Black Cat. Normally, Mason left the televisions in the corners of the café off. He said they disrupted the aesthetic of interior design and distracted the people who came in here to work or study. Today, each television was tuned into a local news channel, and many patrons watched with narrowed eyes or opened mouths.

"One regular coffee, a hot chocolate, and two grilled cheeses with tomato soup dippers," I ordered, counting cash out over the counter. Mason, like everyone else, had his eyes glued to the TV. "Actually, make that three grilled cheeses. I'm starving. Mason— hellooooo?"

He finally tore his eyes from the new story. "Yes, I'm sorry. That was a coffee, a hot chocolate, two grilled cheeses—"

"Three." I gestured to the woman chatting away on the TV. It was on mute, and the captions were too delayed for me to bother reading. "What's going on? Everyone in here looks like a zombie."

"Didn't you hear?" Mason whispered conspiratorially. He glanced over the counter at Sammy then lowered his voice. "Police are saying there's a dangerous stalker in the area."

I handed over my cash. "Oh, please. That's the big news?"

"This isn't something to be so blasé about, Peyton," Mason scolded me firmly. "You should be worried. Stay on your toes.

Apparently, this guy isn't just a Facebook stalker. He's got priors, and he likes abducting women and children."

"Hey," I said sharply, jerking my chin toward Sammy. "I have a kid with me, remember? He's got enough nightmare fuel, if you don't mind."

Mason organized the cash in the old register and counted out my change. "Sammy's a big boy. Besides, he should know it's not safe to go running around without his mom like he's made a habit of in the past."

Below Mason's eyeline, Sammy rolled his eyes. I grinned. I felt like he had learned that from me. "Can I just have my change?"

Mason let the coins clink into my palm and gave me a wink. "You be careful too, Peyton. I'm serious. You're out in the woods all alone, and the Abram Mansion used to be the perfect place for squatters to crash before you and Ben moved in. I wouldn't be surprised if the stalker paid you a visit."

"I'll keep an eye out," I assured him. As I led Sammy to a table, a sense of unease stole over me as an effect of Mason's warning, and like the other people in the café, I turned my gaze up toward the TV for details on the stalker. The man's name was Brandon Lee, and like Mason had said, he'd gone to prison for stalking and injuring women. How he escaped was apparently a mystery, and according to the news program, he had been spotted near Falconwood. I called Ben to let him know, but it went straight to voicemail. He was probably still trying to figure out how to fix Basil's greenhouse problem. Worry began to build in the back of my head. I had too many things on my plate, and it was starting to feel like I was just waiting for something to explode.

As Mason set our grilled cheeses in front of us, my phone rang.

"Hello?"

"Yes, hi. I'm looking for Peyton Fletcher," a soothing, unfamiliar voice said.

"This is she."

"This is Jennifer with the Falconwood emergency clinic," the voice went on. "We have you listed as Theo Baker's emergency contact. Is that correct?"

My stomach dropped. "Yes. What's wrong with Theo?"

"Nothing major," Jennifer replied. "She had a panic attack at work and was admitted to us about half an hour ago. We've given her some medication to help calm her down. She'll be ready to go home soon, but our policy requires someone to pick her up."

"I'll be there in ten minutes," I said and hung up. "Sammy, wrap up your grilled cheese. We've gotta get out of here."

Ten minutes later, Sammy and I paced the waiting room of the emergency clinic together. The last time I'd been here was the first time I'd met Sammy, after he'd broken into the mansion through an old doggy door to talk to Alyssa. It was just a few months ago, but I felt like I'd known both Sammy and Theo for the majority of my life.

"Is Mama okay?" Sammy asked me for the tenth time since we left the Black Cat.

"I'm sure she's fine," I told him. "She's not hurt. She's just scared."

"But why would she go to the hospital for being scared?"

I sat down in one of the plastic waiting chairs and pulled Sammy into my lap. "Sometimes, it's possible to get so scared that you can't breathe. You know when you're running around the playground and you can't catch your breath? It feels like that, but worse."

"Mama can't breathe?"

345

"She can now," I assured him. "The doctor helped her."

Jennifer, who was sitting behind the desk, cleared her throat. "Excuse me? Theo's on her way out."

Sammy and I leapt to our feet as a nurse pushed Theo through the double doors in a wheelchair. Other than the heavy droop of her eyelids, Theo looked okay. As soon as she cleared the doors, she put her foot down to stop the nurse and stood up.

"Apparently, the wheelchair is policy too," Theo grumbled. "I can walk just fine."

Sammy hid behind me, peeking out around my waist. "Mama?"

At the sight of Sammy, Theo's expression went from annoyed to relieved. She squatted down and reached out for her son. "Hey, dude! I'm so glad to see you. How was school?"

He ran into her arms and squeezed her around her neck. "I didn't like it. Are you okay? Peyton said you got so scared you couldn't breathe. What happened?"

Theo lifted Sammy into the air with a groan. "I'll tell you when you're older. Let's get out of here. Is that grilled cheese? It's all smushed!"

THEO DIDN'T WANT to go straight home, so I drove her and Sammy to the nearby park. As Sammy swung around like a monkey, Theo and I sat on the nearby bench. I'd offered her one of my sandwiches and we were sharing the coffee. I didn't ask her about the panic attack. I figured she would tell me about it when she was ready. Sure enough, she opened up on her own.

"I don't know what happened," she said as she ate the crust of the sandwich first. "Actually, I do. The office has a TV in the waiting room, and I caught part of the news this morning. Did you hear about that stalker?"

"Yup. Mason wouldn't shut up about it."

"Neither could anyone at work," Theo said. "Something about it put me off. Maybe it's because we just finished dealing with Dylan, and he was practically a stalker himself. Anyway, I kept thinking about what would happen if this stalker decided to focus on me. That's just my luck, you know? Before I knew it, I was curled up in a ball behind the front desk and hyperventilating." She blushed and shook her head, like she was embarrassed of her reaction. "I couldn't make it stop, and it was so irrational. I mean, why would the stalker come after me of all people?"

"Well, you are adorable," I pointed out. "Plus you're single. No man of the house for him to deal with—I'm not helping, am I?"

"No, not really."

I moved our trash so I could scoot closer to Theo. "Look, if we could deal with Dylan, we can deal with some random guy who may or may not come through our neighborhood. Considering he's on the run, I doubt he'll be making a pit stop in Falconwood to dilly dally."

Theo leaned her head against my shoulder. "Thanks for picking me up today. I don't know what I would do without you."

"You don't have to wonder."

"Yeah, except you're leaving soon," Theo said. "Did you think I'd forget? How long do you have left here? Two months?"

"A little less," I answered sheepishly. "But I don't have plans to leave for now, okay? Don't freak out just yet. We'll figure something out."

She pinched me playfully. "You better."

hen I returned to the mansion later that evening, Basil and Della's tiny electric car was parked in the driveway out front. The neon green vehicle looked like a little bug to me, something you wiped off your windshield instead of drove around the streets, but it fit the Gordons' hippie vibes and eco-friendly lifestyle with weird specificity. I glanced into the window as I passed by and saw Basil's printed notes for the book he was working on with Ben. The stack was about an inch high. Since Ben and Basil had been ensconced in the greenhouse for the time they'd been working together, I didn't know how far along they'd gotten with the book. Ben wasn't particularly into plants, so the current success of their partnership was surprising.

"Hello?" I called through the foyer as I hung up my denim jacket on the coat rack. "Anyone home?"

"In the kitchen!" Ben called.

I followed his voice down the steps at the back of the house and into the basement. The mansion was so old that the underground level had originally been built as the servants' quarters. The kitchen staff wasn't meant to be seen unless they were serving food to the blue bloods upstairs. At first, it was weird to cook and eat in the kitchen, but now the room felt weirdly cozy.

Basil and Della sat across from each other at the table while Ben manned several pots and pans on the stove. He had a dish towel thrown casually over his shoulder, and his curls—which were in need of a trim—were pushed back and restrained with a pink workout headband he had borrowed from my bathroom. The scent of fresh herbs filled the air; Della and Basil must have saved some from the flooded greenhouse.

"Hey, babe," Ben said, glancing over his shoulder. The "babe" habit was hard to break for him. Despite our impending divorce —which should be happening in less than two months—he still referred to me with the terms of endearment we'd been using since our high school sweetheart days. Sometimes, it annoyed me. Other times, it didn't feel like such a bad thing, like maybe we could actually be friends after all this was over. "I invited Basil and Della for dinner. Is that okay?"

"Of course." I patted Basil's drooping shoulders. "How's everything looking at the airstream?"

"Terrible," Basil said.

"He's exaggerating," Della added. "But it's not great. The airstream is fine, but the rain flooded everything. The green-house is completely ruined."

I checked on Ben's expression, confirming the grim set of his lips. "What does that mean for you guys? Didn't you rely on the sales from the greenhouse to pay your bills?"

"No, no, no," Della said. "We have enough money in savings to live comfortably without ever working or selling anything ever again."

Basil coughed. It would have been an innocent enough bodily function had it not been accompanied by an under-the-table nudge to Della's knee. For whatever reason, Basil did not want Della to share the details of their finances with us. I partially understood. Though Della and I had grown close very quickly, we didn't know each other that well. Basil's discretion was a matter of safety. On the other hand, Ben and I weren't exactly the type of people to take advantage of an older couple like the Gordons. Then again, Basil was already overpaying Ben for the work he was doing on the greenhouse book. Maybe I was milking the Gordons for their money more than I thought, but I also had to know how our income was going to be affected by the greenhouse flooding.

"Are you going to rebuild?" I moved away from the Gordons as I asked, pretending to help Ben at the stove while really trying to read the body language of the people behind me. "I know how important that greenhouse was to the two of you. Especially you, Basil. I imagine this is difficult for you."

Basil sighed into his cup of tea. "I should have accounted for flooding when I built it. I won't make the same mistake when I try again."

I tasted the sauce Ben was making. "Are you thinking of rebuilding right away?"

"There's no point," Basil said. "There's too much damage right now. We have to haul away the ruined materials from the old greenhouse, but the ground is practically mush. We won't be able to break ground on a new one until it dries up a little. According to the weather report, that won't be anytime soon."

"What about the book?" I asked, hoping I sounded as casual as possible. "Do the two of you have enough material to keep going?"

"We're going to compile and edit what we already have," Ben answered for Basil. "But we were centering the book around an experiment Basil was doing in the greenhouse, so that's ruined."

"The book is on a back burner for now," Basil said mournfully. "At least regarding additional material. Ben's kind enough to entertain me with structure and editing and all that, but I'm not sure how far we'll get without studying an actual subject."

"Speaking of subjects," Della jumped in, "can we change this one? I don't want to keep thinking about the greenhouse. It's depressing me."

"Did you guys hear about the stalker on the loose?" I said and winced. "I guess that's not much better than the greenhouse, is it?"

Basil looked up from his tea. His brow knitted together, the fine lines of his forehead tracing a maze across his face. "Stalker? What are you talking about?

"Apparently some guy with a penchant for stalking women and children broke out of prison," I told the room. From the look on everyone's faces, it was clear none of them had watched the news that morning. "He was spotted in the Falconwood area. Everyone's freaking out."

Della grasped Basil's forearm. Thankfully, she kept her nails trimmed because of all the gardening work she did. Otherwise, they might be embedded in Basil's skin. "A stalker in Falconwood? What are they doing to catch him? Are we in danger?"

"I think the police are on it," I said. Ben handed me a spoon and gestured for me to continue stirring the sauce while he worked on something else. "But you know Falconwood. There's a grand total of three deputies here."

"This is just what we needed." Della solemnly shook her head. "First the greenhouse. Now this stalker. Basil, I don't feel comfortable being in the woods all alone."

"Me either," I added, nudging Ben to make sure he was listening to the conversation. "Mason reminded me how popular the mansion used to be with squatters. I'm afraid this guy's going to look us up, break in, and make himself at home. This place is so big, we'd never know."

"What about the alarm system?" Basil asked.

"We never armed it," Ben chimed in. "Everyone told us Falconwood's crime rate was so low that there was no point."

Basil harrumphed and crossed his arms. "Oh, please. Sure, Falconwood's a nice place to live, but there's crime everywhere. Hell, a man killed himself in your foyer a few days ago."

Bile rose in the back of my throat at the reminder. Ben caught the look on my face and momentarily abandoned cooking to give me a brief hug. The sauce began to bubble and churn beneath my spoon, so Ben lowered the heat.

"I have an idea," Ben said. "Basil, you used to work security awhile ago, right? Before you started all the horticulture stuff?"

"I have some experience in surveillance. Why?"

"What if the two of you moved here temporarily?" Ben offered. "We have plenty of room, and we could all look out for each other."

Della's eyes went wide. "No, I'm sorry. I don't think I could live in the mansion. I have an unhealthy relationship with it."

"Then bring your airstream," Ben said. "You can park it anywhere you like on the property. Once this stalker is taken care of and your land is a little less waterlogged, you can move back."

"*And,*" I added, picking up the pieces Ben was putting down, "if you wanted, Basil, you could restart your project here. We have so much property. You could easily build a greenhouse wherever you wanted."

It was a good idea, one that solved everyone's problems at the current moment. If Basil and Della moved their airstream onto our property, we would have two extra pairs of eyes to monitor the mansion. I didn't know much about Basil's background in security, but the idea of having him closer to us comforted me. Not to mention, Della maintained a strange relationship with the ghosts inside the house. Sometimes, I wondered if she knew more about Penelope and Alyssa than she let on, but her fragile mental state kept her from sharing intimate details with me.

"We couldn't do that to you," Basil said. "It's too much of a burden."

"Oh, please." Ben waved off Basil's statement. "This house is a burden, not the two of you. Come on, you've been so good to us since the moment we arrived in Falconwood. It's the least we can do."

Basil turned to his wife. "It's up to you, honey. Would it bother you to be so close to an old passion project?"

Passion project was an understatement. Della, a photographer like me, had wasted years at the Abram Mansion, taking pictures of the house from every angle and digging up what information was available on the Abrams. When I asked for her research a couple months ago, she claimed to have gotten rid of it. Her selective memory and wishy-washy willingness to help me were getting old, but I didn't want to push her either. When it came down to it, Alyssa had chosen *me* to help her and Penelope, not Della.

"It's fine with me," Della said.

"That settles it." Ben lifted his glass of wine for a toast. "You can bring the airstream here tonight if you like. Cheers, roomies."

As we all clinked our glasses together, I grinned. This felt like the beginning of a great idea.

IN THE MORNING, Basil and Della's cute silver airstream filled up one corner of the vacuous front yard. It was nice to see it there, the sun glinting off the metallic exterior. The older couple had already set up their portable porch, complete with a picnic table and chairs. By the time I woke up, they were already sitting outside to watch the sun as it rose above the trees and into the sky. They had matching e-readers. I'd pegged the Gordons as book collectors at first, but their cramped, nomadic lifestyle couldn't exactly accommodate a library. If I had to guess, Basil was brushing up on his greenhouse knowledge and Della was cruising through the best and latest sets of nature photography. I made a pot of coffee and went to take some out to them before I realized they had already made their own in a cute little pour over. It rested on the picnic table, looking more like a piece of table art than a coffee maker. As I watched the older couple read, Basil reached across the chairs to take his wife's hand in his. Their fingers clasped together for a brief moment before they each returned to their own business. It was like a little declaration of their love, shared as a brief reminder between the two of them. It was almost intimate to witness it, and I pushed down an annoying sense of longing as I drew away from the window and returned to the kitchen.

I poured the coffee for myself, sat at the table, and put my feet up in the chair opposite of mine. I suddenly wished I had a life partner, an e-reader, and a pour over coffee maker. Ben and I had never been like Basil and Della. Even at the beginning of our relationship, we were hectic in each other's presence. I liked it back then. Ben's sturdy boy-next-door vibes rounded out my rebellious anywhere-but-here attitude. Little did I know that our inherent differences were eventually going to be the cause of our divorce, but before I could go down the rabbit hole of what went wrong in our relationship, my phone rang.

"Oh boy," I muttered to myself when I saw the caller ID tag. I took a deep breath and answered. "Hey, Mom!"

"Don't you 'hey, mom' me," came the reply. "You haven't called me in days. What's gotten into you? What if I'd drank too much and died?"

"I've been busy," I said shortly. "Besides, you only call *me* when you've had too much to drink. What was it this time? Gin or bourbon?"

"Hard soda, but I went through two packages before I hit a buzz," she answered. "The sugar makes you crazy, huh?"

I checked my watch. It was nine in the morning. Either my functioning alcoholic of a mother had started drinking at dawn, or she'd been up all night. "Mom, did you call me for a reason?"

"Yes. No. I don't remember."

"Drink some water," I advised her. "Call me back when you've sobered up a bit."

"I'm not that drunk," she assured me. "Please don't hang up. I miss you. Why don't you come see me sometime?"

I refilled my coffee. It was going to be a long conversation. "You know the deal. I'll come visit when you go back to AA."

"That's a terrible deal. When did we agree to that?"

"Mom—"

"I'm kidding! It was a joke, honey." She sighed, filling my ear with the whoosh of static. "Can I do anything for you? Buy you something? Send you money? I feel like being a mom."

I turned the speaker setting on and set my phone on the table. "You're a mom no matter what, and you don't have any money to give me."

Something clinked together on the other end of the line—glass on glass. "I'm trying my best—"

"Actually, there is something you could do for me," I said, getting an idea. "I want to know more about Andrew Anderson."

She groaned into the phone. "Ugh, why are you suddenly so obsessed with your grandfather? It must be that damn town. People go to Falconwood and disappear forever."

"You mean Grandpa, right?" I said. "He left Grandma for a job in Falconwood. What did he do for his job anyway?"

"He was a—what's it called? The people who arrange art shows."

355

"A curator?"

"Yes, that's it!" The triumph in my mother's voice rang through the phone. "He was a curator, but he wasn't stuck to any one museum. He traveled around the country to lesser-known areas, digging up rare art."

It fleshed with the story I already knew. Andrew Anderson and Percy Abrams had become best friends while they were both in Falconwood. Percy was a collector of fine art while Andrew showed it off. Together, they were perfect partners.

"Did you ever hear of Grandpa's best friend?" I asked Mom. "Percy Abrams?"

"You mean that guy whose house you're living in?" Mom said. "Sure, he was all your grandmother could talk about for a while. If there was one man she hated more than her own husband, it was Percy Abram."

My feet thunked from the chair to the floor. This was news to me. Everyone I'd met—excluding Della—loved Percy Abram to a fault. Why would my grandmother hold a grudge against him unless she'd known what was happening inside the Abram Mansion?

"Why didn't she like Percy?" I asked.

"Why do you think?" Mom replied. "He was the reason your grandfather stayed in Falconwood. Dad was obsessed with that guy. My mother was convinced they were in love with each other. What a scandal that would've been, eh?"

I was less interested in my grandmother's vaguely homophobic theories than I was in Grandpa's life in Falconwood. "Did Grandpa have his own business?"

"No," my mother answered firmly. "He worked for a larger company. Never went solo."

I pulled the Anderson & Associates business card from where I'd been using it as a bookmark in the novel I was reading. "Are you sure?"

"Who's to say?" Something crunched in my ear. Cheetos. They were Mom's hangover food of choice. She was probably leaving orange fingerprints all over her phone. "After he disappeared, your grandmother cut him off. I suppose he could've started his own company later, but I doubt it. He was never much of a go-getter."

"And you never heard from him after he left Grandma?" I asked, speaking slowly to make sure she caught every word. "*Ever?*"

The crunchy chewing paused. "He sent you birthday cards."

"He did?"

"Every year," she went on. "Without fail. They stopped coming when you turned eighteen, but he *did* send you a congratulations card for your wedding. No idea how he heard about it. In the paper, I guess."

I kneaded my forehead, trying not to get mad. "Why didn't you ever tell me?"

"Because I was afraid he would do the same thing to you that he did to me," Mom replied candidly. "He left me, Peyton. He told me and Mom that he loved us, then packed up his life and left. I didn't want you to have to go through that kind of pain."

My heart jumped into my throat. Most days, I forgot my mother's childhood was one of the reasons for her drinking. Still, she'd managed to raise me without regrets. "Did you keep the cards?"

"I have them in a shoebox in my closet."

"Can you send them to me?"

"Sure thing, honey," she said, her voice softening. "Hey, I'm doing something for you!"

I couldn't help but laugh. "Yes, you are."

A knock interrupted the pleasant moment, and I looked up to see Basil standing on the last step of the kitchen stairs with

357

his knuckles resting against the door frame. He mouthed "Sorry!" and pointed to the phone. I waved off his apology.

"I gotta go, Mom," I said. "I'll call you soon, okay? I love you."

"I love you too."

Basil stepped all the way into the kitchen as I hung up. "That was my fault. I didn't see you were on the phone."

"Don't worry about it," I said. "Did you need something?"

"Toilet paper," he admitted, hanging his head sheepishly.

"You don't make your own?" I joked.

He chuckled. "I did suggest washable clothes to Della once. She almost threw me out the window."

I went down the hall to the storage closet and came back with a few rolls. "There's only so much torture you can subject a woman to."

He bowed in thanks as he took the rolls. "She'll be forever grateful. Would you like—?"

An ear-splitting crash punctuated the middle of his sentence. It rocked the ceiling overhead so much that it shook loose some sawdust from the renovations. Basil looked up, alarmed.

"What on earth was that?"

I ushered him up the stairs and toward the front door. "It's an old house. Things go boom more often than you'd think. Let me know if you need anything else! Bye!"

The second I shoved Basil out of the house, someone screamed upstairs. I covered my ears as I ran up the mezzanine and into the east wing. I flung open door after door, searching for the source of the scream, until I finally came to Alyssa's bedroom.

There she was, standing in the center of the room, her mouth dropped open in a never-ending shriek. Her pink scarf had slipped, revealing the terrible gash beneath it. I ran inside.

"Alyssa!" I shouted. "Hey! Stop screaming!"

But she went on and on, not even pausing to take a breath. I guessed that was one of the advantages to being dead. You could throw the world's most annoying temper tantrum without ever losing steam.

"I can't help you if you won't be quiet!" I waved my hand in front of Alyssa's vacant eyes, trying to ignore the chill she always inflicted on my skin. "Hello? Can you hear me?"

My phone vibrated in my pocket. I almost ignored it, too preoccupied with Alyssa's outburst, but when I checked the number, I recognized it as belonging to the elementary school. I plugged one ear, ducked out of Alyssa's room, and answered.

"Hello?"

"Hi, this is Mallory. I'm a front desk secretary at Falconwood Elementary School."

If Mallory could hear the high-pitched screaming in the background of the phone call, she didn't let on. "Hi, Mallory. Is this regarding Sammy? Is he okay?"

"He's fine... physically," Mallory said. "But he threw quite the fit a few minutes ago. He was escorted to the nurse's office to calm down, but we think it would be better if he didn't return to class today. Would you be able to pick him up? I have you listed as his secondary caregiver."

HALF AN HOUR LATER, Sammy was dead asleep in the back seat of my car. While he napped, I stared off into the distance. We'd stopped at Sammy's favorite park. I was hoping it would cheer him up and make him comfortable enough to tell me what had happened at school, but he was snoring before we even arrived. The wind pushed the empty swings, like ghostly children had taken advantage of the park's vacancy. I shuddered at the thought.

Someone rapped on my window. It was Della, holding a paper to-go bag from the local deli. I rolled down the window.

"I saw your car," she said. "What are you doing here? Why is Sammy out of school early?"

I checked to make sure Sammy was still asleep before getting out of the car and waving Della over to the nearest bench to sit with me. She opened the paper bag and handed me half of a roast beef sandwich.

"Don't tell Basil," she said. "But I was dying for a little bit of meat."

"Your secret's safe with me."

"Spill," she said, nodding toward the unconscious six-year-old boy in my car. "What's going on with Sammy?"

I bit into the sandwich first. Spicy mustard squirted across my tongue, awakening my senses. My blood sugar was too low. "He went wild in class today. According to the teacher, he started screaming in his seat, rocking back and forth, holding his head. It took them twenty minutes to calm him down."

Della pursed her lips. "Panic attack?"

"It must be going around," I said. "Theo had one yesterday, and Alyssa decided to give me a heart attack this morning."

Della's shoulders tensed up like they always did when I mentioned the undead inside the Abram Mansion. "What do you mean?"

"Basil was there when it happened," I told her, wiping mustard from my chin. "She knocked something over then started screaming her head off. I got Basil out of the house before he saw anything, but I couldn't get Alyssa to calm down."

"So what happened?"

"I got the call about Sammy," I said. "I couldn't do anything. She wouldn't let me help her, so I left."

Della bowed over her half of the sandwich, almost as if in prayer. "It's getting worse. Something's happening."

"What are you talking about?"

"The more time I spent at the mansion, the more frequently

Alyssa showed up in person." She wrapped the rest of her sandwich up and placed it back in the bag. She'd hardly taken two bites. "It was like she fed off of my living energy, growing stronger the longer she had access to me."

"I feel fine," I assured her. "She's not draining me or whatever—"

"She's affecting *someone*," Della insisted. "Her outburst today is enough for me to know that. These connections are unhealthy for both participants. Take it from someone who knows."

"What am I supposed to do about it?"

Della turned her face to the wind. "Watch. Wait. Be ready for anything."

25

There was a man standing outside my bedroom window.

It happened quickly. I opened my eyes and saw his tall silhouette, the shadow of a beard, the gleam in his eye. Lightning flashed, illuminating his face for half a second. We looked at each other. He smiled...or was it more of a grimace on his face? Was he real? In the next moment, after darkness had fallen again, he was gone

I hurled myself out of bed, pulled on my robe, and ran from window to window in the hallways for a glimpse of him. For no reason at all, I was compelled to find him again, to see him, to know who he was. When I exhausted my search on the first floor, I went up to the mezzanine and ran to the largest window, the one that looked out on the front yard and the vast woods around the mansion. I scanned the grounds for some hint of the man, staring for hours until the moon moved sleepily toward the horizon to make room for the sun. Finally, I saw movement, but it was only Basil Gordon.

He emerged from the airstream wearing thick gloves and

carrying a massive shovel. About fifty feet from their portable home, near the edge of the woods, Basil pierced the wet grass with the shovel and used his boot to shove it deeper into the land. Yesterday, Ben had given him the go ahead to start working on his new greenhouse, the one I'd told the Gordons they could build on our land. I didn't realize he'd be building it right in front of the mansion.

I watched Basil work. His shoulders rolled and lifted as he lithely maneuvered the shovel. He was a diligent worker, and the digging came easy to him, as if he'd done this for a hundred greenhouses before. Within several minutes, he'd turned over a large patch of earth, readying it for whatever he wanted to plant there, but he kept going all the way to the tree line.

"ARE you sure you weren't dreaming?" Ben asked me.

The four of us sat at the kitchen table to have breakfast together. Thankfully, Basil had showered in the tiny airstream bathroom before joining the rest of us inside the house. When he was through with his project outside, he was covered in mud. Even now, a slight earthy smell radiated off of him as he tried our regular coffee pot brew. He wrinkled his nose and passed his cup to Della. Apparently, it was pour over or nothing for Basil. Della took the cup without argument and drank deeply from it.

"I wasn't dreaming," I said. "It felt too real. It had to be this stalker guy, right? But how did he end up at my window? This place is enormous. I don't get how he found my bedroom out of all the windows on the first floor."

"You should put some curtains up," Della said. "I can help you pick some out at the store if you like. Ooh, or better yet, we could make our own."

"I like to look at the sky when I sleep."

"Is no one going to take Peyton's claim seriously?" Basil's voice was oddly rough, as though the moist air had clogged his nasal passages. "A strange man showed up at her window. We have to do something about this. We should inform the police at least."

Ben hopped up from his seat to flip the pancakes on the stove. "I already have. Officer Spaughton is on her way up to take a look around the property."

"Officer Spaughton," Basil murmured. "Nice girl, is she?"

"I don't think her niceness makes her any less capable as a police officer," Ben said. His grip tightened on the spatula, and I noticed his weirdly defensive tone even if no one else did. "She's come up to the mansion for a few similar issues we've had in the past."

"And what, may I ask, did she do about these issues?"

"She patrolled the property," Ben answered. "All night. When we thought we had an intruder in the house, she refused to leave. She was the one who helped Peyton and Theo after what happened in the foyer too."

"All right," Basil said. "I get it. She's competent."

Della poured hot water into her coffee mug before returning it to Basil. "Please forgive my husband. He likes to make everyone think he's a happy-go-lucky guy, but I've never met anyone more paranoid about personal safety."

"I am simply concerned," Basil said. "These days, all this technology makes it so easy for someone to get ahold of your information. Automatic locks on your front door, keyless entry for your cars, sheesh! With the right tools, anyone could break into your home and take over your life. You can't trust anyone until you know them as well as you know yourself."

Ben cursed as he flipped a burnt pancake. "How can you tell if you know anyone that well?"

Basil turned to Ben. "Because a true friend will trust you with all of their secrets."

The two men locked eyes, as if each of them were telepathically arguing their position in a silent debate. Ben looked away first, if only to flip another ruined pancake.

"You know, some of that newfangled technology could be incorporated into your greenhouse plans," Ben said. "You could use it to monitor the health of your plants and keep organized records on your tablet. In the long run, it would be the ultimate way to collect data."

Basil sipped his watered-down coffee in pensive silence. Ben turned toward the wall to display his triumphant grin, but I saw it anyway. Della cleared her throat, ready for a new conversation that didn't involve pitting our generations against each other.

"So, Peyton," she said. "What's on your agenda for today?"

"The usual," I replied. "I'll probably use the morning to work on editing some stuff for my photography portfolio. Then I have to go pick up Sammy from school. Hopefully he makes it through the day this time."

"Oh, yeah," Ben said, setting the stack of blackened pancakes in the middle of the table. "What did Theo say about all of that?"

After my lunch with Della in the park, I'd returned Sammy to his apartment, tucked him into bed, and let him sleep for the rest of the day. When Theo got home, I filled her in on what had happened at school. Initially, she was upset I hadn't notified her at work right away, but I convinced her that Sammy was okay, and it was better that she wasn't distracted while at the office. I didn't mention that Sammy happened to be freaking out in tandem with the ghost of a dead little girl who lived at my house. That was science or magic I couldn't explain.

"She's worried," I answered. "I am too, to be honest. Sammy's always been kind of a weird kid, but he's never had issues like this before. Theo says this is the first time he's had an episode like this."

"But it's not," Ben said.

"It's not?"

"No. Remember that day you brought him here?" Since no one reached for the burnt pancakes, Ben loaded them on his own plate and covered them with enough maple syrup to mask the charred taste. "It was the same day Della—"

He cut himself off when Basil looked sharply at him. Della gazed absentmindedly over Basil's shoulder, almost as if she hadn't heard Ben's sentence. Perhaps it was better for Ben not to mention the strange incident that had happened that day, when we found Della in the empty pool in the courtyard, screaming for no reason like Alyssa had done yesterday.

"Anyway," Ben hastened on, "Sammy started crying out of nowhere. He totally freaked out. No reason that I can remember. It's probably worse now because he watched his dad shoot himself. That's traumatic for any kid."

"Herbal supplements," Basil chimed in. "That's what the kid needs. A good dose of calming herbs. Chamomile, lavender, lemongrass. I could make him a tea."

"I'm not sure a tea is going to kick the PTSD out of his system," Ben commented.

"Helping Sammy is up to Theo," I reminded everyone. "We shouldn't be talking about their business like this. You know how this town is. If anyone else catches wind of what's happening with Sammy, it'll be printed on the front page of the local newspaper this Sunday. Can we respect their privacy please?"

Della rested her hand on top of mine and rubbed my arm until I'd calmed down a bit. "I agree with Peyton. We shouldn't be airing the Bakers' issues all over like it's ours to talk about. I only hope Theo knows what's best for Sammy."

"She's his mother," Ben said with a shrug. "Why wouldn't she?"

"Not everyone's mother know what's best for her kid," Della said.

I clinked my coffee mug against Della's. "I'll drink to that."

WHEN IT CAME TO DISAPPEARING, my grandfather was a professional. I spent hours combing the internet for information on Andrew Anderson, but it was almost as if the man had never existed. I couldn't even find the record for his birth until I bit the bullet and called my mother. It turned out she had been born in the same hospital as my grandfather, but when I reached out to the hospital, they claimed not to keep records from so many years ago. They did, however, recommend a paid service to track down Andrew's birth certificate, so I shelled out $19.95 and was rewarded with the date and time of my grandfather's birth. It didn't turn out to be much good though. I knew Andrew existed. What I didn't know was what had happened to him in those years after he left my grandmother and Mom to fend for themselves. Despite his friendship with Percy Abrams, no one in town was as familiar with Andrew as they were with Percy. I asked practically every local I met in the streets whether they recalled Percy's supposed best friend, but every interaction felt similar.

"Andrew Anderson? Sure, he was that shy fellow that followed Percy around like a puppy. Odd-looking man. Had glasses like owl eyes, and he never went anywhere without his cane."

As far as my mother knew, Andrew had never used a cane in his life, which made me doubt the credibility of the townspeople's recollections. Of course, the people who remembered

Andrew were all nearing the age of seventy. I couldn't count on their memories to be super sharp anyway.

The most beguiling thing of all was that there was no record of Andrew's death. I even called David, the man who was mediating mine and Ben's divorce, since he had been the one to inform us of our obligation to the Abram Mansion. According to David, he only had access to the information regarding Andrew's will. He had never seen Andrew's death certificate, though he did offer me the number of the lawyer that had contacted him about Andrew's will in the first place. When I called the lawyer's number, it was no longer in service. Every road was a dead end.

Days later, the rain still hadn't let up, but the musty weather didn't stop Basil and Ben from throwing themselves into the construction of the new greenhouse. They had brought in bags upon bags of fresh soil to build upon, but the monsoons washed it away in one night. The yard looked less like fertile land and more like the perfect place to host a mud-wrestling event. Basil had to move the airstream farther away from the greenhouse site due to how much the ground was moving. He was afraid the watery earth would wash the airstream into the trees. To avoid the same mistake, they built the foundation of the greenhouse first then filled it with additional soil. I hated to think how much money they had spent on dirt.

Wearing my bright yellow rain slicker, I watched Ben and Basil work from the balcony. It was good to see Ben working in the mud, not because of the filth, but because just a few months ago, it was a challenge for him to stand up. His fall from the balcony put new life in him. Before, he never would have considered taking a job that involved building greenhouses. He was a writer, not a construction worker, but spending so much time with Basil had somehow changed that. I liked the new aspects of Ben's personality. It was as if he were taking on some of Basil's hippie meditation vibes. I leaned against the balcony railing, enjoying the soft tickle of rain against my face. Unfortunately, the peaceful feeling didn't last long.

The window in the door leading to the balcony shattered. I ducked at the sound, pulling the hood of my rain jacket across my face as broken glass flew through the air. Ben hollered up to the balcony from the ground:

"Peyton? Everything okay up there?"

I checked behind me. The wispy trails of a ghostly body scurried away from the window. One of the dead members of the Abram Mansion intentionally wanted to scare me, and I had a good bet on which one it was.

"I'm fine!" I called down to Ben. "A piece of hail hit the window up here at exactly the right angle. We're going to have to replace it."

Ben turned his face upward and squinted toward the sky. "It's hailing?"

"Only a bit."

He shrugged and started shoveling again. "I'll tarp it later!"

"Don't worry. I can do it."

Under the pretense of fetching a tarp from the window, I receded from the balcony. Stepping carefully over the broken glass, I made my way inside. This was the main hallway that led to the balcony, the one Percy Abrams would have used to shepherd his guests to an exclusive outdoor party underneath the stars. The balcony was huge, and there were other ways to get to it, but this corridor was the most extravagant. It also had a few doors branching off from it, which made it easy to track where my temperamental ghost had gone. Penelope, unlike Alyssa, left wispy trails of what looked like smoke in her wake that I could only see from the corners of my eyes. I wondered why her essence was easier to spot than Alyssa's. Did it have something to do with their age difference or was this a fact of the ghostly world I didn't understand?

The trail led down a servants' staircase and into a familiar room. It was once Penelope's craft room, where she presumably sewed or painted or did whatever else she needed to do in order to escape Percy's fists. At first glance, Penelope's ghost was nowhere to be seen, so I pretended like I'd wandered into the room by accident. I let my fingers drift over one of Penelope's unfinished projects, a lily-white lace dress draped over a mannequin in the corner of the room.

"Don't touch that!"

The voice was low and sharp, emanating from the closet that housed all of Penelope's former projects. I had never heard her speak before. Carefully, I lifted my hand from the lace, but I didn't turn around, giving Penelope the illusion of privacy.

"What was it for?" I asked her.

"What do you think?" came the abrupt reply. "It's my wedding dress."

I studied the unfinished train. "But you were already married. Why would you be making another wedding dress? Unless... oh."

Penelope huffed. "Yes, that's right. You've been through *all* of my business. You know I had an affair with another man, but I refuse to let you judge me for it. If you knew what was actually happening under this roof, you would have told me to run to Charles in a heartbeat—"

"I wish you had."

Penelope halted her rant, and I finally turned around to face her. She was as beautiful in death as she had been in life, with long hair that flowed all the way to to her waist, an elegantly pointed face, and eyes that were both kind and stern at the same time. I held my breath as I examined her ghostly figure. Alyssa wore the method of her murder around her neck and covered it up with that atrocious pink scarf. How had Penelope been killed?

"What did you say?" she asked me.

"I wish you had gone to Charles," I told her. "Then you and Alyssa would have been safe, and I wouldn't have to be doing this with you right now."

"You know what happened?"

"I got the gist. Don't *you* know what happened?"

"I got the gist," Penelope repeated back to me in a poor imitation of my voice. "What are you doing here anyway? I've been trying to get rid of you ever since you invaded my home."

I crossed my arms and stood my ground. "I know. You're annoying. By the way, it's my house now. Percy left it to my grandfather, who left it to me when he died. Guess I'm your new landlord. It would be great if you could pass over and leave me alone."

"If I knew how, I would!" Penelope snapped. She vanished from the closet and reappeared close enough to my face to make me stumble backward. "You think I want to be here? You think I want my child to be stuck in this hellhole for all eternity? We have been damned, and all I want is to be left in peace. Don't you hear her?"

"Hear her what?"

Penelope cupped her hand to my ear, and though I couldn't feel her skin, the cold chill of being so close to a ghost permeated my entire body. "She's crying again."

She went quiet and forced me to listen. Sure enough, from another room in the house came Alyssa's wailing sobs. She sounded as if she was in deep, bone-burning pain. Penelope flinched as she listened to her daughter cry and withdrew from my side.

"Don't you see?" she said. "She wasn't like this before you

arrived. It only happens when people come to our house. First, it was that crazy woman. Now, it's you and your husband."

"What crazy woman? You mean Della?"

"Della, yes," said Penelope. "She was the first one who tried to help us. When will you stupid mortals realize we cannot be helped? You're only making the situation worse."

"What do you expect to happen?" I demanded. "You think this house is going to stay empty for all eternity? It doesn't work that way. This place is old money. Someone's always going to want it."

"But *you* don't," Penelope pointed out. "So why don't you leave this place?"

"I would love to!" I told her. "But I can't leave for another month because of my stupid grandfather!"

Penelope swept a small bucket of thimbles to the floor in frustration. "Who is this grandfather you speak of? What's his name?"

"Andrew Anderson," I scoffed. "So if you have a problem with the way I'm dealing with all of this, you can take it up with him! Let me know if you get a hold of him because I'd love to give him a talking to. Tell him to take this house and shove it up his—"

"Your grandfather was Andrew Anderson?"

"Yeah. Why?"

Penelope waved a hand, and the thimbles picked themselves up from the floor and rearranged themselves in the bucket. If I didn't already know Penelope was a ghost, I would have guessed she was actually a witch. Or a Jedi.

"Andrew Anderson was my husband's best friend for a brief period of time," Penelope said. "Percy trusted him with everything: his money, his assets, even his life."

"Yeah, I've heard," I said. "Percy and Andrew were best buddies. So what?"

"So what you haven't heard is the real reason Andrew Anderson moved to Falconwood," Penelope whispered, as if she feared our discussion would be overheard.

I stopped fiddling with Penelope's dress designs. She had my full attention. "Are you saying you know why Andrew abandoned my mother and grandmother?" Penelope shook her head, but the look in her eyes told me a different story. "Penelope, who was my grandfather to you?"

"It's not my secret to tell," she whispered.

"Are you kidding me?"

She turned stern again, squaring her shoulders. "It's not Alyssa's secret either," she hissed, "so don't go prying my little girl for hints again. You won't like what might happen if you do."

"Are you threatening me?"

Penelope disappeared, but not before she knocked over the entire desk. I leapt out of the way as the sewing machine toppled over, tripped over the rug, and landed with a jolt on the hardwood floors. I groaned and rubbed my bruised tailbone.

"Why can't ghosts ever be straightforward?" I grumbled, pushing myself to my feet. "Just tell me what you want, Penelope!"

The answer never came, and I figured Penelope wasn't showing up again anytime soon. I was on my own again, but whether Penelope knew it or not, she had given me something to look for: the true reason for my grandfather's disappearance to Falconwood and beyond. I'd already know Andrew held part of the secrets to the Abram Mansion, but this confirmed he'd been up to something, possibly without Percy's knowledge. Were the two of them actually best friends, or had Andrew been cooking up something behind Percy's back?

Alyssa was still crying, but if I went looking for her, Penelope would surely have my head. I bit the bullet and headed downstairs, using the servants' staircase again. There was something spooky and empowering about the hidden stairs. Using them made me feel like I knew the mansion's secrets more than anyone else. The door to the stairs was even hidden in the paneling of the wall on the first floor. To exit, you had to pull a lever on the inside to pop the panel out of place. With relish, I yanked the lever and stepped into the first-floor corridor—

A hand covered my mouth.

"Don't scream," a deep voice whispered.

I let out a shriek loud enough to pierce the eardrums of my captor, bit down as hard as I could on the fleshy part between his thumb and forefinger, and jabbed my elbow as hard as possible into the gut behind me. My captor grunted and doubled over, and I took his momentary lapse in attention to make a run for it.

My brain was sending me into flashback mode. Just a few days ago, Theo's crazy ex-boyfriend had turned up at the mansion, intent on murdering us all. I would never forget the feeling of Dylan holding me around the neck and yanking me around by the roots of my hair. My breath came in short gasps. Panic set in. As I fled the first-floor corridor, light footsteps padded quickly along behind me. I was being followed.

As I rounded a corner, I chanced a quick glance behind me. It was the man I'd found standing at my window that morning, his long hair and beard masking the true features of his face.

"Wait!" he called in a whisper. "I'm not going to hurt you!"

His declaration terrified me more than anything. It was always the men who claimed not to hurt you who did most of the damage. I pumped my arms and sprinted into the next corridor. My feet slid on the rug, and I went tumbling down. The man advanced, getting closer to me as I scrambled up and ran on.

"Help!" I screamed as I ran toward the foyer. Could anyone hear me from outside? "Ben, help! Help me!"

As we careened into the foyer, the front door opened and Basil Gordon stepped inside. He took one look at the man pursuing me then picked up a fire poker and swung it at the man's head. The man ducked and gave up his chase. He made a run for the back stairs, and Basil followed him into the kitchen. The door down there opened and slammed shut. I waited breathlessly, my hand over my heart as I tried to calm its rapid pace.

The stalker of Falconwood had fixed his attention on me.

26

"*H*e came out of nowhere."

Basil and Ben stood behind each of my shoulders. They both had their feet spread at shoulder-width and their arms crossed, doing their best imitations of the president's bodyguards. Officer Hillary Spaughton, my favorite Falconwood policewoman, sat across from me at the kitchen table to take my statement.

"So you led him through the first-floor corridor into the foyer," she muttered, taking notes on a small legal pad. "That's when Basil came in and chased him away?"

"Yes, thank goodness." I patted Basil's hand when it came to rest comfortably on my shoulder. "I'm not sure what would have happened if Basil wasn't coming inside to get a drink of water."

"And Basil, what happened when you chased the intruder out of the foyer?" Hillary asked.

"He made a run for the back door," Basil said. "I lost him in the garden. It's a bit of a mess out there. As soon as he made it past the first set of topiaries, I couldn't see him anymore."

"It was like he knew where the kitchen door was," I added.

"As soon as Basil went after him, he made a break for it. Do you think he's been inside before?"

Hillary scribbled another note on her pad. "Possibly. We've talked about the lack of security in the house before, and this isn't the first *or* second time I've been here to take your report on an intruder."

"Yeah, but this time it's not some crazy little kid crawling in through the doggy door," Ben said, speaking at last. He'd been quiet for so long, I was starting to wonder if he'd inexplicably become mute. "We can't have some dangerous stalker using our house as his motel. How are the police going to deal with this? I want immediate action."

"You'll get it," Hillary assured him. "This is the first real lead we've had on the stalker. We aren't going to let it go by the wayside. I've already got a team combing the perimeter of your property. If he's still here, we'll find him. Did either one of you get a decent look at him?"

"I was too busy running for my life," I said. "All I saw was long hair and a shaggy beard."

"Color?"

"Light brown and gray."

Hillary wrote more notes. "No eye color that you can remember? Any other defining features?"

"Nope."

"What about you, Basil?" Hillary asked. "Anything to add?"

Basil cleared his throat. "Frankly, Officer Spaughton, I was too busy seeing red to get a decent look at the jerk's face. Besides, I only saw the back of his head. He looked scraggly, but he wore an expensive coat. That's about all I got."

"An expensive coat?" Hillary flipped to a new page and scribbled the note down. "How do you know it was expensive?"

"It was made of mink hair," Basil replied. "I highly doubt it belonged to him. Hell, he probably stole it from one of the closets upstairs. Those coats can sell for thousands of dollars."

Hillary tapped her pen against the notepad. "Hmm. Interesting. Sounds like he might have known how much it was worth. That means he either came from money or spent some time around rich folks."

"Or he was cold," Ben suggested, "and he grabbed the first coat he could find."

Hillary nodded in acknowledgement as she stood up from the table and slipped the notepad into the pocket of her uniform. "I'll let you know if we find any sign of the intruder on the property, and I'll make sure someone cruises by here every few hours. A cop car should scare this guy off. Give me a call if you see him again or if you suspect he's been in the house. You have my number?"

"On speed dial," I said.

She tossed her coat over her shoulder. "I look forward to hearing from you, Peyton. Hopefully, it's to tell me you haven't seen hide nor hair of this guy. You know, I'm starting to think that the only crime in Falconwood happens at this damn house."

THE NEXT MORNING, as I was warming leftover coffee in the microwave because I was too lazy to make a fresh pot, Basil came through the kitchen carrying a shovel, pruning shears, and a huge box of black trash bags. He wore thick gardening gloves and the same boots he used to build the greenhouse.

"Morning, Basil," I said, taking in his haul. "I thought you and Ben were taking a break from the greenhouse building to work on the book today?"

"Ben is." Basil balanced everything in one arm as he filled his water bottle at the fridge. "He says he can at least start editing the first part of the book. It's all about the theory of gardening, rather than the practice. Once we get the new greenhouse up and running, it will be absolutely glorious."

"I bet it will be," I said, sticking my finger in my coffee to see if it was warm enough. "What's with all the gardening supplies then?"

Basil capped his water bottle and took a test sip. "I'm tackling that courtyard of yours today. It's a mess."

"Oh, you don't have to do that," I assured him. "Please, Basil. That's not your job. We can hire someone to take care of the courtyard. It's not your responsibility."

"If I'd been able to see the stone path, I could have caught the man who broke into your house yesterday." Basil's cheeks puffed out and turned red. "I won't let something like that happen again, so I'm cleaning up the courtyard whether you like it or not, Mrs. Fletcher, and you can't do anything about it."

"Well, okay then."

Without further ado, Basil hoisted all of his tools and proceeded to the courtyard. I leaned against the door and watched as he set everything down next to the first topiary. He flexed his fingers to make sure his gardening gloves were a good fit, shook open the first garbage bag, and began hacking away at the topiary's overgrown branches. I shook my head and smiled. When it came to plants, there was no stopping Basil's determination.

My phone rang. I checked the caller ID, half-hoping it was Officer Spaughton calling to tell me they had the stalker in custody, but it was only Theo.

"Hey, you," I answered cheerfully. "Everything okay?"

"Decidedly not," Theo replied, her voice terse. "Did Sammy talk to you yesterday?"

I reflected on my last afternoon with Sammy. "About what? He was pretty quiet for most of the day."

"He had another fit at school," Theo said. "The principal

called me at the end of the day to ask if Sammy had been diagnosed yet."

"Diagnosed for what?"

"I have no idea!" she exclaimed. "But what if he's right, Peyton? What if there's something wrong with Sammy?"

As Basil continued to shape the topiary, I decided I wanted a better view to watch him work. I took my coffee, my book, and my phone and moved upstairs. As I climbed to the next story in the house, I told Theo, "There's nothing wrong with Sammy. Even if he does have something that needs to be diagnosed, there isn't anything wrong with him. Just because a kid might have a behavioral disorder doesn't mean he's broken."

"He really didn't say anything to you?" Theo asked. "The teachers said he was crying uncontrollably. They had to take him out of class again."

"He didn't mention it to me," I told her. "Maybe he didn't want you to know. Why didn't the school call me like they did the first time?"

Theo scoffed into the phone. "I asked them the same thing. They told me Sammy needed to learn how to control his emotions so he could return to class. I think it's bullcrap, but apparently it worked. He calmed down after an hour or so, and they made him do multiplication tables for the rest of the day."

I made it to one of the hidden balcony entrances and emerged onto the terrace. I looked down into the courtyard, where I could see the top of Basil's head as he continued his work on the overgrown topiaries. Already, the one he was working on looked more like a rearing horse than a giant bush.

"That's good," I told Theo. "I know it's hard, but sometimes you have to let Sammy figure stuff out on his own. You're not always going to be around to help him."

"He's only six years old, Peyton."

"I know that," I said. "But soon he'll be ten, then fifteen, and before you know it, you'll have a twenty-five year old on your hands who still lives at home and doesn't know how to wash his own laundry."

Theo groaned. "Don't remind me that he's going to grow up. Just don't."

I let out a laugh. "All I'm saying is to give Sammy a little space. You don't have to be so overprotective. Dylan's gone now, remember?"

"Says the woman who got attacked by a stalker in her own house last night," Theo reminded me. "You're like a magnet for criminals."

"I'm not, but this house is," I grumbled. Down below, Basil mounted a step stool to shape the leafy horse's shoulder. "This place is full of ghosts."

Theo snorted. "I bet. Listen, I'm going out of town for a work thing in a few days. I'll only be gone for one night, but I need someone to watch Sammy. Would you be able—?"

"Of course," I answered before she could finish the question. "You don't have to ask. What's the work thing?"

"It's a networking event," she said. "The office is sending me as their representative. I might make some great connections."

I sipped my coffee. It had already gone cold. "That's great, Theo. Well, I'm more than willing to take care of Sammy. We're best buds. You know that."

"I do," Theo said. "He tells me that you're the best part of his day. I'm starting to get a little jealous."

"Don't worry," I assured her. "I have no intention of replacing you. In fact, we should all hang out sometime! We haven't had dinner in a while."

Theo sighed. "I'd love to, but I'm alway so exhausted after work. It's all I can do to read Sammy a bedtime story before I shower and pass out myself. Maybe once everything calms down, we can get together again. For now, I appreciate how much you've been there for Sammy. He needs someone like you."

"It's no problem at all."

"By the way, don't worry about picking him up from school today," she said. "The office gave me the day off to take him to the doctor."

My whole body stiffened. "What kind of doctor?"

"A psychiatrist," Theo said, trying and failing to sound nonchalant. "I want to make sure Sammy gets the help he needs."

I clenched my teeth. Sammy didn't need a psychiatrist to diagnose him with some disorder he probably didn't have and force medication down his throat that he definitely didn't need. What Sammy needed was to stop being haunted by his imaginary friend Alyssa and the suicide of his own father. A children's therapist would be more helpful than a psychiatrist, but it wasn't my decision as to what to do about Sammy's health.

"I hope it goes well," I managed to say, hoping it came out naturally. Considering my clenched teeth, it probably didn't. "Keep me posted. If you want to, of course."

"I will. See you later, Peyton."

I hung up without saying goodbye and tucked my phone into my pocket to stop myself from chucking it over the edge of the balcony. None of this was fair. Sammy shouldn't be having mental breakdowns in the middle of class. He shouldn't have to be analyzed by a doctor who cared more about pushing medication than the headspace of his patients.

Watching Basil work helped me calm down. He knew his way around the courtyard as if it belonged to him. He trimmed the bushes, pruned the withering roses, and weeded the stone pathways. By noon, he had made significant progress. From the balcony, I could tell what the garden was supposed to look like. The path began at the back door and branched out in two different directions. One led through the rose garden and the other led through the topiary collection. Between the roses and the topiaries was the swimming pool. I imagined what it was like to go swimming on a gorgeous summer day. With the weather finally warming up, I considered asking Ben to fill the pool, but with all the "accidents" that occurred around the Abram Mansion, I wasn't so sure I wanted to swim here after all.

When Basil went inside for a snack and some shade, I decided it was also time for me to come off the balcony. I'd forgotten to put sunscreen on, and now my face felt a little too warm for my liking. As I stepped inside, the corner of my novel caught on the doorway and it tumbled from my arms. My book-mark—the Anderson & Associates business card—fell from the pages. I picked it up and studied the number, remembering what Penelope had said about Andrew Anderson. On a whim, I dialed the number.

The first time, no one picked up. The call simply ended itself. There was no way to leave a voicemail or anything. I dialed again. This time, on the fifth ring, someone picked up.

"Uh… hello?"

"Is the office of Anderson & Associates?" I asked. "I have a business card with this number printed on it."

There was a pause on the other end of the line. Someone cleared their throat. When they spoke again, it was a woman with the air of someone who'd adopted her professionalism in the last ten seconds. "Yes, this is the office of Anderson & Associates. I'm Penelope, the secretary. May I ask who I have the pleasure of speaking to?"

A shiver ran through my body when the woman introduced herself. Surely it wasn't a coincidence that she shared her name with the dead matriarch of the Abram Mansion. "This is Peyton Fletcher. Andrew Anderson was my grandfather."

"Oh, Mrs. Fletcher!" the woman, Penelope or not, exclaimed.

"Yes, we've been expecting your call. When would you like to schedule your appointment?"

"My appointment? Regarding what?"

"Regarding the business, of course," the living Penelope replied. "Your grandfather left it to you. Surely that was covered in his will?"

"The only thing covered in his will was the Abram Mansion," I said. "What can you tell me about that?"

The woman hesitated. "I'm afraid I don't know anything about Mr. Anderson's former address. I was only tasked with passing on Anderson & Associates."

"Fine." I sighed heavily. "Can you at least tell me what kind of business my grandfather ran?"

"I'll happily discuss that with you in person," the living Penelope replied. "Now, would you like to schedule that appointment? We're flexible. I'm sure we can accommodate whatever day you're free."

"How about today then?" I challenged. "Right now. Where are you located?"

From the pause before the living Penelope's reply, I assumed I'd thrown her off track again. "We're located in Hartford. Are you able to make it here by two o'clock?"

I checked the time on my phone. It was only noon, and Hartford was no more than an hour's drive away. "I'll be there. What's the address?" She rattled off a street number in Hartford that I hastily scribbled in the margins of my novel. "Great. I'll see you in two hours. Penelope, was it?"

"Yes, and Mrs. Fletcher? I'm so sorry for your loss."

It was a happy coincidence that I didn't have to pick up Sammy from school today, and it was also an odd relief to get out of Falconwood. I told Ben I was running an errand for Theo and that I needed the car for the rest of the day. He was surprisingly compliant, kissed me on the cheek before I left, and assured me he would have dinner on the table for all four of us—Della and Basil included—when I returned home. It was like he had accepted the older couple as his surrogate grandparents, and I wasn't exactly opposed to the idea. I liked the person Ben was when he was around them.

The drive to Hartford gave me too much time to think. Who was this living Penelope and how did she know my grandfather? Why was there so much mystery surrounding Anderson & Associates? If my grandfather had been missing for so long, who had managed his business for him all these years? None of it made any sense.

Once in Hartford, I made three U-turns before I finally located the street address the living Penelope had given to me. It was one of those walk up offices with an entrance that was squished between two other businesses. The door was barely visible. I parked on the street and yanked the handle, but it was lock. With a huff, I rang the doorbell. Static buzzed through the intercom.

"Anderson & Associates. How can I help you?"

I recognized the living Penelope's voice. "Hey, Penelope. It's me, Peyton Fletcher."

"I'm sorry. Who?"

"Peyton Fletcher," I bellowed into the intercom. "I have an appointment at two o'clock."

The door buzzed to let me open. Rolling my eyes, I went inside. The carpeted stairway smelled like mold and must. At the top of the steps was another unmarked door. Before I could reach the handle, someone else opened it.

"Hello, Mrs. Fletcher!" The living Penelope beamed as she looked down at me. She looked nothing like the actual Penelope. She was a squat, middle-aged woman with puffy cheeks and tightly curled hair that made her look like a chia pet. She waved me up into the office. "It's such a pleasure to finally meet you."

When I crested the top step and saw the official office of Anderson & Associates, I almost turned around and went right back to my car. It looked nothing like the office of a respectable businessman. The windows were blacked out with tarps and duct tape. Filing cabinets were stacked against the walls, over-flowing with papers and folders. The place smelled like mildew and cigar smoke. A single desk had been cleared of debris in the front corner of the room. The surface had been hastily wiped free of dust, as if the living Penelope had arrived here minutes before I did and tried her best to make this place look like someone actually worked in it.

"Okay, what the hell is going on?" I asked Penelope. "If you try to tell me Anderson & Associates is still in business, I'll wring your neck."

The living Penelope flinched at the threat. I didn't realize how convincing it had sounded. "Mr. Anderson told me to tell you that the business *is* still going, but it's important you know—"

"Speaking of Mr. Anderson," I said, forcing Penelope toward the filing cabinets, "When was the last time you spoke to him?"

"Eight months ago," Penelope stuttered as she stumbled away from me. "Right before he died."

"How did he die?"

"I don't know."

"Really, Penelope?" I challenged, cornering her by the window. "Because I can't find any information about my grand-father's death at all, and it seems like you were the last person to see him. Maybe I should go to the police?"

"No!" The living Penelope slammed her fist into one of the cabinet drawers, creating a metallic racket that echoed off the musty walls. This time, I was the one who flinched. "Andrew was adamant that the police could not get involved. He made me promise not to call them, even when he disappeared."

We glared at each other, inches apart. The reek of the office made my eyes water. I let my shoulders and my guard fall then sank into the one and only office chair. "Screw this. We're both posturing, and this place stinks. Do you want to get a coffee? I'll tell you what I know if you tell me what you know, but I have to warn you: I don't know much."

The living Penelope collected her coat from a nearby chair. "There's a good café a block away. Let's go."

A FEW MINUTES LATER, the living Penelope and I found a private booth tucked away in the back section of a noisy café to talk about my grandfather. She ordered a green tea, claiming coffee gave her acid reflux. Then she tried a sip of my cappuccino and proceeded to let out small burps throughout our conversation.

"First of all," I said, keeping my voice low. "Your first name isn't actually Penelope, is it?"

"No," she replied sheepishly. "It's Alice, but Andrew told me it was important to pose as Penelope."

"Apparently, he told you a lot of important things. Who were you to my grandfather?"

"His secretary. I swear!" she added when I gave her a skeptical look. "He hired me thirty years ago when no one else would give me a job. I've worked for him ever since."

"Thirty years ago, my grandfather had already disappeared from society," I reminded her. "He was a hermit."

"He was reclusive," she corrected, "but he hadn't disappeared. Besides, he had good reason."

"What reason was that?"

Alice pressed her lips together, crossed her arms, and leaned back against the booth. If she knew the truth about Andrew, she wasn't telling.

"He was my grandfather," I hissed. "Don't you think I have the right to know?"

"I'm under strict instructions," she replied. "I wasn't sure if you'd ever show up at the office. It all seems so silly."

I stirred a packet of stevia into my black coffee and took a long sip to calm myself down. "Listen, Alice. I'm trying to figure out a mystery that goes back about forty years, and my grandfather, as it turns out, played a huge part in the story. Whatever Andrew told you to tell me, I need to know sooner rather than later, and if you have any additional information you'd like to share, I'd appreciate that too."

Alice studied my expression, and I tried to look as pitiful as possible. At long last, she heaved a sigh. "All right. I'll tell you everything I know, but I'm not sure if it will help you. Let me start by saying I never saw Andrew in person. We spoke over the phone or communicated via email in more recent years. He ran Anderson & Associates from afar."

"What is Anderson & Associates anyway?" I asked her. "What was his business?"

"It was his passion project," Alice said. "As you know, he worked as a freelance art curator around the country. When he moved to Falconwood, he started Anderson & Associates with the financial backup of a dear friend he made there."

"Percy Abram."

"He never mentioned a name," Alice said. "Anyway, his friend —Percy, perhaps—passed away suddenly, leaving everything in his name to Andrew. As a tribute, Andrew kept Anderson & Associates alive. We were successful for a long time, but the art world has changed so much. Without being here in person, Andrew couldn't keep up with the competition. However, he refused to shut down the business. He said he wanted to pass it on to you."

"If that's the case, why didn't he put that in his will?" I asked her.

"He said you needed to earn it."

I pushed my coffee away, and it accidentally sloshed over the lip of the mug and onto the table. "I need *one* straight, non-cryptic answer about my grandfather's existence. For my entire life, he's been the guy that walked out on his wife and daughter for no reason then disappeared off the face of the earth. We knew he was crazy, but not this crazy."

"Like I said, Andrew had his reasons," Alice repeated. "And if I'm not mistaken, one of them was a concern for your safety. Here. This is the only thing he left for you."

She drew a folder from her purse and slid it across the table. Inside, there was a piece of yellowing paper preserved in a plastic sleeve. I pulled it out for a better look.

"An old magazine article?"

"Your grandfather wrote that piece," Alice told me. "You should read it thoroughly. Don't skim."

"This is it?" I asked, holding up the article. "He didn't give you anything else?"

Alice's lips turned downward as she reached into her purse for another folder. "I wasn't sure if you wanted this or not, but I feel as if you need it more than I do."

I looked in the folder. It was Andrew Anderson's death certificate, dated exactly eight months ago.

he old magazine article proved difficult to read because the print was so faded and the page was so yellowed. I sat at the kitchen table with the shades open and every possible light on, holding a magnifying glass in one hand and a flashlight in the other. When Ben walked in on my strangely luminescent procedure, he raised an eyebrow.

"What are you doing?" he asked.

"Don't worry about it. You'll think I'm going crazy."

Ben washed his hands in the sink. As usual, he'd been working on the greenhouse with Basil that morning. He sat across from me. "I knew you were crazy the moment I met you. You're not telling me anything I didn't already know. What's this old paper anyway?"

"It's a magazine article my grandfather wrote," I relented, sliding the article toward him. He almost picked it up with his wet fingers. "Don't touch it! Sorry, it's delicate. Just look."

Ben squinted at the tiny, faded print. "Painting and plants: the link between traditional artistic styles and modern day horticulture. Wow, who would have thought anyone cared about that?"

"Andrew Anderson did apparently," I said. "So did Percy Abram."

Ben narrowed his eyes at me, trying to predict where I was getting at. "I feel like this is going to turn into a lecture."

"Not if you don't want it to."

He sighed, got comfortable in his chair, and checked his watch. "I told Basil I was going inside for some shade and water. You've got four and a half minutes."

"I've asked around," I said. "Percy and Andrew knew each other. They worked together, then became good friends. When Percy supposedly died, he left the mansion to Andrew, but I think something else is happening—"

"Hang on," Ben interrupted. "What do you mean when Percy 'supposedly' died?"

I trapped my bottom lip between my teeth. We were getting into conspiracy theory territory. I didn't have solid evidence to prove Percy faked his own death. It was a prediction based on conversations with people who were either dead or half out of their mind. Neither one bore enough merit to convince Ben of what I thought to be true.

"I misspoke," I said, tapping the article to draw his attention away from my word choice and back to the magazine. "I went to Hartford yesterday to visit Andrew's business. The secretary told me Andrew left this article for me. There has to be a clue in it."

Ben looked perplexed. "A clue to what?"

"A clue as to why he left this house to us," I answered. "The reason he required us to stay here for six months before we could sell it. From the beginning, it didn't make any sense. Don't you want to know why we had to come to Falconwood?"

Ben took a deep breath and braced his hands on his knees as he stood up. "Honestly? Maybe if you had asked me that question at the beginning of all this, I would have said yes. But it's almost over now. We'll be out of here in a little less than a month. We fulfilled your grandfather's wishes. That's all that matters, right?"

"Right," I murmured, my eyes returning to the cramped, faded letters.

Ben paused before he left the kitchen. "Nothing's changed, has it? Between you and me?"

The tentative nature of his question pulled my gaze from the decrepit magazine. "Everything's changed, Ben. In my opinion, we're in a much better place than we were in five months ago. We have a clear idea of how our relationship works now. We're friends, right?"

He gnawed on the inside of his cheek and glanced at the floor. "Yeah, we are. I guess I really wanted to ask if any of our experiences at the mansion have made you reconsider."

"Reconsider our divorce?"

He nodded slowly, a solemn air about his person, as if he already knew the answer to his question. But a flicker of hope danced in his eyes as well. I hated to put that spark out, but it was worse to give him false hope.

"I'm sorry, Ben," I said, watching that spark extinguish itself in real time. "I'm glad we've been getting along here, but I still think we should get divorced."

"You don't think any of this has made us closer?" he said, gesturing around the kitchen. I knew he meant the mansion itself and all the challenges we had overcome since we arrived. "My injury? The break-ins? We've handled everything together. I thought we were learning how to work with one another again to solve our problems. I thought—"

"This *has* been good for us," I told him. "But it doesn't change the fundamental reasons behind our divorce. We're different, Ben. I want things you don't want and vice versa. Say we go home after this and stay together. How long would it be before things got boring again?"

Ben hung his head. "I never thought our life was boring."

"That's because you *had* a life," I pointed out. "You had your jobs and your friends and your family there. I didn't have any of that."

"I had you too," he replied. "And you had me."

"Your partner isn't always the end all, be all," I said softly. "There are other requirements that needed to be fulfilled. I had no friends back home because they were all the same people I resented in high school. I had no family unless you counted my mom, who was always three sheets to the wind. I needed to go out and *find* family."

Ben scratched his fingernail against the newly painted door frame. "I'm not sure I get that. How do you find family?"

"You connect with someone," I said with a shrug. "Some people aren't lucky enough to get a family like yours. We have to make our own."

"You mean like Theo and Sammy?"

"And Della," I added. "Basil, too, I guess. I don't know how to explain it, Ben. Ever since we moved here, I feel like I actually have people in my life that matter."

He winced. "Harsh."

"No, I didn't mean it like that." I abandoned the article in favor of meeting Ben by the kitchen entryway. I took his face in my hands. Usually so clean cut and shaven, he had let his hair beard grow out a little bit. The rugged look suited him. He seemed free. I pressed my thumbs up and over his eyebrows, a little massage trick I used to use on him whenever he was feeling particularly stressed. His eyes floated shut and his frown melted away. "You always mattered to me. You still do. It's not my goal to forget about our marriage or relationship. It's my goal to find the part of me that wasn't permitted to grow in our tiny little hometown. Does that make sense?"

"It feels like you're blaming me for never pursuing your photography career," Ben said, his face tightening again. "That's what it always felt like."

"I'm not," I insisted. "I promise you. Okay?"

He pulled away from my touch, like it was no longer as comforting as it once used to be. "If you say so. I should head back out. Basil's probably wondering where I am." He turned around to go up the stairs and ran into Della as she was coming down. "Hi, Della. Good day so far?"

"Not too bad," Della said, and though Ben might not have heard it, I could sense the lie in her voice.

Ben waved over his shoulder. "See you for dinner."

Della waited until she heard the front door close before turning to me. "It's getting worse."

"What is?"

"Whatever's happening in this house," she clarified. "I'm starting to feel it out in the airstream. It's spreading across the grounds."

"I'm doing the best I can!" My voice exploded across the kitchen and ricocheted off the subway tiles, coming back to me louder than intended. I took note of Della's shocked expression. "Sorry. I didn't mean to yell. I'm frustrated. I tracked down my grandfather's business and all I got out of it was this stupid magazine article."

Della peered around me for a look at the magazine. "What article? Can I see it?"

"Sure, but good luck making any sense out of it."

She sat in my chair and pulled the magazine toward her. She didn't use the magnifying glass like I did. "I've read this article before."

"You have?" I looked over her shoulder, as if something new

might have appeared on the old pages to trigger her memory. "When? How?"

Her eyes flicked back and forth as she skimmed the article. "I'm not sure, but it's definitely familiar." She checked the byline. "Your grandfather wrote this?"

"Supposedly," I said. "I didn't know he was interested in horticulture. Then again, I didn't know a lot about him in general."

"Can I have this?" Della asked, holding up the article with a delicate touch. "I'll return it to you tomorrow. I promise."

"Well, I was going to—"

"One day," Della said. "Twenty-four hours. That's all I need."

Though she meant it as a request, it sure sounded like a demand, and Della was the only other person I could trust with all of this information. If she knew something about the article, it couldn't hurt to let her figure it all out.

"Okay," I said, nodding. "Until tomorrow."

Someone cleared their throat behind us. I looked into the shadowy kitchen stairway and spotted Alyssa's familiar outline. She wouldn't come entirely into the kitchen, not while Della was there. Della and Alyssa's intertwined paths prevented them from wanting to coincide again. Only Alyssa's shoes and socks were visible, since she stood on the next to highest step.

Della tucked the article into the front of her sweater, pushed in the kitchen chair, and left without a word through the back door. As she went, I caught a glimpse of the newly-trimmed garden. Basil had done a phenomenal job shaping the courtyard into its former grandeur. He had trimmed the topiaries into lions that guarded the pool and garden. They prowled and panted around the garden's perimeter. As Alyssa moved into the kitchen, she too peered into the backyard.

"It looks the same," she whispered, pressing her nose and little fingers to the window panes in the door.

"No, it doesn't." I stood behind her to get a better look at the garden, half-expecting to see the condensation from Alyssa's breath on the glass. Of course, there was none. "It looks completely different."

"I meant the same as it used to," Alyssa said. "Mama never liked the lions, but I did. Daddy made them like that for me."

A sour taste flooded my mouth. "At what point did your dad stop cutting bushes for you and start planning your mur—?"

I cut myself off. I had forgotten who I was talking to, as well as her relative age. Sometimes, it was difficult not to talk to Alyssa as if she were a fully grown adult. She was so well-spoken for a five-year-old girl, and she sometimes exhibited maturity that far exceeded my expectations of her. Alas, she was only a child, one that didn't deserve to be reminded of her death.

"Did you need something?" I asked her, redirecting the conversation. "You don't usually come out of hiding unless you want to tell me something."

"I heard someone snooping around in the study."

My blood ran cold. Had the stalker already returned to the mansion for another round of cat and mouse? I fished my phone out of my pocket. I had Hillary on my list of favorites. As I clicked her name and the phone began to ring, I crept out of the kitchen and up the stairs to the mezzanine. As I passed the fireplace, I grabbed one of the iron pokers and swung it over my shoulder like a baseball bat.

"Officer Spaughton," she answered.

"Someone's in the house," I hissed, creeping along the hallway toward Percy's study. "I think it's the stalker."

Her tone changed at once, and I heard the squeak of her chair as she sat up straighter in her seat. "Where are you? Are you safe? Where is the intruder?"

"He's in the study," I whispered, hardly breathing as I approached the door. It was slightly ajar, and I could hear someone shuffling around inside. I kept the fire poker up by my shoulder. "I'm right outside."

"Get out of the house," Hillary advised. Something rustled in my ear, as if she'd pinned the phone to her ear to get her jacket on. "I'm on my way."

"No," I replied, my resolve hardening. "I'm going to confront him."

"Peyton, don't—!"

I hung up on Hillary, knowing she would be here in five minutes anyway. With the fire poker in position, I tiptoed closer to the study's entrance. Something had come over me—an adrenaline rush and the knowledge that this was *my* house as of right now. I'd been scared in my own home for too long, and I refused to be fearful any longer. A wave of anger came over me, forcing my foot up and into the study door. It slammed open, and I charged inside, yelling and waving the fire poker.

"Get out!" I screamed at the figure crouched in the corner, examining Percy Abram's art collection. "This is my house, you piece of scum! The police are on their way—"

The "intruder" turned around. It was Basil. He raised his palms and backed away from Percy's things, trembling with emotion. He eyed the fire poker raised over my shoulder.

"It's me, Peyton," he said, his voice shaking. "It's Basil. I was looking for some old paper to recycle. There's a way to use it as fertilizer. I thought it might make for an interesting chapter in the book—"

I lowered the fire poker. I was shaking too. The adrenaline rush hadn't worn off quite yet. "I thought you were the stalker."

He gave an uncertain laugh. "Clearly. Are you all right?"

I squeezed the bridge of my nose, wishing my panicking body would catch up with my brain. "I will be. Can you do me a favor though? Shout me a warning if you come into the house. This whole stalker situation has me a little on edge."

"Are you sure it's not the house?"

"What do you mean?"

Basil rolled some of Percy's papers up to manage them better and tucked them under his arm. He set his free hand on my shoulder to comfort me. "I know better than most that this house isn't entirely what it seems. I've seen what it did to Della. It took her awhile to come back from that. I don't want that to happen to you too."

I took his hand and squeezed it. "Thank you. I appreciate it. Did you find what you needed?"

He waved the rolled-up papers. "These should do the trick. They're practically disintegrating already."

"Good luck with your experiment."

He touched his fingers to his forehead—since he wasn't wearing a hat—by way of farewell and escorted himself from the study. As his footsteps faded down the hallway, I slumped against the plush green armchair by Percy's desk. A cold breeze tickled my shins.

"False alarm," I called to Alyssa, knowing she was there before I could see her. Sure enough, she peeked out from behind Percy's bookshelves. "It was only Basil."

"Basil," she murmured, elongating the "ah" sound. "Who is he?"

"Della's husband."

Alyssa left the study and crossed the corridor to watch from the window as Basil left the mansion and headed back to the greenhouse foundation. Alyssa peered down at him, her eyebrows scrunched together in consternation.

"Is he your dad?" she asked.

I snorted. "No, my dad is an enigma."

"A what?"

"Never mind," I told her. "Are you okay?"

She stayed at the window, leaning her chin on her elbows.

In the yard, Basil shredded the papers by hand and added them to the fresh dirt of the greenhouse. She didn't answer my question.

"Helloooo." I waved my hand in Alyssa's face. No response. "I'm done. Let me know if you need me, kid. I'll be downstairs trying to restart my heart."

THE HOURS PASSED BY SLOWLY. I skipped the Black Cat Café that day because Hillary's cruiser came screaming into the yard five minutes after I'd called her, and it took me an hour and a half to convince her that the stalker *hadn't* actually returned to the house. She insisted on doing a perimeter check anyway, lingering near Basil's greenhouse to inspect his new work. Basil talked to her for ten minutes or so, his hands moving wildly as he gesticulated his greenhouse plans to her. Hillary, mildly interested, let him go on until she got a call on her radio for someone speeding through town.

"Keep me updated," she said to me as she ducked into her cruiser and started it up. "I want to know everything that goes on out here."

"Will do," I said.

Hours later, the mansion was so quiet and boring that I found myself hoping something more exciting would happen. Without Andrew Anderson's article to examine, I had nothing to go on until tomorrow. For the hell of it, I filled up the pool. The courtyard looked so much nicer after Basil's marathon of gardening yesterday that it seemed silly not to take advantage of it. Not to mention, the sun was warm enough to stick my feet in without freezing to death. I got a towel and a book and set myself up outside. There, I spent the rest of the afternoon until it was time to pick up Sammy. Significantly tanner, I went inside to get dressed and ready. As I rinsed sunscreen off my legs in the bathroom nearest my bedroom, a short, distressed yelp echoed into the hallway.

My first thought was that it belonged to Alyssa. I was starting to expect her freak-outs, especially with what Della said about things getting worse. I hopped out of the bathroom, still toweling off my legs, and listened in the hallway. All was silent.

"Hello?" I called. "Everyone okay?"

No replied.

"Alyssa?" I ventured, hoping no one else was in the house that might question who Alyssa was. "Anyone?"

I slipped on the new flooring but managed to catch myself before I hit the floor, using a table in the corridor to pull myself along. I tossed the towel on the floor and stepped on it to dry my feet before moving farther. The house was eerily quiet. The hair on the back of my neck prickled as I moved into the foyer. There was no sign of Alyssa or anyone else, so where had the scream come from? A small noise—a pained moan—echoed from the bottom of the kitchen staircase. I rushed downstairs.

"Della!"

She was splayed across the kitchen floor, blood pooling from her head. A heavy wooden rolling pin had tracked the blood across the white tiles. Someone had hit Della in the head and dropped the weapon. I dropped to my knees beside her, but I feared moving her. I didn't want to injure her further.

"Help!" I yelled. "Basil! Ben!"

I dialed the emergency number on my phone, and the operator answered.

"My friend has been attacked," I babbled, brushing Della's blood-soaked hair out of her eyes. She looked dazed, and her breathing was ragged. "Someone hit her in the head with a rolling pin."

"Is she breathing?"

"Yes, but she's having trouble."

"Is she conscious?"

"I think so?" I examined Della's eyes again. "Her right pupil is blown. That's not good, is it?"

"It means she needs immediate attention. What's your address?"

I gave her the street address for the Abram Mansion. "Please, hurry."

"I'll have a team there in a few minutes."

As I hung up, footsteps stomped down the stairs, and both Ben and Basil emerged in the kitchen. Basil flung himself to the floor beside his wife, immediately tearing up.

"Della?" he whispered. "My love, are you awake?"

Ben helped me up. My palms and knees were stained with Della's blood. The warmth and tackiness of it made my heartbeat speed up. I took one deep breath. Then another. The air wouldn't make its way to my lungs, no matter how much oxygen I tried to take in.

Ben wrapped his arms around me from behind, squeezing me tight. "You're having a panic attack," he murmured gently in my ear. He turned me to face the back of the kitchen so I couldn't look at Della anymore. "You're hyperventilating. Try to relax. I'm right here. The ambulance will be here soon. Everything's going to be okay."

The reassurance felt false at first. Nothing was ever going to be okay, not until we got out of this damn house. But Ben squeezed me tighter, and the pressure of his arms forced my heart rate to slow. Steadily, my breathing regulated itself. Then Basil grabbed my ankle.

"What happened?" he pleaded from the floor. "Who attacked her?"

"I don't know," I said, hot tears burning the corner of my eyes. "I was in the bathroom when I heard her yell. When I found her, she was already like this."

"The stalker?" Ben muttered under his breath. "It's the only thing that makes sense."

"Why would he attack Della?" I said back. "Unless she saw who he was and threatened to call the police."

Basil draped himself over his wife, his sobs vibrating through his entire body. "This is my fault. I brought her here. I made her move. All for a stupid greenhouse."

Ben, the only one with enough brain cells to do damage control, knelt next to Basil, careful to avoid the puddle of Della's blood. "Help will be here in a minute, Basil. We don't know—"

Sirens wailed in the front yard, and I ran to the foyer to fling the front door open. The paramedics dismounted from the rig and carried a stretcher inside. I sat on the mezzanine steps as they strapped Della in and took her away, keeping my head in my hands. Once they cleared the foyer, I waked over to the front window to watch as they loaded her in the ambulance. Basil climbed in after her, and they were gone in the blink of an eye. When the ambulance disappeared, it revealed the waiting cop car behind it. Hillary Spaughton, shaking her head, came into the foyer.

"So there *was* someone in the house," she said. "I swear, I combed this entire place. I can't believe I didn't find the guy."

"This house is huge," Ben reminded her. "He could still be here."

"I'm done with this," Hillary said. "I'm putting a security team out here in the woods. We're going to catch this guy. I promise. Get yourself in the shower, Peyton, and don't worry. I'm not leaving the two of you alone."

"Thanks, Hillary," Ben said as he steered me away from the front door.

I stayed silent while Ben led me into the nearest bathroom and started the shower. My body and brain felt numb. Basil was wrong. It wasn't his fault that Della had been attacked here. It was mine. I was the one who had invited the two of them to stay at the mansion. I was the one who encouraged Della to face her fears and spend time inside, even though I knew of her rocky relationship with the horrors here. She had been attacked because of me, and I wasn't sure if I could ever forgive myself for that.

AFTER BEN HELPED scrub the blood from my skin, he wrapped me in a freshly-laundered robe and lay me down in my bed. He drew the curtains, made sure I was comfortable, then disappeared for a few minutes. When he returned, he had a cup of tea and a cardboard box in hand.

"Here you go," he said, handing me the tea. "It's Della's relaxation blend. I thought it might help. And this was at the door for you. It's from your mom. Have the two of you been talking again?"

He set the box in my lap. It was an old shoebox, taped shut, with the Abram Mansion's address written on the label in barely legible handwriting. I was surprised the mailman managed to decipher my mother's penmanship.

"I called her to ask about my grandfather." I gestured for scissors, and Ben produced a sharp pocket knife that hung off his keychain. He cut the layers of tape off the box for me. "He sent me letters every year on my birthday. I asked Mom to give them to me."

I pried the lid off the box and let out a surprised gasp. It was full from end to end with unopened envelopes. Some of them were crinkled and worn, as if they'd been in the box for quite some time. Others looked almost new. With Ben's knife, I carefully opened the one closest to me and read the first line aloud.

"My beautiful granddaughter," I said, voice shaking. "This will be the last time I am able to write you, and then I shall disappear. Please don't come looking for me, but if you have it in your heart, go to my house in Falconwood, Connecticut. I have a responsibility to that house and its occupants, a responsibility that I must pass on to you. You may not understand, but you will soon, and for this understanding, I must ask for your forgiveness. I will try to be there for you, but I cannot make any promises. For now, this is goodbye, but I hope to speak to you again in the future. Yours forever, Grandpa."

Ben looked over my shoulder to read the letter for himself. "This is the same guy that your mom said abandoned you and your grandma, right? I thought he never contacted you."

"Mom hid these from me," I said, studying the letter. "Because she was so mad at him for leaving."

"What does he mean about the 'occupants' of this house?"

Ben's face crinkled up the way it did when he was thinking too hard about something. It brought the slightest of smiles to my lips. I used to watch him make that face from across the room in geometry class many years ago. Something about that face made me realize it might finally be time to tell Ben the truth about the Abram Mansion. I could trust him.

"Ben, I think you should know," I began, "there's a reason my grandfather wanted us to come here, and it wasn't so we could sell this old house. Percy Abram—" I stopped dead in the middle of my sentence when I caught sight of the date Andrew had written in the top right corner of the most recent letter. "Can you hand me that envelope?"

With a look of confusion, Ben fetched the envelope from my desk and gave it to me. I pulled Andrew's death certificate out of it and compared it next to the letter.

"Oh my God," I breathed.

"What is it?"

"Look at the dates," I said, handing him the papers. "Andrew's last letter is dated *after* his death."

*T*heo, of course, was understanding about my inability to pick up Sammy from school that afternoon. The office allowed her to leave early like she used to in order to get Sammy herself. I made her call me when they were safely at home.

"That's terrible," Theo said over the phone after I'd recounted the afternoon's events to her. "I can't believe someone could be awful enough to hit an elderly woman over the head like that. Have you heard anything about Della's condition?"

"Basil called us from the hospital," I replied wearily. I was in bed again, drinking tomato soup from a cup. Ben had been checking on me all day. "Apparently, she was hit so hard she had a brain bleed. They had to do surgery to evacuate it. The doctor said it went okay, but she hasn't woken up yet. I don't think Basil's going to leave the hospital until she does."

"And what about you?" Theo asked. "How are you holding up?"

I suppressed a heavy sigh. "I'm fine, I guess. Exhausted. This is getting old. I want to move out of this place and go some-where small. A one-bedroom apartment sounds like such a dream right now. At least I'd know whether the stalker was actually in my house or not."

"Are the police still there?"

"For now," I answered. "The department can only spare one officer at a time because they have everyone else searching Falconwood for this guy. Hillary's pissed off."

Theo scoffed into the phone. "I would be too. This creep has slipped through her fingers one too many times."

"Well, she's making it her personal crusade to catch him." I set aside my empty soup cup and covered my head with the blankets. "Are you still going out of town this weekend?"

Theo hesitated, and I wondered if I wasn't going to like the answer. "I tried to get out of it, but I can't. I don't have anyone else to watch Sammy..."

"Oh, I'm not backing out," I assured her. "You know I don't mind taking care of Sammy, but I am nervous about having him in the house."

Static hit my ear, and I imagined Theo blowing air through her lips the way she did when she was trying to accommodate an unsolvable problem. "I'd tell you to stay at the apartment, but the landlord is having the roof fixed this weekend. It was perfect timing for Sammy to be out of there before all this stalker stuff started."

"We have round-the-clock police watch here." I peered out the window in time to catch one of Hillary's coworkers shining his flashlight across the courtyard for his hourly search of the grounds. "I'm not anticipating any problems, but I wanted to make sure there wasn't any other solution."

"I'm afraid not," Theo said, her voice tight. "The only other person I trust to watch Sammy overnight is Della, and —well—"

"She's unconscious in a hospital right now."

"Exactly."

"I won't let Sammy out of my sight while he's here," I said. "I promise."

"I'll have him all packed up on Friday afternoon then."

I DIDN'T SEE Theo before she left for her trip. It made my heart ache. I'd seen more of Sammy than my best friend ever since her job ladened her with more responsibility, and while I never minded Sammy's company, it was nice to have someone my age to talk to and connect with every once in a while. As promised, I picked Sammy up from school on Friday, where he emerged from the art classroom with his backpack and a small duffel bag that managed to swamp his tiny figure. I got out of the car to help him with it so he didn't drag it along behind him on the ground. In his other hand, he clutched a new drawing.

"Whatcha got there?" I asked as I tossed his duffel into the trunk.

He clambered into his booster seat and did up his seatbelt himself. "My entry for the art fair."

I closed the trunk and went around to the driver's seat. "Isn't the art fair here at the school? Why are you bringing it home with you?"

"I stole it," Sammy said. "I don't want anyone to see it."

I peeked at his forlorn face in the rearview mirror as I pulled out of the pickup loop. "Why don't you want anyone to see it?"

"Because they don't understand."

"Am I allowed to see it?"

Sammy pinched his lips together. "Maybe."

WHEN WE ARRIVED at the house, Basil was outside working on the greenhouse. It was the first time I'd seen him all week since Della had been admitted to the hospital.

"Can you grab your bag, Sammy?" I said. "Wait here for a moment."

"Why can't I go inside?"

"Because I'm not taking my eye off you this weekend." I got out of the car and jogged over to Basil. A light, misty rain coated my skin. "Basil! How's Della?"

He kept working, not looking up from a blueprint of a greenhouse frame. He didn't have any of the pieces yet. "Unconscious. Doctor said she should've woken up by now. If she doesn't soon, she could have brain damage or amnesia."

An invisible fist clenched around my heart and squeezed, but I knew Basil must be feeling a hundred times worse than me. "I'm so sorry."

"I'd rather not talk about it," he replied, pushing his hands beneath the soft ground. "I can't think about it. Please."

He was so hunched over the earth, he looked like he might become one with it. I left him to his work and returned to Sammy, who was struggling to pull his duffel bag out of the trunk.

"What's wrong with Basil?" he asked.

"He's sad about Della," I said. "She's hurt."

"What happened to her?"

The memory I'd made up in my head flashed before my eyes. The man from the window—tall, shaggy, and violent—coming into *my* kitchen, Della at the table drinking tea. Did she spin around at the sound of his footsteps? Did she try to defend herself as he grabbed the rolling pin from the drawer and swung it at her head? I squeezed my eyes tightly shut and watched the lights dance behind my eyelids, focusing on the imaginary fireworks rather than the intrusive thoughts in my brain.

"Don't worry about it," I told Sammy, guiding him inside. "Let's get you settled. I put a kid-sized bed in my room so you don't have to sleep alone tonight. Is that okay?"

"Sure."

I showed Sammy the room and put his stuff in the corner by his bed. He placed his drawing on top of the new comforter and smoothed the paper from corner to corner. I caught a glance of it over his shoulder and felt my courage disappear. He had drawn a self-portrait, but he had added Alyssa's neck injury to it, resulting in a garish depiction of his own death. I picked up the drawing.

"Hey!" He made a jump for it as I held it out of reach. "That's mine!"

"We should talk about this," I told him. "I don't want you to be thinking about stuff like this. You're not going to end up like Alyssa."

Sammy sank onto the bed and tucked his knees into his chest. "I can feel her inside me."

"Now? At the mansion?"

"All the time," he whispered, staring blankly at the wallpaper. "Like she's a part of me."

I knelt next to the bed and tugged on Sammy's knees until he released them willingly. I rested my chin on his lap, and he put his tiny fingers in my hair. "What happened to Alyssa will not happen to you. I won't let it."

"But it already happened to her," Sammy said. "That's the problem."

"I know, buddy. I'm trying to fix it."

"Maybe it's too late to fix it."

He gently wormed away from me and left the room, but with my promise to Theo about not letting Sammy roam around, I had no choice but to follow him. He went right to the kitchen, opened the fridge, and found an apple on the bottom shelf. Then he poured himself a glass of water, climbed up into a chair at the table, and proceeded to enjoy his apple while quietly admiring the cleaned-up courtyard out back. I made myself a cup of tea and sat across from him with the shoebox of letters from my grandfather, slowly working my way through them as the afternoon passed.

IN THE EARLY EVENING, I got a call from Ben. He'd gone to Hartford earlier that day to have lunch with a potential employer. It was the first job lead he'd gotten in a while, and I could tell he was excited about it. The lunch had gone well, and the man he'd met with wasn't ready to let Ben go home yet. They had dinner and drinks planned as well.

"I'll probably be home late," he said. "Is that okay? I feel bad leaving you alone with Sammy. If you need help, I can ask Mike for a raincheck."

"Don't do that," I told him, though my heart sank at the thought of not having Ben in the house as darkness fell. "You might not get a chance like this again. Have your dinner. Stay for drinks. We'll be fine."

"The cops are still there anyway," Ben said. His confident tone sounded more like he wanted to assure himself than me and Sammy. "You won't have any trouble."

I didn't want to tell him that the last officer to check the mansion's property for intruders had informed me the department was understaffed that day and he had to go back to the precinct to address more pressing matters. He promised Hillary would drop by later when she had time, but I had yet to see her cruiser pull into the driveway.

"We'll be fine," I said.

"Great! I gotta go. Mike wants to show me this new project he's working on before we get to our dinner reservations. Bye!"

He hung up before I had a chance to reply with a farewell of my own. I was sad and happy at the same time. Though working on Basil's greenhouse book was a decent source of income, it wasn't what Ben was truly interested in. Ben also didn't share the details of the new job with me at all. Usually, he recounted every single thing to me a hundred times until I was sick of hearing about it. This job represented the first step of his actual separation from me. In less than a month, Ben and I would be officially divorced, and he wouldn't be under any obligation to tell me anything. It was what I wanted, and yet it still felt like I was losing something.

"What's that?"

I jumped out of my chair as Basil's voice resonated over my shoulder. He was covered head to toe in dirt, as if he'd tried to bury himself under the greenhouse. He gestured to my shoe box.

"They're letters from my grandfather," I said, holding an envelope up for him to see. "My mother kept them from me until now."

"Oh."

He ambled to the sink to wash his hands and arms. Sammy watched Basil as he scrubbed away the dirt. Each of them reflected the mood of the other. Both were forlorn and at a loss for what to do with themselves. Did that make me tonight's sole caretaker of the Abram Mansion's broken occupants?

"Basil?" I said. "A few days ago, Della borrowed an old magazine clipping of mine. Do you happen to know what she did with it?"

Basil tapped his hands against the sink to shake off the excess water. "I don't believe I've seen it, but I'll have a look around. Are either of you hungry? I have some leftovers from yesterday that keep rather well."

"I can take care of dinner," I said, blocking Basil's way to the fridge. "Why don't you sit? You've been working all day. I hope you wore sunscreen."

Basil gratefully drew out the chair next to Sammy's, who

unabashedly examined the older man. "How are you, son? Hanging in there?"

"You look different," Sammy said instead of answering the question.

Basil shifted in his seat. "I haven't changed."

"Yes, you have." Sammy leaned forward and pointed at the lines around Basil's mouth. "These didn't used to be here."

"Sammy," I said. "That's not nice."

"It's not mean either."

Basil chuckled, but it was more for Sammy's sake than anyone else's. "You're sharp, aren't you, Sammy? Is that why you have so much trouble at school?"

Sammy dropped his head onto his chest. I paused in setting the table to tap his chin, encouraging him to look up again. We exchanged a small smile.

"Sammy's different than the other kids." I took Basil's leftovers—an exquisite kale and mushroom pasta—from the fridge and spooned it into a microwave-safe bowl. "And the other kids don't understand him."

Basil propped his elbow on the table as he turned to Sammy. "You listen here. There's nothing wrong with being different, do you hear me? Being different—being smarter—means you're better than the rest of those kids."

"I'm not sure that's the kind of lesson we want to teach him," I said, patting Basil's shoulder. "But I'm sure he appreciates the sentiment."

Basil took Sammy's shoulder, almost as if he hadn't heard me. "Focus on you, boy. Don't pay attention to anyone else. You want to be successful? Worry about yourself. Put yourself first. That's important."

Sammy stared back at Basil. A split-second later, his eyes filled with tears. His bottom lip trembled. The first tear dropped, followed shortly by a waterfall. His lips parted, and he let out an anguished howl.

Basil yanked his hand away from Sammy's shoulder. "I—I didn't mean to upset him. Peyton, I swear."

I turned Sammy's chair away from Basil and took his plump cheeks between my hands. "Sammy. Sammy! Look at me, buddy. Focus on me."

His chest heaved spasmodically as he tried to catch his breath, but he looked me in the eyes as asked, even grasping my forearms in his tiny hands to steady himself.

"Breathe," I said, remembering how Ben had instructed me in my moment of panic. I took Sammy into my arms and hugged him closely. "Just relax. Everything's okay."

It took Sammy several long minutes to calm down, but his breathing eventually slowed. Basil had left the kitchen without eating, and if his bowed head was any indication, he couldn't take the emotional outburst he'd unintentionally inflicted on Sammy. Once Basil was gone, Sammy lifted his face from my tearstained shirt.

"You okay?"

He sniffed and wiped his nose on the back of his hand. "I think so."

"What was that all about?"

"I don't know."

TO MY SURPRISE, Sammy fell asleep in a matter of minutes that night. He snoozed soundly on the opposite side of my bedroom, his tuft of hair the only part of him that was visible above the blanket. I'd plugged in a nightlight by his bed so I could keep an eye on him, but as the hours passed and the moon rose in the sky, my eyelids grew heavy. I propped my head on multiple pillows, hoping to stay away a little longer, but it didn't do the trick. I dozed off.

A light knocking woke me from my slumber. I checked on Sammy first, but he hadn't moved. Paranoid, I stepped out of bed and stood over him to make sure his chest was rising and falling with his breath. The gentle knock sounded again. I followed it out into the hallway. The cord dangled from a table lamp, swaying against the wall. The lamp was unplugged.

"Alyssa?" I whispered warily. These days, I didn't know if it was the ghosts or the stalker making noise in my house. "Is that you?"

"Afraid not," came the answer.

I whirled around to see Penelope leaning against the door to my room.

"Come with me," she said.

I followed her up the corridor and into the east wing of the house. I had never been on the first floor of the east wing because I had always gone upstairs to the mezzanine first. Not to mention, the door between the south and east wings was locked shut. Neither Ben nor I had ever found the key. Of course, Penelope made no issue of the door. With a simple wave of her ethereal hand, the door opened itself for her—or rather me—to pass through.

"What's this about?" I asked her. "You never want to talk to me."

"In here."

She gestured me into the first room in the hallway. It was yet another sitting room. The mansion had dozens of them, each with different interior design patterns. This one was all palms and florals. The pink couch was accented by the green leafy curtains. Penelope went to the window to look out on the courtyard.

"You're running out of time," she said, gazing away from me. "A man has come to your house, a dangerous one."

"Yeah, the local stalker," I said. "The police are on it."

"I'm talking about Percy Abram."

I wrinkled my nose. "What?"

Penelope rolled her eyes. "Multiple people have made you aware that Percy is still alive, have they not?"

"Yes, but—"

"He's back," Penelope said. "He's been in this house."

"Why didn't you tell me that sooner?"

She stood quickly, and a vase on a nearby table toppled over as if a swift breeze had catapulted through the room. "Because I didn't recognize him!"

The vase rolled off the table and shattered on the floor. I flinched as the ceramic showered my bare feet. Penelope rolled her shoulders back, reining in her frustration.

"It's difficult to explain," she went on. "When you exist like this" —she presented her own body— "your perspective on the mortal world is skewed. It's why we appear and disappear at random. It's impossible for us to exist in a place where we don't belong, and yet we still do. Caught in between this world and the next one makes keeping your facts straight a bit difficult."

"It's definitely not a science," I said.

"It took me a month to notice you and your husband had moved into this house," she said. "Similarly, I did not realize my own husband had returned. I have yet to encounter him."

A portrait of Percy Abram hung on the wall. I turned on my phone light and studied the picture. "So he's the stalker, huh? No wonder he won't leave the house. He must feel like it's still his. No one's going to believe this."

Penelope snapped her fingers to regain my attention. "Listen to me. The only reason I know about Percy is because he's affecting Alyssa. She, unlike me, is more tuned into his presence, and she hasn't been herself ever since he returned here. You should know. She's projecting on that boy."

"Who, Sammy?"

"Yes," she answered. "Alyssa's *friend*. If you didn't notice from his little freakout at dinner, he's getting worse. That's because Alyssa is getting worse. The two of them are connected. Sammy won't be at peace until Alyssa is, and if they don't find that peace soon, I fear both of them will descend into madness."

"Madness, huh?"

"This is not a joke," Penelope said. "If Percy gets his way, you'll be dead too. Mark my words."

*a*s always, Penelope vanished without warning, leaving me to find my own way back to the wing of the house I actually lived in. I was wide awake, mulling over all the things Penelope had told me. This ghost stuff wasn't an exact science. From what I gathered, Penelope and Alyssa had less control over their own apparitions and emotions than I originally thought. And then there was the matter of Percy Abram. According to Penelope, he had returned to the house, but she wasn't able to see him. A blind spot, per se.

I paused at my bedroom to check on Sammy and let out a sigh of relief when I saw him sleeping safely in bed. A second later, I jumped out of my skin. Alyssa sat at the end of Sammy's bed, half-hidden in the shadows. Moonlight reflected off of the tears on her cheeks.

"Alyssa?" I whispered. "What's wrong?"

Her fingers hovered over Sammy's feet, as if she wished she had the tactile ability to tickle his toes. "Everything." She wiped her tears on her nightgown and moved away from Sammy. "Keep him safe. Please."

"I am. Alyssa, wait—!"

She, too, popped out of existence. All that remained of her was a cold draft. I covered Sammy's shoulders and tucked the blanket underneath his feet. It floored me that he slept through the night with Alyssa at his bedside. Every time I felt a ghost nearby, it gave me goose bumps.

I pushed Sammy's hair back, pondering Alyssa and Penelope's warnings. "What's happening?" I muttered. "Am I going to lose you? I can't do that, Sammy. Your mother would kill me."

Sammy, of course, didn't answer. He slept on, blissfully unaware of the stress that crept through the mansion like a horde of spiders. I left him be, knowing it was unfair of me to loom over him like an extra ghost. With my shoebox of letters from Grandpa, I went into the foyer to spend the evening by myself.

With a huff, I lowered myself onto the sofa and wrapped the throw blanket around me. I chose the next letter in the box and carefully tore it open. One by one, I was working my way through them from the newest to the oldest ones. It was an eye-opening experience. For all the times my mother and grandmother had told me that Andrew had abandoned his family, there was a letter from him apologizing for his absence. Though he never revealed the reason for his disappearance, it was plain to see he had not severed all connections as my family had had me believe.

Halfway through another birthday letter—one from my sixteenth that was accompanied by a large check I wished I'd had the opportunity to cash back then—the lock in the front door clicked. My heart stopped and restarted when I remembered that Ben had been out late last night.

"Hey," I said when I heard the door brush against the rug in the entryway. "How were drinks with your soon-to-be boss?"

"Excuse me?"

I glanced over my shoulder. It was not Ben, but Basil who

had come into the house in the middle of the night unan-nounced. "Oh, hi. I didn't know you had a key."

"You gave one to Della," Basil said, stomping his boots on the mat to make sure he didn't track mud into the house. "In case of emergencies."

"Is everything okay?" I asked him. "Did the doctors call you?"

"Not yet," he answered. "I couldn't sleep though, and I've run out of tea at the airstream. Yet another problem with my wife being indisposed. I don't have her wonderful healing hand to help me."

His voice broke on the last sentence, persuading me out of my seat. I guided him from the entryway and into the foyer, where I made him sit in front of the empty fireplace. "Wait here. I'll get you some tea. I think we have a little left over from Della's last batch."

In the kitchen, I found a single sachet of Della's homemade tea, so I put the kettle on. After the water boiled, I let the sachet seep for an extra minute so Basil's tea would be a bit stronger than normal. Hopefully, it would soothe his fears about his wife, but I had a terrible, instinctive feeling that Della would never wake up. I took a moment to compose myself before returning to the foyer.

"Here you go," I said, handing the cup to Basil. "Careful. It's piping hot."

Basil blew across the surface, took a tentative sip, then set the mug on the coffee table. "Ah, that's good. Thank you."

I settled down next to him, pulling the knitted throw over my knees. Despite the spring weather, it was drafty in the mansion. "Basil, can I pick your brain about something?"

"Sure, honey."

"You've lived here for a while, right? You know about Percy Abram and Andrew Anderson and all that business?"

Basil tipped his head. "A bit, I suppose. We moved here after all that hubbub had subsided, but it's impossible to live in a town like Falconwood without learning of its history."

"Did Della tell you her hunch about Percy Abram?"

"Let me guess," he said, leaning back against the sofa. "She told you she thinks he's still alive."

"You think she's wrong?"

Basil struggled not to roll his eyes. "I love my wife. I really do. But when it comes to this house and the people who used to live in it, she's always been a bit—" He made a funny whirling motion with his hand. "It's a conspiracy theory. Percy Abram was declared dead a long time ago. Why go digging up the past? What's the point?"

"Because he killed his wife and daughter." I was done dancing around the subject. The time to be open was long past due. "Maybe you think Della's out of her mind, but it's not true. I've been going through the facts, and—"

"Why?" Basil demanded, his voice rising. "Why would you do that? I knew it was a mistake bringing Della here. The two of you are too similar, always sticking your noses where you don't belong. Just let it go!"

His voice echoed to the top of the mezzanine. I slid an inch or two away from him but kept my ground.

"I can't let it go," I said, "because it's affecting the people around me. Riddle me this, Basil. If Percy Abram isn't alive, then who's the man who keeps breaking into the mansion and trying to kill me?"

"*That*," Basil said, darting close to my face, "is your absolute *dolt* of a grandfather. And he's not trying to kill you. He's trying to tell you about *me*."

He lunged across the sofa and wrapped his hands around my neck, pressing his thumbs against my windpipe. Caught completely off guard, I didn't think to defend myself. I just sat there with Basil's full weight on top of me, his knee in my stomach. The blood rushed to my face, but he was holding off. I knew why: he wanted me to realize who he really was.

"Y-you?" I choked out. "*You're* Percy Abram?"

His lips tweaked into a smirk, and I noticed the slightest gap between his teeth, the same gap I'd seen in old photos and portraits. No wonder Basil only ever cast tight-lipped smiles. It was a dead giveaway, but there wasn't much else to pinpoint him as the old owner of the Abram estate.

"I did an excellent job of disguising myself, wouldn't you say?" he said, his pride evident in his braggartly tone. "It took some work. I dyed my hair a different color, *and* I had a plastic surgeon alter my nose. I had a deviated septum anyway, so I thought two birds with one stone, eh?"

"Why would you ever come back here?" I fought against his hold, but he was too strong. "After what you did to Penelope and Alyssa?"

"I came back because I've been waiting for this very moment," he replied. "You only figured out bits and pieces of the story, my dear. Everyone thinks your grandfather and I were the best of friends, and we were until he betrayed me."

"He knew, didn't he?" I gasped. "He found out you were abusing your family."

"And like you, he inserted himself into business that wasn't his," Basil snarled. His nails dug into the skin of my neck. "I have no idea how long he was watching me, how long he was conferring with my wife behind my back."

"That's why he moved to Falconwood," I said, realization engulfing me. "To protect Penelope and Alyssa."

"They didn't need his protection!"

"Shut up! Sammy's asleep."

To his credit, Basil—Percy, whatever—actually checked the hallway to the bedroom to make sure Sammy hadn't woken up.

Then again, Sammy's unconsciousness worked to Basil's advantage. He didn't need a witness to this.

"Ben will be home any minute," I warned him. "We're right in front of the door, Basil. He'll see everything. You won't get away with this."

A creepy smile spread across Basil's face. "Oh, I think I will. You see, I was the one who sent Ben to Hartford. I hired 'Mike' to keep him busy, and when he arrived home an hour ago—yes, an entire hour—I caught him from behind."

"No," I begged. "You're lying."

"I can drag you to the window if you like," Basil said, "so you can see his body in the yard. I hit him with the same rolling pin I used to dispose of my precious wife."

"*You* attacked Della?"

"She was a flaw in the plan," Basil said. "I knew it as soon as I saw that magazine article you'd given to her. I helped Andrew write that article. When she read it, she connected the dots, and she came into the house to warn you about me. I couldn't have that, could I?"

"You tried to kill your own wife."

"I'd done it once before. I had the strength to do it again."

"You're crazy."

"I'm committed," Basil hissed through his teeth. "The problem is that no one ever commits to me the way I have for them. Not my first wife, who bedded some other piece of work. Not my daughter, who began to fear me before she started school. Not Della, who cared more for this house than she did for me—"

"Because you're an ass," I replied. "And a madman. No wonder my grandfather had to step in—"

My voice cut off with a splutter as he tightened his grip around my throat again. "Your grandfather was a traitor, watching me for years. I couldn't possibly continue living in

Falconwood, so I faked my own death and set off to get the best of your grandfather. Unfortunately, he was always one step ahead of me. He disappeared in the blink of an eye, so I waited an appropriate amount of time then returned to Falconwood as a different person to watch over my estate. Then, of course, *you* showed up. I thought it was a fluke, but now I understand. Your grandfather lured you here on purpose."

Eyes streaming, I gasped, "To get rid of you?"

"To ruin my reputation," Basil snarled. "To destroy everything I've worked so hard to rebuild. I was a fool to leave this house to Andrew, but it was too late to alter my will. The decision became my ultimate downfall. For years, I've been waiting for him to return to it, watching from that pitiful little van."

"So the airstream isn't your dream home after all?"

"*This*" —he gestured grandly to the mezzanine— "is my dream home. I never wished to leave it, and after I'm through with you, I won't ever have to again."

I scoffed with what little air was left in my lungs. "Good luck with that."

"You're mocking me?" he said, letting enough pressure off of my throat to let me draw breath again.

"You killed two people," I reminded him. "Plus you've attacked me, Ben, and Della. You think the police are going to let that go so you can live in your dream home?"

"The police won't find out," he said. "Hillary's the only one of them with half a brain. I'll convince them the local stalker made his way into the house once again, that he murdered you and Ben, leaving only me alive in the airstream."

"Sammy—"

"Ah, you would be worried for the boy." Basil tsked and shook his head. "Don't you see? I can't leave him alive, Peyton. He's a loose end. What if he's listening at the bedroom door right now? Don't worry though. He and Alyssa can stay friends. After all, those who die in this house can never leave it."

"You know?" I said. "About Penelope and Alyssa?"

"Of course I know," Basil spat. "Della went on and on about them for years. I thought she was delusional until she began recounting things about my family she never could have known without meeting them. Personally, I've never seen them, and I'm glad of that. To look at my wife's face again after she's soiled herself with another man?" He shuddered. "Disgusting."

"But killing her isn't?"

He sat back on his heels, loosening his hold on me yet again, almost as if he was lowering his defenses. He didn't expect me to put up a fight, not when he had taken everything from me. "You're hyper-fixated on the murder aspect. Think of what they did to *me*. But you don't understand either, do you? That's why I'm going to enjoy killing you, Peyton."

"Like hell you are!"

The deep declaration came out of nowhere, as did the enormous figure that catapulted over the back of the sofa and knocked Basil off of me. I took a deep, gasping breath as the two men landed on the coffee table. The legs of it flattened beneath their weight, and the glass top shattered. As the men wrestled, I flung myself off of the sofa and made a run for the bedroom. Sammy was finally awake, sitting straight up in bed.

"Peyton?" he asked groggily. "What's going on?"

"Don't you dare leave this room," I commanded. "Promise me!"

He held up a hand as if he were swearing on the Bible. "I promise!"

I locked the door from the inside, slammed it shut, and made sure the handle was fixed in place. To get to Sammy, Basil would have to bust the door down or go through the courtyard to break the window. Anything to slow him down—

A hand came down on my shoulder. I screamed, but when I whirled around, it wasn't Basil who stood behind me. It was the same man I'd seen at my window and in the house a few times before.

"He took off up the mezzanine," the man said. "But he'll find us again. He knows this house better than anyone else. Our best bet is to hold down the fort in the foyer. Come on."

He took me by the elbow but applied no force. Ultimately, it was my decision whether or not to follow the tall stranger into the center of the house. Something instinctive drove me to go with him.

"It's you, isn't it?" I whispered as we rushed down the hall-way. "Andrew Anderson?"

He tossed a mischievous wink over his shoulder. "You're a marvelous human being, Peyton. I wish I'd been around to watch you grow up."

"All this time," I said, "Mom and Grandma told me you had abandoned them, but you were trying to steer clear of Basil."

"Percy," he corrected. He led me into the foyer and dragged the sofa against the wall. He gestured for me to join him behind it. If Basil came into the foyer again, he wouldn't immediately be able to see us. "And yes, you're correct. I gave up my family to bring this one peace. It was a difficult choice to make."

"You can see Penelope and Alyssa too?"

"On rare occasion," he replied. "I've spent most of my life trying to track Percy down. He threw me off for quite a while, what with the name change and all. Do you have your phone? We should call the police before he returns."

I checked my pockets then grimaced. "It's locked in the bedroom with Sammy."

"The child is here?"

"His mom's out of town."

Andrew's beard rustled around his mouth. "Damn. That

changes everything. We gotta get the kid out of here." Something tinkled overhead on the mezzanine. Both of us snapped our heads up to look. Andrew muttered something under his breath. "He's watching us. Can you get Sammy on your own? If Percy comes back this way, I want to be ready for him."

"Are you sure—?"

"Don't worry. I'll have your back. Sammy's the priority. We have to keep him safe."

I nodded firmly, scanned the mezzanine for any sign of Basil, then crept out from behind the sofa. As soon as I cleared the foyer, thunderous footsteps came up behind me, and I burst into a run to reach the hallway. The sofa scraped across the floor as Andrew made his move. Once again, he tackled Basil. As they went down, someone's fingers clutched my ankle. Stumbling, I yanked myself free, but my ankle twisted and popped.

"Go!" Andrew yelled.

A second later, he let out a groan of pain, but I didn't look behind me to see what had happened. I limped into the hallway, reached the bedroom, and hammered on the door.

"Sammy?" I called. "It's me, Peyton! Unlock the door."

"You just told me not to come out," came the small voice from the other side.

"I know, buddy, but we gotta get out of here," I pleaded. "Can you let me in?"

"Okay."

The lock almost clicked out of place before Basil tackled me from the side. My knee buckled inward as he flattened me out on the floor, and I screamed as he intentionally twisted my ankle between his hands.

"Where's your grandfather now?" he hissed, throwing himself on top of me to keep me rooted to the floor. "Not here to save you, huh?"

"What did you do to him?"

426

"Let's just say he's closer to God now."

I wrestled one hand free and pressed Basil's face away from mine, raking my nails across his cheek. He howled in pain as three deep gouges opened in his skin. He grabbed my wrist and slammed my hand against the carpet, pinning it in place. Sammy banged on the door from the room, shouting incoherently.

"Stay inside!" I yelled to him hoarsely.

"So noble," Basil said, displaying that terrible grin again. "You and your grandfather love being the heroes, don't you? God, it's annoying."

He let go of my hand to reach for something behind him: the cue ball from the pool table in the study upstairs. He gripped it firmly and raised it above his head. With my free hand, I tried to grab his elbow, but he stayed out of my reach.

"Maybe I'll see you again," he said, "but I hope not."

I squeezed my eyes shut as the cue ball came hurtling toward my head, not wanting to see the moment it thunked against my skull. The blow never came. The ball bounced off the wooden floors and rolled away. Basil collapsed on top of me, forcing the breath out of my lungs.

"Ugh!"

Panting, I shoved Basil off of me and rolled to my knees. Basil was completely unconscious. Like Della, he bore a dark mark on his head—close to his neck—one that quickly spread blood across the new carpet. Something thunked to the floor—the rolling pin. I whirled around.

"Penelope?" I whispered.

She wasn't her usual sparkling, incandescent self. She flickered in and out like a faulty fluorescent light as she stared down at the unmoving body of her husband.

"Did you do that?" I asked her.

She nodded silently. I moved forward and pressed two

fingers against the inside of Basil's wrist. "He doesn't have a pulse."

"Leave him," Penelope whispered. "Come with me. Into the bedroom."

"He's dead," I murmured. "I have to call the cops. I have to check on Andrew and Ben!"

Penelope leaned down, placing herself between me and Basil. Though she had no physical body, the cold radiating off of her forced me away from her once husband. "This is more important," she said. "We're leaving."

"What?"

She gave me no answer, instead floating through the closed door and into the bedroom. I stood on shaky feet, using the wall to prop myself up. Both my right knee and ankle were too damaged to put weight on. I checked the door. Sammy had unlocked it.

Inside the bedroom was a spectacle I never expected to see. Sammy stood between Penelope and Alyssa, his hands—somehow—clutched in theirs. Was it an illusion? Could he actually feel the ghosts on either side of him? He stared up at Penelope in amazement. I did too. The light that made up the ghosts' presence had changed. They no longer looked gray and gloomy, but radiant and white. The moonlight from the window made Alyssa's skin glitter and shine.

"You did it," Alyssa told me, beaming from ear to ear. She was no longer wearing her trademark pink scarf, but the wound on her neck had also disappeared. She looked like a regular five-year-old kid, except for the fact that she was transparent. "You helped us."

"I didn't do anything," I said, unable to tear my eyes away from the child. "It was my grandfather. It was your mother."

"I would have never been able to see Percy without your help," Penelope told me. "He suddenly became visible to me when he tried to kill you. We've been waiting for this moment for forty years, Peyton. You made it happen."

I furiously shook my head. "It wasn't me."

Penelope floated toward me and cradled my face in her hands, but I wasn't like Sammy. I couldn't feel anything except the cold. "You changed everything, and for that, I can never repay you. We have to go now. I can feel it pulling me away."

"Feel what?"

She shrugged and smiled. "Whatever comes next."

Alyssa turned to Sammy. "Everything's going to be okay now."

Sammy's bottom lip trembled. "Am I ever going to see you again?"

"Sure," Alyssa said. "I'm always going to be with you."

"But it won't be the same."

"No," Alyssa said. "It'll be better. Thanks for being my friend, Sammy."

He reached out to give her a hug, but his arms went through her. Alyssa laughed as they mimed a hug instead. "I'll never forget you, Alyssa," Sammy whispered.

"Me either."

When they parted, Alyssa smiled and returned to her mother. Penelope took her daughter's hand. Together, they floated to the window, where the moonlight shone through them. Sammy threw his arms around my waist and I hugged him to my side as Penelope and Alyssa gradually faded from view. Right before she disappeared, Alyssa waved goodbye.

When I waved back, she was already gone.

"*I*t's the one at the end of the street," I directed the airport taxi driver as I pointed over his shoulder from the back seat. "That blue one on the corner."

I smiled at the sight of the familiar house. It was a small cottage with a three-paneled sitting window in the front. The yard was freshly mowed and blooming with marigolds. A tree loomed over the roof in the backyard, a rickety swing hidden in its leaves. The driveway was packed with cars, so the driver parked on the curb instead.

"Are you having a party?" he asked.

"A family reunion," I replied, hurriedly unbuckling my seatbelt. "And a very important birthday."

"You must be excited to be home."

I handed him a gracious tip. "You have no idea."

"Need help with your bags?"

"Nope. Someone should be out any minute—"

The white front door blasted open, and Sammy came running down the front walk. As I stepped out of the cab, he flung himself into my grasp. I hugged him tightly and ruffled his hair.

"Holy crap!" I said. "Did you grow again?"

"Probably! I'm the tallest kid in my class now."

With a year and change, Sammy looked like a totally different boy. Not only was he taller, but he wasn't so skinny anymore. He did sports now too—baseball and karate—and he didn't go anywhere without a ball cap. Half the time, he had a few bruises or scrapes to show off and a story to go with each one. Theo had finally let up on the reins, meaning Sammy was free to try a range of new things.

"Hey, Peyton!" Theo was the next person to come flying out of the house to engulf me in a hug. "Welcome home!"

Like Sammy, Theo had changed for the better. She'd cut most of her hair off. It sat near her chin rather than around her shoulders, something she claimed made her feel more free than she had in years. With Sammy taking more responsibility for himself, Theo had the time to do the same for herself. She had toned up at the local gym with weight-lifting and yoga classes.

"Thank you," I said. "Everything okay here?"

"Totally." Theo grabbed my suitcase from the trunk and handed it off to Sammy. "Where are your manners, kid?"

As the cab driver carefully pulled away from the curb, Sammy tried to roll my suitcase up the front walk toward the house. "Gosh, this is heavy. What's in this? Bricks?"

"Your birthday present, actually," I told him. "Unless you don't want it?"

"No, I want it!"

"Guess you gotta get the suitcase inside then."

He put on a burst of speed as if the suitcase had suddenly become featherlight. Theo chuckled and linked her arm through mine. "How was Namibia? I don't suppose they have Wi-Fi over there yet. It's terrible not talking to you."

"It was great," I said. "We got some amazing pictures, and Adele wrote the most moving article. It's going to be huge."

"Who's publishing it again?"

"The New Yorker."

Theo squealed as she dragged me inside. "I'm so excited for you."

"I'm excited to be home."

The house smelled like cinnamon, as it did on the day we'd originally stepped inside. When Theo and I first decided to rent a house together, it seemed like a weird plan. After Ben and I finalized our divorce, I needed a place to call home base as my photography career took off. Likewise, Theo wanted a place where Sammy could have his own room and space to grow. It worked out that the perfect blue house in the quiet Falconwood neighborhood was up for grabs. Maybe it wasn't a permanent situation, but it was the perfect one for now.

The living room was decorated for Sammy's birthday. Theo had gone for a samurai theme, no doubt playing up Sammy's recent brown belt acquisition, but the paper plates had sumo wrestlers on them. As I fully entered the room, a rambunctious cheer went up. Sammy's friends were playing Twister in front of the TV, and Bryce—a particularly lanky boy from Sammy's third-grade class—had just taken out the rest of the kids with a right hand on yellow.

I caught sight of Ben's laughing face. When he saw me, he raised his beer in a salute. His new girlfriend, Mallory, sat beside him. I'd met her a few times before. She was nice and pretty, and more importantly, she wanted the life that Ben wanted to give to her. They lived together in mine and Ben's old house, a few hours away, but Ben had wanted to visit Falconwood for Sammy's birthday.

"Do you want a drink?" Theo asked. "Your mother's tending bar."

"Of course she is."

We went out to the patio, where my mother chugged fruit

punch beside the backyard bar. "Peyton, honey! I didn't know you were back in the States."

"I said I would be here," I reminded her. "What's in that fruit punch?"

"Fruit punch," my mother insisted. She reached in her pocket and tossed something at me. It was a sober chip. "Ninety days, kid. Proud of me?"

She offered me the cup. I took a whiff. No hint of vodka.

"Nice job, Mom."

"Thank you! What would you like? Old Fashioned? Manhattan? I'm living vicariously through everyone else today, but I've got a hankering for bourbon. Please, Peyton. Just let me uncork the Bulleit."

"I'll have a water," I said pointedly. "Where's Grandpa?"

Mom narrowed her eyes and nodded toward the towering tree. Andrew—Grandpa, as I was getting used to calling him—inspected the trunk and the attached swing. I wandered over to him.

"Peyton!" he said, clasping me to his side. "I was just having a look at our boy's swing here. These bolts are getting rusty, you know. They could break while he's on it. What if he falls off?"

"I'll change them," I promised. "How are you getting along with Mom?"

"I think I'm wearing her down." He took his sunglasses from his forehead and placed them over his eyes instead. "Every day, she forgives me a fraction more for leaving her and your grandmother."

"But it's working out so far?"

"So far. I'm glad to be home with her." He looked over my head to watch my mom as she chugged a bottle of water while eyeing the bourbon wistfully. "I was a terrible father to her. It's time I make up for it."

"I'm sure you will."

The sliding door opened, and Della Gordon stepped out. She smiled widely as she made her way across the backyard. Shortly after the events that had occurred at the Abram Mansion that fateful night, she had awakened from her coma. Though she walked with a limp and a cane now, she got around on her own just fine.

"I thought I heard your voice," she said. Like everyone else, she gave me a big hug. "It's so good to see you. I want to hear all about your new project."

"How long do you have?" I joked. "You're the only person I can gush to about it."

"As long as you need," Della said. "I'm so glad you got this opportunity."

Sammy appeared at the back door, holding the wrapped present he'd unearthed from my suitcase. "Peyton!" he yelled. "I'm going to open it, okay?"

"Not until I come inside," I replied. "I want to watch."

"Come inside then!"

"Are you telling me what to do?"

"...No?"

I grinned and patted Grandpa on the back. "Shall we?"

Everyone gathered in the living room to watch Sammy open his presents. There was a pile of them stacked around him, but he kept the one from me in his lap. Theo sidled up next to me.

"What'd you get him?" she muttered in my ear.

"You'll see."

The other kids clamored around Sammy, craning their necks to get a look at the brightly wrapped packages. Sammy bounced up and down, unable to contain his excitement.

"Can I open it?" he asked, his eyes sliding between me and his mom. He needed permission from both of us.

"Yes," we chorused.

Sammy tore into the wrapping paper and unearthed a worn

leather bag. Once he realized it was an antique, he moved with more caution. Tentatively, he unzipped the bag and unfolded the top part. When he reached in, he drew out the first camera I'd ever used, the one I'd actually stolen from my high school photography class. It was an old Pentax k1000, a classic starter SLR for anyone who wanted to pick up the hobby.

"An old camera?" Bryce said. "Lame."

Sammy shoved Bryce's shoulder. "Shut up, Bryce. It's so cool!"

With complete familiarity, Sammy checked to make sure a roll of film was loaded, lifted the viewfinder to his eye, and snapped a picture of me and Theo as we leaned against the kitchen counter. Then, just as quick, he snapped one of Bryce. The attached flash bulb went off in Bryce's eyes.

"Agh!" Bryce yelled. "I'm blinded!"

"That's what you get," Sammy said smugly. He pulled the neck loop over his head so the camera bounced around his chest, shot to his feet, and ran over to me to give me another hug. "Thanks, Peyton! I'll take good care of it."

I grinned and stole his baseball cap. "I know you will."

Made in the USA
Columbia, SC
09 May 2021

37650815R00239